PRAISE FOR CHRIS FABRY

"A mesmerizing tale . . . [*Almost Heaven*] will surprise readers in the best possible way; plot twists unfold and unexpected character transformations occur throughout this tender story."
PUBLISHERS WEEKLY

"Fabry has a true gift for prose, and [*Almost Heaven*] is amazing. You'll most definitely want to move this to the top of your 'to buy' list."
ROMANTIC TIMES, 4½-STAR TOP PICK REVIEW

"Fabry is a talented writer with a lilting flow to his words."
CROSSWALK.COM

"[*June Bug*] is a stunning success, and readers will find themselves responding with enthusiastic inner applause."
PUBLISHERS WEEKLY

"An involving novel with enough plot twists and dramatic tension to keep readers turning the pages."
BOOKLIST

"Engrossing and entertaining . . . [an] unforgettable tale."
ROMANTIC TIMES

"A captivating story. . . ."
CHRISTIANBOOKPREVIEWS.COM

"Precise details of places and expe⋯⋯⋯⋯⋯⋯ in the story, and the complex, likable ⋯⋯⋯⋯⋯ *Bug* the enduring quality of a classic."
TITLETRAKK.COM

CHRIS FABRY

FROM THE BESTSELLING AUTHOR OF *Dogwood*

NOT IN THE HEART

Tyndale House Publishers, Inc.
Carol Stream, Illinois

Visit Tyndale online at www.tyndale.com.

Visit Chris Fabry's website at www.chrisfabry.com.

TYNDALE and Tyndale's quill logo are registered trademarks of Tyndale House Publishers, Inc.

Not in the Heart

Designed by Jacqueline L. Nuñez

Edited by Sarah Mason

Published in association with Creative Trust Literary Group, 5141 Virginia Way, Suite 320, Brentwood, Tennessee 37027, www.creativetrust.com.

Scripture quotations are taken from the *Holy Bible*, New Living Translation, copyright © 1996, 2004, 2007 by Tyndale House Foundation. Used by permission of Tyndale House Publishers, Inc., Carol Stream, Illinois 60188. All rights reserved.

This novel is a work of fiction. Names, characters, places, and incidents either are the product of the author's imagination or are used fictitiously. Any resemblance to actual events, locales, organizations, or persons living or dead is entirely coincidental and beyond the intent of either the author or the publisher.

Library of Congress Cataloging-in-Publication Data

Fabry, Chris, date.
  Not in the heart / Chris Fabry.
    p. cm.
  ISBN 978-1-4143-4861-2 (sc)
  1. Fatherhood—Fiction. 2. Heart—Transplantation—Fiction. I. Title.
PS3556.A26N68 2012
813'.54—dc23
                                2011031337

Printed in the United States of America

18 17 16 15 14 13 12
 7   6   5   4   3   2   1

For the addicted and those who love them.

Part I

Life is a gamble, at terrible odds—if it was a bet,
you wouldn't take it.

Tom Stoppard

CHAPTER 1

30 DAYS BEFORE EXECUTION

The trouble with my wife began when she needed Jesus and I needed a cat. Life can be that way. That's part of the reason I was on Sanibel Island in the cottage I had always dreamed of owning and she was in Tallahassee tending to the sick son of our youth. But it's more complicated. There was more troubling me than religion or people who think problems can be solved with a leap of faith.

Said cottage was a tiny house that seems to be the rage among those who believe we are warming the planet with each exhale. I didn't buy it because of that, but I recycle my Coors Light cans. My little contribution to the cause. Lately it's been a hefty contribution. There was one bedroom in the back and a little bathroom, a walk-through kitchen, and a living area that I used as an office.

Murrow usually sat in the window looking out at the beach with as much interest as I have in paying both of my mortgages. It's not that I don't want to pay. I can't.

I was on the bed, surfing news sites, fueling the ache about my lack of direction and lack of a job. The satellite TV company disconnected me a few months ago, so I got my news online from the unprotected network of a neighbor who can't encrypt his wireless router.

I could see the downsizing coming in every area of the conglomerate media company. I knew it would hit the newsroom, but I always thought when the music stopped, I would have a chair. What I got was severance, a pat on the back, and a shelf full of awards I stuffed into a suitcase that sat in the attic of a cottage I couldn't afford.

I closed my laptop and told Murrow I'd be back, as if she cared, and walked barefoot out the front door and down the long, wooden stairway to the beach. I bought this cottage for these long, head-clearing walks. The sound of the waves crashing against doubts and fears. The smell of the ocean and its salty cycle of life and death.

A mom and a dad dressed in white strolled along the beach with two kids who squealed every time the water came close.

I walked the other way.

The phone rang as I passed a dead seagull. Not a good omen. "Tru, it's me."

The woman of my dreams. The woman of my nightmares. Everything good and bad about my life. The "I do" that "I didn't."

"Ellen. What's up?"

"How are you?" She said it with a measure of compassion, as if she weren't holding back years of boiling anger. As if she didn't have something else she wanted to ask me and wasn't just setting the stage for the coup de grâce.

"I'm good. Just taking a walk on the beach."

Wish you weren't here. Wish you weren't still in my head. Wish you hadn't called. Wish the last twenty years were something I could bury in the sand. What were you thinking marrying a guy like me? My life is a sand castle and my days are wind and water.

"Hear anything back yet? Any offers?"

"There's nothing plural about my job prospects. Not even singular. I did hear from the Fox station in Des Moines yesterday. They went with somebody with longer hair and bigger lungs."

She spoke with a wry smile. "It's only a matter of time; you know that."

"Right. It's always been a matter of time, hasn't it?"

She let the irony hang there between us, and I could picture her in her wedding dress and without it. Then the first time we met in the university newsroom, big glasses and frilly blouse. Hair that smelled like the ocean and felt like silk. A sharp wit, infectious laugh, and the tenacity of a bloodhound on every story she covered. I thought we were always going to be on the same page, but somehow I kept chasing headlines and she moved to the Life section.

"I have something that might interest you," she said.

"How old is she?" I'm not always a smart aleck with the people I love. When I'm asleep, they tell me I don't say much of anything.

"It's not a she. It's a he with a pretty good story. A great story. A life changer."

"Not into guys."

She sighed and plowed ahead. "Have you heard of Terrelle Conley?"

That was like asking a history major if she'd ever heard of Alexis de Tocqueville. "I know he's facing the needle."

"Right. Next month."

"Wonder what his last meal will be. How do they choose that anyway? Shrimp and steak or lobster bisque? Macaroni and cheese? How can you enjoy a meal knowing you only have hours left? Or what movie to watch? What would you choose?"

"I know his wife, Oleta. She wants somebody to write the story from his perspective. The whole family does."

I laughed. "In thirty days or less."

"They've scraped up some money. Not much, but it could probably help."

"How much is 'probably'?"

"I don't know exactly, but I was thinking you could call Gina and find out if—"

"I'm not with Gina or the agency anymore. She dropped me. Said it was a hard decision on their part. I guess they took a vote."

"I'm sorry."

"Just another bump in the literary highway. I don't think writing is my thing, anyway." I said it halfheartedly, coaxing some kind of compliment.

"You're a great writer," she obliged. "You haven't had as many opportunities lately, but . . ."

"I haven't had any politicians who want to be president or sports stars who've been accused of steroids approach me in a few years. That's what you mean," I said. "Where did you meet Olatha?"

"Oleta. I met her at church."

Groan. How did I know that was coming?

I paused at a sand castle that had been constructed with several five-gallon buckets. Towels and chairs had been abandoned for the moment. Water filled the moat, and I heard laughter from a bungalow perched like a lighthouse above. A couple in love.

"You must have some idea of how much."

"A few thousand. We didn't talk about that. The important thing . . . it's not just an opportunity for you. It's for Aiden."

"Now you're really getting cryptic. You want to back up?"

"Terrelle's wife is in a study group with me. She's known about Aiden's condition for years. Always asks for updates. Terrelle came up with the idea—he wants to be a donor. A second chance for Aiden."

I should have been doing cartwheels. Our eighteen-year-old son could get a new lease on life? Instead, I was skeptical, like any good journalist. "Ellen, there's no chance. Do you know how long something like that would take?"

"It's been in process for a while."

"Why didn't you tell me?"

"You haven't exactly been available."

"The prison system, the authorities, they'll never let this—"

"The governor is taking it seriously. I've heard he's working with the legislature. It's not a done deal, but there's a chance."

The governor. The hair rose on the back of my neck.

"Ellen, there's some law firm in Tallahassee salivating at all the appeals and counterappeals that are going to happen. This is less than a long shot."

"Yeah, but right now it's looking like a pretty good long shot." There was emotion in her voice and for the first time I noticed noise in the background.

"Where are you?"

She swallowed hard and I imagined her wiping away a tear. My wife has had plenty of practice.

"At the hospital again," she said. "ICU."

I cursed under my breath and away from the phone. Not just because of all the hospital bills I knew were coming my way, but also because this was my son. I'll be honest—the bills were the first thing I thought of, but picturing him hooked up to tubes and needles again crushed me.

"How is he?"

"Not good. They're monitoring him. Same story."

"How long have you been there?"

"Since late last night. He was having trouble breathing. Lots of pain. He asks about you."

Guilt. She had to get that in there, didn't she?

"Tell him to hang in there, okay?"

"Come see him. It would mean so much."

"Yeah. I will." I said it fast, though I knew I'd have to launder all the cat hair from my clothes because Aiden's deathly allergic to cats just like I'm allergic to the inside of the death chamber.

Someone spoke over the intercom near her and the sound took me back to those first days when I wasn't as scared of hospitals. Back then I could watch a movie or a TV show with a medical setting. Now I can't even watch the TV promos. My chest gets tight and the smell of alcohol and Betadine and the shape of needles invades, mingling with the cries of a young child in pain and another memory of a man on a gurney.

We discovered Aiden's heart malady by accident. Ellen was into natural food, natural medicine, whole-grain seaweed sandwiches and eggs that came from free-range chickens who had bedtime stories read to them each night before they settled into their nests. Natural childbirth with a midwife. All that stuff. She was convinced antibiotics were the forbidden fruit, so she didn't run to the HMO every time our kids were sick. But something told her to take Abby in for some chest congestion she couldn't get rid of. Aiden was with her, and on a lark the doctor placed the stethoscope on his chest.

Ellen cried when she tried to explain the look on the woman's face. They'd missed it when he was born.

That sent us on a crash course of congenital heart defects and a series of surgeries and treatments that would change our lives. Ellen hates hospitals as much as I do, but you do what you must for your kids.

"Terrelle has the same blood type," Ellen said. "He's about the same size as Aiden, maybe a little smaller, which is good."

"Ellen, you know this is not going to happen, right? There are so many hoops and holes. They don't let doctors execute people."

"There are guidelines, but they don't have a problem harvesting organs from an already-deceased donor."

"Anybody who's pro-life will howl. I thought you were pro-life."

"I am, but this is something Terrelle wants."

"Doesn't matter. They harvest organs from prisoners in China, but we're not in China." Though you wouldn't know it by shopping at Walmart.

"I know all that. But I also know my son is going to die. And Terrelle and his wife want something good to come out of their tragedy. They asked if you would write his story. I got to thinking that maybe . . ."

She broke a little and hearing her cry felt like some lonely prayer drifting away and hitting the empty shores of heaven. Not that I believe there is one, but you know, metaphorically speaking.

"You were thinking what?" I said.

"Maybe all of this is not really for Aiden. Maybe all we've been through in the last eighteen years is for somebody else. If they deny Terrelle's request and Aiden doesn't make it, maybe writing this story will make a difference for someone down the road."

Her altruism was more than I could handle. "Look, I don't care about all the people with sick kids. I don't care about prisoners who want to make up for their crimes. I don't care about protesters or the politicians who've found a wedge issue. I just want my son to live. Is that asking too much?"

The emotion surprised me and I noticed the family in white had changed direction but now quickly herded their children away from me.

It was Ellen's turn to sound collected. "Do you have time to work on something like that in the next thirty days? It would at least pay a few bills."

"If they're trying to get a stay of execution, they need to go straight to the press. Forget a book deal, forget a magazine exposé—it's already too late. Get somebody at one of the local stations to pick it up and run with it—"

"Tru, they don't want a stay. He wants to give his heart to Aiden. And somebody has to get the story down before it's over. No matter how it goes, this will make a great story."

I was already mulling titles in my head. *A Heart from Death Row. Change of Heart. Pitter-Pat. Life in Vein. Aorta Made a Better Choice.*

She continued, "They know your history. What you've seen. How you're against the death penalty and why. For all your faults, Tru, you're the best reporter I've ever known. You get to the heart of the story like nobody else. I think you should consider it."

The Heart of the Story. Another good title. I could tell she was buttering me up. I love being buttered up by lovely women. But I hate the complications of life with beautiful women.

"I don't write evangelical tracts."

"Why are you so stubborn?" she whisper-screamed at me. Her voice had an echo like she had moved into the bathroom or stairwell. "Why do you have to look at this as some kind of spiritual conspiracy against you instead of a gift? This is being handed to you on a platter. Don't push it away. I don't care if you agree with them about God. You didn't agree with every sports figure or politician."

"The only way I know how to do this job is to ferret out the truth and tell it. Flat out. The way I see it. And if you're expecting me to throw in the third verse of a hymn every other chapter and quote the Gospel of Terrelle, I can't do that. Call somebody from the Christian right."

"Tru, it's because of who you are and how you tell the story that they want you. Just talk with her. Let her explain. If you don't like the situation, they'll go somewhere else. But they have to act quickly."

The sun was coming down behind me and the wind picked up off the water. I could smell the first hint of an impending storm. Or maybe I forgot my deodorant.

"I'll think about it."

I hadn't been gone that long, but as I walked up the stairs, I heard a vehicle pulling away from the house. The taillights had disappeared into the distance by the time I made it to my front door.

Murrow was still in the window, looking down on me with that superior look. *Humans are such a waste of oxygen,* she seemed to say. Maybe she was right. Maybe we are a waste of oxygen and the best thing would be for us to be wiped from the planet. But something inside said that wasn't true. Something inside pushed me to keep moving, like an ant dragging a piece of grass along the sidewalk until a strong wind blows it away. The ant picks up another and starts over. I get exhausted just watching them.

On the front door was a legal document stating that whereby and forthwith said mortgage company had begun said process with an intent to foreclose and otherwise vacate said occupant's tail onto the street to wit and wheretofore so help them God, amen. I had received several such letters in the mail, filing them carefully, hoping the rising tide of foreclosures would save my little cottage until I got a new job.

I ripped the notice down and used it to wipe the sand from my feet. And then a thought struck. A horrible, no-good, bad thought. The newspaper. They published my name with each intent to foreclose. That meant others would know where I was. Others, as in people I owed. Bad people.

Another car passed, slowly. Tinted windows. A low rumble of expensive metal and fuel.

I hurried to the back of the little house and pulled out every suitcase I could find and stowed everything of value. Books. Pictures of me with newsmakers. Cloudy memories of trips abroad, war zones, interviews with generals and dignitaries who went on to fame or perished in motorcades that didn't make it through IEDs.

It was hard not to sit and absorb the memories, but the passing car gave urgency. I jammed every journal and notebook in with the pictures, then put one suitcase with clothes in the trunk of my car and took the rest on my shoulder down the sandy path to the Grahams' house. Sweet people. He retired from the Air Force and they moved for the sun and salty air. Both should have died long ago from arthritis and other maladies, but they were out walking the beach every day like two faithful dogs, paw in paw.

Jack and Millie were on the front porch, and I asked if I could borrow some space in their garage for a suitcase or two. "I need to take a trip. Someone new will be living in my house."

"Relatives coming?"

"No, someone from the Bank of America wants it."

Millie struggled to get out of her rocker and stood by a white column near the front door. "If you need help, Truman, we'd be glad to."

Jack nodded and the gesture almost brought tears to my eyes. "How much are you short?" he said.

"Just a spot in the garage is all I need."

"What about your cat?" Millie said.

"Murrow's going with me."

"If we can do anything at all . . . ," Jack's voice trailed.

"I appreciate it. I appreciate both of you. Thanks for your kindness."

"We pray for Aiden every day," Millie said.

The garage was spotless. Everything hanging up or neatly placed on shelves. I should have joined the Air Force. In the back I found an empty space near some gardening tools. I shook Jack's hand gently and gave Millie a hug. I only turned and looked at them once as I walked back to the house. They stood like sentinels, the fading light of the sun casting a golden glow around them and their house.

When Murrow saw the cat carrier, she bolted under the sofa and I threatened to sell her to the local Chinese restaurant. An open can of StarKist and my tender, compassionate voice helped coax her into the carrier, and we were off.

I texted my wife: Will call your friend tomorrow. Can I use Abby's room?

The phone buzzed in my shirt pocket as I drove along the causeway into darkening clouds. Key under frog. No cats. The next text gave Oleta's number and a short message. You were made for this story.

Maybe she was right. Maybe I was the one for this job. One loser telling the story of his kindred spirit. I sure didn't have anything better to do. But with the window down and my hand out, being pushed back by the cool air, it felt less like the start of a new chapter and more like the end of one.

CHAPTER 2

I awoke with the distinct feeling that I was someplace I shouldn't be, mainly because Michael Jackson and Justin Timberlake stared at me from opposite walls. I've had this feeling a few times, waking up in places where I didn't remember the previous night. The pink covers were disconcerting, but not half as terrifying as the knock I heard at the front door and the fact that I'd left my suitcase in the car and stripped down to my underwear, leaving my clothes outside in order to observe the "no cat" rule.

I jumped from the bed and moved toward the kitchen, glancing out the front window. The only clothes of mine in the house were stored in a closet in Ellen's room. I had taken everything else or it had been given away. I found Ellen's robe in the bathroom, something Aiden had given her a few Christmases ago, and threw it on. My manhood isn't diminished by the color pink, but I try to avoid going out in public in terry cloth.

"Mr. Wiley?" a woman said at the front door.

Another creditor? I reluctantly moved to the door and noticed Ellen had relocated our wedding picture from the mantel to the piano. Was that good or another dead seagull?

I opened the door and the humidity of the morning hit. I had driven through rain most of the night and the morning sun made it sauna-like outside. I'd meant to get Murrow out at sunup. So much for good intentions.

On the front step was a woman in her late thirties, I guessed, though to me African American women always look about ten years younger than they actually are. She was nicely dressed in a brown pantsuit and hoop earrings that spun like an amusement park ride when she moved. She cradled a leather Bible in one arm and had a full shopping bag in the other. I half hoped she would ask to come in and talk about the Bible so I could just close the door, but I guessed the bag wasn't full of *Watchtower*s.

She did a double take at my robe, then glanced down at the clothes I had laid over the frog the night before. Part of me wanted to explain, but the best of me decided to let her think the frog had fashion sense.

"Can I help you?" I said.

"Depends on whether you're Truman Wiley or not."

"I am." I extended a hand.

She smiled and shook it firmly, like some old deacon had taught her well. "Oleta Conley. Your wife said to come over this morning. We need to get moving."

She whisked past me into the house as though she owned the place.

"Yeah, come on in and I'll make us some coffee," I said.

I followed her to the kitchen as she walked, resolutely, as if to an appointment with the Almighty. She plopped the bag in one of the chairs and scanned the cupboards. "I think Ellen keeps the coffee in here," she said, opening the right door on the first try.

"If you don't mind, I'm going to grab some clothes. I'll be right back."

She lifted a hand and waved me on without turning. By the time I returned, the aroma of freshly brewing coffee filled the kitchen. The smell instantly transported me to happier days with Ellen, sharing morning coffee over scattered newspapers. Oleta had cleaned a few dishes left in the sink and was firmly planted at the table scanning something from the middle of her Bible. The book looked thick enough to stop a bullet.

"How's Aiden?" she said to the page. "Have you heard anything today?"

"Not yet. I know Ellen's still at the hospital with him." The information didn't seem to impress her.

"I've been praying for that boy almost as long as I've prayed for my own husband. Doesn't seem fair sometimes, the way God works."

I peeked in the bag and grunted some kind of acknowledgment, but I wasn't about to go down the holy highway.

"That's all you're going to need as far as background," she said. "Just about every scrap of newspaper and magazine reports from the time of the murder to all the years he's been in prison. There's transcripts from the court proceedings—at least the ones I could get my hands on. Video of the news reports that came out at the time and what was used at the trial. I had it put on DVD not long ago. And there's a recording of Terrelle's testimony. His spiritual journey."

"Mrs. Conley, we need to back up a little. I don't know what my wife told you, but I'm a little skeptical about this project."

"Skeptical? To tell you the truth, I'm a little skeptical myself."

"How's that?"

"Skeptical of a man who doesn't visit his son in the hospital. Skeptical of the heart of a man who lets a wife fend for herself. Skeptical of a man who would rather play the slots."

How insulting. I never play the slots, unless I only walk in with change.

"Skeptical of a man who would bring a cat in here when he knows his son is allergic to them."

"I didn't bring her inside. That's why the clothes are out on the frog."

"You left your cat outside in a rainstorm?"

"Look, I don't have to explain any of this to you."

She rolled her eyes. "You're going to find some way to mess this up. I know that."

"If you're looking for perfection, I'm not the guy," I said, grabbing the bag and holding it out to her. "Looks like you need to find somebody else."

"My feelings exactly, before I heard about your past. And Terrelle seems dead set on you. I tried to talk some sense into him, but he wouldn't listen. Said God told him you were the one."

I thought about the irony of her husband being "dead set" on anything. My arm got tired holding the bag and I set it on the table between us. "Well, this is just going to have to be another disappointment in his life, won't it?"

"You're turning us down?"

"I think that's a fair way to put it."

She took the bag and moved it to the floor, keeping the sight lines open. "I didn't mean to come on too strong, but you seem like the kind of person who appreciates a straight shooter. And I'm shooting straight. I don't like what's gone on in your family, but I also know there are two sides to everybody's story, so I'm willing to give you the benefit of the doubt."

"I don't need you to give me anything, Oleta. Now if you'll leave, I'll feed my cat and get over to the hospital."

"Mr. Wiley, sit down."

"No, this is my house."

"This is not your house. You left your house and shacked up at the beach with some young thing."

"Is that what Ellen told you?"

"Why else do men leave their wives and families?"

"Apparently someone has misinformed you. I didn't shack up with anybody. I needed some time to myself, to figure out life."

"And you haven't done enough traveling to Kosovo or Baghdad or Afghanistan or any of the other places? Let me ask you this: How many birthday parties have you missed? How many Little League games? Piano recitals? Your daughter's first prom?"

It showed how much she knew—Aiden never played Little League.

"Your point?" I said.

"My point is, you've been a lousy father. Whether you shacked up or not isn't important. But you have a chance to do something with the talent you've been given. You can do something that will make a difference."

"And the chance you're giving me is to prove your husband is innocent in thirty days or less."

"It's twenty-nine now," she corrected. "And I'm not asking you to prove anything."

Oleta rose and got a mug from the cupboard like she could just ignore me. She poured a cup and sat.

"I know Terrelle's not coming out of Starke in anything but a hearse," she said. "When he's out, he'll have a tag on his toe. I am resigned to that fact. And so is he."

"So he admits he did the crime."

"No, he doesn't admit it. He didn't kill that woman."

"Then why don't you want me to prove that?"

"If you can, more power to you. I'd love to have Terrelle back again, but I'm not holding my breath." The coffeemaker gurgled and hissed. "I would be a fool to hire you to prove my husband innocent when your son is in line for his heart. What do they call that—a conflict of interest?"

I nodded, still standing. Clearly this was a bulldog of a woman. Smart, too. I hate smart bulldogs.

"I'm not trying to stop his execution. If the Lord wants to intervene, I'm good with that. More than good. But I have enough faith to believe this path we've been put on is bigger than Terrelle's guilt or innocence. Joseph was thrown into prison for something he didn't do, and he wound up saving his entire family and the whole Jewish race."

I vaguely remembered the story of Joseph's coat and somehow Donny Osmond's face flashed across the synapses along with Yul Brynner saying, "So let it be written; so let it be done." Another sip of coffee brought me back.

"I want Terrelle's story told because it's going to help somebody," she said. "The truth always does that. Might even help you."

"Oh, I get it. That's your plan. You conspired with my wife. Prison ministry from the inside out. Terrelle tries to save my soul before he goes to the death chamber."

She slowly shook her head. "Ellen didn't even come close to describing how mean you can be."

"Me? You accuse me of infidelity and I'm the one who's mean?"

She rose to dump out the contents of her coffee mug in the sink and switched off the coffeemaker, as if I would forget.

"Looks like we got off on the wrong foot," she said. "I apologize for how I sounded—"

"That's fine and I forgive you, and here's your Piggly Wiggly bag and good luck with life."

She took the bag. "Just like that. You walk away just like that." Her back was straight now, and she looked me in the eyes like a persecuting attorney. I know it's *prosecuting*, but the word seemed to fit her.

"Good-bye, Mr. Wiley," she said as she walked out and closed the door.

I stood there, fuming, until I heard my cell phone ring in the back bedroom. I answered and glanced at Justin and Michael.

"Are you up?" Ellen said.

"Yeah. I met your friend Oleta."

"Did she give you the check?"

"We didn't get around to talking about money, unfortunately."

"What happened?"

"Let's just say we didn't hit it off."

The doorbell rang.

"Tru, you need to go after her."

"No, I don't."

"Don't mess this up."

I walked toward the front door. "Look, there's not enough money in the world for this job. I can't work with people like her."

Through the small window in the door I saw brown hair and circling earrings.

"She's back; hang on."

"Talk with her, Tru."

I opened it. "Yes?" It wasn't the most polite *yes* in the history of door openings, but it was all I could muster.

"Just thought you'd want to know your car's gone."

There was an empty spot on the driveway where I'd parked.

Oleta turned toward the sidewalk and I called after her, "Did you see who took it?"

"Some guy in a tow truck. You might want to call the impound lot."

I put the phone to my ear. "I have to call you back."

Chapter 3

I wish I could say Murrow was the only thing I thought about at that moment, but I will not lie. My laptop came to mind a split second or ten before her. I grabbed my sandals from the entryway and ran into the street. I had the sinking feeling that I wouldn't retrieve the car. Ever.

Oleta sat in her aging Lincoln Town Car. I headed down the sidewalk, trying to remember any of our neighbors' names. There was Todd with the immaculate lawn, who pulled crabgrass with tweezers and put out his USC flag every weekend. I could remember a handful of others but the prospect of knocking on a door and trying to explain the situation overwhelmed me.

Hi, it's Truman from down the street. Remember me? I'm the guy who abandoned his wife and kids after my job fell through and went to live like a hermit. Can you help me? There are some things you can't spin.

The Town Car pulled forward and stopped. Oleta leaned over in the front seat and opened the passenger door. The car sounded like it had arthritis and lumbago and maybe ulcerative colitis. But I had to remind myself that Oleta still had a car and I didn't.

"Are you going to stand there or are you going to get in?"

She moved the paper bag to the backseat and I swallowed my pride.

The interior of the car didn't look much better than the outside. There was the requisite number of Burger King and McDonald's bags smashed into the floorboards. Two empty Diet Coke cans in cup holders. Yard signs wedged between the seats made things cozy.

"Did you have car problems?" she said with a certain knowing, smarmy tone. "Is that why they towed it?"

"It's a repossession. Been dodging that bullet."

She fell silent and I noticed Christian music crackling through the speaker that still worked. It just happened to be on my side. Something about blessing God in the desert and wilderness and blah, blah, blah. Had Oleta preprogrammed her songs to reach me? No, a deep-voiced announcer gave the time and temperature.

She told me the location of the closest impound lot. "That's the direction I saw him go, but if he went someplace else, I might have to drop you off and let you find it on your own. I can't be late for work."

"Where do you work?"

She told me the street.

"No, I mean, what type of work do you do?"

"Real estate company. But back in the day I worked at the impound lot, so I know the drill. I've had just about every job you can think of the past few years, trying to hold the family together." She laughed and it sounded like exercise for her lungs.

"You and Terrelle have kids?"

"We had two little ones when he was arrested. It was because of them that I told him to get out. His drinking took over. I wanted a big family, you know. Lots of kids coming over for Christmas dinner and . . ." Her voice trailed as we pulled to a stop sign. "Two kids grown and flown now. Didn't raise them the way I wanted, but they seem to be doing pretty well, all things considered."

"That's an accomplishment."

She sped up to make it through a light and looked at her watch. I spotted a tow truck ahead, but it wasn't pulling my car.

I stared out the window and felt her eyes on me, hate and pity. I'm not accustomed to that. I'm more into the adulation of people who say, "Aren't you the guy on TV?"

Her voice sounded soft enough to be a prayer, and it cut through the music and air conditioner rattle. "I want to apologize for coming down on you so hard. I had no right. Part of it is probably how angry I still feel about Terrelle. All the crazy choices he made that put him where he is. I put that on you."

"What choices?"

"You know, the people he ran with. The dependence on alcohol and drugs and the womanizing. People around me told me to just let him go, divorce him, but I couldn't do it. And in a lot of ways my life is better because of all we went through. I don't know that I would have ever found the Lord if we hadn't gone through that. And I know he wouldn't have."

Asphalt and palm trees and the climbing sun. These were the visuals as I endured her onslaught of faith.

"I don't know your side of the story and I shouldn't have jumped on you. It wasn't the best way to hire somebody."

"I appreciate you saying that."

But like every Christian I have ever known, she didn't know when to stop. "I identify a lot with that wife of yours. I see her pain. I see her on the edge of collapse with Aiden. To be honest, when you opened the door, I half expected to meet a monster. I've seen you on TV, but I figured I'd see the Mr. Hyde side, if you know what I mean."

"I can be a monster."

Her laugh was a gurgling, clucking chuckle that sounded like it emanated from somewhere deep. "I'll just bet you can be."

"I wasn't exactly civil to you, either," I said.

She turned left and we headed toward a part of town I tried to avoid, with storefronts boarded up and bars on the windows. People made a vain effort to stay in the shade as the sun rose higher and the streets below heated to blistering.

"Ever had a car repossessed before?" she said.

"Happy to say this is my first time."

"Well, the bad news is, you've lost those four wheels, but the stuff inside is still your property. They can't take that away. Surprises me that they'd tow it if they saw an animal inside."

"They probably didn't see it. I left her cage behind the front seat and draped my shirt over the top to keep the sun from being directly on her. If I happened to sleep in."

She pursed her lips. "You should have set your alarm."

"Yeah, I can see that."

"Well, if we can find it, they'll probably let you take—look there. We're in business."

My BMW was making a wide left turn into a chain-linked lot that looked like something out of a postapocalyptic movie. It made the term *junkyard* seem upscale. Oleta did a U-turn and parked on the street in front of the office and accompanied me inside.

The girl behind the desk didn't recognize her, but someone from deep inside the building let out a screech. "Oleeeeeta! What are you doing here, girl?"

The two made small talk and I stood behind her, watching out the window as a bearded man in dirty coveralls unhooked the car. When I pulled out my keys, Oleta snapped her fingers and gave me a mama bear look. "You stay right where you are."

It is not in my nature to wait. Making things happen is a specialty, whether it's tracking down a news source or getting past people whose job it is to keep me away from the interview. But I watched the man loosen the chains from the flatbed trailer and open my front door. Seconds later he came toward the office with the shirt-draped cat carrier.

"Get me some water—I think I got a dehydrated cat," he said with a thick drawl.

"What kind of fool would leave a cat shut up in a car like that?" the woman behind the desk said.

Oleta pointed at me. "That's him. But don't judge him too quick. We spent the last thirty minutes trying to catch up with you."

The man looked at me. "I never take a vehicle with an animal in it. I didn't know."

I nodded. "I believe you. Does that mean I get the car back?"

He smiled through yellowing teeth, some darkened, some gone. "Sorry, not my call."

Oleta ran interference and I took Murrow, the laptop, and my big suitcase. We got back in the Town Car and drove away. Instead of taking me to her real estate office, she made a turn and we wound up in front of Tallahassee General.

"I can't go here," I said.

"Sure you can. Your son's up there."

"You don't understand."

"Well, I understand that I'm late for work and I can't loan you my car. Go see your wife and son."

I opened the door and grabbed Murrow's cage.

"Leave her with me," she said. "There's a PetSmart near the office. I'll get her some food and water and a litter box. You don't need to carry cat dander into the ICU."

Murrow seemed more irritated than anything. For some reason letting her go with a stranger felt cruel, but maybe it was just me trying to hang on to what I couldn't keep.

"All right. That would help a lot. I'll be around to pick her up when I get a car."

"Take this." She handed me the Piggly Wiggly bag and wrote her phone number and address on the side. "You could look through some of the material in the meantime."

Like airports, hospital drop-offs are busy places that don't allow long chats. With my back to her and the door open, my feet on the hot pavement, laptop in my arms, I mulled the decision.

"Ellen said something about payment. That you're prepared to put some money up front."

She rummaged in her purse and pulled out an envelope. "It's made out to you. Probably not what you're used to, but it's a start."

I took the envelope, but she held on until I was forced to look her in the eyes.

"It's taken a long time to get that money."

I opened the flap and looked at the check. She was right—it wasn't even a third of the advance for my last book, but that had been a couple years ago. It was enough to pay some debt. When you have no income and you're wading through a swamp of bills, anything green is gold. I didn't have the heart to tell her this is not how it works. You don't just pay somebody to write your book; there are agents, there are contracts, there are publishers, etc. And it takes at least a year or maybe two from the time you begin. I've fast-tracked a few projects, but those are exceptions.

"If you saved all this, why didn't you get a writer sooner?"

"This'll be hard for you to believe, but God brought this money to me. He impressed it on my heart to save some, but with all the bills and how tight things were, I just couldn't. But he had a plan. It just kind of dropped on me, and I knew it was supposed to be for a writer to tell the story. And if I had come to you back when you were flying high, I doubt you would have given me the time of day."

She let go of the envelope. "I believe we're prepared for the hard times in ways we don't even know. 'For just such a time as this.' You were meant to be here, Mr. Wiley. You were meant to do this. And I have enough faith in the Almighty to put this in your hands and let it go."

That's a lot of faith.

"If I decide to do this, when can I meet with him? I have to be on a visitors' list, approved by the prison. Right?"

She smiled. "You're already on it. I'd say we could get you in within the week. The warden isn't too happy about reporters, though."

"I'm not a reporter. I'm a friend of the family."

"That's good. And you're father of the boy Terrelle wants to help."

A security guard waved a hand at Oleta to pull forward.

"You think I'm going to uncover his innocence."

"There's no doubt you're going to find he's innocent because that's the truth. But deliverance doesn't always look like the prison bars flinging wide open. I'm not expecting a last-minute miracle. I'm trusting in the Lord to do what he does best."

"Which is?"

"Work everything for our good."

I'd heard it before, but I'd lived something wildly different. God, if he was even up there, had never worked everything for my good. Or for my wife, son, and daughter.

"Mr. Wiley, God has a plan. He has a purpose for bringing you here. He brought you low and to the end of yourself so he could start something new."

Whoopee. God sure is good. It was all I could do to keep from raising my hands and dancing in the spirit and shouting, "Hallelujah."

I stuffed the envelope in the bag, climbed out of the car, then leaned down to the window. "Get a message to your husband. Tell him to write as much as he can remember about the case. Details. Stuff he wants people to know about his life. Last words. Ten life lessons from death row. Anything."

Tuesdays with Morrie's Electric Chair.

"So you'll do this?" she said.

I nodded. "We should put a contract together."

The security guard approached with a stride that said he would move us, and he looked big enough to pick up the Town Car and fling it to Georgia. The one near Ukraine.

"We don't need a contract," she said. "You give me your word right now that you'll get this done before Terrelle . . ." She couldn't finish.

"I'll do it," I said. "It's not going to change what will happen, but at least you'll have his story down the way he wanted in his own voice. I can't promise you it'll be published. But I'll write it with everything in me. I'll make it readable and compelling."

She wiped away a tear and nodded. "I believe you. Thank you."

Sometimes the hardest questions come at the least opportune moments. Shouted questions at a president walking toward a helicopter or at a shackled convict heading for a squad car.

"Why is he doing this for my son?" I said to her.

She looked at me through tired eyes, brimming with tears. A middle-aged black woman who had been through hell and a half. "He's not doing this for your son. He's doing something good from the heart, making sense out of the bad. Your son is just the recipient of the grace of God."

I nodded, then said good-bye to Murrow and hello to Tallahassee General.

Chapter 4

Ellen Wiley sat by her son's bed feeling helpless. Again. She had spent so much time in hospitals, doctors' offices, and examination rooms, waiting for test results and praying God would simply stop the insanity. But he had not. He had left her in this garden of doctors and nurses and orderlies where medication flowed like water. And the end result was the drawn face of her son, listless and colorless.

This was not how she had written their story. In the inverted pyramid of their lives, she and Truman would have four children, a nice house, lots of money, and they would live to a ripe old age. Their favorite pastime would be watching grandchildren on weekends. They would take long walks on the beach and die in each other's arms.

The only long walks she took now were alone around the nurses' station or to the cafeteria for food she couldn't stomach. And it had been so long since she held Truman in her arms. It had been so long since she wanted to hold him.

The heart monitor had been muted by one of the nurses, but Ellen could still hear it. She heard it in her sleep. She heard it even when they weren't in the hospital. Her days were dictated by a constant flurry of pills, medication, and monitors—and it was all totally and irrevocably out of her control.

It was in a hospital ICU like this one that she'd encountered a mother of a child with similar cardiac maladies as Aiden's. Though Ellen was filled with constant worry and fear, this woman seemed to have quiet peace. Over the next few weeks as the faces of doctors became more grim, Ellen sat with this woman, drank copious amounts of coffee, and watched the family walk through the death of their daughter with unwavering faith.

Ellen wept bitterly for the loss, more than this mother, and she marveled at their response. When the woman returned after the funeral to check on Aiden, Ellen asked her to explain how she had achieved such peace in the midst of her loss.

That day Ellen knew she wanted what that woman had. Before, she had only wanted to be on the other side of all the problems, to be "past it all," looking back at some bad storm season, sailing into calmer waters. She had been raised by parents whose faith was best described as "God helps those who help themselves." God takes care of your life as long as you manage your own details. Her father's political career had been legendary in old Virginia and their spiritual life as a family had the veneer of religiosity, but as soon as Ellen had the chance to spread her wings and attend UVA, she left the church and all the imposed rules, regulations, and conventions. She didn't rebel against it as much as live the logical conclusions of her parents' unbelief. If God was the god of self-sufficiency, then she would simply take the throne and hold the scepter.

She met her true companion, Tru, after several relationships that didn't work, and her life felt complete. Whole. She'd never experienced the euphoria of another like she experienced with him. Their lives together, as she could conceive it, would be spent working up the journalistic ladder, her in print, him in electronic news gathering, and they would wind up with a cushy existence in DC. She would write a column and he would anchor a Sunday morning talk show, and they would live in Georgetown or outside the Beltway, in two- and four-year cycles like everyone else.

Then Abigail came along, unexpectedly, in 1989. Sweet Abby, their child of love, child of hope, and child of crisis. Ellen never considered abortion, though Truman did. But four years later, when Ellen walked the aisle of the church she had grown up in, Abby spread rose petals before them and Ellen knew her decision had been right.

What no one in the congregation knew at the time was that Aiden was already growing in her womb. And this heartbroken child would eventually help lead her to something much greater than her own plan.

Now, when things seemed at their worst, she sometimes prayed not for God to heal Aiden but to just take him. To end his suffering. Not hers, but his. She knew where he would be, totally healed, totally happy on the other side of the veil. This selfless prayer lasted a moment or two, and then she returned to pleading with God for just one more day, one more hour.

She felt even more conflicted, if that was possible, about Abigail and Truman. And therein lay the irony. Her son had been knocking—no, leaning against the bell at death's door countless times, and her inner life alarm pegged when she thought of her daughter and husband.

Aiden gasped and suddenly opened his eyes. He looked at her and ran his tongue over cracked lips. Before he could speak, she had the cup over his chest and the straw to his mouth. He lifted his head slightly and took a sip, then lay back and closed his eyes. He put a hand to the railing and she took it in her own, feeling the cold, clammy skin and wishing there were something she could do. If she could crawl inside his skin and take his own heart, she would do it. If she could place her heart in his chest and go without, she would do it, even if it meant only a moment of health for him.

"I had a dream," he said. It was nothing more than a whisper, but she had become fluent in the subtleties of Aiden's speech.

"Was it about Melody Swanson?" Ellen said, smiling.

Aiden's eyes remained closed, but the corners of his mouth inched upward. "Not that kind of dream, Mother."

"What was it about?"

A pause. Intake of air. "Dad and I were on a trip." Wait for the next breath. "Some news story he was doing. And he took me along."

"Sounds like fun."

"Yeah. We talked. A lot. Didn't just read a newspaper or look at his laptop. It was cool."

Ellen put her chin on the railing.

"Then something happened," Aiden said. He opened his eyes again and lifted his head an inch from the pillow. "Something happened to Dad and there were all these people. And I got scared."

"Shh, it's okay. It was only a dream. Your father loves you a lot, Aiden; he just does a really bad job of showing it."

Her son shook his head weakly. "You always say that. If he doesn't know how to show it, why can't he figure it out?"

"He will. One day he will."

"I don't think so. If he can't even come see me, how's he going to figure it out?"

She patted him on the arm. This was something she couldn't fix. Truman had built a chasm between himself and the children she knew he loved. He just wasn't able to get the drawbridge of his heart down far enough to get across.

Aiden motioned for another drink and she held the cup close. His eyelids fluttered. "You think I'm going to get out of here this time?"

"I'm sure of it. Melody needs a date for the prom."

He smiled, and that effort was all she needed. The slightest glimmer of life from him was like an electrical impulse. The trailer of a coming attraction.

"Tell me the story again," Aiden said.

"What story is that?"

"Come on. You know. How you met."

He was like a little kid, thirsting for drops of the father he didn't know. So she told him. Not all the gory details, but with enough flair to satisfy. How she was coming off a relational plane crash and she saw him in the newsroom. Tall and handsome and that smile that could melt polar ice caps. Aiden had to know what songs she listened to and what movies they saw, details that gave him an anchor to their past.

She never held back from him that they had moved in together in college. Or how her parents felt about Truman. The truth was better.

But there were things about the present she did not reveal.

For example, that the mounting medical bills had put them so far behind they would probably never recover. Or the fact that even with the medical insurance, the transplant cost would be astronomical. Or the truth that financial rescue was only a court procedure away. Her parents had told her they would assume responsibility for all her debts and work to pay for the transplant if she would simply divorce Truman and end the debacle. It seemed cruel at first. They had dug in their heels as deeply as she had and now it was a test of wills. Who would cave first?

She couldn't divorce him. Not now. She understood her parents' perspective and at times agreed with their assessment. She had threatened divorce a number of times. But something deep inside said, "Hang on. Don't give up." Embracing faith also meant she had embraced possibility. God raised the dead to life. Like Lazarus, Truman could one day have his own come-to-Jesus moment. She held on to that hope like a child holds the string of a leaking balloon. Shrunken, shriveled, and dragging on the ground behind her.

"Why did you choose that song at your wedding?" Aiden whispered.

"'True Companion'?" The words echoed through her mind. "I don't know; it was probably our favorite album that year. Everybody loved the song 'Walking in Memphis.' I almost took a job at a newspaper in Memphis and I wouldn't have even considered it except I loved that song. I wanted to walk on Beale Street and report Elvis sightings. It seems frivolous now, but that's how my mind worked."

"Back to 'True Companion.'"

"Sorry. I called your father Tru, and once we were an item on campus, we spent every waking moment together."

"Did you text all the time?"

"We didn't even have e-mail, as I recall. Cell phones were a luxury and even if I had one, he wouldn't have. Our dinner dates were the salad bar at Wendy's. Your father was the poor church mouse."

"Without the church."

"Right."

Her cell phone vibrated and she ignored it, staring into Aiden's fading eyes. One thing she had learned early was that any waking moment was Aiden's time. She would focus on him until exhaustion or the medication overtook him. Or both. And each time he fell asleep, she feared it might be the last time she would ever see those eyes.

Aiden looked out the window and the morning light reflected on his face. Teeth grinding now. Jaw set. "He doesn't care."

"Sure he does."

"Then why doesn't he come see me?"

She took a deep breath. "Well, what do you think?" Questions were always better. Hearing what was going on inside him was best.

"Could be because he just cares more about his work. But it doesn't make sense that he wouldn't come around. Maybe he's allergic to hospitals."

She put a hand on his head. He always responded to her touch. Truman hadn't given him that. Couldn't give him a hand on the shoulder with all the miles of separation.

"I don't think he's allergic to hospitals. Or you. But I do think it's unusually hard for him to come into these places." The phone beeped. A new voice mail. "He does love you. I know that. It's just that his love is imperfect."

"Like his love for you?"

She smiled. "Both of us are imperfect. And I never want you to feel that he's the bad one. I've made my share of mistakes."

"But you stayed. You've been here through everything. You're a rock, Mom."

She took his hand, a pale, small thing now, just skin and bones, and squeezed it. "I've been the lucky one. He's missed out. But I think part of his absence is because he can't stand to see you in so much pain."

Aiden closed his eyes and opened them, turtle-like. "There wouldn't be as much pain if he were here. I mean, that would help me forget it a little."

A tear coursed down his cheek and Aiden shut his eyes. Her heart melted. He always said something that did that. Something that pointed toward the truth and the ache of life, the ache of love, of eternity, or some mundane desire, like buying his own car.

She leaned forward. "There's a quotation by Longfellow I read years ago that I cling to about your father. It's a popular quote about men I've seen in a lot of books. Other writers agree with old Henry."

Aiden stared at her, his eyes focused, and she closed hers to get the words right. "'Every man has his secret sorrows which the world knows not; and often times we call a man cold when he is only sad.'"

She opened her eyes and saw another tear making its way down Aiden's cheek. For a moment she couldn't speak, the pain of her own voice echoing the heartbreak.

"That pretty much sums it up, doesn't it?" Aiden said.

She nodded. "That your dad hasn't been around doesn't have much to do with you, I don't think. He's just tired and angry and at odds with himself. Which doesn't make it any easier. It still feels bad. But to know he's in pain helps me. And to know the wounded always wound those they love the most. They don't mean to; it just happens."

She stroked his head, parting his hair the way she had when he was a child.

"Is that why he goes to casinos?"

"I suppose."

"Did he do that when he was in college?"

She took a deep breath, remembering the excitement in Truman's voice when he would call from some gambling triumph. "I knew he was drawn to gambling. It actually paid for some of his schooling. I encouraged it for a while. But I had no idea how destructive it would become."

"That sounds like something a psychologist would say."

She laughed quietly and stared at the acne around his face. Aiden was much older than his years, but his body didn't know it.

"He's searching. And it's been a long search I hope will end soon."

"Me too." His breathing became more shallow and for a moment, when his chest seemed to hover and stop, she thought he had slipped away. Instead, he squeezed her hand and said, without moving his lips, "I'm tired. Gonna get some sleep."

She kissed his forehead. "I'll be here when you wake up."

"I know."

She quietly left the room and stood in the hall, leaning against the wall and staring through the glass at him. She checked her phone and saw the missed call was from Truman.

"Hey, it's me. I'm in the main lobby here. Had a problem with my car. Can you come down when you get this? I assume you're upstairs."

Ellen shook her head and rolled her eyes. She wanted to throw the phone against the wall.

He was sitting behind a pillar, riffling through pages from a paper bag. Her first instinct was to scream, to ask what he thought he was doing, to yell that his son needed him. But she took a deep breath and watched him work.

There had always been something about Truman Wiley that caused a stir in her heart, good or bad. When she first met him, he had the big, wiry hair that framed his Tom Hanks–like face, narrow and long, and when he smiled, it was like a caricature of some lovable, squinty-eyed fur ball. He wore tight jeans and walked with that air of confidence that few in college seemed to possess. Long-armed and lanky and a laugh that was as genuine as a summer rain. She saw only echoes of that now. The years had edged his hair back from his temples. He was nowhere near balding, but he kept it close, though now he looked a bit shaggy. She saw he had lost weight. His cheeks were sallow and when he stood, his sweatpants sagged. And his eyes betrayed a tiredness, a weariness that comes not just from lack of sleep but lack of rest. A life of questions and nowhere to turn for answers.

"Why didn't you come up?" she said, trying to keep the edge from her voice.

"Good to see you, too."

She bit her lip. She had prayed this wouldn't go badly. All the way down the elevator.

"He's not doing well. He was asking about you before he went back to sleep. I think it would help him if you—"

"I've been with Murrow. I didn't have a chance to change."

"You didn't go in the house with those clothes, did you?"

"No, I stripped down last night—it's a long story. The house is fine, I promise. But my car was towed. Repossessed. And Murrow was in there."

He spoke about the cat like it was a person. Someone he cared for. It was all she could do not to head for the elevator.

She looked at the paper bag. "Is that from Oleta?"

He nodded.

"So you're taking the job?"

"She paid me and I'm going to deposit the money and get started. But I need a car."

"You can't take a cat in my car. If you can't come up and see him, you can't ride in the car."

He ran a hand through his hair. "There's a Target a few blocks from here. I'll get some shorts and a shirt. Will that work?" There was bite in the question, as if she was the one causing the problem. She could tell he was in get-it-done mode, but there was still fear in his eyes—or something close to it.

"If you want to use the car, you have to come to the room. By the time you get back, he'll be up for lunch."

He stared at the floor and nodded. "Okay. But I can't lug this stuff to Target and back. Let me have the keys."

She crossed her arms and stared. "Grab your stuff and follow me."

They walked outside to the parking elevator and the Florida heat hit them. Stretching her legs felt good even though she walked into an oven. It had been more than a day since she had been outside.

"You and Oleta didn't hit it off?" she said.

"She was a little abrasive. Distrustful. She probably has reason. I just hope she doesn't take it out on Murrow."

"She's a good woman. And she'll be a reliable resource. Picked anything up from the Piggly Wiggly files?"

He smiled and pressed the Up arrow at the elevator. "The evidence is overwhelming. Looks like I don't have any reason to fear."

"Fear what?"

"That I'll get into this and find out he's not guilty. Which is what they all say. Especially the ones who are looking at the needle. That would throw a wrench in the transplant plans. . . ."

"Carlton's on our side," she said. "But those around him—"

"Carlton? You're on a first-name basis again?"

She rolled her eyes. "Governor Townsend. Don't tell me you're still jealous."

"Have you talked with him?"

She checked her watch and nodded. "With his office, his chief of staff. And he and I have had a couple of conversations about Aiden's situation. His intervention in this will also be part of the book, I assume."

"Which makes me wonder *why*. You know he's not going to do anything to derail his chances of the White House."

They stepped out at the top floor and Ellen led him to her Sequoia. He stowed his computer and the bag in the back.

"I don't see how this could hurt him. He wants to help, Tru."

"If the far-right crowd thinks this is a bad idea, they'll turn on him. The liberals, too. This could stir up party dissension. The leadership won't want that, especially with him rising in the polls."

"This is not about polls. He's on board. Why are you trying to steal the last hope we have?"

They rode back down the elevator in an uncomfortable silence. When the door opened, he stopped near a white pylon, shading his eyes from the sun. "I'm trying to be realistic. I don't want you to get your hopes up."

"You think I'm not being realistic? That I haven't thought through all the possibilities? With every surgery I get my hopes up. With every new drug. I've gotten my hopes up about a lot of things that haven't come through, so don't worry about me."

Ellen turned away. The icy silence was broken only by the traffic pulling into the garage and the people shuffling past them on the street.

"There's no doubt I'll need to talk with him," he said. "Maybe you could set it up. And I should make contact with the detectives on the case. Family of the victim, too."

"Truman, this doesn't have to be a Pulitzer prize winner. This is one man's story of change inside an ugly place. Don't get every angle. Don't make it a personal crusade."

"Personal crusade? Telling different sides of a story is a personal crusade?"

"I'm not suggesting you do a bad job, but you don't have to make this so hard."

"You asked me to do this. Now you want me to phone it in?"

"I'm glad you're suddenly sold on the idea. I just think there's more going on. Maybe all this happened because you're supposed to be here for Aiden. Maybe you could make him a priority."

"I love my son. I know I don't do that as well as you do."

"Don't make this about me."

"If you and Oleta want me to throw something together and print Conley's death row gasps and be happy with the money, you asked the wrong guy. You know I don't do things halfway."

"Yeah. Most things."

She wanted the words back, but there they were, hanging in the air like a circling hawk looking for prey. This was the content of the last few years of their marriage. The hurts of the past seemed to rise up at even the slightest hint of a meaningful conversation. The further toward faith and reliance on God Ellen moved, the more Truman seemed to pull back. He became angry, more aloof with Abigail and Aiden, taking hardship assignments and flying to foreign countries for stories that made him a household name but not a fixture in his own home.

"I need to get back up there," she said, turning toward him. She put out a hand and touched his arm. "Tru, I think you should do this with everything in you. Full speed ahead. And I know this has fallen in your lap for a reason."

"Oleta said the same thing. Purpose and all that God stuff. I hope you're right."

She moved toward the front door and he called out to her. "You think I could have the keys? I told Oleta I'd get Murrow. . . ."

She couldn't believe it. Another dodge. "You're not carrying that cat in any part of my car. You know you can't do that. And whether you like it or not, you need to see your son."

"Ellen, you don't know what you're asking."

"What *I'm* asking?" She shook her head and dug into her purse, threw the keys hard at him and turned away. She didn't care anymore. *Take the car. Get the cat. Go. Get out of our lives.* She held her tongue as the automatic door opened and she walked toward the lobby.

She didn't look back until she reached Aiden's floor and saw her car still sitting atop the parking garage.

CHAPTER 5

THAT CERTAINLY WENT WELL. Funny how a tender conversation can bring out the fangs. But I will say this: Ellen's key-ring fastball on the outside corner left a bruise on my right hand. That girl could've pitched in the minors.

I walked to Target in the blistering heat, cursing the sun, Ellen, and myself. Part of moving to the cottage was to alleviate the strife and bad vibe I brought around the house. Even Ellen didn't know I had bought the cottage until I moved there about six months ago. Maybe it's a cop-out to say I went away to make things easier for them. Maybe I was just doing it for myself. But I felt it was better for everyone if I wasn't around. When I was at home, we fought. When I was gone, we fought about me not being home, just over the phone. And I can always hang up the phone.

It was one of those SuperTargets with produce and baked goods in the front, and I grabbed a sandwich and found some shorts, a shirt, and even picked out new briefs and socks within five minutes. I am past the point of worrying about how I look.

I ate the hoagie on the way back, all changed into my new clothes. White shirt, gray shorts. I threw the others into the bathroom trash. No sense in taking a chance with cat hair.

The sandwich tasted like a rock and hung somewhere in my esophagus, a dry clump of meat and cheese and yeasty bread. Maybe it was my digestive system, but I tossed the remainder of the sandwich into a culvert and stuck the wadded-up wrapper in my pocket. Some hungry animal would eat that sandwich, but the plastic wrap would have been a detriment to the earth and I wasn't about to have that on my conscience. No, sirree, even if I can't visit my son on his deathbed, I recycle.

With check in hand, I drove to our bank. I'd tapped out my credit cards and I needed cash. I didn't recognize the teller. Turnover is heavy there. She seemed concerned with the large amount I wanted, but I explained I had my eye on a used car. That's what I figured I'd do: get something cheap at a dealer and away I'd go. That's what I told myself.

She handed me the envelope stuffed with hundred-dollar bills and I stuck it as deep in the pocket of my new shorts as I could and returned to Ellen's car. I had bought her an Escalade years earlier, but she'd traded it in on a Toyota Sequoia that she said got better gas mileage. Someone in her church owned a Toyota dealership, so I'm sure she got a good deal. That should sound sarcastic because it is. The only thing worse than a Christian who wants to help save your soul is a Christian who wants to save your soul *and* sell you a used car.

I'm a fast reader and after my foray through the stack of pages in my new paper-bag briefcase, I decided I only needed to talk with one man at the police station, a detective named George Chandler. Judging from the picture in the article, George was probably at or near retirement, if he hadn't succumbed to heart disease from beer and donuts. After a couple of calls I found out he was across town and still on the job. It took me forty-five minutes to get there.

George was not only nearing retirement, he had a bandage on one discolored arm that looked frightfully close to a melanoma emergency. He walked outside with me, heading to his car with his partner in tow, a thin man who looked like he was just out of high school. I don't think George would have given me the time of day if he hadn't recognized my face from a report I did about a slain officer's tribute a few years earlier. I told him I was writing about the Conley case and he wanted to know what angle I was taking.

"I'm telling it from his side."

He raised an eyebrow, which looked like the only exercise he'd gotten all day. Maybe he was doing eyebrow Pilates. I've heard it can strengthen your core.

"That should be interesting," George said. "Finally getting the truth out of him?"

"I don't think he's ready to give up his innocence."

The detective cursed. "What he put that mother through. Unimaginable. That was the easiest conviction we ever gave the DA. Ever."

I got the point with the first *ever*.

"Every shred of evidence pointed to him. If there's anybody who deserves the death penalty in the history of this state, it's Terrelle Conley. You can quote me. More evidence than Bundy and the rest of them put together. And I'd be glad to pull the switch on Old Sparky or stick in the last IV. Tell that *guy* what I said."

Only George didn't say *guy*; he said another word that I guess could mean *man*, in a loose translation of his French.

"Were there ever any doubts in the investigation?"

"None. Not one. Ever."

There it was again. He was an everaholic.

"Did you consider another suspect?"

"Didn't have to. He buried her in the dump near where he was sleeping. We found the murder weapon in his cabinet. What more do you need?"

I had made a note and pulled out a name I'd scribbled down. "What about your partner at the time, Sawyer?"

That got a rise from him. Lines formed on his face at the mention of the name. Advanced forehead Pilates.

"Yeah, you need to talk to Dennis if you want Conley's side. Dennis was always the defense's best friend on capital cases. Bleeding heart. Against the death penalty. Could have ruined us but he didn't." He opened his door. "You should definitely talk to him."

"How do I find him? He still on the job?"

"Hey, you're the *guy guy* reporter, right?"

Only he didn't say *guy guy*. You get the point. I reached for the door before he closed it and he looked at my hand like it was a raw chicken. With lice.

"One more question," I said. "You ever find a motive? She wasn't sexually assaulted. Why would anybody kill a hairdresser?"

"You haven't seen the video, have you?" George said. "Take a look at the video from that case and ask your friend Conley to explain it."

He closed the door and the two drove away, George's mouth running in a rampant and obscene tirade.

During the conversation I had ignored my cell. Now I pulled out the phone to listen to the message and noticed that another had come in earlier.

"Mr. Wiley, this is Vanessa from Tallahassee General's billing department." She sounded like she was twelve and was reading her mother's recipe for Ding Dong pudding. "Your wife gave me this number and said I could reach you here. This is to confirm the notice we sent to you last week that your balance will be referred to a collection agency if—"

Get in line. I pushed the 7, the one for delete. I don't know a lot about my phone but I do know the delete button is 7.

"Truman," a male voice said on the next message. "We see you've relocated." It sent a shiver through me, something akin to racking, bowel-loosening fear. The kind of feeling you get when you see a dark figure in the yard at midnight staring at your house and holding an ax. I wanted to hit the 7 but knew I couldn't.

After a pause he said, "I understand you're having some personal problems. And a colleague there in Tallahassee tells me your son isn't well. Sorry to hear it. But, Truman, we need to deal with this little matter of the loan. My *heart* goes out to you, but my patience trumps my heart. I suggest you contact me quickly. Otherwise we'll be contacting you."

There was heavy breathing at the end of the message and I could picture Mickey "The Vault" Luchesi's face. I had met the man on an investigative story. I'd weaseled my way into an interview, with the caveat that we wouldn't show his face, give his name, or in any way expose him. He spoke candidly about a string of recent murders near gambling establishments on the East Coast.

I didn't know it at the time but he was using the opportunity to send a message to his colleagues. I had stayed in touch with Mickey afterward, unfortunately, and took a loan from him at a particularly dark point. That decision only compounded my troubles and exponentially increased the darkness.

The hospital's collection agency was bad. Mickey's agency didn't send letters. They came in person.

I've learned in reporting that when your back is against the wall on a story, you have to just do the next thing, take the next step, get more information. You can't worry about what you don't have; you have to focus on what's in your Piggly Wiggly bag, proverbially speaking. If I ever write a book about reporting, that will be one of my maxims: do the next thing.

I called the realty office and Oleta picked up. She assured me Murrow was fine. She had bought a litter box and food at the pet store and Murrow now had the rule of their storage room.

"How's Aiden?" she said.

"He's good. Stable."

"You didn't see him, did you?"

Why do all the women in my life have antennas? Even their friends have it. Maybe I'm paranoid, but I felt even Vanessa from the billing office could have guessed my blood pressure and pulse rate.

"I haven't gone up yet, but I did see Ellen. Have you heard anything about getting me into Starke?"

I could tell a *tsk-tsk* when I heard one; then her voice became animated. "You're on for this Friday morning. You have one hour. The chaplain set it up for me but they're regimented over there. It's like being in the military. You come in late, you don't go in."

"I'll be there. But about Murrow, is there any way you could—?"

"Don't worry about her. I'll take her home with me if I have to. She'll be fine. Just concentrate on your son. And the book."

"Great. That puts my mind at ease. And for what it's worth, I'm sorry we got off on the wrong foot. I appreciate what you're doing."

"We're praying for Aiden. He's the most important thing right now."

I asked her if she remembered a Detective Sawyer who worked on her husband's case and knew how to get in touch with him. I felt naked with my laptop in the back. She took down the name and said she'd call.

The well rose as I drove back to the hospital. A familiar feeling like a river cresting against the banks of life. I knew I had to see Aiden, but I couldn't get past the obligation, the responsibility, the guilt of the past, the desire for my wife, and the shame of my choices. Once you've failed your family, you live on a different level. You're always trying to fill in the missing stairs. You try too hard to live up to expectations or to not fulfill the negative ones.

I pulled to a stop on the street across from the hospital and guessed which was his room. Shades were drawn. I wondered if my son was waiting. I imagined him hooked up to tubes, swollen face, sunken eyes. I focused on monitors and blips when he was young. Scars down his chest. Sharp silver plunging into pale skin.

Instead of pulling into the parking garage, I drove past it and headed for I-10. Like a magnet I was drawn to the broken white lines, east toward the coast, toward the water and the old familiar way to lose myself. With each exit I had the urge to turn around, to return and sit with my wife and son. But I managed to push those urges down.

CHAPTER 6

OLETA CALLED with the number for former detective Sawyer, who was now a private investigator and probably chased divorce cases. That's what I assumed when I heard his voice mail for "Sawyer Investigative Services." I left a message and felt glad he wasn't in. I couldn't focus on the story or the book, and I told myself I needed this release. I needed the inner demons exorcised. And I needed to take the $15,000 in my pocket and turn it into $50,000. I'd done something like that in college, back when I could quit when I was winning, but in recent trips I hadn't been as successful. I promised myself if I made it to $30K, I would walk away.

I figured Jacksonville was safely out of Mickey's territory. There had been a floating casino that went belly-up a year or two before, but that was replaced by another cruise ship under different ownership with a catchy name and top-of-the-line accommodations. Every one of these places had nice-looking women at the front welcoming you with that breath-of-fresh-air feeling that you were in a place built for beautiful people. I knew there were usually two cruises each day and the evening one left around seven. Since traffic was light, I made it before they set sail. Lucky me.

I quickly changed my cash for poker chips and headed toward the tables, stretching my legs. My ticket paid for food and a few drinks, though I made a point of not mixing business with pleasure. And when I sit down at a table, it's all business.

My phone rang a couple of times, but I don't take calls when I'm in the zone. I silenced it so it only vibrated, but even that was a distraction. In the first few hands I'd made several hundred dollars and the old mojo was back. Just like I'd experienced in those early years at college when I turned my father's insurance money into tuition, rent, and an old Toyota with enough miles to reach the moon. My heart raced; the endorphins pumped; my mind was fully alive. It was like reporting from a fully engaged battlefield.

Then the mojo left. Fast.

With only an hour left on the cruise, twinkling stars reflecting on the water, I had lost all but a handful of poker chips. Funny, I had planned when to stop if I won, but not when to stop if I was losing. I cashed in the chips and lost that money at the slots. As I said, I never play the slots, and for good reason. About the only thing I took away from the boat was a charge for my cell phone. Not a good return on a $15K investment, but there it is. In previous excursions I had lost more than that. My worst night . . . I don't think about my worst night.

It's hard to describe the compulsion to someone who has never experienced it. It's like when the carnival barker gives you three darts to pop two balloons, and you can't stop buying darts because all you can think of is that other balloon and how easy it will be to take the big doll home if you just spend two more dollars on another dart. Only I wasn't spending dollars, I was spending thousands, which made the high even better. The bigger the risk, the more adrenaline, the better the feeling, the greater the rush.

Those looking in at my life from the outside would say I've seen it all. They're right. With my experiences in war zones, disasters, calamities, mudslides, earthquakes, all the loss of life and devastation, I'd say I've seen too much. Most envy living on the edge, sucking the marrow from life, but that's romanticizing my travels. When I wake up in the middle of the night, I'm not thinking of the exotic locations or international celebrities I've interviewed. I think of events I've witnessed and tried to describe. Spaces of time that have numbed me to the core.

A good friend accompanied me to the interior of Africa, flying in a small plane and driving over unimaginable roads. It could have been any year, any decade, you pick the famine. I wore plastic gloves and the three-year-old child I held weighed not much more than a newborn back in the States. I don't know how he'd made it that long. His ribs were draped with a thin layer of skin and his pulse lightly flickered at his neck. His breath was as shallow as a bird's, deep brown eyes as wide as the coastline and searching. He just stared at me as I did my stand-up in front of the camera, and when I looked down at him, right before I said the tagline with my name and the network's signature, I noticed there was no movement on his neck and his pupils were fixed.

I finished my report and handed him to the aid worker nearby and threw up in a trench. That was the second time I'd stared death in the face. The effects have lasted.

That's what greets me in the middle of the night when I awaken. And it's part of the reason why writing Terrelle Conley's story didn't hold the allure it might once have. I've seen the eyes of men and children about to die, and I didn't relish seeing another set.

If you want to know, I don't gamble for fun. I don't use it to pass time. Gambling is something that makes me *feel*. It's nerve on nerve rather than the dull plodding that passes for the rest of my life. Food has lost its allure. Even sex has lost its edge.

I found the Sequoia and sat inside, trying to descend from the high and realizing what I'd just done. It would take a long time to deal with this guilt. So I decided to use my time wisely and at least check my messages.

"Tru, where are you?" Ellen said. Her voice was tight and edgy, like she thought I might be at a casino. "I need the car to get a change of clothes at the house. I thought maybe you could give me a break here for an hour or so. Call me. Would you?"

I checked the time stamp, then my watch. Not good. It was early morning now and a good three-hour drive to the hospital. I tried to formulate some kind of cover story about working on the book or doing research or getting lost in the writing and losing track of time as the next message played.

"This is Dennis Sawyer," the man said with more than a hint of a Chicago accent. "You called about the Conley case. I got plenty to tell you. Call me."

I put my head back. I needed sleep. I reached for the keys and noticed movement outside. Someone pecked on the glass and motioned for me to roll down the window. The guy was silhouetted in the lights above and wore a hooded sweatshirt. All I could see of his face was a handlebar mustache and a sick grin.

I'm used to winos and the homeless stopping me. I have no

problem giving them a few bucks, but I wasn't in the mood and all the cash I had was on the boat.

"Sorry, pal; I'm tapped out."

The man banged the window with the bottom of his hand and it ticked me off. I made a gesture of goodwill to him with one of my fingers and started the car. In the rearview I noticed a vehicle that was little, loud, and expensive blocking my exit. To my left, a glint of light flashed off the chrome of a silver tire iron. Glass shattered and scattered onto my lap and into the front seats.

Call it a reporter's intuition, but my gut told me this was not good. The mojo was definitely gone.

CHAPTER 7

28 DAYS BEFORE EXECUTION

I was asleep in the hospital waiting room when Ellen found me. She shook me awake.

"When I take your hand, I'll watch my heart set sail." The words of the Marc Cohn tune came back as I looked at her face. Waking up to see her did something inside, like the old days when we'd wake up in each other's arms. Why had I abandoned this beautiful creature? Why had I chosen this path?

"Truman, what happened?"

I'd played out the conversation on my way back to Tallahassee with the wind in my face—not that I had a choice to have wind in my face.

"Have you had that treated?" she said.

Another hospital bill was the last thing I needed. "I'm fine; it's just a scratch." Of course I could still taste the blood in my mouth from that scratch, but then it was easy to spit it out the window that wasn't there. I didn't know how to tell her about her car, but I'd stopped at a self-serve car wash and vacuumed all the glass from the seats. Like a cat, I like to keep my living space clean.

She touched the goose egg under my eye and the bandage over the gash in my cheek. "This is going to get infected. You need stitches. Was it a car accident?"

I shook my head. *Note to self: don't shake your head when you have a hole in your cheek.* "I got jumped. Guy with a tire iron."

"A carjacking?"

"They didn't get your car, but they left you without a driver's-side window."

There. I said it. She was too focused on the wound to worry about her car, which was a good thing. My first question would have been about the car. I hoped I could use her selfless concern to divert her from the truth. That a couple of Mickey's goons had tracked me down to a casino boat and were trying to extract a payment. But I had fooled them and lost everything before they showed up. Serves them right. Perhaps it wasn't Mickey's goons. Maybe his tentacles didn't reach that far. Didn't really matter, but I still wondered.

The crashed glass and the gash on the face were only the beginning, of course. A warning. And if the Marine who had just gotten back from Afghanistan hadn't been there, no telling what else would have happened. This was the guy who had won about $5K of my money at the poker table. After the little car with the big price tag sped away, the man offered to call the police but I waved him off. I didn't want the police involved. He drove me to

Walgreens and poured a whole bottle of hydrogen peroxide on my cheek as I listened to it bubble and fizz. The Betadine stained my white shirt and shorts, but the way he bandaged the open wound made me think he'd done this before on the battlefield. He used a knife from his boot to cut strips and pulled the skin on my cheek tighter than a drum. It felt weird but didn't look half-bad in the rearview.

"What did those guys want?" the Marine said. I found out he was from Alabama and that he had a hard time sleeping. The boat helped calm his nerves. Didn't hurt his bank account either.

"I assume they wanted money," I said to him. "I should have sent them your way—you have all of mine."

He laughed and shoved a hundred-dollar bill in my shirt pocket, the one with Betadine all over it. If the boat had been open, I would have gone back.

"Did they get the money?" Ellen said. "You didn't cash all of Oleta's check, did you?"

I have scruples. Maybe about a handful. I don't out-and-out lie to my wife, even if divorce is a possibility. "It's all gone." Technically that was telling the truth.

"Did you file a report?" she said through her hands. I could tell from the tone of voice that she suspected something. Maybe this was why I had abandoned this beautiful creature. She could read me better than I could read the morning paper.

"I'm talking with a detective this morning." Another subtle piece of information that would ease her mind but not necessarily give her the truth.

"Where did this happen? Were you just driving along the street?"

I winced, though it was more from the pain of not being able to think of the answers I had planned. Sleep had clouded my mind. I said something about driving around, thinking about the Conley case, drinking coffee (which was true), and getting lost in the story.

"You need to go to the emergency room right now." She grabbed my arm as if it were a fait accompli.

I waved her off. "I'm meeting Sawyer in half an hour. I just wanted you to know I'm sorry I wasn't able to spell you yesterday. How's Aiden?"

That took her aback. "He made it through another night. His vitals have stabilized."

"So he's going to pull through."

This time her eyes betrayed her. She dipped her head. "I keep thinking that his only hope is in death."

I thought she meant the sweet-by-and-by, Jesus-in-the-clouds kind of thing Christians sing and talk about, which is part of my problem with the leap of faith. Jumping into the darkness of death for your hope in this life is not my idea of a good way to live. I would rather hope in something I taste and feel and experience.

Then she surprised me.

"I feel guilty about what has to happen in order for him to live. Someone else has to die. That doesn't feel fair, even if God provides a heart."

"Kind of like people praying for a clear day for their picnic while the farmer prays for rain," I said.

She gave me that quizzical look. There was probably some verse, some pearl of wisdom I could say to calm her heart and send her into my arms. Unfortunately for me, all I could think to say was "It's the circle of life."

My wife was not into *Lion King* theology.

"Look, after I meet with this detective, I'll come give you a break," I said. "You can take the car and—"

"I got a ride to the house from a friend at church. I'm fine."

Great. These church people were everywhere.

My cell phone alarm rang and the sound made my head feel like an inferno. My eyes burned from too little sleep, and my mind went from the $15K I had lost to those hooded men to the hospital billing department. If they knew I was in the lobby, they'd probably send nurses in hooded sweatshirts to pummel me with bedpans.

"I want to do this for you," I said. "When I get back, you take the rest of the day and do whatever you need. Go to a bookstore. Go to a movie. I'll stay with him. I'll work on the book while he's sleeping and check out the hospital food."

"I can't leave him," she said, but there was some light that came into her face and it wasn't just the sun trying to get through the heavy shades in the lobby.

"I need some time alone with him," I said. "Just him and me. It's been too long."

"I know he'll really like that, Tru. He mentioned you again last night when he woke up."

"So prepare me. How does he look?"

"I feel like I need to prepare him for what *you* look like."

I grinned and it felt like the Joker had taken a knife to my cheek and opened the smile a little wider, like back to my ear. Of all the things I needed right then, an estranged wife who made me smile was not one of them.

"He's lost a lot of weight," she said. "His color is off. His eyes are dead and lifeless most of the time. It's hard for me to see it because I've been so close to it for so long. Friends come and see him and act concerned because of the change, but it's been gradual."

But will be terrifying to someone like me who hasn't seen his son in months. That's what she was saying.

"The heart is mysterious," she continued. "Everything in the body depends on it and we take it for granted."

"He's going to get through this. Ten years from now, this will all be a bad dream."

I reached out to touch her hand and she pulled back. She tried to mask the instinctive move, but my observational powers are superior to those of mere humans.

"Do you want to get something to eat in the cafeteria?" she said.

As hungry as I was, I imagined the pain of chewing Cap'n Crunch with my loose molars and it felt like torture. "I'd better hold off on that. Expect me back before noon, okay?"

She nodded and stood. "And get that looked at, Tru."

CHAPTER 8

DENNIS SAWYER PULLED UP to the Denny's in an ancient Toyota Camry. Not exactly the image of the grizzled ex-cop/crack PI I'd expected, but at least he was on time. Portly and balding, he wore white Dockers, open-toed sandals, and a tentlike Hawaiian shirt that hung loosely over his belly. With the sunglasses and mustache he could have passed as an aging rock star. I waved at him from the back of the restaurant, but he seemed to know where I was as soon as he hit the front door.

He shook my hand and glanced at my face. "Run into some trouble?"

"Yeah, IHOP got jealous."

He snickered and the waitress arrived. He ordered without ever looking at the menu: coffee and the special. I wasn't sure how the food would sit on my acid-filled stomach but I was starving and ordered pancakes. Easier to chew. The orange juice and coffee were probably a mistake, but I couldn't help myself.

My head still felt cloudy without much sleep. I needed to focus. I thanked him for meeting and he seemed uninterested in small talk. *How are the kids? Do you have kids? What's your favorite color?* It wasn't his style, which I appreciated.

"Why are you so interested in Conley?"

"He and his family asked me to write a book. It's what I do."

He seemed unimpressed. "A little late to change the outcome, isn't it?"

"I think he's resigned to the needle. He's actually trying to become the first heart-transplant donor from death row."

"Who's the lucky recipient?"

"My son."

He stared at me. The coffee came and we both partook, our first station of Denny's communion service.

"How much do you know?" Sawyer said.

"What I've read from the news clippings and court transcripts. Chandler said it was the cleanest conviction he'd ever had."

"Is that what George said?" He pursed his lips like someone had squeezed a lemon into his coffee. "Well, he was right. It was the easiest."

"You had doubts about Conley, though."

"Still do. Everybody congratulated themselves. Made a lot of people happy to catch a perp and get a conviction that fast."

"Chandler called you a bleeding heart. Against the death penalty."

Sawyer gave a wry smile. "I got no problem with the death penalty for people who deserve it. And I don't know about Conley.

Something tells me he probably deserved being behind bars for a lot of things, but not the murder of Diana Wright."

He used her name, not just "the victim." Interesting that after eleven years he still had a connection. "What happened with the investigation?"

"We got the missing-person report from the mother. We interviewed people who worked at the shop. There had been some kind of altercation with a drunk on the street. We got the surveillance video from the salon and the pet store next door, made a positive ID on the guy, and traced Conley to a junkyard."

"He lived there?"

"Slept in a little pop-up trailer toward the back of the lot. The owner said he'd hired Conley as a night watchman, if you can believe it."

"How'd you find the body?"

"A dog. Took her about a minute to find it. Shallow grave by a '67 Mustang. Out in the open, like he wanted us to find it. Yellow tape went up and that was it."

"And he was asleep in the trailer?"

Sawyer nodded. "Still had half a bottle left, too."

"What about a car? If he was just a drunk on the street, did he have transportation?"

Sawyer nodded. "Rusted-out Mazda. Looked a lot like him. It wouldn't even turn over. But that little piece of the puzzle wasn't important."

"Chandler and the prosecutor said he found out where she lived, waited outside, snatched her, and killed her. But why?"

"He threatened her. It's in the court transcript."

"Was there forensic evidence in the car?"

He opened a grape jelly packet and scooped it into his mouth with a butter knife. "We found her hair. Her purse. One shoe. It felt conveniently haphazard. Looked like a drunk had tried to pull off the perfect crime. Ineptly meticulous. To me, it didn't fit."

"You find a dead girl in the dump and evidence everywhere and you don't think it fits?"

"How did he abduct her without anyone seeing? How did a drunk get her back to the dump? And why bring her back there? Why not dump her body in a river or the swamp?"

I shook my head. "The case was open and shut. The guy's guilty."

"Maybe so. But I've got more questions. Where did he get the revolver with the serial number filed down? And who keeps a murder weapon in a kitchen cupboard? What about the owner of the salon where Diana worked? That guy is a piece of work."

I gave him my best reporter's quizzical stare, the one where I furrow into a unibrow. Always worked with political figures and heads of businesses to get them to elaborate without me even asking another question.

"The manager of the salon owned three of these places across town. Now it's just one. *Shady* is an understatement. Actually, it would be a compliment. I heard he had the girls do more than cut hair, if you know what I mean. Sleazeball. And he had a brother who's now in jail."

"What's the manager's name?"

He folded his napkin and closed his eyes. "Curtis Tompkins. Brother's in prison for dope dealing, but that was the plea deal. He was guilty of a lot worse."

He gave me the name of the salon, but I had that in my notes.

"What did Chandler say about these inconsistencies?" I said.

"Two and two make four, and when things fit as neatly as this did, investigations shut down. But it wasn't just Chandler. The prosecutor, Boyle, was up for election that year. He wanted a quick conviction. Push it through. Get the ink dry on the headlines."

My cheek throbbed and I popped a couple more Advil and washed them down with the watery orange juice.

"It smelled to me like something else was going on but for the life of me I don't know what. As soon as we found the body, the reports were written and everybody went home."

"If you were so sure it wasn't right, why didn't you follow up?"

He shrugged. "Like I said, he was probably guilty of something. And I did have other work. But it's bugged me over the years. Why did he pick her? There were other people on the street. Why go for her?"

"Did the defense bring any of this up?"

"The defense was inept. Conley got shafted on all sides. Unless he really did do it."

"Which makes the most sense to me."

The food arrived and he dove into his eggs with abandon. I dove into my pancakes like a timid swimmer, pushing small bits to the right side of my mouth, away from the pain. Despite the good detective's concern, the conversation made me think Sawyer was a sour-grapes guy who didn't mind stirring things up for his old partner. Maybe Chandler had cheated him out of a dozen donuts. Still, there was something about his questions that felt disconcerting.

"Is this why you left the force?"

Two pieces of bacon went into the bottomless pit and Sawyer wiped his fingers on a napkin. "I'm no saint. I didn't leave over some moral problem if that's what you're asking. Let's just say it was a mutual decision between my superiors and myself."

"So he might be innocent but you'll just let him die?"

He spread grape jelly on a biscuit this time. "Nothing's going to stop the wheels of justice. Short of some action from the governor, Conley's dead. Which puts you in an interesting position with your son."

"Yeah. Interesting."

Sawyer leveled his gaze and spoke softly. "If he needs this kind of procedure, he must not be doing well."

The man's sensitivity surprised me. Almost choked me up. Almost.

I changed the subject. "What was Conley's motivation? Revenge for not giving him money? The autopsy said she wasn't sexually assaulted."

"Ask Conley. Ask Chandler. I got no answers to that, other than what he yelled at her and what witnesses saw and testified."

"I haven't read that yet."

"Witnesses outside the salon say he approached her and asked for money. He followed her, begging. He finally got in front of her, and when she refused, he screamed he was going to kill her. She got by him and climbed on a bus. The next day she didn't show up for work. Then we found her body in the junkyard."

He wiped his plate with the remainder of his biscuit and popped it into his mouth. All done. Good boy. The waitress brought the check and I tried to ignore it, but it just sat there. He remained quiet until I pulled out the hundred-dollar bill. It still had some Betadine on it.

"When do you see Conley?" he said.

"First meeting is Friday morning."

"Buy some new clothes. Don't walk in like that. And get your face checked. Looks like it's infected."

Thanks, Ellen.

"How'd you get that?" he said.

"I had a run-in with a couple of guys who think I owe their boss some money."

"Do you?"

I nodded.

"Must be quite a loan." He gave me a look like he'd seen this type of thing before. A sad look. "Did you get the authorities involved?"

"Not yet. I think I can handle it."

"Does your wife know?"

I hesitated.

"Friendly advice if you'll take it," he said, pointing at my face. "That was a message. And the next one won't be as subtle. Pay the bill. Fast. I'd hate to get a call from your wife asking me to look into this after you're in the morgue, which is where you're going to wind up."

He rose and shook my hand. "Good luck getting the story. And with your son."

CHAPTER 9

FROM THE PICTURES among Oleta's clippings, the row of shops near the salon hadn't changed much. The pet store was now a tanning salon and there was a convenience shop on the corner. On the other side of the salon was a locally owned office supply store that seemed to have more employees than customers. The street looked like it was something from a Mayberry reunion show with awnings that shaded the sidewalk and a brick facade. Across the street sat a public parking lot. Same as before.

Mane Street Hair and Nails sat in the middle of the block, a narrow building with the usual signs outside stating they were full service. Hair and nails, walk-ins welcome. I decided to test them and walked in.

The front section was set up for nails, while two women and

one man were styling hair toward the back. All three were busy. Only one Asian woman was doing nails and she was occupied with a blonde woman whose hair seemed to stretch in prayer toward the water-stained ceiling tiles.

Two middle-aged women in plastic chairs leafed through magazines, the requisite bottles of designer shampoo, conditioner, and hair coloring stacked in glass cases behind them. A thirtyish, jowly woman sat at the front desk and didn't look up when I approached. Her short hair was colored several hues of yellow.

"Name?" she said.

"Truman."

She wrote it on a pink slip under a row of names that had been crossed out. "Haircut?"

I looked at the prices and gulped. It had been a long time since I cared what it cost to cut my hair. With my dwindling funds, I was a little protective.

"Yeah, just a cut today. I do my nails on Thursdays."

"Fifteen minutes," she said.

I leaned on the counter and took off my sunglasses, waiting until she glanced up to speak. "Are you the owner?"

"Is there a problem?" she said, staring at the bandage on my cheek. In the mirror behind her I could see what a hideous sight my face had become.

"I'm just looking for who's been here the longest. Would that be you?"

"I've been here a few years."

"Do you remember Diana?"

A cloud came over her and she cocked her head. "You here for a haircut or something else?"

"A little of both," I said.

"A few more days and all of this will be over. We'll finally have it behind us."

I nodded. "You were the witness at the trial, weren't you? You saw the whole thing."

"No, that was Wanda. But we don't talk about it. She gets upset."

She went back to whatever she was doing and the ladies held their magazines. I smiled, though it hurt a lot more to smile than frown, disproving that saying about the muscles in your face.

A tall man was led to the front by the male hairdresser and they exchanged pleasantries. Either the sitting women were having their nails done or they were waiting on the female stylists because the man came toward me. He seemed not to notice my injury.

"I'm Dexter. Is this your first visit to Mane Street?"

"It is. How long have you worked here?"

"Going on four years," Dexter said. He was a small man with a slight build and a pleasant face. He buttoned the cape around my neck and looked in the mirror, lifting his hands to my head as if preparing to sculpt a work of art. "So what are we doing today?"

I love it when stylists talk in the first-person plural. "Let's just do a three on the side and a five on top and call it good."

He frowned. "Really? That drastic? Are you sure? A man with all your hair should show it off."

"Shorter means less gray," I said. "Plus, it'll take the attention away from my face."

He laughed. "I'm not sure any haircut could do that, my friend. All right, five on top, three on the sides, and I'll blend a bit."

He began the small talk dance of hairdressers and I wondered if they took Chitchat 101 in beauty school. Make a connection. Form a verbal bond.

"You have the day off today?" he said.

"I'm actually working right now. On a project about the lady who used to work here. Diana."

He turned off the clippers and stared at me in the mirror. "I thought I recognized you. Didn't you use to work for—oh, what's that news network . . . ?"

I told him and he snapped his fingers. "Yes, Truman. The reporter. It fits." He turned and looked at his coworkers. "Wow, we have someone famous in the shop today." He giggled and his eyes twinkled. "Weren't you the guy who got caught in that melee in San Francisco between all the protesters?"

I nodded. "You have a good memory."

He pursed his lips and rolled his eyes. "No, I was there. What a night." He told me much more than I wanted to know, but it was clear he really had been there.

"How did you wind up in Tallahassee?" I said.

"Series of life changes, choices. My partner moved here for his work and then we split. Left me for someone taller. I always said he only loved me for the free haircuts. He had such a lovely mane. I hope it all falls out. Well, that's not true. I don't wish him ill."

"I know the feeling."

"So how did you get the bandage and bruise? Covering another riot? Shark invasion?"

His quick wit made me smile. And then wince. "Let's just say it was a misunderstanding."

"Oh, I've had my share of those. All right, I won't pry." He leaned close to my face and I could smell the coffee on his breath. "But you really should get that looked at. It could get infected."

He finished the back and sides and began blending with scissors. "You covered the execution in South Carolina, too."

"You have way too good of a memory."

"The bane of my existence. I remember too much. Bits of conversation. Meaningless details. Latin words. Middle names of presidents. Which company makes which candy bar. It's not photographic, of course—I'm not that talented. God wouldn't give me anything I could actually use. Just enough to swirl my mind and keep it going when I'm trying to get to sleep. And to win at Trivial Pursuit. Most people won't play me."

An older woman came into the shop and trudged through as if walking in a snowdrift. Someone said, "Hey, Wanda," and I deduced that this was Wanda. This is why I'm such a good reporter. She gave me a quick glance in the mirror as she slipped past the falling hair and closed the door to the office.

"Round or square in the back?" Dexter said.

"Surprise me," I said.

He finished his masterpiece, unfastened the cape, twirled me around, and handed me a mirror. "What's the verdict?"

"Guilty of the perfect haircut." I pulled some cash out of my pocket and handed it to him. He was about to lead me to the front when I gave him another five and said, "I need to use the restroom. It's in the back, right?"

Dexter nodded. "I'll have your receipt at the front."

I knocked lightly on the office door and Wanda said something from inside I couldn't decipher. When I opened it, she looked up, cigarette smoke swirling. "Can I help you?"

I closed the door behind me and sat. I told her my name, that I was in town to write a story about the Conley execution and needed to ask a couple of questions.

"You need to talk with Curtis and he's not here."

"You testified, didn't you?"

"There's nothing I have to say to you that I haven't already said a million times. And if you're trying to make that monster seem human, I don't want any part of it."

"You saw the confrontation on the street, right?"

"I heard the commotion and went out just as he said he was going to kill her. It was a vile, vicious attack. I hope he burns. Forever."

"Did you speak with Diana about it?"

She shook her head. "She got on the bus. I called her house later, but her mother said she was in her room. I never talked to her again. If there's anybody on the face of the planet who deserves to die, it's Terrelle Conley. Print that in your story."

The office had that male touch, meaning *Playboy* calendars and *Hustler* magazines. "Is this your office?"

"I do the books for Curtis. We share this space."

"Tell me about Diana."

She took a draw from her cigarette. "Tell you what?"

"What was she like? A hard worker? Did she have a boyfriend?"

"She was the sweetest girl I ever knew. Never said a mean thing about nobody. Took care of her mother, so she didn't have much time for a life. And she never missed work, except for some personal time she asked for."

"Personal time?"

"I think she had business on the side. I didn't pry. Her mom was sick, so she needed some extra cash."

"Is her mother still living?"

"As far as I know."

"Boyfriend?"

She shook her head. "She never talked about anybody and I

never saw her with anyone. She was always one of our most popular stylists because she really got to know the people, you know? She even took that guy cookies, that's what kind of person she was."

"You mean Conley?"

"Yeah, she felt sorry for him. She'd take him food around the holidays. A sandwich or a cool drink on a hot day. Just the sweetest thing."

I got the point about how sweet she was.

"Do you remember that last day? Was there anything different about her?"

She shrugged. "She was a little antsy. Agitated. I think it was because she saw Conley."

"Why would he make her agitated?"

"I don't know—maybe he threatened her or something."

"She said that?"

"No, I'm just guessing."

Wanda seemed a little impatient and I decided to drop the bomb. That's the main reason you come for the interview—the question you want answered when you walk in the door, that you wait to deliver when the mood is right. My conversation with Sawyer made me at least mildly curious about the boss.

"How did she get along with Curtis?"

The cigarette hung on her lips like a bird on an electric wire in a hurricane. "What's he got to do with it?"

"I've heard stories that he likes to dip in the company pool. Did he and Diana have a relationship?"

"All right, you can leave now," she said, struggling to get out of her chair. And it was a struggle. A civil war of hips and leg muscles that finally led to her opening the door beside me and blowing smoke in my face.

I lifted my hands. "I didn't mean to offend you. I just wondered if she and Curtis knew each other well."

She pointed like I was a dog. "I said get out."

Dexter was holding my change when I passed him.

"Keep it. Sorry for the trouble."

Wanda berated Dexter as I headed for the door and into the street. I looked at the surveillance cameras near the front and then walked the sidewalk where Terrelle had verbally accosted Diana. I wanted to get a feel of the area so I could put it down well. Capture the uneven concrete, cracking and filled in with makeshift patches. Parking meters leaning like Towers of Pisa. Storm grates that didn't fit properly, jutting up like a waiting lawsuit. Trash cans filled to overflowing. Happy bees that should have been spreading pollen sucking from empty Dr Pepper and Coca-Cola cans.

In my head I was writing the scene, watching Diana come out of the salon, Terrelle accosting her, Wanda following in polyester. Though, for the sensitive, I would have left out the polyester. A smell of stale beer hit me from a nearby bar. Men in long-sleeved shirts stood by a liquor store in the heat, hoping for a drink or a smoke or both. Dogs barking in the pet store window. Let the reader taste and smell the story.

The bus stop was at the end of the street, with a bench sporting graffiti over several layers of paint. I turned and looked back, seeing nothing out of the ordinary. I closed my eyes and listened to the sounds of life. This was where the death of Diana Wright had begun.

Chapter 10

I drove toward the hospital but passed a Toyota dealership and had to check with the parts department. I explained I needed to replace the driver's window and asked the cost. I wasn't sure which hurt worse, the crowbar to the cheek or the estimate from the three-whiskered kid behind the counter. I couldn't keep driving around with no way to lock the car, but for the moment I would have to settle for duct tape and plastic.

This was the same feeling I had when my writing wasn't going well. There's nothing like having a project stall in the middle of the work. The key is momentum, whether it's working on a story for TV or print. You move forward, gathering information and writing as you go. Most people don't realize you're writing in your head all the time—I was writing as I talked with Wanda, though

83

she had no idea. But there comes a point when you not only get up to make a cup of coffee, you go to the store to get the exact brand of coffee that sparks your creativity. And when you settle in afterward, with the cup of coffee in your hand, you hear the mail truck pass and you walk to the box and pull out the bills that simply have to be paid. This is the dance of the creative mind, putting off the pain of sitting in front of a screen that beckons to be filled.

But this Toyota procrastination had nothing to do with writing. I was avoiding the hospital. I knew I had to go there, see my son, and live up to my part of the bargain. Sitting next to him and talking felt like writer's block squared. Life block, I guess.

I passed a car-parts store and thought of comparing prices but kept the vehicle on the road and made it to the hospital parking garage, where I sat for a few minutes. My head pounded and my cheek felt like someone had hit me with a tire iron, which I had always thought of metaphorically. It was way past noon and I could see the hurt and disappointment in my wife's eyes even before I entered the building.

I stopped at the information desk and received a confusing series of directions from a geriatric helper who seemed not too far removed from the critical care ward. Maybe she was doing this to help pay her bill. I heard eighth floor, south elevators, and wandered down a series of pathways, meandering through a maze of people and sterile hallways with soothing music. At best, hospitals are designed as positive places to die.

I finally located the right elevators and rode up looking out at the palm trees and landscaping through the windows. Men in light-brown work clothes manicured the lawns and shrubbery, as if the scenery would cheer up anyone walking into this cesspool of germs, radiation, and hopelessness. My lungs seized up and my heart beat faster and the skin on my face produced toxins. Not really, but my imagination had taken over.

I told you I don't like hospitals.

Ellen was at the nurses' station talking with three women who acted like she was the sweetest person in the world. I couldn't get that phrase out of my head. I guessed she was talking about how good the Lord was and how he was always there for her, unlike her husband, and how he had been there for Aiden every step of the way, unlike his father. You can always trust in God, but husbands will always let you down.

The choir seemed to know instinctively it was me because they all went quietly back to what they were doing and Ellen turned, her face a pool of hurt. More like the Atlantic.

"Sorry I'm late. Has he had lunch?"

"He couldn't eat much. He's asleep again." She led me back to the waiting room. "I don't think it's a good idea now. Why don't you go home and get some sleep?"

"I wouldn't be here if I didn't want to be." That actually sounded a bit like I meant it, and the conviction surprised me. "You're the one who needs to go home and get some rest. Come back later tonight after we've had dinner and a chance to watch some baseball."

Her face lightened a little. "Are you sure?"

"Yeah, go. Just ask one of your friends there to get me when he wakes up. I'll camp out here until then."

She touched my arm. "I told him you would be coming by and he seemed really excited."

It felt like Aiden was seven again and we were going to his soccer tryouts, though I never took him to one of those. I was in Afghanistan talking to Hamid Karzai or in Syria trying to track down Mahmood Bahoody or whatever the guy's name was who happened to be a Hamas leader ready to give an interview. Like I said, I've been all over.

"I'm here," I said, handing her the keys. "I'm working on getting the driver's-side window fixed."

I plugged my phone into the charger and settled in for more of the life and times of Terrelle Conley. The orange chair was more comfy than it looked at first glance and it was easy to sink back and leaf through clippings. There was enough in that bag for a couple of books, but the articles brought out vicarious facts tossed about on the waves of journalistic integrity.

I read as much as I could, making notes in the margins as the fire in my face burned on and the noise of the hospital waiting room increased. A family had gathered to await news about someone in surgery. It made me long for a big family. For at least two minutes. Then came the little kids who bounced off the walls until they got enough money for a soda from the machine. And then they did the sugar dance.

No thank you.

The buzz of the waiting room provided the background noise I needed to rest. Unfortunately when I awakened, the family was gone, my shirt had a drool stain, and even worse, a man who reminded me of my father sat next to me. I tried to discreetly wipe my chin.

"Truman Wiley?" the man said. He had a voice like God's. Deep and sonorous. Precise.

"Yeah? Is something wrong?"

He smiled. "No, I'm sorry to disturb you. I'm Nelson Miller. Your wife and son attend our church."

Great. Ellen sent the God squad. I glanced at the clock. Dinnertime. I wiped my eyes and wished I'd had a bib.

"Nice to meet you," I said and shook his hand. He wasn't what I expected. From what little Ellen had said, I thought he would be older and wearing a Republican lapel pin, but he didn't even wear a suit. Just a polo shirt and shorts. A thirtyish guy with piercing eyes and a day's growth of beard.

"I was visiting another family in the hospital and thought I might find Ellen here. The nurse told me who you were."

"They were supposed to get me when Aiden woke up."

I gathered some pages from the floor. I was really out of it. And when I bent over to get them, my cheek lit up again and the blood pulsed like a lightning bolt.

"So you're going to do it?" the man said. "You're going to write Terrelle's story?"

Of course he would know about the whole thing. "I'm researching now. Hope I can finish it in time to do some good."

He patted my shoulder. "I'm glad. It's quite a story. I've been inside to see Terrelle. It's brutal. But he's right with God. His heart's in the right place."

What's that supposed to mean? That mine isn't?

"I've also spoken with the mother of the victim. Helen."

"How did that go?" I said.

He shook his head and his eyes betrayed him. "I wish there were some way to let that woman out of her misery."

"Like a confession?"

"I've encouraged Terrelle to tell it all. Maybe you're the one who can get to the bottom of it."

"You don't think he's telling the truth?"

"The human heart is deceitful and desperately wicked. That's what Jeremiah says."

I wondered who Jeremiah was and why his opinion was so

important. "If Terrelle is born again, washed in the blood, why would you doubt him?"

"He became a Christian inside the prison. His conversion was genuine, no doubt. You'll see that. But there are very few people inside those prison walls who will admit their guilt. You give up all hope if you do."

"I don't see any way he'll confess. Wouldn't make sense."

"I don't know . . . I think you may be the one God sent to get the truth. You know, to finally help him become free."

"Is the mother of the deceased open? Would she talk with me?"

"She's a pretty tough customer. Hardened. Still grieving. But I believe while there's still breath, there's hope. She lives only a short distance from here."

I nodded.

"I know Ellen is glad you're back. Aiden, too. He's a special young man."

No matter how sincerely he said it, his words left a bad taste in my mouth, like one of those energy bars that are supposed to give you the nutrients you need but just leave you feeling full of oats. I couldn't imagine this guy having more input in my son's life than I had, but somebody had to fill the void.

Suddenly jealousy reared its head. What if this guy had given Ellen more than spiritual encouragement? I could picture it. The late nights sitting in the waiting room, praying, holding hands, giving comfort. Maybe a ride home. My mind wandered and I imagined them at my catless house.

"Thanks for being here when I wasn't," I said, peering closely to discern any guilt or shame.

"Would you mind if I prayed for you right now?" he said.

Would I mind if he rammed shards of glass underneath my fingernails? How about shoving my head into a bowl of acid?

"Sure, go ahead," I said.

He put his hand—the one with the ring on it—on my shoulder, and I wondered if that's how it all started with Ellen. A hand on the shoulder, his soft, soothing voice in her ear, whatever that cologne was he was wearing, and me out of her life. She needed a soul mate to walk through those dark nights. It was easy to see what had happened. The soft hands of a pastor, a spiritual mentor, compared with the hard heart of her husband. A furtive glance during a sermon. Clandestine meetings at the hospital coffee shop. It was all so innocent, so unavoidable. But what about the good pastor's wife? How could he do this to her?

". . . I ask you to give Truman the ability to walk through this story and get to the truth. . . ."

He had his eyes shut tight, not caring who walked by and heard every word as this quarterback prayed in his holy huddle.

". . . give wisdom to the doctors. . . . Guide the governor and those making decisions about the transplant. . . ."

He had transitioned smoothly from one subject to another and all I could do was hope that he'd come to the end of his spiritual half nelson and let me go.

". . . in Jesus' name . . ."

Finally. The Christian incantation. The bibbidi-bobbidi-boo of the faithful. Ties everything up into a nice little bow at the end and everyone can feel better.

"Amen."

"Thank you," I said.

He patted my shoulder. "You want me to take you back to Aiden's room?"

"I'll find it. I'm sure there are others you need to see."

He nodded and slipped me a card. It was tastefully printed with just a splash of color. Not one of those gaudy cards with every Christian symbol known to mankind. The fish next to a lion next to a lamb with golden rainbow light shining down and a dove flying over an open Bible with a crown made into a communion tray.

"I understand," he said. "If you need anything at all, this is my cell phone. Give me a call."

His shoes squeaked as he walked toward the elevators and I couldn't imagine Ellen falling for anyone with squeaky shoes. I pushed my fears away and focused on the pages from the Piggly Wiggly bag.

"Mr. Wiley?" a nurse said a few minutes later. She was younger and folded her hands primly in front of her. Hair tied in the back and a nice face like most nurses. White teeth and crinkly eyes. "Your son is up and asking for you."

"I'll be right there," I said. "Need to visit the little boys' room."

I opened the door to the lobby, took the stairs, and headed to the street.

Chapter 11

Ellen drove home, leaning closer to the vent and reaching out a hand for a little cool air to counter the hot wind whipping at her hair. It made no sense to use the air conditioner but she did it anyway. Full blast. It was like putting an ice cube in a volcano.

Her thoughts turned to Truman and his offer to relieve her for the day. She didn't need a break from Aiden; she needed him to pay attention to their son. She knew what it would mean to him. And while she questioned if Truman would really follow through, she had to at least give him a chance. She had prayed for this. So why did she feel conflicted?

She had prayed for more, of course. That Truman would lose his addictions, turn into a better husband, a better father, and be the man she wanted him to be. Complete healing for Aiden, that

Abby would become interested in spiritual things, and that God would give Ellen herself the ability to hang on and believe in the midst of the unbelief.

Deep within she knew that a turnaround for her husband could only come from God. Truman couldn't work all of his addictions away; he had to be changed inside, and frankly, that possibility seemed as far away as complete healing for Aiden. The tiny spark of hope she'd carried for Truman was just an ache now, a fleeting thought. Like trying to cool a car in the Florida heat and humidity with all the windows down.

Lost in her thoughts, she pulled into the driveway and sat a few moments, staring at the house, unable to move. The weight of life pressed her into the seat and it was like moving buckets of sand to open the door and move both feet. Fatigue was one thing. That was with her every waking moment as the fear and dread of Aiden and what might happen next washed over her, even through her dreams. The crushing weight was knowing what needed to happen and that she could do nothing but hope and pray and wait.

As she opened the front door, she sensed someone behind her and turned to see two men. One held a knife to his chest. The other pushed her into the house. She didn't have time to scream— or the energy. They closed the door behind them.

"What do you want?" she said breathlessly.

The one with the knife nodded to the other, and she studied their faces. The big one had acne scars and dark hair that piled on his head. The one with the knife was thinner with eyes like a fox. Cunning. Calculating. He moved toward her and she backed into the kitchen.

"Sit," he said.

She fumbled with a chair and obeyed, staring at the knife and the man's face. When he reached out, she recoiled, but instead of touching her, he grabbed her purse and pulled out her cell phone.

"What's this about?" she said, her voice shaking.

"Where's your husband?"

Books falling in the bedroom. Things being scattered.

"He's not here," she said.

"We know that. Where is he?"

"My son is sick," she said, then regretted it. Endangering Aiden was the last thing she wanted.

The bigger one returned, shaking his head. Fox leaned forward and put the knife to her neck.

CHAPTER 12

I WANDERED THROUGH THE LOBBY looking for a local map but
found none. Finally I got desperate and asked the newcomer at the
information desk to help me find Oak Street. I could have hailed a
cab, but with the cash running low and my legs aching for movement, I decided to hoof it.

It doesn't matter what you think of me for leaving without
seeing my son. Nothing you could say or think would make me
feel any worse. And as I walked along the streets, carrying the bag,
I couldn't help but think what a depressing sight I was to even the
casual bystander. With the bandage on my face and the black-and-
blue eye, all I needed was a guitar and a harmonica and I might
have been able to make cab fare.

Pastor Miller was wrong. Helen Wright's house wasn't even

close to the hospital. What I thought would be a few blocks turned into too many. The sun was still beating down when I reached an older section of town that had suffered through the recent economic downturn. The Wrights' house had aluminum siding that had been painted white, but dark brown showed through chips and cracks. There was a chain-link fence around it and the rickety porch swing hung at an angle. Metal chairs looked like they had survived WWII.

A button hung on the doorjamb by two thin wires, so I knocked and heard a dog bark and scratch at the door. Moments later a woman wearing an apron over a ratty nightgown opened the door. The nightgown covered a misshapen body. A kindred spirit. I could tell it in her eyes. We were both like living babushka dolls, all frump outside and hollow inside.

She looked through the screen at my paper bag. "I'm not buying."

"I'm not selling."

A small, arthritic poodle sniffed the air and I heard the faint sound of sizzling meat.

"What's in the poke?" she said.

It took me a second to realize what she was asking. "Just some articles. Newspaper clippings."

She kept her head down, staring at the poke. "What do you want?"

I'm not above manipulation and letting people believe something that isn't true in order to get information, but standing on Helen's porch made it seem a bit unethical not to shoot straight. Yes, even to me.

I told her my name, as if that mattered. I told her I wanted to talk about Diana. About Terrelle Conley's execution.

"You a reporter?"

"I was," I said.

"What are you now?"

"A guy looking for answers."

"I ain't got nothing to tell you," she said. She closed the door and the dog jumped up to a worn spot on the back of the couch by the window and barked, but you could tell his heart wasn't in it. It could have been from the pain in his legs as much as his aversion and distrust of me.

The mangy thing followed me to the next window and all around the house as I walked the overgrown path. Weeds were as tall as the windows and the back step was just a cinder block or two.

Helen Wright was neither slight nor pretty, but she had long dark hair that was streaked with the requisite gray of the grieving. She must've known I was at the back door because her curly-haired alarm barked at the top of its lungs, which sounded like they were giving out. She kept her back to me, hovering like Escoffier over her stove turning greasy chicken legs and livers with a greasy fork. I'm an experienced reporter; I could tell by the smell through the screen it was chicken. I was also a very hungry reporter. I hadn't had anything since the pancakes.

That's when I spied the beautiful thing in the window squinting its eyes at every bark. Disdainful of the noise and smells and surroundings, she sat with her paws curled underneath and only moved to breathe, content, peaceful, solitary. Such a placid sight, it reminded me of Murrow and made me wonder where she would spend the night.

"Is that a Himalayan?" I said through the screen.

Helen didn't turn around.

"What a beautiful cat. Why would you want to keep that mangy mutt around when you could give her free reign of the house?"

"That mangy mutt saved my life last year. I've never had a cat do that; have you?"

"I'm not sure. I think my cat may have saved my life several times, but she doesn't usually put out a press release like dogs do."

She spoke without looking at me, facing a yellow-coated oven fan. "What do you have against dogs?"

"I'm just not a dog person, I guess. Too much work. They need your attention. They need you to tell them when to shut up and when to go to the bathroom. Too dependent. I like the independence and who-cares attitude of cats."

She turned a little and gave a wry smile. "That's what Diana always said."

"Smart girl." I opened the back door and Fluffy or whatever her name was jumped down from the window and came outside to sniff everything she could get her nose near. I gingerly moved in, and since Helen didn't object, I felt I was on safe ground. I put my Mr. Piggly on the table. I always name my projects and that seemed as good as any at the moment.

"You wouldn't have enough for two, would you?" I said.

She didn't acknowledge the question. Her feet were swollen and crusty, white in that diabetic, lack-of-circulation way, with blue veins showing and ankles that looked like sledgehammers.

Finally, when the silence was killing me, she said, "This look like a homeless shelter?"

I looked around the kitchen. To be honest, the health department would probably shut it down if it were a homeless shelter.

"I could run out for a bottle of wine," I said. "What goes best with fried chicken? Two-buck Chuck cabernet?"

Without missing a beat, she said, "I'd go for a zinfandel, that pink stuff." She pronounced it emphasizing the middle syllable like it was wine made from ceiling fans. "You can join me if you want. Can't promise it'll be good, but it'll probably fill your stomach."

"It smells like a five-star restaurant in here," I lied. It smelled more like a Kentucky Fried Chicken, but I wasn't complaining.

"I'll feed you, but I won't answer your questions about that man."

"I understand," I said, pulling out a chair. "Then tell me about Diana."

Her fork hovered over the skillet. "What do you want to know?"

"What was she like? What do you miss the most? Did she have dreams about the future?"

She didn't speak for a moment. Then she looked out the side window with a long stare. "Every Thursday night she would pick up Chinese from this little restaurant near the beauty shop and we'd watch *ER*. That was her favorite show."

Another hospital drama. Diana and I would not have gotten along.

"She loved that Dr. Ross. Every time he came on the screen, she would wave her hand like she was having a hot flash." Helen chuckled and her lungs rattled until she had to support herself with one hand on a cabinet. "I miss just having her here. I miss her talking about what was going to happen when she got her big break and went to Hollywood and became a hairstylist for the stars. What she wouldn't have given to get her hands on that man's hair."

She shook her head, then turned the chicken a few millimeters. "I've got some potato salad in the refrigerator if you want it."

It was more of a demand than an offer, and when I discovered the plastic tub in the refrigerator, I knew why. I nearly threw my back out carrying it to the table. Helen kept her potato salad in five-gallon drums. I left the plastic top on because there were ample flies providing air movement in the kitchen.

"Did she ever date?" I said.

"She had some boyfriends in high school. Guys who were just out for one thing. But unlike me, she managed to avoid anything too devastating."

"You mean your husband wasn't a good man?"

She gave me a look over her bifocals. "Honey, to me those two words don't go together. 'Good man' to me is like 'jumbo shrimp.'"

An oxymoron. She didn't know the term, but she had the concept. I wondered if Ellen felt the same way. Or Aiden. Or my daughter, Abby. Did they think men could be good after living with me?

Helen continued. "After she finished beauty school, there were a few relationships, but nothing serious. At least not that I knew about."

"What about Curtis Tompkins?"

She worked at the meat, poking and prodding it. "I don't talk about that man much either."

"Did he make advances?"

"She said he did. She told him to go jump in the lake."

"One with gators, I hope."

She clucked. "Diana knew it wasn't personal. He was after all the younger women. And after what he did for me, I'm not going to run the man down."

"What did he do?"

"He and some others at the shop got together and paid for the funeral. Even brought a gift over afterward. I never forgot that."

"Some people think what happened . . . that he might have had something to do with it."

She set two bloodshot eyes on me. One was opaque. The way she cocked her head made me think she could only see through one.

"The man who killed Diana is locked up. I hope he dies a slow and painful death." The chicken sizzled hotter and gave an eerie charge to her words. "They ought to bury him alive like he did to Diana. Did you know that? The coroner said she was probably still alive when he covered her up with that junkyard dirt. Still breathing. Do you have that in your Piggly Wiggly bag?"

"I didn't know that."

"Well, it's true. Nothing good can come from telling this man's story."

Instead of withholding the information, I told Helen that Terrelle wanted to donate his heart.

"Anybody who takes that man's heart will be cursed the rest of their lives."

I watched a fly land on the potato salad container, rubbing two legs together in hope or hunger. Maybe in prayer. I had to weigh my reaction to her words and decided, in an unguarded moment, to just tell her.

"My son is actually going to be the recipient. He's the one who will be cursed."

She picked off a piece of meat with the fork and blew on it before she stuck it in her mouth. "What's wrong with your son?"

I touched my chest. "Bad ticker. He's had heart problems since he was little. We've always known he'd need a new one, but we didn't think it would be this soon."

She shook her head. "I wouldn't wish that man's cold heart on my worst enemy, let alone my kid. Tough choice to make, I imagine."

"It might be if we weren't out of options."

"So you know him. The condemned. You're writing a friendly story about him to get people's sympathy."

I shook my head. "My wife knows his wife from her church. He was a match for my son."

"And you want me to feed you information about Diana to make his story look better." There was a hardness to her words, like these were the only weapons she had left.

"You don't have to give me anything. This transplant could save Aiden's life. The book will try to get at the truth."

She rolled her eyes. "As if you people care about the truth."

She put several paper towels on a dish and forked out the dripping chicken. The poodle sat in the corner, dark circles under his eyes.

"If your son is so all-fired important, why aren't you over there at the hospital?"

"He's asleep," I said. "I needed to take a break and found your house."

She put the chicken on the table and grabbed two plates and forks from beside the sink. Napkins were in a rooster-shaped holder. I could tell we were going to need them.

"You want to say grace?" she said.

Her request surprised me, but I took it in stride. I folded my hands and closed my eyes, trying to remember my mother's prayers when I was small. I guess some things stick with you even though you decide to move on.

"Father in heaven, we thank you for this food and ask you to bless it to the nourishment of our bodies. And we pray you would bless all who are gathered around this table. And those who aren't here. In your name, amen."

I opened my eyes and saw Helen biting into the chicken, the breading falling off the meat. She had been watching me the whole time.

"Do you have pictures of her I could see?" I said.

"Of Diana? I took most of them down, but there are some photo books in her room."

I wolfed a piece of the chicken and in the process bit my cheek and tasted blood. Not a good way to start dinner. I tried the potato salad. It was creamy, with celery, pimentos, olives, boiled eggs, and a few mystery vegetables. The coolness of it felt good against my cheek and I complimented Helen on the texture. She said she had made it for a family gathering she didn't attend a couple of weeks earlier. "Got to get rid of it before it goes bad."

Great to know.

She asked what had happened to my face and I told her my cat scratched me. She pressed and I said it was nothing. "Just a misunderstanding."

"Looks more like a lawsuit."

"Is this where Diana grew up?" I said, deftly switching topics. Don't try this at home. I'm a professional.

"No, she grew up in Ocala. After my husband died, we took the little money from the insurance and moved here, closer to my sister. She would cut hair in the front room for people in the neighborhood. Sometimes out on the front porch of the evenings. She'd do it for free to the kids and the older folks. The parents usually came and gave her a few dollars. I was on disability. Then she finally got hired over at the salon. She was always working and trying to help pay the bills. Never did one selfish thing in her life."

We ate in relative silence with nothing but the poodle's whine and the residual skillet sizzle. I noticed some muffled street noise—cars passing, kids squealing, and the *thump-thump* of booming bass notes drivers wanted to share with the world. It reminded me of the days when Mom and I would sit down to a meal of macaroni and cheese or hot dogs and pork and beans and have it interrupted by my father. He would head straight for the refrigerator and grab a beer, grousing about how tough it was being on the job all day, but you could tell from his eyes and his breath that he'd been "working" at the local bar.

I would usually take my plate to my bedroom because I could predict within a few seconds the exact moment when something would break or a fist would go through the wall or a door would be kicked in. Call it my early reporter's instinct.

I vowed I would never be that kind of father. I would never terrorize my family and make them fearful. That was at the back of my mind when Abby came along. And I accomplished at least that much. My family did not dread my appearance in the doorway of their lives. Instead, I had left them to wonder if I would ever return, a phantom lurking in the shadows. I had abandoned them. For what, I wasn't exactly sure.

"Is that your phone ringing?" Helen said.

I hadn't noticed the buzz in my shirt pocket. Some memories run deeper than others. "Yeah, you're right."

It was Ellen. I looked at my host at the wobbly kitchen table, then back to the phone and wondered how I was going to explain to my wife. "I'll be right back," I said to Helen.

"Tru, where are you?" Ellen said. There was an extra-sharp edge to her voice, and I wondered if I'd missed my chance with Aiden.

"Is he okay?"

"Yeah, no change, but where are you?"

"I took a walk," I said as I moved through the hall past a bathroom and into the tiny living room. Helen was right. There weren't any pictures of Diana. Just knickknacks and paddywacks and trinkets of a lonely, grieving old woman. "What's up?"

"You took a walk?" She said it like I'd told her that I was preaching Sunday at her church. "Tru, did you even see him?"

"I met your pastor," I said, hoping that would quell her disgust.

A pause and sigh. I could see Ellen's face, though I wanted to see Diana in a cap and gown from high school. Or cutting hair on the front porch.

"Tru, I need you," Ellen said. "Two men came to the house."

"What men?" I said. The room spun. I held the phone tighter but it slipped because of my greasy fingers.

"Two guys who asked for you. They pushed their way inside and went through the house."

I took some tentative steps toward the front door. There was the smell of old wood here. Old memories trapped like dust in the curtains. "Did they hurt you?"

She didn't answer.

"Ellen, did they *hurt* you?"

She began to cry and I closed my eyes, imagining what they did. After the tire iron incident I should have known they would follow me. It made me wonder if they'd gone to the hospital.

Aiden. What about Aiden?

"What did they do to you?" I said, teeth clenched and a bit more desperation in my voice.

"He had a knife," she said, her voice cracking.

The arthritic poodle limped into the hallway, looking at me with runny eyes. I was trapped in the creaky old house with the sun going down on my life and every bit of stability shaking beneath me.

"Where are you?" she said.

"I'm working on the book, getting some background. Ellen, what did they do to you?"

"I'm okay. But they made it clear I wouldn't be next time. Who are these people, Tru? What have you done?"

"I'll get back to the hospital. Just make it back there and I'll explain everything. Don't worry; it's going to be all right."

"No, it's not," she sobbed, and the dam burst on the other end. "It's not going to be all right. Our son is dying, Truman. Your son. He's crying out to you and you act like you can't even look at him. Abigail is floundering. I'm barely holding on here."

My face flushed and even the dog looked like he was ashamed to know me. Where was Murrow when I needed her? These feelings would send me for a run on the beach, wondering what it would be like to run into the water and not stop until my legs and arms gave out. A peaceful and quiet end. Nothing too dramatic. Just a slow, meaningless slide into the dark. Eventually my body would be discovered and the insurance payment would go out and everyone would mourn and *tsk-tsk*, but my family would finally have some closure and provision. Or maybe the sharks would get me. Even better. At least I would contribute to the food chain.

"I'm sorry, Ellen," I said. It was the best I could do. "I'll see you at the hospital."

I flipped the phone closed and tried to shake her words from my skull. Sometimes it helps just to do your job, so I surveyed the front room that led to a small bedroom. A white bed with white bedspread and white walls and white bookshelves. A Bible on the nightstand. Things looked untouched except for a round spot in the middle of the bed. The poodle followed me in, stepped onto a stool at the edge, and curled up on the spot. With those sad eyes, he put his head down and licked his paws a few times.

On the nightstand were a couple of sticky notes with faded to-do messages. There was a receipt from a beauty supply store. I was about to open a drawer when the floor creaked behind me.

"I don't want you going through her things," Helen said.

"I wasn't going to," I lied.

"What's wrong at home?"

I pointed to my cheek. "The misunderstanding showed up at my house. I need to get back to the hospital."

She waddled toward the door and I followed, the dog not even lifting his head from the bed. On the way out, I picked up a framed picture from a shelf on the bedroom wall, a small one of Diana and her mother, their heads tilted toward each other.

"Is it all right if I borrow this while I'm writing?" I said. "This is such a good picture and the newspaper reports all have the same one."

Helen took the picture and held it at arm's length, studying it like some ancient hieroglyph.

"Just make sure I get it back," she said. She held the picture for a moment, then finally let go and headed toward the kitchen.

I followed and placed the picture in the bag.

"You want me to wrap up the rest of your dinner for you?"

"I'm good. Thanks for the meal. Maybe I can ask you some more questions along the way. To fill in the gaps."

She pushed some potato salad with her fork. As soon as it clinked against the plate, toenails clicked on the wood floor behind me.

"The truth has a way of filling in the gaps."

Chapter 13

As I walked back to the hospital, I gathered myself for the phone call I knew I needed to make. I pictured Mickey Luchesi at his club in Metairie, Louisiana, sitting behind his mahogany desk, his bare feet sinking into the carpet. He kept the room cold enough to store meat.

He would be looking at the parking lot, counting the money he would make that night with each car that pulled in. His personal chef would be serving him salmon, shrimp, and a bowl of gumbo, along with a tub of butter sauce and a couple of longneck beers. Mickey would twist the heads of a few crawfish tonight, sucking out the spicy juice inside.

"Luchesi," the man said on the other end.

"Mickey, this is Truman Wiley." I said it with all the confidence I could muster.

His voice turned soft and there was a smile, just enough to get under my skin. "So good to hear from you. How's the weather in Tallahassee?"

"I'm working on getting your money, but you have to call off the dogs."

"Well, Truman, you've been working on that for quite a while. I'd say paying me back hasn't been a priority. The deadline has passed. We had an agreement."

"The agreement was you'd get paid. And that's what I intend to do. But I need more time."

"Did I delay in lending you the money? Did I hold back? No. All I ask is the same courtesy. I am a professional and I deserve to be paid for our arrangement."

"You're only causing trouble you're going to regret," I said.

"Oh, really? How have I caused you trouble?"

"I know you sent those guys to my house."

Mickey paused. Probably wondering if I was recording this. Wondering if I had gone to the authorities. "I don't have any idea what you're talking about. What happened? And what is it exactly that I'm going to regret?"

I gave him a sigh. "I've got multiple situations here. You know I have a sick kid. I just lost a house—"

"Yes, the little beach home you failed to mention. You know, Truman, I'm having a difficult time dredging up sympathy for someone who's had two homes, a boat—"

"I sold the boat."

"Wonderful! Then you can use the proceeds to pay your debt. Unless you've already used that money for something else. Tell me, what happened to the money from the boat sale?"

"It's gone. But I'm going to get your money. I just need more time."

I heard him chewing now, his mouth smacking. "Hmm. That's twice you've mentioned needing more time. You know, you have assets that could be used. Your automobile, for example."

An ambulance passed and I had to wait to talk. Mickey jumped on the opportunity. "I would have taken your car or your boat. Maybe both would have paid down a significant portion of your debt."

"You're a terrorist, you know that?" I said. "A terrorist with nice shoes and all the coke you can snort."

"Truman, why the pejoratives? I've always treated you with the utmost respect."

"I can cause you problems, Mickey. A lot more than this is worth."

"If this is penitence, I can assure you it is not moving me."

I gritted my teeth and stopped walking, turning my face from the street. "Leave my wife out of this. She had nothing to do with it. She doesn't even know."

"Ignorance may be bliss, but it's no excuse. She's part of this whether you like it or not. Now, the last thing I want is to see someone get hurt—"

I laughed. "Too late."

"But I do have my business interests to consider."

"My debt to you is chicken feed and you know it."

"It's not the amount, Truman. It's the principle. A high-profile client such as yourself who is allowed to simply walk away? What would my other clients think? That's not good business. No, you and I have a deal and I expect you to follow through."

"I have enough information to blow you out of the water. I still have contacts with the DA's office."

"Well, join the club. Who do you know? I'm probably friends with them as well."

I didn't answer.

"You're being rather vague," Mickey said. He lowered his voice and imitated me. "*I know what you're doing and I'm going to tell.* Everything I do is aboveboard; you know that. There's nothing you can say to the authorities that they don't already know. Some of them are my clients."

"Like the governor of my state?" I said, fishing, hoping there might be something there. "I know everything."

Mickey laughed from the gut. "So that's what you've been doing? Trying to ferret out information about your political friends? That's priceless. The journalistic bloodhound has his nose to the trail. Well, keep sniffing. You won't find anything between the two of us, unfortunately."

Gritted teeth again. "Call off your goons. I'll get your money. But if you so much as look at my wife from across the street, the whole thing falls apart. I'll go to the Feds and tell them everything. You'll be running your operation from Angola."

Mickey paused. "Thirty more days. That's final, Truman."

"I can do thirty days."

The phone clicked and I was alone with my thoughts as the hospital came into view.

CHAPTER 14

HEARING LUCHESI'S VOICE was like seeing that a former college flame has gone on a multistate crime spree. That's never happened to me, but I've heard of such things. You can't help thinking about what life would be if you had made that choice, if you had chased that dream.

The problem was, I *had* chased a dream, and Mickey and I were entangled even deeper than two old flames. What would my life be like today if I had stayed away from the casino? That epic losing streak would have no power over me. Instead, it does have power and follows me every waking moment.

Mickey was right. I hadn't spent my downtime in self-flagellation and pity. My nature is not to wallow or despair; it's to pull myself back up to a sitting position and then, in some way, to stand. I had spent my downtime looking for leverage. My strength has always been an ability to discover information others wanted to hide. That makes me good at what I do. My problem is a lack of ability to use that for my own life. I was consumed with the debt I was in with Mickey, while ignoring the epic loss of relationships. I believed I could somehow pay back the mountain of money I owed, but I had given up on the hearts of the woman and the children I loved.

One thing at a time, I told myself. One compartment of my life to clear up before I go to the next.

The scene at the hospital was not good. I was hoping some of that gooey Christian love would seep into the conversation. The gentleness and humility and concern. But I drew the tough-love ace of spades. A spurned woman brought forth her fangs. She had sharpened them since last we'd seen each other. And how could I blame her? I was accused of being heartless. Guilty. Uncaring. Pathetic. More concerned about myself than any other human on the planet. You bet.

"How do you live with yourself?" Ellen said. "How do you get so close to your only son and then just walk away?"

I made the mistake of pointing out that she was the one who wanted me to work on the Conley book. The fangs had extensions.

"I should never have married you," she said.

Of course, I agreed with her wholeheartedly there in the main lobby of the hospital. Everyone nearby tried to act as if they were more interested in back issues of *Popular Mechanics* and *People* but I could tell they were listening intently and cheering Ellen on. It was only when the security guard approached us and asked if we would take our disagreement outside that I could see the others look a bit disappointed that they weren't going to see how all of this would end.

She threw the car keys at me. Slider, low and inside. A passed ball.

"I'm going back up to him," she said.

"Let me go," I said halfheartedly, weakly, with a certain amount of guilt mixed with hope, expectation, and dread. A toxic soup of internal angst.

She shook her head and walked to the elevators. I picked up the keys and followed but was stopped by the security guard. Not so much stopped as I was blocked. He looked a bit like the linebacker who was the subject of my first book. A brick of a man, solid and unmoving.

"Why don't you let things cool off?" the man said. "It was getting pretty heated over there."

He studied my face. I guessed the hospital had provided training in de-escalation of conflict or perhaps knowing how to spot trouble in the lobby before it headed up the elevators. What could he see on my face other than the gauze and tape? Maybe he saw fear. Maybe he just wanted to make it to midnight, when he could go home.

I smiled. "She's upset because I haven't been there for my son. Or for her. He's dying."

"Why don't you go home and give it another try tomorrow?" he said, cracking his gum and putting his hands on his belt.

"I want to give it one more try now. I want to see my son. I promise I'll head back down if it falls apart."

A radio squawked at the desk and he lifted both hands as if in acquiescence to his inability to stop me. "What room is your son in?"

I could only remember his floor and I gave it to him. "Heart problem?" he said.

I nodded and walked to the elevator. *Yes, we both have a heart problem. We all do in some way,* I thought. I wax eloquent in lonely elevators. Ascending gives me a feeling of how far I have to go.

When I saw Ellen weeping at the nurses' station, I wanted to get right back in that elevator and visit the security guard again. But I fought that impulse with everything in me and walked past them carrying my Piggly Wiggly bag. With resolute aimlessness I meandered the brightly lit corridor, peering into rooms, searching for vestiges of my son. Older men with tubes in their noses, their veins hooked up to IVs, their eyes filled with the flickering images of flat-screen TVs. Averted glances. Furtive stares of exhausted family members who needed a shower, a change of clothes, and three days of sleep.

Toward the end of the hallway I finally noticed the little plastic holders mounted beside each room with the patients' names. Another observation from a crack reporter. Two doors from the stairwell, I saw *A. Wiley.*

I turned, thinking Ellen would be back there, her arms crossed, her hopes high, but she wasn't. Just the empty hallway.

I moved to the stairwell exit to see if there was an alarm if I needed to bolt. Sometimes you just have to have an out. Of course that's not something I look at when I walk into a casino. I only look at how many ways there are to get in the place.

Aiden's room was the edge of something, a ledge of sorts, and I knew this was my last chance. I would never get this opportunity again. Likewise, if I went forward, there was no turning back. Funny how you can walk up to a total stranger and have a deep conversation but to do the same with a blood relative seems like such a frightening prospect.

I gathered myself outside the door. The TV was on and I could hear the familiar rise and fall of the play-by-play announcers trying to fill in the gaps of nine innings of relative inactivity punctuated with bursts of action.

I closed my eyes and put a hand on the door and it all came flooding back. The nights in the hospital, not knowing if Ellen and I would go home alone, if Aiden would be in the morgue or on the playground the next day. The distance that the illness of a child brings to the parents. The isolation of the one who bears the brunt of the work. The guilt the provider feels, the one who keeps going with his life out of necessity or obligation or the inability to deal with reality. High walls were erected in those days, haphazard edifices that grew thicker with each new day as Aiden languished.

I pushed the door open with a final burst of will and found an empty bed with Ellen's purse at the side of the rumpled pillows and covers. The curtain was drawn on the other side and the familiar blip of the heart monitor comingled with cheers of a crowd.

"Bottom of the ninth, Mom; you'd better hurry."

His voice had grown deeper. A guttural, raspy depth that could have come from hormones or just the trauma of all those tubes and respirators. His feet stuck out from the covers, bony and pasty white. Like a skeleton's feet in some professor's biology classroom. I wondered about his face. Was he past the stage of pimples?

"Did you hear from him?" Aiden continued.

The Cubs were playing the Brewers, probably a meaningless game at the end of the season but vitally important to the standings now. At least, that was my professional opinion. I pushed the curtain back a little and stuck my head in, as if I were a magician pulling my own head out of a hat.

"Dad!" Aiden said, and his face lit up.

I was struck first that the wavy, thick mane that had been his trademark was gone. Instead, the lion had been shaved down to the scalp. His eyes were sunken and there were dark circles underneath as he sat up and fumbled to find the Mute button. His smile stretched over his jaws and I wished I could loan him a few excess pounds. But I didn't have any. The stress of the past few months hadn't made me the picture of health. Phone calls from creditors, the foreclosure and repossession, all the bills surrounding Aiden's hospitalizations—it was a weight loss program that worked for me but I couldn't recommend.

Despite the gaunt look, the old Aiden light was there. Somewhere in his eyes, his face, it shone. That was one of the reasons it was so hard to look at him. As sick as he was, as sick as he'd always been, there was an irrepressible light, a glow inside that couldn't be killed. At least not yet.

"How you doin', Tiger?"

"Better now. Mom said you were in town."

I wasn't sure whether to shake his hand, hug him, or keep my distance. He reached out and gathered me tightly in the embrace of a desperate son. He patted my back a couple of times and wouldn't let go.

"Missed you, Dad," he whispered.

"I missed you too."

When I stood again and looked into his eyes, I could tell he was captivated by my cheek.

"Didn't get that in Afghanistan, did you?"

"No, closer to home. Your mother has a vicious right hook."

He smiled and looked at the floor. "I like your new briefcase. Stylish."

"And better for the environment. Fewer trees and endangered

animals are hurt when you carry your vital papers in a Piggly Wiggly bag."

His teeth had gone the same way as the rest of his body. You can always see it in the teeth. In Africa, Asia, the Middle East, Appalachia—the teeth go bad first. There's a reason you look a gift horse in the mouth.

I pulled a chair from the foot of the bed to his side, where I could see the game. Why had it taken so long just to come in the room? This wasn't so bad.

"Nice to have the room to yourself," I said.

"There was an older man here when I came in the other night, but he didn't make it."

"Sorry to hear that."

"He had a nice family. And a cute granddaughter."

"That's my boy. Using a problem as a stepping-stone to the ladies."

He snickered. "Is that how you attracted Mom?"

"No, you have to have a heart in order to have a problem with it."

We focused on the game and watched it slip into extra innings where one error, one passed ball, one wild pitch could manufacture the winning run. The future hangs on small things.

I stared at the machines around Aiden's bed and recalled how ominous they'd looked when he was young. Back then, he was just a kid in Winnie the Pooh pajamas in a sea of cords and cables. The hospital had to bring in extra power strips to plug in all of the devices to monitor him. Now they at least seemed more proportional to his frame.

"So you heard about Mr. Conley and what he wants to do," Aiden said.

"Yeah."

"You're going to write his story?"

"I'll try. Me and Mr. Piggly hold all the information in the universe about him."

"Kind of sad to think somebody has to lose their life in order for me to have one," he said. "What do you think the chances are? I mean, of it all actually happening?"

I knew he was looking for something more than Vegas odds. But I didn't feel competent to answer. "That's a tough one. You've got a political hurdle with the governor and the legislature. Then there are the religious nuts who want Conley to either fry or have his sentence commuted to life. If they don't throw wrenches and if the other authorities don't raise a stink, then your chances are good."

Single to left and the runner took a wide turn at first, then scrambled back when the throw came in behind him. Aiden wasn't paying attention to the game anymore and I could tell that wasn't the answer he wanted.

I put a hand on his shoulder and leaned toward him. "A lot of people are pulling for you, big guy. Hang in there."

He turned away.

"Did I say something wrong?"

"No, your breath stinks."

We both laughed and a nurse came in and pulled back the curtain. She looked at me with the quick glance of someone who knows too much but is trying not to let on. He had meds to take and she had some nursely things to do and asked me to wait in the hall.

"Come on, it's extra innings," Aiden said playfully.

"Obey the nurses," I said. "That's in the Ten Commandments somewhere."

"You'll be back, right?" Aiden said.

"Wild horses couldn't drag me away."

I walked into the hall and looked into the moist eyes of a wild horse. My wife. "How did it go?" she said.

"Fine. He looks good. Better than I expected."

She stared daggers. "You know this is as bad as it's ever been. He doesn't have much longer."

"You missed your Zig Ziglar conference. That's not the positive thinking he needs."

Wish I could have that one back. *Start over. Breathe.*

"What's up?" I said, using one of my best journalistic questions.

"There are problems with the governor. He wants to meet with one of us."

"Well, I promise you he's going to be disappointed if I show up."

"Tru, this is no time for petty jealousy."

"You're right; I should stick to plain jealousy with nothing on the side."

"Can you be serious?"

"I'm just saying that given the choice, I think he would listen to your request over mine."

"Both of us can't go and this might be your only shot at the governor for the book."

"What does he want to talk about?"

"He's going to take a political hit for this either way. I think he wants to know what we can offer in the way of support after the surgery."

"What we can offer? You mean to his campaign? As if he needs us. I couldn't care less about his run at the White House, and frankly I think it could be the worst thing to happen to this country since . . . I don't know, Katrina? The Bangles?"

"Keep your voice down." She leaned her shoulder against the

wall. Her hair was a mess, eyes bloodshot; she wore no makeup and her clothes were rumpled. She was still the most beautiful thing on the planet.

"He wants to see you tomorrow morning, early, so you should go back to the house and get some sleep and some fresh clothes."

"You go back to the house. I'll sleep here tonight and catch up with him. Seriously, I'd rather you went and met with . . . Governor Townsend." You don't know how hard it was to say those words with anything but utter contempt. I wanted to say, "the Weasel in Chief."

"It needs to be you," she said.

This was a song that wasn't about to end anytime soon and we would have gone round the mulberry bush a lot longer but the nurse rushed out of the room. She looked at Ellen and said, "He's having a reaction."

Ellen hurried into the room and I followed. She pushed me back out and I stood, helpless in the hall. My first thought was *Murrow*. Then I remembered Helen's cat. I must have picked up some dander and Aiden had hugged me. I could see the news story. "Eighteen-year-old reunites with father and dies from reaction."

My life is filled with thoughts like this, populated with ideas, choices, and decisions. A tweak here or there and maybe I wouldn't be standing alone.

Maybe it's God's fault. Maybe he was punishing us for having children out of wedlock. Maybe he visited the sins of my youth upon the son of my youth. That would be just like God, to punish an innocent for someone else's sin.

No, that's twisted. We give God too much credit. People simply get sick and die. They have allergies. We don't need God to explain that. The best we can hope for in life is not divine intervention, positive or negative, but human acquiescence to reality. Accepting the way things are and dealing with them.

Standing outside the door, watching another nurse and a guy with a stethoscope hurry to Aiden's room, my philosophy solidified. You make your own breaks. Don't trust luck or God. Nothing is a substitute for hard work and a daily search for the mojo, the groove of life where you plod and do your best. Anything else is wishful thinking, and the world eats wishful thinkers like wild animals eat their young. You have to move forward, one step at a time, and let momentum carry you. Call it redemption, salvation, or just human inertia, you have to move.

And so I did.

To the back stairwell and down, a step at a time, all the way to the parking garage and the car without a side window. The wind stung my face but I didn't slow. At the house I fell into Ellen's bed and felt guilty for sniffing her scent on the pillows and thinking of how it used to be before the wars of our lives erupted.

That thought led to a dream or perhaps a memory. I use these to help me sleep and crowd out the images of men with hoods and tire irons and a hollow-eyed boy hooked up to tubes and heart monitors. Collegiate hormones raging, young skin unveiled, blood coursing, and two hearts in rhythm. Laughter and passion and whispered words. Pure love, with wild abandon, inconsiderate of consequence, acting on impulse and emotion surging forward like the ocean surges toward the shore, toward release.

CHAPTER 15

My cell phone awakened me. I walked stiffly to Ellen's dresser and fumbled for it, noticing the birthday card I had given her years ago stuck in the corner. Interesting. I noticed a text message from Ellen that came while I was asleep. He's okay was all it said.

"This is Truman," I said, my voice giving me away, groggy and cloudy as the Florida sky.

It was someone from the governor's office confirming my appointment for eight thirty at the governor's mansion. Reginald somebody gave a staccato, prim rehearsal of the governor's schedule. Every minute accounted for. I looked at my phone for the time and saw 7:55. I was a good forty-five minutes away and I hadn't even brushed my teeth.

"Eight thirty is good. I'll be there," I said.

A better man with a shred of pride would have at least showered and shaved and looked for a decent outfit. I did grab a pair of sunglasses and Aiden's NY Yankees baseball cap, figuring that was a way to subtly tick off the good gubner. The closer I got to the mansion, the better I felt about my appearance. I was glad he would need to stare at my cheek wound and the hair on my legs.

I made good time despite the rain that came down sideways and leaked through the plastic over the driver's-side window. I still pulled up to the mansion a few minutes late. Making Townsend wait gave me a sense of control. That's something I lost a long time ago.

There were concrete barriers near the entrance, but so far terrorists weren't interested in Tallahassee. A guard met me and gave my cheek and the missing window a concerned glance. He found my name on the guest list and told me where to park with a point and a grunt.

I was met at the door by a perfectly dressed male assistant who checked his watch and my soaked shirt and shorts. He handed me a card that said, *Reginald Gentry, Aide to the Governor.*

"You're late, Mr. Wiley."

If you hadn't called, I wouldn't even be here.

"Traffic was murder," I said.

He walked me through the immaculately decorated hallway, checking his watch again. "The governor is on a tight schedule."

"Yeah, me too."

He led me to a dining room with an atrium that had been redone to look like a Rainforest Cafe. "He's on an important call now but he said he will meet you for a light breakfast shortly. Please, help yourself and have a seat."

Reginald motioned to one of the staff members, who immediately uncovered silver serving platters filled with enough food for a large Haitian village. Or maybe the whole island. I hacked my way through the jungle to get to him and used the silver tongs for some fruit and sausage, then topped that off with eggs and a sweet roll. The server poured orange juice so thick it rolled into the glass. He smiled genuinely, not as though he was being paid for it.

I had taken my first bite of the sweet roll, part of it adhering to my upper palate, when a woman entered, greeting the server by his first name and smiling wistfully. I felt the immediate inclination to stand as if I were in the presence of royalty. She had shortish auburn hair and a pleasant face, as immaculately prepared as the table. Her teeth sparkled like a glass chandelier. She wore a tight-fitting dress that reached her knees, and even a casual glance from a disinterested observer could tell you this was not a common woman. In the way she walked, the way she carried herself, everything said she was a woman of distinction.

I took off my sunglasses and rose to shake her hand. Then I remembered the sticky sweet roll, so I discreetly put my fingers in a glass of water and wiped them dry.

"Mrs. Townsend, I'm Truman Wiley. A pleasure to meet you."

"I know who you are," the woman said, sparkling and twinkling. She shook my hand firmly and invited me to continue my breakfast. "I just came by for my cinnamon raisin bagel. Can't start my day without one."

She turned and the server had a plate prepared. "Has my husband left you down here all alone?" she said.

"I'm to blame. I'm late."

"Nonsense, he should have met you at the door."

"I think he's on an important call."

She rolled her eyes. "Probably setting up a golf game. Another campaign expense." She took a bite of the bagel and closed her eyes in ecstasy. "Now don't report that. It's strictly off the record."

I laughed. "If I had a job, it would be at the top of the newscast."

Her face turned placid. "Yes, I heard about the downsizing. I'm very sorry. I'm surprised you weren't snatched up by another network by now." She pulled out a chair and sat primly. "I also heard about your son. I'm so sorry. You and your wife have been through so much. How is he?"

Jennifer Townsend was well known for her philanthropic work with ailing children of various diseases. From my cursory observance of her life there wasn't an unfinished hospital wing in the state she hadn't visited. But she also cared for injured dolphins and hyperactive otters and seagulls with ADD. If it hurt, the First Lady would have her picture taken near it or trying to soothe it. As far as I could tell, the only humanitarian thing she had left to do was adopt a dog with prostate problems from the local animal shelter. To me, that's the ultimate, but the Townsends really didn't seem like animal people. Too busy.

Still, I didn't recall her having a photo op with Aiden at the hospital, and her genuine concern almost choked me up.

"He's up and down. It's the story of his life. I saw him last night. Things will even out, and then he goes downhill."

"And there's no hope outside of a transplant?"

"That or divine intervention, but I'm not holding my breath."

She nodded. "Well, I know that my husband has this on the front burner. I assume that's what you're talking about today."

"That and Conley."

She shook her head and stared at the bagel. Deep in thought. Or perhaps the random pattern of the raisins looked like Elvis.

Finally she said, "It's hard to understand how people can cause so much hurt and pain and then want to atone."

"You mean Conley?"

She nodded. "I suppose it makes logical sense to want something good to come from the end of your life. Why not help someone else if yours is being taken? Maybe he thinks that will get him into heaven."

"You think a murderer has a chance at heaven?"

She shrugged. "I don't judge people. Who can? I'll leave that up to God or the courts. But his life seems to have changed for the better."

"How do you know about him?"

"My husband gets the reports, the requests for a stay, all of that. Plus the newspapers and TV have been rehearsing the case before the execution."

"You know I'm helping him write his book."

She looked up at me. Maybe it was the scar that drew her eyes, but she seemed genuinely surprised. "A book?"

"His wife wants me to tell his story. What happened to him early on, the bad choices, the murder—and then the come-to-Jesus moment."

"I hope he confesses to you."

"I haven't met with him yet, but his wife still swears he's innocent."

"Isn't everyone on death row innocent?" She took a bite of Elvis's forehead. "That would be the final insult, you know. To the memory of that poor girl. Him trying to put himself up as some kind of martyr. How would you write something like that?"

"I'm just going to tell his story. I'm the pen he doesn't have."

I couldn't believe I'd just said that. It sounded cliché, like I was the wind beneath his wings.

"Don't you have any compassion for the mother of that girl?" Her tone changed, brow furrowed and blue eyes white-hot.

I took a bite of the sweet roll to give myself a chance to think of a good answer. In the meantime, back at the cinnamon raisin bagel, things weren't going well. She picked off Elvis's right eye and put it on her plate. Strange way to eat a bagel, but perhaps that's how she kept her figure.

"Have you ever spoken with the mother?" I said. "I saw her yesterday and she feels the same way. Like putting his story down is a sin."

"You feel differently."

"Like you, it's not for me to judge. It's like one of those announcers your husband uses on commercials. Does that guy really think his opponent is a demon in disguise or that your husband is pure as the driven snow? He just reads the copy put in front of him."

"You're comparing my husband to Terrelle Conley?"

Sure I was.

"Of course not. I'm saying everybody has a right to be heard, especially when their life is coming to an end in thirty days."

"Twenty-seven." Her eyes darted from my cheek to my food to the remains of Elvis's sideburns. "You say you'll just write the story, but your son's life depends on getting that man's heart."

Before I could answer, or even think of an answer, voices in the hallway signaled the arrival of His Royal Highness. Jennifer's demeanor changed with the expensive leather footsteps.

"In the telling, Mr. Wiley, be careful that you don't lose your own soul," Jennifer Townsend said as her husband entered the room.

Her words left me with a feeling of dread. Who needs writer's block with friends like this? Not that she was a friend, but still . . .

She rose to meet her husband. Townsend's face brightened in a calculated way, and as he took the phone from his ear, he hugged her and gave one of those side kisses popular with the effete. A feigned connection that might have once been there. Knowing Townsend's past and the whispered stories behind the scenes during our collegiate years, I would have bet the connection was tenuous at best.

"Jennifer, good morning, darling."

I felt the eggs coming back up but managed to hold them down.

Governor Townsend looked like the picture beside the dictionary entry for *electable candidate*. Jet-black hair strategically graying at the edges, tanned skin but not to the point of a concern about skin cancer, teeth that sparkled equally with his wife's, a body that looked frighteningly similar to the one he had in college—only a fuller chest and bigger biceps.

Townsend was known for his perpetual positivity, even then. He would sit in the student section until the bitter end of every football and basketball game, encouraging the team through any insurmountable deficit. There was always something to learn, some takeaway in each devastating loss, some silver lining behind each black athletic cloud. Not that he ever experienced the same—winning for Townsend came as easily as putting his name on a piece of poster paper.

When I first met him, the very first day, he let it be known that he would be the future governor of Florida. Somewhere along the line the next rung of the ladder had appeared and he now aspired to a bigger house farther north. After making several decisions that sent his name to the top of the charts in his party, the talk now among the political pundits was that he had more than a fighting chance in the upcoming primaries. Unless something untoward surfaced.

Jennifer gave me a wave good-bye and then spoke with Reginald, Townsend passing her off to him like a baton at a track meet. The governor locked eyes with me and winced at my wound. He shook my hand with the firm conviction of a man who would lead no matter what the cost.

"Truman, what happened?"

"Car accident." I was out of snappy, funny answers.

"That might need some stitches. Have you had it checked?"

"I'm good," I said.

Townsend sat, removing his jacket and unbuttoning the cuffs of his long-sleeved, perfectly pressed shirt. I guessed he had worn it once and wouldn't be wearing it much longer. The server brought his plate. Three strawberries, two slices of cantaloupe, and unbuttered toast. No wonder he was still the same weight.

"It's been a long time," he said. "How's Ellen?"

He was dashing the cantaloupe with two micrograms of salt as he said it, not looking at me.

"She's been better. We've been better."

"Your son's not doing well?"

I bypassed the concern and small talk about his condition, most of which I wouldn't have been able to tell him because I didn't know. "What are the chances of this Conley thing coming through?"

"You mean the odds? You looking to put some money down?" He laughed and held the piece of toast like a cigar. "That wasn't funny. Sorry. I'd say right now we've got a fifty-fifty chance. The legislature will have to approve it. We might have the votes. But the sentiment in this state about the Conley case makes it touchy."

He bit an atom-size chunk from the toast and continued, hesitantly. "I need to know that you and Ellen will be available to help me convince the public this is a good path."

"I don't think a PR campaign is in the cards. She's at the hospital full-time and I'm working on a book."

"What book?"

"Conley wants to tell his story."

"The jailhouse conversion?"

"That and his background, where he came from . . ."

"And the Wright woman. Will he come clean on that?"

He and his wife really should compare notes. I told him the same thing I told her.

Townsend shook his head. "You know, that's exactly the kind of thing we don't need. Every crazy, anti–death penalty crusader is going to be on my lawn the week of the execution. This story will only fuel that fire."

"You'll have the backing of your NRA crowd and the conservatives who want this guy to fry."

He ate approximately one-third of a strawberry and pushed the plate away. It's a wonder he had the energy. "This is not just about Florida. Every move I make now has the national spotlight. This kind of thing can either show the compassion of my administration or be exploited by my opponents."

"So you're saying you really don't care about Aiden, you just care about the campaign fallout."

He leaned against the table and looked me squarely in the eyes with his square jaw and that no-nonsense, Reaganesque familiarity and candor. "I care about your son. In a perfect world I could offer him something without so many complications. But the truth is that any effort I make on his behalf has a political reality attached. I'm simply asking if you're willing to be on your son's team."

As he sipped his orange juice, testing its viscosity, I said, "I'm fine being on my son's team; I'm just not sure I'm on yours."

He nearly spilled the juice on his starched white shirt. "What does that mean?"

"I don't want you to use my son to score political points. He's had enough people poke and prod and stick him in his life without having you join in."

He placed his napkin by his plate, which was evidently the secret signal for the server to take it away because the man did so with lightning speed.

"Why the animosity, Truman? Seriously, I'm trying to save your son's life."

"And I appreciate that. I just don't want to be used."

"Does your wife feel the same way?"

He stared at me and I matched him. I won the no-blink contest. "I don't speak for my wife. I learned that a long time ago."

"She seems a little more pliable than you on this." He said *pliable* with a bit of irony, like there was a double meaning.

"I don't want Aiden in the middle of some power play. And at the last minute to have his aorta ripped out because you get cold feet."

He stood and Reginald returned on cue, handing him his jacket. "Press conference in fifteen," Reginald said.

The governor looked at me with eyebrows raised. "I'm a man of conviction, Truman. I can assure you, if I decide to help push this through, there will be no cold feet. Have you interviewed Conley?"

"Supposed to go there Friday."

"I'll speak with the warden. He's a good man. You shouldn't have a problem."

I nodded and shook his hand.

"My best to Ellen. I think about her often. Aiden as well."

There are some men I've met or interviewed who leave you richer than you were when you walked into the room. Generous people who treat you with dignity and courtesy and show you what it's like to treat other humans well. But sitting with Townsend brought back all the old memories, the rivalries. Being with him always left me inadequate, like I was losing part of my soul just being in his presence. It's hard to explain the feeling.

It would be even harder to explain to my wife.

CHAPTER 16

25 DAYS BEFORE EXECUTION

Florida State Prison at Starke stands as a monument to justice, sur-rounded by razor wire and the requisite swamps. God help anyone who is put there. God help anyone who escapes. I won't bore you with how many doors I went through or the invasive search by the guard who said my cheek looked infected or the flips my stomach was doing as I walked into the belly of the beast. Just the smell of the place brought back memories I have tried to flush, but my memory's toilet must be broken.

The warden didn't appear for a handshake, but knowing the governor had greased the skids, I sat down with a yellow legal pad (they allowed this but no recording device) and prepared for our first meeting. I had one pad, one pen, and one hour.

Terrelle Conley shuffled into the room, his ankles shackled. He sat behind the Plexiglas and picked up the phone. His hands looked calloused, like sandpaper, and I was struck by how different he looked from his pictures in the paper and online. He wore a blank stare at trial and the mug shot after his arrest was hideous—his eyes puffy and swollen and dark patches of beard scattered across his face. I had seen him in action on the DVD Oleta provided. The footage was chilling, though I hadn't watched the entire altercation.

The man was once as lean as a running back, but the effects of the prison food had added to his weight and hardened his arteries. The same arteries I hoped would go into my son's chest. Eerie.

"Thank you for coming," Terrelle Conley said. His voice was thick. He had chapped lips that seemed to hang from his face, a broad nose, and rheumy eyes.

"You've got an hour," the guard said. He stayed inside the room, his eyes locked on Conley's back. I wanted to be alone, but I wasn't about to start demanding.

A guard appeared behind me and handed me a single sheet of paper, folded once.

"I got your message about writing down what I remember," Conley said.

In childlike print he had scrawled details, words that meandered about the page, some reaching the edge, others barely making it to the center. His writing was continued on the back, but just a few lines.

"This is it?" I said. As soon as I did, I regretted it. His face showed pain.

"I don't do too good with writing. I thought that's why you were here."

I nodded. "It is. I just thought you could . . ." I did a flyby of the thought. "You're right. That's why I'm here. Let's get started."

He sat forward. "Before we do, tell me about your boy. How is he?"

I studied the man's eyes, which seemed to me an oasis of memory and regret. "He's back in the hospital. But he's a fighter."

Conley smiled, revealing broken and rotting teeth. He patted his chest. "I'm doing all I can." He laughed and the phlegm rattled.

I clicked the Bic and wrote the date at the top of the page. Anything to keep from looking him in the eye. I asked a couple of easy questions about his early life to break the ice. Stuff about his mother and family. I wasn't prepared for how hollow his voice sounded as he spoke. We didn't have much time to tiptoe through the backwater.

"What do you remember from that day?"

"What day is that?"

"The day you saw Diana Wright on the street."

"Man, I don't remember none of it. That was a long time ago, and if you'd have asked me the next day what happened, I probably couldn't tell you."

"Did you ask a lot of people for money? On the street?"

"No, I never did that. If I had the money, I'd go get me something."

"Never?"

"Well, if they saw me and wanted to give me money, I wouldn't refuse it. But I wasn't one of those street guys who wanted to wash your windshield for a dollar."

"Then why would you go up to Diana?"

He looked at the table. "I don't know, man. I mean, I know

that's what they say I did and they showed it on the TV, but I don't remember it."

"You were drunk?"

"Yeah, or close to it."

"Do you remember her bringing you cookies? On holidays?"

"Yeah. I do remember sometimes she would bring out these plates with brownies and stuff like that. But I don't remember that day."

"So if you can't remember, maybe you did kill her."

He shook his head and squinted. "I didn't kill that woman. Why would I?"

"The prosecutor seemed to think you did and the jury agreed with him, and the judge and all of America. You were mad at her and found out where she lived."

"I know what they accused me of, Mr. Truman. I've had a lot of years to go over it."

"And what have you come up with?"

He lifted a palm from the table. "That there's a white girl who's dead and a black man who's gonna die. And the only thing the two of us have in common is that we're both innocent."

I lifted the yellow page and folded it behind the pad. "A lot of people might read this book looking for some closure. Diana's mother. People on the jury. They just want to know if you take responsibility. Even if you don't remember the specifics."

"And you're saying that kind of thing would make people want to buy it?"

"Sure. That you're finally coming clean. Part of your redemption."

"Well, I guess nobody's gonna buy it, because I can't say something that ain't true. And as far as my redemption goes, I got that taken care of a long time ago."

"We'll talk about that later. I need to know what really happened, and if all you can tell me is you don't remember, that's going to make a really short book."

"That's why I need you, Mr. Truman. I want you to put the truth down plain and straight. I want you to tell people what the Lord has done in my life and the freedom he's given me."

"Terrelle, people don't want to know what the Lord has done in your life until they know why you committed the crime you're dying for. How do you explain her body at the junkyard? Buried, what was it, fifteen feet from the trailer where you were living?"

"There's not a day goes by that I don't think about that and wonder on it. Who could do something like that? And why did they bury her there? I don't have an answer except for wild theories I come up with on my bunk at night."

"Like what?"

"Sometimes it's space aliens. Sometimes it's demons who were after me. Or liquor store owners that wanted me out of their stores."

"You think they'd want to chase away a good customer like you?"

"I told you they was wild."

"Terrelle, everybody in here is innocent, right? And so are you. But they found the gun in your trailer. They found Diana's hair and fibers in your car." I locked eyes with him. "It's not a flimsy case. It's open and shut. Isn't there part of you that just wants to let it out?"

He studied his hands. "You mean me saying I did it."

"I mean you telling the truth. If you shoot straight, I can tell your story. I'll tell it well and people will want to read it. Some good might come out of it. Your words can echo into hearts."

Saying stuff like that made me cringe, as if I could make a

Nicholas Sparks story out of the train wreck that was Terrelle Conley's life.

"I think you want your last gesture in life to be giving," I continued. "I have to get you from that junkyard and what happened there to the gurney in the death chamber and the team prepared to harvest your heart. But I can't do what I need to do with this." I held up the folded piece of paper. "The most important thing in this whole process is truth. Reality. Your transparency." I could tell from the look on his face that word was too big. "I don't care how much it hurts you to tell it; I don't care what it does to your chances of a stay of execution or what your family will think of you or the public or anything else. I need you to just open up and spill it."

He looked up with tears in his eyes. "I'm telling you the truth. I'm doing everything I can. I swear to you, I didn't kill that woman. If I had, I'd tell you straight up. I can tell you about other stuff they never caught me doing. I'll tell you how I hurt my wife. How I broke her heart time after time. I know she's going to live with that for the rest of her life. And my kids . . ."

A tear coursed down his cheek and disappeared into the forest of stubble. His chin quavered. He wiped at his eyes with the back of his big hand.

"Your wife is okay," I said with as much compassion as I could muster. "She's a brick. She believes in you."

Instead of comforting, that made him melt into the table and it was a couple of minutes before he composed himself.

"God has done something in my life in here that he couldn't do out there. I don't know why it took this, but it did. I couldn't see it back then, but I do now. It took this place to get me to come to myself, just like the Prodigal Son."

Terrelle began a discourse about a biblical parable, but all I could think about was how much time we were wasting. Every errant word was taking us in a bad direction. I pretended to jot down notes and listened halfheartedly about a son who squandered his inheritance and slept in a pigpen and eventually ran into the arms of a loving father who had been waiting and looking and blah, blah, blah. The guard glanced at his watch and shifted in the corner as if he had heard the story before.

"Terrelle," I interrupted. "This is something you can write down for me, okay?"

He reached out and touched the glass in front of us and locked eyes with me. "No, this is the important part. The most important. You gotta put this in there. I'm not mad about being convicted for something I didn't do. I'm glad I was put here. This prison became my way to freedom, you see?"

The guard approached. Evidently a hand on the glass wasn't allowed. Terrelle apologized but the guard said it was time to go.

"We still have time," I said.

"Interview's over. Get up, Conley."

I protested some more but it was like arguing with a paper bag with a badge. I mentioned the governor and the warden and would have thrown in the president and First Lady if I had thought he'd listen. I told Terrelle to write down anything he could think of that would help the book. I told him not to worry, that his story would be told. He nodded and put the phone down and shuffled into the white light of the hallway back toward death row.

The door buzzed behind me. I picked up my legal pad and followed another guard.

"He only has a few days to live and you guys won't give him a break."

The guard snorted. "Right. They're all innocent in here, Mr. Reporter. Every last one of them."

"I didn't know you were at the trial," I said. "Heard all the evidence?"

"Read it in the papers. Plus, I keep my ears open."

"What's that supposed to mean?"

He turned as we reached another metal door. "You want to believe Preacher Man over there, go ahead. If he does something good for you and your boy, that's fine. But no matter how sick your boy is, I wouldn't want that man's heart in my kid's body. No way."

CHAPTER 17

I'VE HEARD THAT THE WAY you treat the person in the room who can do the least for you says a lot about your character. As a reporter who has to get the story, get it right, and get it quick, I didn't spend a lot of time thinking about anyone in the room but myself and the person I needed to interview, and if I had to step over someone in the process, it didn't bother me. Not a pretty picture, but the truth. The other truth is that gambling is the perfect pastime for a person willing to walk over other people to make money. And the dirty little secret is that though I hate myself every time I walk into a casino, I can't stop.

At the beginning, money was at the center. I was good at cards, had a sharp memory and the ability to categorize things and remember who had played what when and the probabilities of a flush or straight or full house. But after college, the tentacles began to grow around me until I didn't just want to gamble and take chances, I *had* to gamble. I *needed* the adrenaline. This put a crimp in my marriage and every relationship, but I never let it interfere with my work. I knew at some point, whether I was in Israel, Afghanistan, or Haiti, I would make it back to a table and let the conversation and laughter and sound of the chips roll over me.

Sitting in the back of the casino, watching the ebb and flow of the room, the anthill nature of the craps table and those who only ventured as far as the slot machines, I had a bird's-eye view of the easy marks and the hardened gamblers. I had maxed out my credit limit long ago, but I felt like I had won the lottery when I discovered a couple hundred dollars in the strong box in Ellen's closet. They were actually savings bonds for my daughter, Abby, which we hadn't cashed.

A balding guy with a comb-over tossed a newspaper toward the trash bin next to me but didn't make it. I glanced at the headline and saw the words *Governor* and *Condemned*, which piqued my interest.

The story looked like it had been written by a PR firm and vetted by Reginald Gentry for accuracy and tone. It painted Townsend in the best possible light, struggling to keep the balance between the interests of the public and the concern he had for a young man who needed a heart transplant. *"These are the times that try men's souls. We need a leader with the wisdom of Solomon."* All that trash.

A photograph of Townsend and his wife on the rear veranda of the mansion showed him pensive but calm, focused but caring, and his wife was the perfect woman to peer compassionately over his shoulder—gorgeous, supportive, every hair in place. Understanding reflected in her eyes. She looked as if she could relieve his stress with the curl of her hair. It was almost Madonna and Child, except the child wore a suit more expensive than most people's cars.

Made me sick, to tell you the truth, but at the same time it gave me hope for Aiden. If this was the kind of press they got (or manufactured), maybe some of that political clout would rub off. Maybe the energy used to push through bills for snail darters and the safe importation of gefilte fish would be funneled to my son.

There was no word from Helen Wright included. It was as if she didn't exist. There was only a cursory mention of the groups that had arisen to protest. Groups dedicated to stamping out the death penalty ramped up their criticism. Religious right-wingers held press conferences and stated they would fight all the way to the Supreme Court. And then there were those who needed something to be against. It didn't matter which side they were on; they just needed to break through the red rover line of life and join hands with somebody.

Buried toward the end of the story was a quote from Ellen about Conley's execution and his sacrificial gift. It was filled with grace and mercy and a nod toward the man who would soon die. Ellen was invested in the outcome of this case, but it was clear she was fully leaning on God's providence.

Religion has always seemed an opiate to me, something to numb a person to reality. But as I stared at the newspaper article, processing the past few days, it seemed that certain people in my life were in prison and others weren't. Ellen was entombed in a hospital. Terrelle was locked up tight in maximum security. And yet both of them had a freedom I didn't. I wasn't bound by physical constraints, yet I felt more subdued than both. This was not an easy truth to acknowledge, and I wouldn't have made the connection without a heavy dose of introspection that comes on the gaming floor when you have lost your last two hundred dollars that was really a birth present from the grandparents.

I tossed the paper in the trash and walked up to the guy with the comb-over. "This watch was given to me as a present from President Karzai of Afghanistan. You can have it for fifty bucks."

He pushed his glasses back to see it in the dim light. "I wouldn't give you fifty if it was from Kennedy. Karzai's like all the rest of those third-world leaders."

I didn't have much energy to argue. "It's a good watch."

He waved me off and went back to the slots, and I walked outside for some air. Too much perfume and alcohol and losing inside. The only other thing I had of any value was Ellen's car. If I'd had the title with me, I probably would have made a deal. There was my cell phone. Or maybe if I ran into someone on dialysis, I could promise them a kidney if they'd advance me a thousand. I even considered dialing Mickey—that's how desperate I was. Walking that casino floor, I felt like a dog without teeth, a golfer without clubs, a journalist without a computer. I was a starving man looking for crumbs on an overgrown path. Or maybe I was just trying to push down the pain.

Smokers hung around outside, their habit fouling the fresh air. I walked toward the parking lot, hoping to find someone who might need Karzai time. I had interviewed the man in a tent on a mountainside where it was so cold I couldn't feel my toes. The five-minute interview for a twenty-second sound bite turned into a three-day ride-along with him through the rocky countryside. In the process—don't ask me why—he gave me his watch. I wanted to give him something of mine and I expressed this, but he grabbed my arm and looked me in the eye.

"The best gift you can give me is to tell the world the truth about my people."

I told him I would. And I tried.

The evening had descended like a cloud and it was dark, the only sounds coming from inside the casino and the *tick, tick* of shuffling feet on windswept concrete and the occasional emphysemic cough from the group assembled by the door.

I should have been more careful. I should have known there, lurking in the dark, was someone watching my every move. Looking back, I should have just gotten in the car. But I was thinking too much about how to get a little more money, just a little more so that I could turn things around. I didn't hear the footsteps behind me. Didn't feel the impending dagger.

Someone touched me on the shoulder and when I turned . . . the world stopped, oxygen left the planet, and I stared into two angry, neglected eyes.

"Hey, Dad," Abby said. Deadpan, no emotion, like she was in one of those places she didn't want to be, dragged to a classical concert by a well-meaning parent when she wanted to hear the Black Eyed Peas.

"Abby? What? How did you—?"

"You want me to go through the five Ws? At least I learned that much in school. Who? It's me, your only daughter. What? I've come to see you. When? Now. Where? Right here outside the casino. Why? Because I really don't have much else to do since I got kicked out of school for nonpayment. And so close to graduation it's a shame. Just one of those things that Mom thinks is God's will but I think stinks. What do you think?"

Her delivery was rapid-fire and it brought back all those times we argued about whether to go to McDonald's or Burger King.

She always won those arguments and I figured if I got into one here, I would lose again.

"Yeah, it stinks; you're right. How did you find me?"

"Come on, Dad. It was either the topless bar or the casino."

I studied her face. It was framed with beautiful, dark-brown hair that stretched toward her shoulders but didn't quite touch. Dark eyebrows. She didn't wear much makeup, but she didn't need to. She had the beauty of someone who doesn't have to work at it. Milky-white skin and full color in her cheeks. A tiny mouth like her mother's, with full, red lips that women in Hollywood used injections to achieve. The only flaw anyone could pick at was the black-framed glasses, thick and heavy, and she crinkled her nose to push them higher as she spoke. In my mind, the glasses didn't detract; they made her look like a schoolgirl who desperately wanted to look older. She had one of those faces you could pick out of a sea of a million people, it was that memorable. And though I hadn't seen her smile yet, I remembered it from the pictures I had by my computer back at the beach house.

"Okay, sorry about the topless bar," she said, crossing her arms and shaking her head. "Mom said I might find you here. She said you went to the prison to meet with that Conley creep."

I nodded. "You don't think I should have?"

"I'm not making a value judgment about you; it's about him."

My mind raced with questions—not for her; my own. Her presence brought things to the surface. Difficult issues. Maybe if I backed into them.

"You look good," I said. "No, really. And I'm sorry about the school thing. We're going to get back on track with that, I promise."

"It's too late."

"No, don't say that. I'll call the finance department tomorrow or at the very least get you another loan."

"Stop it, Dad. You've been saying that for a year—when we can track you down."

"Things are going to change."

"He said as he stumbled out of the casino."

I smiled. "You and Aiden were the best things that came out of our lives. I can't believe how lucky we were to—"

"Stop it! If you thought that, why didn't you spend more time with us? That's like saying Roscoe was the best dog you ever had. There was a reason he growled every time you came home. He didn't know you."

"He was blind."

"A little, yeah. But he could still smell you."

I laughed at the memory of that mangy hound. "Why did we name him Roscoe?"

"*We* didn't name him Roscoe; *I* did. It just seemed to fit his personality. And Mom cleaned up the poop from the backyard and I fed him and Aiden dug the hole in the yard after he died. I don't think you did much of anything except get his blood pressure up when you walked in every few months."

She not only had her mother's brown eyes, she had her memory as well. Like a steel trap. Even an errant word spoken ten years earlier was recalled with the precision of a prosecuting attorney.

"You hungry?" I said, trying to lighten the mood. "You want to grab something to eat?"

"Not in there," she said.

"No, I saw a couple of restaurants back toward the interstate."

"The Olive Garden and an IHOP?"

I nodded. "You like IHOP."

She rolled her eyes. "Yeah, when I was eight. I think you took me there for my birthday one year. I've moved past the pancakes in the shape of Mickey Mouse, *Dad*. I don't eat whipped cream for dinner."

"Okay, it's Olive Garden then."

It began to sprinkle and she took out her car keys. Subtly I made my move. "I just need to finish up in here. I'll meet you there in ten minutes."

She gave me a blank stare, slack jawed and incredulous. I continued, digging my grave a sentence at a time, unable to help myself.

"You wouldn't happen to have any cash on you, would you? Just for a tip." As soon as I said it, I knew I would hear it from Ellen—this little scene would be talked about in the family, in counseling sessions, a small group where Abby would stand and tearfully describe the night her father hit her up for money outside a casino. Maybe at my funeral. Or as I walked her down the aisle at her wedding, she'd look at me and subtly mention what a dolt I had been on this night.

"Forget it; I don't need to go back in," I said.

"I don't believe you," she muttered, turning.

"Your car or mine?" I said.

She waved a hand, dismissing me. "You don't have a car. You're driving Mom's car, which she needs." She stopped and turned. "And if you don't have enough money for a tip, how are we going to eat at Olive Garden?"

"Abby, let's not—"

"Don't call me that. It's Abigail. I haven't been Abby since fifth grade. You should know that." She turned again. I followed.

"You're right. I'm sorry. I always think of you as my cute little Abby."

"You mean fat."

"You were never fat."

"I was a hog. The boys used to call me Fat Abby."

"I bet they wouldn't be calling you that now."

She glanced away and I noticed a crack in the armor.

"Abigail, let's get out of the rain. Get in your car and follow me, okay? We can talk at the restaurant."

CHAPTER 18

I PARKED UNDER A ROW OF EVERGREENS, duct-taped the plastic trash bag over the open window, and found Abby—I mean Abigail—already seated in a booth.

I threw on the old TV charm and told her how good it was to see her and how beautiful she looked and what a spitting image she was of her mother, and she just stared at my wound and asked if it was infected.

"How did you get that, anyway? Wait, don't tell me. I don't think I want to know."

The server took our orders and pleasantly memorized every change Abby made, which was also like her mother. There wasn't a menu on the planet that couldn't be improved upon by a substitution here or a deletion of a certain ingredient there. Making the meal your own, I guess, but sometimes it got to me. Especially when she didn't want croutons on the salad we were going to share. I decided not to let that bother me and we continued.

"So your mother sent you to rescue me?" I said after the breadsticks arrived.

"She didn't send me for anything. She needs her car back. She has a life, you know. Or at least part of one. It puts a serious damper on a person's lifestyle when you take away her mode of transportation."

"Your mother's a big girl. You don't have to run interference for her. You shouldn't take care of us."

She stared at me with those brown eyes as she pulled on her raspberry lemonade. "Maybe I feel that way because you did such a lousy job of being a dad. Maybe I feel I have to run interference because you're out of control. Maybe I feel like I'm the adult and you're the kid instead of the other way around."

Wow, don't hold back because I'm your dear old dad.

"I'm sorry you feel that way," I said.

"I'm sure you are. But that's the problem. Your sorrow only covers your narcissism."

"I thought you were a journalism major, not psychology."

"You're not really sorry; you're sorry I feel this way. You're sorry I'm upset. You're sorry about everything but what you've done to your family. You don't *own* any of your sorrow; you put it on us."

Her voice was getting more animated and people around us were noticing. I used my most calm voice, even and measured in tone. "You're right. I should just be sorry."

That sent her over the edge. She gripped the table with both hands and scooted forward, her knuckles white. This was a long time in coming.

"I'm sure you want me to say you've been a great father and a great man and all those awards you brought home make you a wonderful humanitarian. But I was thinking about your life as I drove down here and there's a common denominator."

So it was a math minor.

"You want to know what it is?" she said.

I wiped all irony and sarcasm away. "Please, enlighten me."

"You are a taker. Anything good you've done, reporting from whatever far-flung place you've been assigned, you never gave, you always took. You took the words of the earthquake victim. You took the pictures of people devastated by wars. You gave the story, but it always came with a price and that price was never paid by you. It was somebody else who had to ante up. And it was the same with Mom and Aiden and me. You provided for us, at least until recently, but every time you came around, you always took more than you gave."

Her hands shook and she grabbed the green napkin as if it were the safety restraint on a wild amusement park ride. There was real emotion here and I let her words hang for a moment as I set aside my stiff and tasteless breadstick.

Searching for words, some way to get through the anger that her words dredged up, I tried to get past myself and my guilt. "Abigail, what do you need from me? What can I give you?" It sounded hollow coming out.

The server came with our salad and placed it between us, then grated some mozzarella cheese into an empty plate so I could spread it at my leisure.

"Can I get you anything else?" she said pleasantly.

Yes, another life, a heart for my son, Mickey Luchesi off my back, a marriage salvaged—any of that.

"We're fine," I said.

After she walked away, Abby said, "You want to say that again? I think I might be in shock. I thought you'd be defensive and make a joke."

Deep breath. Serious. "I see this differently than you, but you're right about everything you've said. And if I tell you I'm sorry, it's going to sound like I'm just placating. I don't want to do that."

"Thanks," she said softly, looking at her empty salad plate.

"I know I've hurt you. And probably the best thing to do now would be to just listen. So tell me. Anything you want. And what I can do to help."

She put some salad on her plate and waved a hand at the past like it was gnat. "You think it's that easy? I tell you what to do and you make up for everything? There's no magic wand here, Dad. It's taken you a long time to dig the hole you're in with us and with your life."

"I know that. I'm trying hard to get things together."

She cursed. "That's what Philip says."

"Philip?"

"You are so clueless. My boyfriend. The guy I've been dating for two years. The love of my life. Everything you haven't been to me."

"And you're figuring out he's as big of a jerk as I am?"

"I'm figuring out there are similarities to the species, yes. But there are glimmers of hope with him."

"Do you give Philip suggestions about how he can better himself?"

"Fortunately he doesn't need me to tell him. He figures it out on his own. Like real men do."

She could turn from gentle and sweet to acerbic again, just like her mother. Endemic to that species, perhaps.

"Sounds like Philip is a real catch. Is he wealthy? Maybe he could help us with a loan."

"His family comes from a mixture of coal miners and truck drivers."

"Nothing wrong with hard work."

"He'll be the first to graduate from college in his immediate family."

"Good for him."

"He offered me every cent of what his family has saved. And don't ask me how much because I know what you'd do with it." She shook her head. "That's what you did with the Conley payment, right? You've lost it already."

"What makes you think that?"

"Let's say it's a strong hunch, especially when you ask me for cash in the casino parking lot. Is it true?"

I wiped my mouth, though it was more of a nervous reaction. Where was the entrée when you needed it?

"Things are a little tight right now."

She took a sip of her lemonade and moved in for the kill. "You asked me what I needed. If you were serious about that and not blowing smoke, here's something. Tell me the truth. I ask you a question, and you don't flinch or hesitate. You don't hedge or make up something or try to get me to laugh."

"Okay, you got it."

"Did you lose all of the Conley payment?"

"Yes."

She paused, staring at me. "How did you get the scar?"

Deep breath. "I owe some money to a man in New Orleans. He sent a couple of his friends to tell me I needed to pay him as soon as possible."

"How much do you owe them?"

I told her. Her mouth dropped.

"It's going to be okay," I said. "It'll work out."

"Dad, you have a serious problem. This is not something that just works itself out."

"My first priority right now is Aiden and seeing that he gets the operation. Part of that is writing the Conley story. For whatever reason, that's what I have on my plate. And this time I'm not just doing it for career advancement or personal aggrandizement, as you probably think, but to help your mother and brother."

She did that thing with her eyes, the incredulous young woman who laughs and casts her eyes around for something they can light on, like the extra-virgin olive oil. "I'm sorry, Dad. I'm still back on how much you owe and whether those two guys might be out in the parking lot right now hooking something up to your ignition."

"I took care of it. You don't have to worry about them."

Our entrées came, but sadly neither of us were interested.

"You saw him, right?"

"Yeah, I went to the penitentiary and had a good chat."

"No, not Conley. Aiden."

"Yeah, I saw him."

There was something more than vulnerable about her face now. Fear mixed with sadness and hurt. "I've never seen him this . . . close, you know?"

I put a hand on hers and she pulled away. It was like trying to comfort a frightened bird. All she could do was protect herself and I couldn't blame her.

"He's a fighter," I said. "Always has been. It's going to be all right."

She leaned forward, squinting like she was three. "How can

you say that? He could have gone into cardiac arrest ten minutes ago and you'd never know. We could be attending his funeral this weekend, unless you find a hundred-dollar bill on the sidewalk and get a poker game going at the mortuary."

"That's cruel, Abby."

She ignored the misuse of her name. "Seriously, is there anything you'd consider more important than gambling? Is there anything you wouldn't toss under the bus in order to get the high of throwing your life away to people you don't even know? People who just want your money? How do you gamble while your son is dying?"

"It's taken a long time to get to this point. It's not easy to control."

She pushed the marinara sauce and noodles around her plate. "I'll bet it isn't."

If I were more of a man, I would have let her grill me about the feeling, about why I got lost at the casino. Instead I said, "Tell me about school. How close were you to finishing?"

"Twenty credits. This quarter and summer school and I would have been good. But when the money runs out and your dear old dad has spent enough at the craps table for a doctorate, the kid's just out of luck, I guess."

With all the generosity, hope, and honesty I could muster, I said, "I'm really sorry for what you've been through. For what I've put you through. I'm going to make it up to you. You'll finish school. I promise you that. And I'll be there to walk you down the aisle. All the way to Philip or whomever. And Aiden is going to be standing beside him as best man. We're going to get all of this behind us and start living again."

"You can't wait to start living, Dad."

"Excuse me?"

"If you wait to start living, it'll be gone. You have to start now."

It sounded like something she read from a motivational book, but as clichéd as it was, she was right.

"What about you and Mom?"

Strangely, of all the things on the plate to fix, that one seemed the most unlikely to work out.

"I think I may have put her through too much."

"Dad, you two were made for each other. I know she can go off the deep end on the religion thing. She's done it to me, too. Praying for me on the phone, sending me books and links to sermons. But she loves us. You know that."

I nodded.

"You can't just flush all those years together."

"I don't want to. But I don't know how to right the ship. And we've been sinking a long time."

"So you're telling me you can help get Aiden his transplant, you can pay off all that money, kick your gambling addiction, pay for my schooling, but you can't put your marriage back together? That's the one thing too tough to handle?"

"I want us to stay together, but it takes two people to make a marriage work."

"Dad, she's into the God thing and God supposedly doesn't like divorce, though you'd never know it from the statistics of church people."

"That's supposed to give me hope?"

"I'm saying that Mom is serious about the faith thing. All she needs to see is a little movement."

"This Conley book was her idea. She's the only reason I'm doing it. That's movement."

Abby sat in thought and I wondered how she and Philip spent their evenings. Did they have these kinds of conversations? Had they been intimate? Of course they had. Were they living together? What kind of a guy would she go for, and was it partly because of the deficiency she had in a father?

"Dad, I don't know how to get you two back together. That shouldn't be my job. But you've never given up on anything. Whatever you've wanted to do, you've gone after."

"Kind of reminds me of someone else I know."

She looked up and smiled. "Stop it. You're not going to win me over with compliments."

"No, there's nothing you've ever wanted to do that you couldn't. Plays at school, the spelling bees . . ."

"You don't know all the stuff I've tried and failed at."

"Welcome to the human race."

The server came and took our plates, just as I was getting hungry. But it was cold anyway.

Abby scooted forward. "You haven't asked why I'm here. Why I wanted to find you instead of waiting at the house until four in the morning."

"I assumed Mom sent you. You said she needs the car."

"She does. But when I told her my idea, she said I should go for it."

"Which was what?" I had the distinct feeling that I wasn't going to like her idea.

"Since I can't finish school right now, I do an internship."

"Good. I like it."

"With you."

"What?"

"I help with your book. You have to write it fast and I can do background and investigate, do the legwork while you write. It's the perfect way for us to get back in touch. Work together."

"I thought Conley was a creep and you couldn't stand the job I've done at being your father."

"So? I learn how to put a book project together and you get some time with your only daughter. It's a win-win."

She was something else. The light in her eyes. The life in her voice. What had been caustic and full of acid toward me had turned sugary sweet with hope and possibility.

"Yeah," I said a little too hesitantly. "You could look stuff up on the Internet."

"No, I want to do the next interview with you. Or track down some witness who saw the whole thing. And I'll drive you around in my car."

"Abby, you're romanticizing this. Writing is a solitary, lonely experience. It's not a tag-team event."

"You don't have to put my name on it. Maybe just a little acknowledgment or part of the dedication."

"Maybe the next project. This one has a lot riding on it."

"All the more reason for me to be involved. Start living, Dad. I can help you."

The tide was turning in her voice, moving from the confident, sure intern who knew she could do the job to a bit of manipulative whining.

"Let me think about it."

She took off her glasses. "No, let *me* think about it. I'll call Mom right now and tell her you blew all the money. Better yet, I'll call Oleta and tell *her*."

I held up my hands. "Okay. You're hired."

"Seriously?" She looked more excited than the day I pulled her first car into the driveway, the old Honda she was still driving. "You mean it?"

"You drive a hard bargain, Abigail."

"Okay, so what's my first assignment?"

"Hand me your purse."

She handed it over and I took out her credit card and put it on the check. "You pay for dinner. That's first. Then we get Mom's car to the hospital, you take me home, we wake up in the morning and figure it out."

She held out her tiny hand and we shook. Father and daughter. Just like that.

What had I gotten myself into?

Part II

Guard your heart above all else,

for it determines the course of your life.

Proverbs 4:23

CHAPTER 19

Abigail Wiley spoke briefly with her mother at the hospital about her "internship" with her father.

"I'm sure you'll learn a lot," her mother said. She seemed excited but a little surprised. "You'll certainly get to spend more time together."

"You think that will be good?" Abigail said.

"I'm sure if he said yes, he'll put you to work. You two will make a good team."

Always positive, always the encourager. Abigail sensed that her mother might be a little jealous, but she wasn't going to let that stop her. She was her own person now and if this brought her and her father together, however briefly, it was worth it. Plus, she

169

really did want to know how to do what he did. It was one thing to study journalism in a classroom and entirely another to do it in the real world.

For one, broadcast journalists weren't supposed to be able to write. Her father mentioned someone named Charles Kuralt, whom he'd watched in class, long ago, marveling at the way the short man with chubby hands could string sentences together like a roving Shakespeare. The fluid rush of words came with bad teeth and a double chin that jiggled as he delivered his weekly sonnets.

"Kuralt taught me it didn't matter what people said, didn't matter how you looked. What mattered was the substance of the story," he said.

The knock on broadcast journalism majors, he continued, was that they were all pretty people with perfect teeth and hair and not much upstairs except the ambition for fifteen minutes of fame. They could write a stand-up for the end of a report and fill in the blanks between sound bites, but as for actual writing, they weren't *real* journalists like those in print.

"Professors taught students it was more difficult to boil a story down than get every bit of information, but those at the *Cavalier Daily* didn't buy it."

Abigail was enamored with these slices of life from his past, which quickly turned to questions about his first as-told-to book. She learned the publisher was also skeptical of his abilities. When it sold half a million copies, their skepticism turned to faith and he produced a string of memoirs, some more successful than others, but none that did as well as the first.

"I gained confidence with each project," he said. "I shoehorned them in between assignments and wrote on the road. The most important thing in the publishing game is to be able to hit a deadline. If you can do that, you'll be in the top 10 percent of the writers out there. Due dates never bothered me; they pushed me to become better."

"What's the hardest part of the writing?" she said.

"Getting up the courage to begin. To set the first words on the page and let them rest. There's always a fear I'll go in a wrong direction, veering into forbidden territory and getting lost. I usually wake up one morning and decide that's the day to begin."

He pulled two tables from the craft room to set up shop in the living room. Abigail couldn't tell if it was too painful for him to use Aiden's room. There were pictures and cards on his bed, and helium-filled balloons hovered above the air-conditioning vent. Perhaps it signaled all the things he had missed, or he could have just disliked the view.

Her mother returned from the hospital that afternoon, took one look at his L-shaped work area next to the couch, and disappeared. After conferring with Abigail, they put their heads together and fashioned the craft room into a journalistic oasis with a door he could close.

The sky-blue ceiling and walls were cheery without being too positive. It gave the feeling that one could float away from one's troubles, and Abigail thought that might be the best thing for her father to do, given he was writing such a depressing story.

"Did you want to write when you were in school?" Abigail asked her mother, aligning one of the craft tables under the window.

"I had career ambitions, but those mostly flew away when you two came along. Something about children causes you to shuffle your priorities."

"Must feel like giving up."

She winced. "Thanks a lot."

"No, I didn't mean it that way. I meant that Dad goes to all these exotic places and gets awards and you have to stay home."

"I know it seems unfair. I don't claim it was easy, but I felt I had the more important job. Raising you and Aiden had perks I could never get reporting on some city council meeting or even a White House briefing."

Abigail placed memory books on a shelf in the closet and closed the door. "Really? Like what?"

"Watching your first steps. Hearing your first words. How do you get that back? The only way to experience it is to be there when it happens." She stopped, placed a fake flower arrangement on the windowsill, and said, "Tell him to come in here."

When her father saw it, the look on his face said it all. He spent most of his life distant and consumed with himself, but she had to admit that for a moment he seemed to get past it. "This is perfect."

"I can sleep in Aiden's room and you can have my room," her mother said.

"No, I took care of that already. I picked this up at Walmart." He pulled out an air mattress and put it on the floor in the corner. "I'll sleep here, whether I need it or not."

Abigail retrieved a set of twin sheets from the laundry room and made his bed. It felt good to do something domestic, just to see what it felt like. She had done this for Philip, though the two hadn't gotten as far as moving in together. Just cleaning up at his apartment, providing a feminine touch here and there. But her father didn't notice her efforts; he was already focused on the story. She hadn't told her mother about his losses and probably wouldn't. Unless he did something that really ticked her off.

She could handle this getting-to-know-him thing. It felt strange but good.

Chapter 20

After she and Ellen set up the writing room, I filled Abby in on what I knew about the murder, hitting the high points. I didn't want to get bogged down in the mud of a lot of questions.

When I'm in the writing zone, I find sleep distressing. Closing my eyes feels like a waste. The ticking clock is not my friend, especially when the subject of the book can't be reached by e-mail after his execution. That pressure propelled me forward like no other project had, plus the added pressure of knowing I needed to get Terrelle's voice right. A guy who would give his heart to my son at least deserved that. I took time out to eat, but I consciously kept my e-mail closed and tried not to open Internet Explorer to the several gambling sites I frequented.

I missed Murrow. Like Hemingway, I suppose, I enjoy the

company of cats who couldn't care less if I'm writing a bestseller or a family newsletter. I like creatures who are absorbed with themselves, probably because I am one of their own. They exude an infectious peace and contentment. Oleta informed me that Murrow was firmly ensconced in her daughter's old room, and even though Terrelle would have fed her to the gators if he had been home, Oleta did enjoy the sign of life in the house.

Abby was full of questions. I tried to reward her inquisitions with real-life lessons, but I made it clear that I couldn't spend time explaining the process, that it would simply slow me down.

"You have to look at this like a spectator at a NASCAR race," I said. (One of my best books was with a driver who told me his story while playing his Xbox. He was killed in an accident at Talladega and book sales increased for a few months.) "I can't spend time talking about how I do this. I have to do it. If you want to help, you'll watch and learn and find ways to fill in the gaps."

"Great," she said, holding up a picture. "I want to fill in the gaps by nailing this guy."

"Who's that?"

"Curtis Tompkins. Diana's boss. You told me about him."

"Abby . . ."

"One of the first things I learned in J-school was to follow the story. Answer any questions that come up. And this guy is one big question mark."

"So you think Terrelle is innocent?" I said.

"From what you say, he thinks he is. And so does Oleta. What's the harm in doing a little more research?"

"You're right about following the story. But there will always be questions. And everything you discover won't work itself into the book. We only have a limited amount of time and I need you for more important things."

"Like coffee and sandwiches? Come on, Dad. We should at least ask him a few questions."

"Tompkins may just be a question that will always be there. What I need is to get to the dump where Conley was living, where Diana's body was found."

"Fine. You keep writing and I'll take pictures at the dump. And then set up an interview with Tompkins."

"No, you stay away from him. But find out what you can online. And the pictures at the dump would help."

Her eyes lit like a kid going to Disney. She left with Aiden's digital camera in tow and came back that afternoon with a memory stick full of pictures I used the next morning to put down the first chapter. Choosing to use third person for that chapter to give the feel of objectivity, I began in a flurry.

Diana Wright's body was found in a shallow grave less than five yards from the trailer where Terrelle Conley slept. On the morning of April 29, Conley was awakened from a dead sleep by Detective George Chandler. He was led outside past abandoned cars and rusted equipment and shown the mound of dirt where a cadaver dog named Thunder had signaled the presence of a body. Thunder watched Conley being led to the mound, while inside the trailer Detective Dennis Sawyer located the murder weapon, a .38 wrapped in an oily rag and stashed in the cupboard above a dish-filled sink. The trailer was described as "a trash heap" littered with spent bottles of wine and the occasional whiskey flask.

These are the facts about the day Terrelle Conley's life changed forever. But there are other facts. His blood-alcohol level when he was booked later that morning was twice the legal limit, and that was after a night's sleep. There were clothing fibers, hair, and blood from Diana Wright's body found in Terrelle's aging Mazda that, by all accounts, coughed and sputtered more than he did—when it started at all. Every shred of evidence investigators discovered in and around the trailer pointed to Terrelle's guilt.

Nearly a year to the day later, a jury deliberated for a little less than three hours and brought back the expected verdict. Terrelle was sentenced to death a week later by Judge Henry Coursey.

His conviction was consistent with the facts of the case. Investigators said it was open and shut. The district attorney never had such an easy conviction. But the other consistent point about the Terrelle Conley case is that from the first interrogation through interviews conducted for the writing of this book, he never wavered in claiming his innocence. Not once in his long incarceration did he ever hint that he might be guilty. When offered a plea deal that would have spared his life from the death penalty, Conley's court-appointed attorney, Dawson Kenyon, a man who had an equal battle with strong drink, stood and shakily said, "The defendant pleads not guilty, Your Honor."

Culling information from the court transcript, I tried to present an overview of the case to give a compelling look at the mountain of evidence Conley was up against, and that I was up against if I wanted the reader to come away with even a hint of question as to whether or not Terrelle Conley had actually killed Diana Wright. If I could at least provide some tension with this point, I figured this would drag the reader kicking and screaming to know the answer and would also propel them through the section I dreaded writing the most, the religious conversion. This part would be fawned over by the faithful who thrill to see God changing a depraved heart, but I hoped my mainstream readers would skip that section or at least be able to stomach it. I wanted a broader audience than the church-pew type who bought a book and passed it to ten others.

I knew I had something good going when Abby showed up at the end of the first full day of writing, pulling the pages off the printer and reading them like they were lost scrolls found in some Qumran cave. She was seeing the translation of life onto a page and her interest invigorated me, though I instructed her not to get the pages mixed up.

"How do you know his attorney had a problem with the bottle?"

"He had a couple of DUIs after the trial. I have to check it out more. Maybe that's something you could clear up for me."

After once losing the first half of an entire manuscript to a computer crash, I vowed to never again let that happen and set in place a regimen every day that I followed as religiously as Ellen or Oleta followed their "quiet times." Each day, and sometimes twice a day when an interview happened in the middle, I would save the file, save it in another destination on the hard drive, save it to my desktop, save it to a removable thumb drive, e-mail it to my Yahoo! account, and then print that day's work. If my computer crashed, I had a backup. If the house burned, I had the files waiting for me somewhere in cyberspace. Abby couldn't understand my anal tendencies until I told her about the crash and the work I had to redo.

"It was probably a better book the second time around," she said. "That happened to Hemingway."

She proceeded to tell me a story I already knew, about Hemingway's lost works that his wife Hadley had brought to him in France. She piled all of his manuscripts *plus* the carbon copies in a suitcase, which was stolen or lost, and he had to begin everything again. Hemingway credited that crisis as one of the best things that happened to his writing. But I'm not Hemingway, no matter what he thought about cats.

She took the next page and pulled at her lip as she read, a nervous habit or force of concentration. I remember coming home from a trip when she was a teenager, days after the latest Harry Potter book had been released, only to find she had finished it in two days. And those were big books. She pulled the next page from the printer tray and read. Then the next. And the next. She was hooked.

Halfway through the chapter she stopped. "So you do think there's a chance he's innocent."

"You and I both know he's not, but I'm leaving that door open for the reader. I'm finding out just like they will. Stories are about tension. Conflict. I have to keep that going."

"But, Dad, that's a lot of conflict for us. If you find out Conley is innocent, Aiden's chances are over."

"It's not going to happen. There's no smoking gun here but the one found in Terrelle's trailer. I'm hoping he'll confess by the execution, but we may never get the whole truth. I need to tell what we do know as well as I can."

"So you're manufacturing the tension, getting us to believe there's a possibility that he's innocent and then pulling the rug out?"

CHRIS FABRY

"No. I can't change what happened in Conley's life. I can't change whether he killed Diana or not. The only thing I can control is how well I tell the story and follow the truth. Whether I'm writing politics or sports, I've found the truth will always lead you to a good place."

She pulled at her lip and picked up another page.

I wondered if I really believed what I had just said.

CHAPTER 21

Abby drove me to Oleta's home early on Wednesday morning and I phoned Aiden on the way. I felt guilty for not going to the hospital to see him, and hearing his hoarse voice didn't help.

"How's the writing going?"

"Good. Plowing through. How's the heart?"

"I'm taking it one beat at a time."

I could see the smile on his sallow face and skin hanging on bones.

"I hear you have an intern. How's she working out?"

"She's intern, chauffeur, barista, and research assistant."

Abby bristled a little, or maybe she liked it. I couldn't tell.

"You should see your sister track down information. She's a natural."

"Can't wait to read what you two come up with."

"You should write the foreword," I said. "Or the epilogue. If everything goes as planned."

"Yeah. That would be cool, wouldn't it?"

His voice was getting weaker. I told him we were at Oleta's and he said to say hello to Murrow for him.

"Love you, Dad."

"Love you, too, Son."

Murrow was on the windowsill of Oleta's daughter's room, looking out at the world with casual indifference. The cat glanced at me when I walked into the room, blinked twice, stretched, and went back to sleep.

"Good to see you, too."

Oleta cooked two omelets and set out a plastic container of banana nut muffins with a Sam's Club sticker on the side. She and Abby hit it off and while they talked about Aiden's condition, I moved about the house searching for pictures of Terrelle. There were a couple on the mantel—their wedding and a shot of Terrelle in his prison uniform. I found an old photo album by the spinet and blew away dust. It was like finding a treasure box with images from his life.

Even in the earliest pictures, the ones of him in a bib, drooling over a plastic dish, face covered with oatmeal, he looked angry. The chip on his shoulder was apparent in his high school football picture. He posed in a blocking position, his shoulder pads bulking up his wiry frame. From his number and build I guessed he played in the secondary.

One picture showed him in a military uniform, another in a graduation cap and gown, and various faded snapshots at backyard parties. I walked back to the kitchen clutching my find and passed Oleta's bedroom. There was a rickety, prefab desk someone had thrown together, and above it was a corkboard covered in three-by-five cards with people's names and various maladies. At the center I saw Aiden's name surrounded by notations and dates. A yellow sticky note said *Ellen* at the top and underneath was written, *Abigail—salvation, Truman—salvation and reconciliation.* There were also cards with verses written out in longhand. Beside the desk was a little bench with a severely worn place on the carpet. This woman was serious.

"I see you found my prayer room," she said.

Her voice startled me. I turned and held out the album. "I wasn't snooping, just looking for pictures."

She nodded. "Your wife says you get in your own world when you're working. You can take it with you if it will help."

I pointed to the board. "Is this your hit list?"

She gave the Oleta chuckle and I thought that was a nice sound to have in a house. I hadn't heard that sound in a while.

"I guess you could look at it that way. Only this is a 'love hit list.' You don't make it to my wall until I really care or you're desperate."

I pointed to my name.

"Some people are both," she said.

"How much time do you spend in here?"

"Praying? It depends on how long I stay in bed. But I find the successes or failures I have begin right here." She laid a hand over her heart. "This is where the biggest battle is fought." She looked inside me—at least it felt like that, like she knew my faults and failures, my losing her money, and she didn't care. Not surprisingly, I took off for the kitchen because it was getting a little uncomfortable in her prayer room.

The omelet was waiting and Abby had buttered some toast. I plied Oleta with questions about Terrelle's early life, how they met, what attracted them. She answered the questions but also took the conversation in spiritual directions as often as possible. Just when we got on the expressway to the story, she'd take the off-ramp to the Bible. Without prompting, Abby veered the conversation to the on-ramp again.

"I've been reading the clippings and I know he claims innocence. But if your husband didn't do this, who killed Diana Wright?"

Oleta cradled her coffee with a far-off stare. Her eyes were a little bloodshot. "To think there's a killer loose is more than I can bear, especially because my Terrelle was locked up for it. But I take heart in the fact that God knows. The Word says, 'Vengeance is mine, saith the Lord.' And 'everything that is hidden will eventually be brought into the open, and every secret will be brought to light.'"

So much for trying to keep her off the spiritual stuff. Oleta was an evangelical bloodhound that always came back to the Bible trail.

"Can't you ask God to show you who did it?" Abby said. "If he knows the truth and he loves you, why wouldn't he want you to know that information?"

Instead of being offended, Oleta seemed to welcome her question. "Exactly my feelings. And I've been pleading with the Lord to show me the truth, to bring it to light. Bring the killer to my real estate office, show me his picture in the paper, give me some kind of sign. But so far I haven't found any wet fleeces."

"Wet what?" Abby said.

Oleta explained something about a guy in the Bible who put out a blanket at night and it got wet or didn't get wet. I didn't follow it, but it seemed to make her happy to tell it. Sounded like a lame excuse to me. From her standpoint, it doesn't matter what God does to us because he uses everything for his purposes. Oleta said God had used Terrelle's imprisonment for good in his life, and if she had the choice, she'd let him get convicted of the crime again because his life had been changed. If it were me in prison for something I didn't do, I would be ticked off at God for not having a better plan.

". . . and then I thought that maybe God has brought your father into the picture for just this purpose," Oleta said.

"What purpose is that?" I said.

"To find out the truth. To reveal what's been hidden."

"What do you think of that, Dad? You might be an answer to prayer."

I've always felt pretty much like I was the *reason* people prayed, not the answer, so I let that slide.

It was Oleta's turn to bring up something. "After reading through all of the court material and articles, do you have any ideas, Truman?"

I took the last bite of omelet and chewed on my left side, which still ached from the injury, but not as bad. "Abby has some questions about the salon owner. And the junkyard owner. Don't know much about him. It wouldn't be outside the realm of possibility for a police officer to plant evidence, somebody who needed a quick conviction, but I don't see any officers with a motive. In fact, motive in this entire case is missing."

"What do you mean?" Oleta said.

"As inept as the defense was, even he keyed in on the fact that the prosecution's theory about Terrelle being motivated by revenge never added up. They contended your husband tracked Diana down and made her pay for spurning him."

Abby jumped in. "They said he planned to do something sexual, but she resisted and he just killed her and tried to hide her body."

"Who would kidnap and kill a hairdresser who brings you cookies?" Oleta said.

"Maybe she knew something about someone," Abby said. "Something she wasn't supposed to know. Something about the salon business."

"I've always thought that Tompkins guy was shady."

"There's another possibility, of course," I said. "Maybe your husband, who can't remember much about anything from those days, really did kill her. Maybe the reason the gun was in the trailer and the evidence was in his car was because he's responsible. He killed her, buried her, and he's guilty."

I thought Oleta would jump up and tell me to get out of her home, that I was from Satan, but instead she just studied the table-cloth patterns.

"I've thought of that too," she said. "Believe me, I have. But you don't know the man. I was with him when he was wrapped up tight in the drink, like one of those boats in a bottle. There was no way he was going to escape. He was like the Gadarene demoniac."

Another biblical reference that went over our heads. Oleta saw the looks on our faces and she hurried to her room and came back with her Bible, heavy enough to be declared a lethal weapon in forty states.

She read verses from one of the Gospels about a man who lived in the tombs and wore chains on his hands and feet. No matter what the people did, he broke his chains and cut himself with stones and cried out at night.

"This man was possessed by demons," Oleta explained. "His

life was miserable and he had no hope until Jesus stepped out of his boat. That sent the demons scurrying because they knew who he was."

She could tell my eyes were glazing over, so she skipped to the end, where the man was dressed and sitting in his right mind.

"Nobody could help this man. Nobody could deliver him from all the voices inside. But when he met Jesus, they didn't need chains. The demons left. That's what Jesus did in Terrelle's life. He took away even the desire for alcohol. He put him in his right mind."

"Your point is . . . ?" I said.

"If he had killed that girl, he would be the first to admit it. He wouldn't drag us through all of this. He's confessed everything he's done. Things I didn't even suspect. But God set him free, even from the need to be proven innocent."

I got up to refill my coffee mug. "Which reminds me: I need to talk with the defense team. You have some lawyers from Florida State working on this?"

Oleta was silent for a moment, recovering from my rebuff of her Bible lesson, I guess. I needed to ask a few questions about the spiritual side of his story, but as pushy as she was being, I didn't dare bring it up or she'd think I was showing interest.

She wrote down the name and number of the lead law professor at Florida State on one of her three-by-five prayer cards. "They've taken an interest in the case since nobody else did. I spent a lot of money on a lawyer but it was like flushing it down the toilet. But now that the transplant is really an option, these people are backing off."

When she handed the card over, she looked hard at me. "He can do the same for you, Truman."

I looked at the card. "The law professor?"

She shook her head. "Jesus can free you from what's binding you."

I took the card and glanced at Abby, who seemed to be enjoying the church service. Or maybe she was enjoying watching me squirm.

"Don't turn away from him," Oleta said.

Sunlight sparkled through a stained-glass wind chime on the front porch and Murrow chased the light across the living room floor, pawing at it. She couldn't catch the light. It was always just out of reach.

CHAPTER 22

Ellen was surprised when her husband showed up in the hospital waiting room. At first she thought his fear of the place had subsided and he was there for a visit with Aiden. Then she noticed the stack of pages and the red pencil.

"You've always been a better editor than me," Truman said. "Would you mind taking a look?"

"What is it?" A little cold, a little distant and put off. She regretted her tone as soon as the words were out.

Truman sighed. "Don't take this as interest in spiritual stuff, because it's not. I've just gone through a long, rambling recording of Conley's 'testimony'—" he said it with quotation marks in the air—"and I want to see if this makes sense. I don't want to offend the faithful."

While Truman went for coffee, Ellen spread the pages on her lap and took the red pencil in her hand. It was written in first person, from Terrelle's perspective. Truman had captured the voice of the man behind bars without sacrificing the English language.

I had been in prison for about six months, feeling empty and hopeless, just going from one day to the next. I had the guilt of years wasted hanging over me. I had been separated from my wife and children without any hope of ever being a free man again. I didn't want to live.

There was a chaplain at the prison who would meet with people, but I wasn't having any of it. I've heard about jailhouse conversions and inmates who talk about God just to get favors from people on the outside. But several of the guys who went to the chapel services seemed like they had something I didn't. I went one Sunday and listened to the singing and the message. It didn't do much to me because I felt God hated me. I always believed there was a God; that wasn't my problem. I just didn't think he cared.

I don't remember the songs or what the preacher said that day, but one thing stuck out to me. There was this little pamphlet—they call it a tract. It had fallen on the floor under my chair and I picked it up. It quoted John 10:10: "The thief's purpose is to steal and kill and destroy. My purpose is to give them a rich and satisfying life."

That's when I realized my life had been stolen. Actually, I had given it away to booze and other women. My life was anything but satisfying and rich. And when I looked around at these guys, it was clear that nothing had changed for them. They were still in prison. None of their circumstances had changed. But they were singing to God and thanking him.

I prayed, *God, is this for me? Can you give me a life here in Starke?*

When the service was over, I stood up and took that piece of paper with me, holding it like it was a ticket to the outside. And the chaplain met me at the back of the room. He asked if I had enjoyed the service and I told him I had. He saw I was holding the little piece of paper and asked if I wanted a Bible.

"Sure," I said, "I'll take one."

He handed me a New Testament and just before I walked away, I pointed to the verse on the page and asked him where I could find that verse.

He opened to the Gospel of John, the tenth chapter, and stuck the piece of paper in there. "This is a good place to start reading. Just go through all of John and look at how much Jesus cares."

I went back to my cell and started reading. I swear, for a whole week it was like opening a window to my soul. I had heard about Jesus before, heard his name used a lot on the street, heard about him from my wife, but I had never encountered him the way I did that week.

When I got back to the chapel that next week, I was ready. I didn't care what people thought, whether they believed me or not; I wanted to pray and ask God to change me. The truth was, he already had. He was doing something inside of me with just me being open enough to read the Bible.

When Ellen finished reading the section, Truman was there with his coffee, looking over her shoulder. She had heard Terrelle's story from Oleta and couldn't help but hope and pray this would one day be her own husband's story. Not the prison part, of course, but the longing for life represented in what Terrelle wrote.

"I wouldn't change anything," she said. "But are you going to include his completion of the Bible studies he did, the correspondence school?"

"I'll probably mention it later, but in this chapter I just wanted to give people the feel of the freedom he felt. Even inside the prison."

The obvious question was why Truman wouldn't want that same freedom. It was lost on her. But she held back.

"It's good. You did a good job with that one verse. I wonder if you could include anything else. Does he mention any other Scripture?"

"He talks about John 3:16 and putting his name in there, but it felt kind of clichéd."

"No, don't cut that. That will hit home with a lot of readers, especially the ones who feel like God couldn't care less about their lives."

Truman sipped his coffee and nodded. "Yeah, I can work it back in. I just don't want to stall the story. This section can get people bogged down."

"But you can't understand why he would give his heart to Aiden if you don't get a glimpse of this."

"Sure you can. You don't have to have a religious conversion in order to do something good. Who wouldn't want to help somebody else if your life is being taken from you?"

John 15 flashed through her mind. *"There is no greater love than to lay down one's life for one's friends."* That was what Terrelle was doing and Truman couldn't see it. But Ellen couldn't *make* him see it.

She handed the pages back. "This is going to be a great book. I'm glad you're doing it."

CHAPTER 23

Aiden was having tests, and as my next interview with Conley approached, I was in the writing groove—like a pitcher in the zone. Food and coffee were the fuel now and I had my head down as the words flowed. It was partly because I was through most of the spiritual logjam. I knew I had to fill in a few blanks Ellen had pointed out about his conversion, but I had the guts down about the trial and most of the pieces of the puzzle were there.

I try not to judge my material as I write. My approach is to purge myself of the story, to spill it on the page and not be concerned about the order or the form of the first draft. But even though it was raw, I had the feeling this was some of the best stuff I had ever written. Something akin to Ernest Gaines's *A Lesson Before Dying*, which had moved me. There were holes, of course, like the ending, but I had a great hook. I hoped the end would result in him giving life to another, but I couldn't be sure of that yet.

I didn't watch much television during this time, but the snatches of news I saw played up the story. There wasn't a hint that anyone was writing a book about Conley's life, and I was happy to fly under the journalistic radar. But I cringed when I saw a picture of my son, then a photo of our family. In the same newscast, the governor stepped to a podium amid flashing lights and a gaggle of reporters. Protesters outside the capitol building were shown holding "Thou shalt not kill" signs.

With his wife beside him, smiling and beautiful, the governor announced his desire for a new office and address.

"I don't know that there's ever been a time when we were more in need of strong, principled leadership. Unemployment issues, a faltering economy, and crushing debt have threatened our way of life. Forces outside our borders threaten us. Porous borders allow entry to those hungry for freedom and, in some cases, those with a desire to destroy. At this critical time, we need someone uniquely prepared to address these issues and unite our country with a single vision, with a voice of hope, and that is why I am announcing my candidacy for the presidency of the United States of America!"

There was wild applause, then wild protesting, then obligatory reactions from people on the street, saying, "Yeah, I think he would make a good president," or "He can't hurt us more than the one in there now," and the giggling younger woman who said, "I think he's hot. I'd vote for him."

I tried hard not to think about that while I wrote, but as I crawled to my air mattress late at night, exhausted, I couldn't help wondering what this would do to our transplant chances.

It was midmorning, in the middle of one of those stretches of unbridled creativity when I'm not writing word by word but bleeding pages, that Abby walked in all smiles and sunshine. She really was a beautiful girl. No wonder Philip wanted to pay for her schooling. She was a bright light, but at this moment I wanted to pull the shade. She picked up a stack of pages from the night before and hovered, like a moth around a campfire.

"I did it," she said.

"You did what?"

"Got an interview."

I looked up from the screen. "For what?"

"A job. At Mane Street. He posted it on craigslist. Can you believe it?"

"Abby, no."

"Dad, yes. It's with Tompkins himself. Tomorrow."

"No way. You're not going in there."

"How many times have you called him?"

"It doesn't matter."

"I can get information, Dad."

"He knows my name. He'll connect the dots."

"I'm not using my real name. He only knows me as Cheryl. I'll make up a last name."

I gave her my best fatherly stare.

"This is my chance to do some real reporting instead of being a gofer."

My fingers itched to get back to the keyboard. "And how are you going to do that? You don't even know how to cut hair."

"It's not a stylist position; it's for a receptionist."

"So what are you going to do, write down your social security number and give him your work history and then say, 'By the way, did you kill Diana Wright?'"

"Of course not. I might not have a chance to ask many questions in the first meeting, but you have to admit, it gives us access. And we haven't had that."

"It's too dangerous. It's highly unlikely he was involved in Diana's murder, but if the detective was right, this guy will protect himself at all costs. If he finds out you're connected to a reporter . . . I don't want you to do it."

She cocked her head and looked at me through those black glasses. "What are you afraid of? That I might show you up?"

"No, I don't want you to get hurt."

"Is it that, or are you afraid I might find something you haven't been able to? I think that threatens you more."

"That's absurd."

"Mom said you're territorial. That I should be careful because you want to control everything."

Her mother was a vindictive, heartless person to say such an incriminating thing about her husband. She was also dead-on. And of course, being the self-respecting American male, full of pride, vinegar, and misguided zeal, I had to defend myself against this vicious attack.

"I don't want to control you. What have I said no to so far? I've let you follow every idea you've had, and your instincts have been good."

"I get you coffee, Dad. My best instincts have been to hold the mayonnaise on your ham and cheese. I haven't done anything of substance and you know it."

I tried to think of a good argument for that. She had helped with a lot of the research into Conley's past. But that wasn't glamorous. She also made good coffee, but I decided not to bring that up. I may look like a dolt of a dad, but I'm not that stupid.

"I thought you wanted to learn what it was like to put a book together. That's what I've been trying to do. Putting your life on the line is not part of the deal."

"How is going for an interview and asking a couple of questions putting my life on the line?"

"What if he offers you the job?"

"Great. I'll have more access."

"What if he offers to take you to dinner?"

"Even better. It'll give me a chance to catch him when his guard is down."

"Abby! You don't get it. At best he's a creep with some shady business dealings. At worst, he could have shot a woman in the head and buried her body in a garbage dump."

"But you said yourself that's a very small chance."

"Yes, but if he did it, he was smart enough to frame another man for the crime. I don't want a guy like that to have access to *you*."

She moved closer, a vein in her neck pulsing. "Exactly. If this guy is the evil killer, I want to know it before Terrelle Conley is executed, don't you?"

I thought about that for exactly two seconds, then turned back to the computer screen. There are some things you just don't want to know or to think about when you're in the middle of writing.

She cursed. "You don't trust me at all. You still think I'm that little girl you used to take to the library for story time. I'm a grown woman. I have good ideas, good instincts. I have a gut feeling this is something I need to do."

"I don't think of you as that little girl. I know you're grown and you can make your own decisions, and I'm proud of you. But I don't want to put you in this position."

As I spoke, she shook her head and looked down, as if all the praise I gave rang hollow.

"Why, because you care so much?" She laughed. "You wouldn't know where I was or what I was doing if I hadn't found you at the casino. I had to follow you around like a hungry puppy to get you to notice me."

"Abby, I think about you every day—"

"Abigail," she snapped. "And *thinking* about someone doesn't mean you care about them. It's not the same. You think a lot more about gambling than you ever have about your children. I used to think that if I had something wrong with a vital organ, maybe you'd notice me. Maybe you'd care. But then you drew away from Aiden, like you were more concerned with protecting yourself than helping Mom carry the load. What's that like, Dad? Caring about someone by thinking about them but never coming to see them, never calling them? You don't want me to have contact with Tompkins because you care? Sorry, I'm not buying it."

She whisked out of the room and I sat staring at the computer screen. I knew I had to go after her, but I was glued to the chair, glued to the screen with all the letters and lines running together and my vision blurring from her words.

I see myself as good at dialogue, coming up with the next question for the interview or press conference, boiling the conversation down to one cogent question, so I went through our next scene in the kitchen, me putting a hand on her shoulder, remembering to call her Abigail, telling her I was sorry, thinking of some other assignment to divert her from her plan to wear tight jeans and a clingy blouse that I knew the guy couldn't resist. Something that would keep her satisfied but safe.

Before I could try out my snappy dialogue, my phone buzzed with a restricted call on the screen. An uptight and overly caffeinated voice said, "Please hold for the governor."

I sat, listening to the hustle and bustle of the wheels of government churning.

"Truman, how's the writing going?" Townsend said. I could see the flash of white teeth, the tweezed eyebrows, the perfectly tanned skin crinkling as he smiled.

"Making progress. Maybe one of these days you'll let me write your story. You seem to be in the news."

"Things are getting a little crazy, I'll admit that. But I have a favor to ask. Could you meet with me this evening? I have something important to talk about that I can't do over the phone."

"What time?"

"I'm open at eight fifteen. Oh, and I'd really like Ellen to join us. She should be in on this."

"That might be tough, given Aiden's condition."

"How is he doing?"

I told him the latest prayer request Ellen had sent to her Facebook prayer group, and Townsend gave a concerned grunt/groan that showed he was feeling our pain. But as soon as the calculated amount of time had passed, he said, "I think we really need her in on the conversation."

"I'll see what I can do."

"Thanks. I'll see you two tonight then." He gave me instructions on how to get through security after hours.

I hung up and went to the kitchen to see Abby. The coffeepot was going strong and I heard her engine fire outside. By the time I made it to the door, she was gone.

CHAPTER 24

WITHOUT A WORD about our previous conversation—nor many words at all—Abby dropped me off later at the hospital. While I met Ellen, Abby hurried up to Aiden's room.

I do not have a good history of being a passenger with my wife driving, and she instinctively headed to the passenger side. Our worst experience had been a few years earlier when she picked me up at the airport. Instead of a mutually satisfying conversation, which I'm not sure I have ever enjoyed, she put the car in park at a red light and climbed into the backseat. Sadly, that was not the low point of our marriage. From that point on, I parked my car at the airport and drove myself. But tonight I would allow her to drive us to the governor's mansion as penance for infractions past. I decided this small gesture would show her how much I had changed.

With trepidation, she started the car. She tried to hide her fatigue and worry but I could see through the fake smile. I asked her how Aiden was doing and she gave a curt, quick answer, as if she was really wondering why I didn't leave enough time to go up and see him.

"Looks like they did a good job on the window," I said.

"It does cut down on the street noise," she said. She mentioned that the guy from her church was a gem and had taken care of several automotive problems she'd had over the years, which immediately made me feel like a failure as a husband. I'll bet the guy even did his own oil changes at home, crawling under the engine and getting his hands dirty, something I had never done. I am not a guy who tinkers in the garage on weekends. Nothing mechanical relieves me of stress.

"How's the writing going?" she said.

I'm never sure how to answer that question because writing is a process of momentum. It's a lot like learning to ride a bike and you do it anew with every project. In order to keep the bike up, you must have speed, but you can't have speed until you're sitting on the bike, pedaling with all your might. Time away from the page is a momentum killer. Riding to the governor's mansion after dark was time I wasn't writing, so it frustrated me. But how can you explain that? How do you describe an obsession?

"It's going well," I said.

"How is it with Abigail?"

I tried not to read anything into the question, but honestly, how can you not? She could have said, "Abby says it's going well" or "Abby says you're a jerk." I couldn't help but think I was being set up.

"She's a pistol, like always. I can't believe how smart she is. She's a great kid." I was really laying it on now. I believed those things about my daughter, but the voice didn't sound like mine.

"I can tell she's impressed with you."

"How so?"

"She says you eat, drink, and sleep the project. You're an animal. When you get committed to something, you won't let go."

Meaning that if I were half as committed to my marriage and family as I was to my work, I would win Father of the Year? I saw a sign for a casino and was glad Ellen was driving. I needed some release and it had been, for me, a long time since I had visited a gambling establishment.

"Tell me more about what Carlton said," Ellen said. Her voice was calm and she seemed more comfortable behind the wheel.

I told her the verbatim conversation, leaving out his tan, white teeth, and all the stuff that runs through my head when I think of the toad. I know that last statement was unkind, so in fairness to toads everywhere, consider it withdrawn.

"Sounds kind of ominous," she said. "What do you think he wants?"

"Knowing Townsend, it'll probably be something simple. Firstborn child. A piece of my anatomy. But I don't think it's a coincidence that I have another interview with Conley tomorrow."

"It has to be about Aiden."

"I assume. But given his designs on the White House and what the pundits are saying, he may want to invite you to the inauguration."

She drove in silence, a little slow for the middle lane, but I didn't say anything. No sir. Not going to mention the fact that cars were passing us on both the left and the right. I just looked out the window, trying to keep my lips tight and my spleen from exploding.

"Maybe he wants you to be his press secretary," she said. "Have you thought about that?"

The thought had crossed my mind, but I laughed. "I can't imagine a less satisfying job. Trying to come up with creative answers as to why Townsend would do anything would be impossible. I'd rather be unemployed. As for why he wants you there, I think he wants to get another look at your legs."

She gave that Ellen laugh, the one with all air and a tilt of her head back and a smile that could melt the hardest heart. Yes, she was older and she hadn't had the "help" that Jennifer Townsend had, but she was genuinely beautiful. Not a great driver, of course, but you can't have everything.

"You don't have to worry about my relationship with the governor because I don't have one," she said.

"You could have. Come on, your parents wanted you to marry him and you know it."

"That's such an old burial ground, Tru. I chose you."

"To your everlasting regret. How long did you two date before I found you in the newsroom?"

She shook her head. "Let's not go there."

"No, we've never really talked about this. It was serious, wasn't it? I mean, think about it. You could be sitting in the governor's mansion tonight getting ready for a move to Washington, DC. Your life would have turned out drastically different. You might not have had children, but you could have raised several porpoises and saved the life of endangered marsh scum."

"I don't have to live in a mansion to have everything I need."

"What about everything you want?" A car passed on the right and a guy with more bling than an NBA all-star told us we were number one in his book. Ellen was oblivious.

"I don't think about what my life might have been. I'm too busy with what *is*."

"And what *is* right now is pretty bad."

She sighed. "I'd pretty much say I hate my life. The stress. The uncertainty. The struggle with Aiden. With Abigail. With you."

She said it in a melancholy way that matched the night sky. A lonely, unloved woman sitting beside a lonely loser. We should have been the perfect pair, but we were Naples and Fort Lauderdale, on different sides of the peninsula but with no relational I-75 to help us meet. Highways of the heart can't connect souls when there is so much distance.

"But I'll tell you this," Ellen said. "I wouldn't trade places with Jennifer Townsend."

"Why not? All the stability you can handle and the only stress you'd have is where to store your furniture for eight years."

"Truman, this is going to come as a shock to you, but I wouldn't trade the uncertainty or the stress. I've learned things about myself through this that I never wanted to learn, would never have learned if it all hadn't crashed down around us."

Our exit was coming up and she was still in the middle lane, but I was able to bite my tongue. I think it was a test and I passed. On the right side, of course.

She continued, "There are things you learn about life and your-self in the valley that you can't learn anywhere else. And yes, God is there."

"So you're telling me God gave Aiden a bad heart so you could learn more about life? Couldn't you just have gone to one of those women's seminars? That would seem a lot more fair to Aiden."

She gave her signal and crossed two lanes to the exit. It nearly caused me to speak in tongues.

"I don't presume to know why God does what he does. But I know I would not be the person I am today if I hadn't gone through this."

"So does that mean I was a mistake? I'm trying to make sense of it. Was I God's punishment to you? Did he zap Aiden because you married a heathen?"

She drove in silence and I knew I had touched a nerve, though I didn't have designs on that nerve.

As we neared the governor's mansion, she pulled over, without giving her signal, and threw the car into park. "I don't look at you as a mistake, Tru. You've given me two beautiful children. All of our troubles caused me to run to God, and I don't think that would have happened if everything had gone smoothly. I'm not happy about our problems, but they've had a deeper effect. I know I can't get you to understand, but it's true. And I still have hope that somehow we can work this out. But I'm tired. It feels like we're in a boat and I'm the only one rowing. And we're going around in the same circle."

She looked at me without tears, without drama, without longing or anything but that hollow reckoning of a woman who has been alone. Just a blank stare. But even with the stare, there seemed to be an invitation, something drawing me inside the pain.

She didn't say anything else. The prosecution was resting. And the defense had no believable witnesses.

"I'll bet Oleta and Terrelle don't have these kinds of conversations."

"I'll bet they wish they could," she said. "She's told me she'd give anything just to have dinner with him and hold his hand or argue over which movie to watch on a Friday night." She looked into the night. "Abigail tells me she thinks there's a chance Terrelle might be innocent. Do you agree?"

I shrugged. "In the universe of chances, that's one of them. I don't see what it matters at this point."

The LED clock clicked over another minute. We were already late for the meeting, but that didn't concern her. She was always the one who played loose with the clock. I watched my seconds and she lived by the hour hand.

"Tru, I haven't told you this yet, but Oleta and Terrelle didn't want to write a book. I suggested it."

"What do you mean?"

"I gave her the money for the book."

I stared at her, trying to think of the next question at the press conference that had become our marriage.

"It was manipulative and dishonest," she said.

"But it worked. You got me into the story."

"I knew if you got onto the trail, you'd be able to follow it. That you wouldn't give up."

"You knew what I would do with the money."

She nodded.

"And that I would feel obligated."

"And that the work would fill in the blank places. That you'd work at it with the same passion as your gambling."

"And you knew this would get me home."

"I hoped it would."

A warm feeling mixed with disgust. "What about Abby? Did you set that up?"

"I was as surprised as you were when she showed up."

"But you sent her to the casino."

"She asked where I thought you were."

I sat with the confession for a moment. "So I lost your money."

"Our money."

"Where did you get it?"

"I had savings. There was a life insurance policy my father had paid fully. I took the cash value. Sold a lot of your stuff on eBay." She smiled. "Just kidding."

In the midst of this revelation, when my default was to excoriate her for her devious, conniving ways, reach out with my fangs and slice her open, I realized how much it took for her to take this step—or leap of faith. She *wanted* me back in her life, which made me concerned for her sanity and judgment. Perhaps she knew this was our last, best chance.

I processed this and had nearly formulated my response when my cell rang. "It's him," I said as I answered.

She nodded, put the car in gear, and pulled out without adequately looking at oncoming traffic.

CHAPTER 25

ABIGAIL HELD AIDEN'S HAND and patted it like she had when they were young. When he was a baby, her mother had allowed her to be a "big girl" and sit with him on the couch with her arm tucked gently behind his head. She would pat his hand when he was in his high chair waiting for food. Pat his hand sitting next to his car seat as they drove to the hospital for another procedure. His hand still seemed just as fragile.

A game was on TV, but he had the sound muted. He watched haphazardly, as if he knew the winner and loser didn't really matter. *How could you become emotionally invested in baseball,* she thought, *in your condition?*

"I admire you," she said out of the blue, staring at his pale hand. She traced a blue vein with her eye until it disappeared under his wrist.

"What's to admire?" Aiden said.

"The way you've handled all of this. Even when you were little, you just took everything in stride. One day at a time."

"It's the only way I knew how to live. What else was I going to do?" His voice was shallow, supported by short puffs of air.

"Don't sell yourself short. It's admirable. I wish I could live that way."

"You do. You just don't see it."

"Not like you, though."

Aiden turned on his side and the effort made him wince. "Well, maybe you're seeing something else and not just me."

"Don't start," she said.

"Don't start what?"

"You know what—the God stuff."

Aiden smiled.

"Mom has been working on me nonstop. And Philip's mom and dad are really into the religion thing. I'm getting it from all sides."

"Religion gets you nowhere—"

"I know, I know—if I hear one more time that it's a *relationship*, I'm going to hurl."

"It's true, Abby. Why don't you give your dying brother just one chance to explain?" He said it with a twinkle in his eye, as if he could guilt her into listening to something she knew was real, knew had made a difference.

"You looking for a pity conversion?" she said.

"That's funny. A new witnessing tool. Evangelism Implosion." His thin rib cage shook through the hospital gown. "Get sick and lead your whole family to faith."

She laughed with him, then looked away as a tear formed.

She didn't want him to see her weak and doubting. She had to be positive and upbeat and believe the best and all that. That's what he needed now. But just hearing his voice made her sad, made her think of what might be in the coming days. What it would be to not have that voice around anymore.

"Truth is, I admire *you*," he said.

"Now there's a shocker," she said. "What little brother in the history of the world has ever said that?"

"First time for everything."

"So what do you admire?"

"Going after your dreams. How smart you are. Gorgeous. You're going to take the world by the tail one day and sling it around, big sister. I can tell."

"You think so?"

"I know it. I just hope I can be there to watch."

"See, that's why I admire you," she said. "You can get outside of yourself, even when you're in pain. Most people would just wallow in self-pity. Do you know how rare that is?"

"Do you know how rare it is for somebody not to take a compliment?"

She tossed his hand aside, feigning disgust.

"How's Philip?" he said. "I'll bet he misses you."

"We needed a break anyway. I think he's more ready to settle down than I am."

"Usually it's the other way around."

"You're just going on the only example you've ever known: Mom and Dad."

"No, I read. I watch movies. I have friends. Most of the time the guy doesn't want to be tied down too soon and the girl wants the long-term commitment. Philip sounds like a nice guy."

"He is. I just don't know if he's the one. I want to make sure that he's as good as my little brother."

"You might wait a lifetime for that." Aiden laughed and coughed a little. He rolled onto his back and coughed again and something didn't seem right.

He waved her off when she asked if he needed a nurse, but when he couldn't stop coughing, she ran into the hall. She could have just punched the button by the bed, but coming out here felt better. She hated to see him suffer, hated to see him struggle. But that had been his whole life, one long struggle.

Abigail got halfway to the nurses' station and listened for his cough, but all was quiet.

CHAPTER 26

ELLEN PULLED UP to the guard at the front gate. The man leaned down and looked past her, recognizing Truman and nodding. He told them where to park and shuffled them off to another guard, who walked them to the front door, bathed in splendorous light. The governor's aide, Reginald, met them there.

The man showed them into the dining room and Truman told her it was the same he had seen earlier. The house had the feel of a mortuary to Ellen, muted in its subdued lighting and the classical music that played in the background, just loud enough to be heard above the fountain in the next room. There was tea, decaf, and cookies at the side table in a serve-yourself arrangement, and Truman did, offering to retrieve something for her. But she just rubbed her hands, gazing at the tasteful decorating.

"You reconsidering your choice in husbands?" Truman said.

She smiled nervously, memories flooding back of the time she and Carlton had spent together. She had mainly been against a relationship with him because her parents were all for it. Then, with his charm and perseverance, he had slipped into her life.

"Feels a little too nice, doesn't it?" she said.

"Makes you wonder how he keeps that youthful physique when there are cookies every night." Truman glanced about the room. "I get the feeling there's some guy in uniform watching our every move."

Reginald returned and stopped just inside the door until Carlton Townsend appeared, still in his suit coat, though he removed that and put it on the back of a chair as he glided forward. There seemed to be no wasted motion in anything he did. Ellen recalled feeling the same way as he studied for tests while sipping coffee. Watching him sign an executive order in some statehouse ceremony was maddening in its circumspection and fluidity.

He crossed the room and gave Ellen an elegant hug and a passing kiss, standing back and looking her in the eye, beaming. "You haven't changed a bit, Ellen. Beautiful."

She could see Truman rolling his eyes and sticking a finger toward his throat.

Carlton turned and shook hands with him. "Thank you both for coming on such short notice. I really appreciate it." He took three steps to the table, tore off half a cookie, grabbed a chair, and turned it around. "Jennifer hates these but they're one of my guilty pleasures."

"Reagan had his jelly beans; you'll have cookies in the White House," Truman said.

"So you saw the announcement."

"Yeah, just happened to catch it. Shame you didn't get more press."

He smiled, then looked at Ellen, turning serious. His voice dropped. "How's Aiden?"

It felt calculated to her, a little too Hollywood. "He's holding his own," she said with a slight tremble.

"He's going to make it, right?" Carlton said. "We only have two weeks to go."

"The doctors are doing everything they can."

"Good. Tell them to keep it up." He dipped his head like a prizefighter before a weigh-in. "With God's help we're going to get this thing done."

The words felt designed. His body language showed empathy, but Ellen could tell something was brewing.

"So what's this about?" Truman said, breaking the somber mood.

Townsend pursed his lips as if weighed down by the enormity of the situation, while at the same time exuding confidence and resolve. He rubbed his hands to dust off the cookie crumbs and turned the chair once more to face them.

"You both know that the wheels of justice grind particularly fast at this point in the legal process. There are usually appeals and requests for a stay—all perfectly legal and certainly among Conley's rights. If it were me facing death, I'd fight for every second."

"What does that have to do with us?" Truman said.

Something rose up in Ellen and she gave Truman a quick glance. *Shut up and let him talk. Don't goad him. Don't make this about you.*

"Nothing, per se," Carlton said. "However, your family is now inextricably intertwined with his story. And you have access to him and his wife like no one else."

Truman stiffened but didn't speak.

"Therefore, I have a request. I know you're meeting with him again. Tomorrow, I believe."

"How'd you guess?" Truman said.

Ellen could hardly hold back, but she managed, keeping her eyes locked on Carlton.

"I want this procedure for your son. I want this for you, Ellen. But there are certain realities of the political world that must be understood. . . ."

Truman jumped in. "You want Conley and whatever lawyer from Florida State he has now to stand down. Not try to block the execution."

Townsend brushed aside the remark like a lion shaking a fly from its mane. "I simply think it will be best for all of us if the process goes on unimpeded. Aiden's chances are much better the smoother this goes in the courts and in the court of public opinion. You can understand that."

Ellen finally spoke. "From what Oleta has told me, there aren't going to be any further appeals. She and Terrelle are resigned to the inevitable."

"That's good to hear. If it's true, then what I have to ask next shouldn't be a problem."

Ellen felt in the pit of her stomach that whatever would come next was going to be a huge problem.

The governor paused for dramatic effect and looked at Truman. "I need a confession."

"What?" Truman said, his mouth dropping.

Ellen put a warning hand on his arm. "Carlton, you know he won't sign a confession."

Carlton showed his palms as if in supplication. "Then my hands are tied."

Ellen dug her fingernails into Truman's arm, trying to stem the rising tide she knew was coursing through her husband. "If you know there won't be any further attempts to drag out the process, to get a last-minute stay, what could possibly go wrong?" she said evenly, unemotional.

Carlton leaned forward, elbows on his knees, his index fingers together and touching his lips. "There is intense pressure about this issue from every side. The right is up in arms that we are coddling a murderer. We're setting a dangerous precedent. The left is agitated that we'll begin using death row inmates as organ factories. You can't imagine the phone calls, e-mails, protests—and not just to me. This filters through to members of the legislature."

Ellen couldn't help thinking that those members wanted reelection more than anything. Something that would have occurred to her husband as well.

"It would be much easier just to let this train pass without trying to step in front of it. Some in my camp are suggesting it's political suicide. But I'm willing to fight for your son."

"You're not willing to fight for anyone but yourself," Truman spat. "You never have been." He shook away Ellen's hand. "If you had any concern for anyone but yourself, you'd do the right thing and tell the right and the left to shove it. But you won't. You stick your finger in the air and Reginald and your other bean counters calculate the cost of votes from one county to the next. And if it's convenient, you'll use my son's life to show how compassionate you are, but we both know it's the polls that will decide this."

The governor's aide appeared as Truman concluded and locked eyes with his boss. Carlton lifted a hand and smiled. "We're fine; we're fine."

Reginald stepped out with an indignant air.

"I like your spunk, Truman," Carlton said evenly. "I always have. That bulldog mentality of getting the story and getting it right has served you well. Remember when you pushed your way into that hotel meeting room? First job out of college and you were already making headlines with your tenacity."

Ellen remembered the incident and was impressed that Carlton did. Something about a quorum and the public's right to know. Truman had read the rules and knew a new city manager was being courted. An aide opened the door and Truman pushed through with the cameraman behind him, capturing horrified faces around a poker table. His stock went up in journalistic circles and down with local politicians, most of whom were tossed out in the next election.

Carlton continued, "You've never been able to understand that tenacity must live in communion with reality. We can't be idealists. I wish we lived in a perfect world where black and white are always distinguishable. Where the good guys win and the bad guys lose. But we do not live in that world. We live in a place where every move is calculated against us by someone with their own agenda. That's the world I live in every day. I don't like it. I want to change it, but I can only do so much. At the end of the day, I have to put my head on the pillow and try to sleep. And I would sleep much better if I knew that Aiden Wiley had a regular heartbeat and that I helped a convicted murderer do something good with his life. One last good thing."

Ellen sat back, looking at Carlton's eyes. It didn't feel like a speech. It didn't feel rehearsed. It felt genuine and from the heart.

"This is what I hate most about you, Townsend," Truman said.

"What's that?"

"Your ability to sway even the most skeptical crowd with that smug superiority that's always bathed in narcissistic compassion."

"What do you want us to do?" Ellen said.

"I would like both of you to talk with Oleta and Terrelle." He said their names like he was an old friend from their neighborhood. "If they know this is the only way the transplant can be done, they may accede to the confession. You both know every man on death row is holding out for a miracle. That's not going to happen. This book you're writing can explain in detail what a heroic thing it was for Terrelle to sign a confession and waive his rights. He's doing this selflessly, putting others' interests ahead of his own."

"He's not going to say something that isn't true," Truman said. "He's come too far."

"That's why you have to get him to look at the big picture. Is it wrong to lie? Yes. Is it ever for the greater good? You need to convince him that this is the only way we can move forward."

"Why now?" Truman said. "Why didn't you bring this up before I met with him the first time?"

"I didn't have the information I have now. I'm meeting tomorrow afternoon with members of the judiciary subcommittee. They've indicated support for this effort if—and that's the operative word here—Conley waives his final appeals and automatic requests for reprieves or stays."

"And if he signs a confession," Ellen said.

"Yes."

"You're saying it's a done deal?" Truman said.

"You learn very early on that nothing is a done deal in the political realm. But if I were a betting man—" he looked at Truman—"I would say your son has a very good chance."

"What if he won't confess?" Truman said. "Isn't there middle ground I can offer?"

"What middle ground?"

"Let's say he agrees to waive his right to a stay and all the petitions. Isn't that what you really want?"

"If we don't have a confession, that hurts us down the road, or at least the potential is there to be hurt and I'm not willing to risk that. It's not in the best interests of the state or my own future political goals."

"That's what this comes down to?" Ellen said. It was her turn to challenge. She had been listening intently and now shifted to the edge of her seat. "You're not really concerned about justice or compassion or benevolence. Truman's right. You're concerned about what kind of plus or minus this gives you in the polls."

"Ellen, I want this as badly as you do—"

"No, you don't. You have no idea how badly we want this."

"You're right." He held up both hands in surrender. "I can only imagine what you've been through and I'm sorry. So sorry. But I do know that this is your best chance at a new life for your son."

Ellen deflated, seeing the dead end this truly was. A political leader can only offer so much. They will always stop short of your humanity. She slumped in her chair, staring blankly at the pristine table with its perfectly polished silver.

Carlton stood and turned to Truman. The meeting was over. He didn't hold out his hand or pat her husband on the shoulder or make any kind of physical gesture, just a few words to charge him. "Get the confession. I'll get your son a heart."

Ellen's phone rang with the tune that signaled it was Abigail. "Who Let the Dogs Out" clashed with Chopin, but she didn't care. She fumbled with her purse and retrieved it.

"Mom, something's wrong," Abigail said. Alarms were going off in the background. "I'm scared."

"We're on our way."

"Is everything all right?" Carlton said from the doorway.

Ellen pushed past him without speaking.

CHAPTER 27

I DROPPED ELLEN at the emergency entrance and headed to the garage. There was a valet at the front but I didn't have a tip, plus I needed a few minutes to gather my thoughts, my resolve. I try to project the image that I'm together, but underneath there is always a need to escape, to rush to some other place where the pain and trouble aren't rising like a tide, ready to engulf.

Like a firefighter who walks into a crowded theater and looks for the nearest exit, I checked the parking garage and nearly bolted, but I knew that was cowardly. I also knew there were two women on the eighth floor waiting, ready to judge me harshly if I abandoned them. If I showed up, they would still judge me harshly for all the times I hadn't, but I decided not to let that stop me.

Perhaps it's the antiseptic smell of hospitals that turns me away.

Perhaps something happened when I came out the birth canal that makes me want to run. Or it may be flashes of that night and the vision of a guilty man strapped in and awaiting the electrical impulses. So many parallels of things I've seen and things I wish I hadn't seen go into this. Of course, it might just be the fact that I have an aversion to the pain my son has been through in such places.

I found Abby and Ellen embracing in the waiting room on the eighth floor, nurses busy in the background. I couldn't help feeling like an intruder. As usual, Ellen had sized up the situation, had spoken with the head nurse and received the report. A specialist was hurrying in to consult and I saw the money spinning toward the jackpot on the medical slots. It's where my mind always went, not to the heart of my son, not to the possibility of losing him, but to the resultant bills. I hate it that I always think about money.

Ellen spoke in the same technical jargon as the doctors. She was familiar with the big words that separate patient from medical professional. She saw the look on Abby's face and explained, "That means his heart can't find its rhythm. It's under stress. His body can't get the blood it needs."

"Has this happened before?" I said.

"Yes, but there are complications. The medication they've given him to thin the blood and help the heart pump is working against them."

"A catch-22."

"Exactly."

"Is he going to be okay?" Abby said. "They can fix this, right?"

A man in a white coat emerged. He recognized Ellen and she introduced Dr. Andrew Fanelli, one of the top heart surgeons in the country. I had read on several of Ellen's blogs what an answer to prayer this man had been and how the Lord had transferred him to this area at just the right time for Aiden. I thought it would have been a lot better if the Lord would have just healed Aiden, but I wasn't about to say that as I shook his hand.

When all of that was over, Dr. Fanelli put his hands on his hips and shook his head. He spoke with a Middle Eastern accent, precise and delicate. "I thought we had lost him two times." He looked at me. "Your son would not give up. But we have come to a pivotal point."

Ellen moved closer, studying his face.

The man said some things I didn't understand but Ellen kept up with him. "You're suggesting the artificial heart?"

"I'm suggesting we keep him sedated and let the machine get us to the point of transplantation. Do you have an update from the donor?"

"We're hopeful," Ellen said. "It looks like the heart will be ready on the twenty-first."

I could tell just saying the words was distasteful to her. One transplant date is another's execution date.

Dr. Fanelli glanced at Abby, then at the floor. He tried to smile. "I know how much this means to each of you. Aiden is in good hands here. The best of care. But you need to prepare for the possibilities that lie ahead." He looked at Ellen. "Time is not on our side. If the transplant does not come through, there will be very little we can do. I just want you to know the realistic picture."

"I understand," Ellen said. She was the only one of us who could actually form words.

"You may see him, but he obviously won't be able to respond."

The doctor and Ellen disappeared behind the forbidden doors and I collapsed in a chair. Abby sat next to me and took my hand.

"How are you doing?" I said.

"Not good." She held a crumpled tissue and wiped at her nose. "It was awful, Dad. His face got so pale and he couldn't breathe. He reached out to me and I couldn't do anything." Abby dissolved into tears and I pulled her close.

"I'm so sorry, honey. You shouldn't have had to go through that."

"I'm glad I was there," she said through the tears and the anger. "I wanted to do something."

"You did. He appreciated you being there." I imagined the chaos of his room, the alarms and nurses running.

"It's like he's been reaching out his whole life for help but there's no one. He just lays there reaching out." She rubbed her forehead with the heel of her hand till her skin was white. "I can't get the sight of him out of my head."

I patted her shoulder and she put her head on my chest. "This is not over. You heard the doctor. As long as Aiden doesn't give up, I'm not going to either."

When Ellen returned, she gathered Abby in and held her. The two cried and Ellen whispered words of encouragement, telling her how lucky her brother was to have her as a sister. All the things I couldn't come up with. Finally Ellen pulled away and through the tears asked if we wanted to see him. I wanted to run. Jump out a window. Throw the dice on some other floor, deal the cards to some other waiting room. Instead I stood and followed, feeling my own heart skip.

We entered the darkened room and I could barely distinguish my son from all the cords, tubes, and machines. It wasn't him, just a pallid shell of the boy I had taken to the playground when he was younger. I tried to recall my last words to him and his to me.

Was this the end? Would I see his pale face staring up from some casket, mercifully unhooked from the hospital's umbilical cords and ushered into forever?

Abby drove me home and Ellen decided to stay at the hospital, though the doctor and nurses assured her there was nothing more she could do. She had invested too much in Aiden to let him go through the night alone.

I got in front of the computer screen but all the words seemed jumbles. I jotted a few notes I'd been thinking about Townsend but gave up on the writing and collapsed in the corner, staring out the window at the stars that managed to peek through the light pollution. I couldn't get the sight of Aiden out of my mind.

I thought I heard Abby crying and went to her door and stood there, listening, trying to get up the courage to knock. I've interviewed terrorists in enclosed campgrounds in Yemen and heads of state who were targets of assassination and didn't think a thing about it. Why was this so hard?

I returned to my air mattress and went over the conversation I would have the next day with Terrelle. I ran through several scenarios, ways I could bring up the confession, but none of them left me feeling anything but coldhearted.

I lay tossing and turning about the years I had wasted chasing stories and fame and making a name. Where had all of that gotten me? What did I have to show for those years except regret and a gravely ill son?

I heard a car pull up; then the front door opened and closed softly. I hit a button on my watch and saw it was 3:12. Why would Ellen be home? If Aiden hadn't made it, surely she would have phoned. I listened to the movement, footsteps outside my room, holding my breath, hoping she didn't come inside with news, knowing I would have to hear it eventually.

The shuffling subsided and I tried to breathe. When I couldn't take it any longer, I wandered into the kitchen, lit only by the stove light. Ellen's purse sat on the table and her shoes were parked next to her bedroom door. What used to be our bedroom door.

I got a drink from the refrigerator and turned on the light, hoping that might lure her back. When it didn't, I walked to her room and found the door slightly ajar. I pecked on it and whispered her name. The door pushed open on its own and I heard the trickle of water from the walk-in shower, something we both had wanted, along with the big Jacuzzi. The fact that she was showering showed the state she was in. She couldn't get the strength up to run a bath.

I knew the only chivalrous thing to do at this point was to turn and wait in the kitchen. Estranged spouses keep their distance, particularly when showers are involved. But something inexorable drew me into the darkened room. It wasn't just the sound of the water trickling; there was something else: soft sobs, quiet tears escaping a crushed soul. There is nothing worse than the pain of a caring woman crying alone.

I sat on the edge of her bed and listened, letting my eyes adjust to the dim light from the bathroom. My eyes lit on the pictures on her dresser. The old birthday card she still had from me. Photos of Abby in cap and gown and Aiden beaming by her side. Where was I when Abby graduated from high school? Haiti? Cuba? The Balkans? I couldn't remember. I went through the list of stories I had covered that spring and cataloged the other photos. I was in so few of them. For all purposes, my wife had been a single parent during these years, and it struck me how unfair that had been to all three of them.

The shower stream stopped. I didn't want her frightened when she stepped from the bathroom, so I rose and headed for the door.

"Hey," she said behind me, softly.

I turned to see her silhouette in the muted bathroom light, one of her thick towels covering her.

"Sorry; I heard you come in. I was afraid something might have happened."

She shook her head and inched forward. "He's stable. I just needed a shower and a change of clothes."

"You should get some sleep."

"So should you. It's a big day with Terrelle."

I nodded and looked at the floor. It was hard to see her in this undressed state. Any move toward her would seem predatory. "Yeah, I've been running that conversation over in my mind."

"Maybe if I talk with Oleta. If she understands, maybe she could talk with him or send a note. . . ."

I pointed at the graduation photo. "Do you remember where I was when this was taken?"

She leaned down to see and water fell on the glass, like raindrops. She didn't hesitate. "Suicide bombing in the Middle East."

"How do you do that? Remember every detail?"

"I don't remember everything. They say the memories you have are stamped on your brain through the emotional markers. Times when you feel pain or loss."

I found myself staring at her legs, at knees that turned slightly inward. That's not a knock—I loved seeing those in-turned knees.

"I'll let you get dressed," I said.

"Don't go."

She wrapped the towel tightly around herself and sat on the bed. I sat next to her, unsure of myself, as if we were wading into waters where the ground might give way and we'd be engulfed by the slipstream.

"Are you going to ask him for the confession?"

"I want to, but I don't know how to do it."

"I think you'll know what to say when the time comes."

"I hope you're right."

I watched the water droplets fall from her hair onto the bedspread. Finally she said, "Thank you for coming to the hospital tonight. I know that's never easy."

"Can't be easy for you, either. Especially when you've had to do it alone for so long."

She shrugged. "I don't know. In some ways I've gotten used to the place, to the comfort of it."

"Comfort?"

"The unpredictability. Having to give him over to the doctors again. There hasn't been anything in this whole process I can control. In the beginning, I thought I could and tried hard to do everything right, to have him eat right, take the best medication, stay away from anything that could hurt him. But now, with every trip to the hospital, it's like I'm abandoning him to God. I have to lean on and trust in something bigger than me or the choices I make."

It made sense. "Kind of like couples who fight all the time and yell at each other. They get addicted to the conflict and it becomes the script. Something they know and are comfortable with."

She let my words hang there between us. Had I said something wrong? Misinterpreted?

"You know, Tru, no matter how this ends up, I'm glad you came back. It's good having you here."

"Other than me losing all your money."

She gave me the Ellen stare. Sometimes that's good; sometimes it's bad. This time I was just glad she was looking at me. "I figured that would happen."

"If you knew I'd blow it, why let me have it?"

"I don't know. Maybe because deep down I still believe in you. That all of the things that hold you back aren't the real you. That somehow, someway, we can make up the distance between us."

"So it wasn't a test?"

"If it was a test, you failed big-time. But no, it wasn't."

"You were trying to lure me back with filthy lucre."

She laughed. "I've missed you, Tru. Your sense of humor. The way the kids light up when you're there."

"Ellen, I'm never going to be the man you deserve."

She took the tone. "I'll agree with that."

"What?" I feigned shock and pain.

She pulled me closer. "My ideal guy doesn't exist. The person who can always be there, always make me happy. Don't get me wrong—I'm still hurt by your choices. But I've come to see that I can't just walk away from us. I can't let you walk away. That's why I needed you back. I need us to make one last try."

"I can understand that. I'm quite a catch. No job, my car's been repossessed, lost the cottage to foreclosure, gambling addiction. Can't pay the medical or college bills. You hit all the numbers in the husband lottery, babe."

She laughed. Short and abbreviated, but there it was.

"Things are going to get better," she said. "I really believe that. I don't know why and I don't know how, but I believe it."

She put a hand on my leg and something electric shot through my body. Maybe it was the smell of the shampoo in her hair. Maybe it was the combination of all my senses. Our eyes met for a moment, and then I turned away as the door swung open.

"Mom, why are you here?" Abby said. "Has something happened?"

Ellen stood like an embarrassed schoolgirl and embraced Abby. She explained that she was headed back to the hospital. I stood and moved past them.

"I hope I didn't interrupt anything," Abby said sheepishly. "I heard voices."

"You didn't interrupt anything," I said, heading back to my room, back to my air mattress, back to my self-imposed cocoon, back to my thoughts and confusion.

Thirty minutes later the Sequoia's engine fired to life. I dreamed about us on the beach in some exotic locale, locked in an embrace, a gentle breeze through the palm trees, water lapping and enveloping our bodies, our mouths finding each other.

It was only a dream.

CHAPTER 28

Terrelle Conley stared at me through the Plexiglas, holding the phone to his ear. Three pages of scribbled recollections sat before me. A meaningless, rambling concoction of words and memories filtered through the sweat and hysteria of death row.

"I got more stuff about the early days if that will help," he said.

"This is good," I lied. "Background gives a context for who you are. It helps the reader identify with you."

"So you've been writing it?"

"Yeah. It's actually going well." I pulled out my notes and asked some questions Oleta wasn't sure about. Details of a life slipping quickly away. We were down to counting the grains in the hourglass.

"How's your son?" he said.

"Not good. He's had a couple of setbacks."

"Sorry to hear that. I've been praying for him."

I nodded and looked Terrelle in the eyes. "I've been trying to figure out how to ask you this and I haven't come up with anything. I work with words like a bricklayer works with mortar and stone. But I don't know how to say what I'm about to say."

He squinted at me and sat up straight. "Best way is just to say it."

"Okay. The governor called my wife and me. Had us come to the mansion last night. He said he's up against some opposition with the organ donation."

"Doesn't surprise me. Let me guess. He wants to help but his hands are tied. He wants to be president."

Smart man. "Sort of. There's opposition and support on every side. But even though his presidential aspirations are big, he wants to help. He thinks he can get this pushed through."

"Do you believe him?"

"He's an astute guy politically. If he says it can be done, it can."

"Then what's the problem?"

"There's something he needs if he's going to take the risk. One thing he needs from you to make it happen."

"From me? I'm giving my heart. What else does he want, my liver?"

I smiled. "He wants to make sure there won't be last-minute appeals, last-chance efforts to drag this out."

"I can give him that. The attorney we hired gave up a long time ago. The professor at Florida State has appeals ready to file, but I'll give them up. We all know what's going to happen here; no sense fighting for a month or two, especially with your son's condition."

I shifted in my chair and leaned toward the glass, wondering who else had used this phone in the past and who might use it after me. "Terrelle, he doesn't just want promises."

And then a cloud of knowing came over his face as if the curtain had parted and he had looked behind, where the wizard worked the controls.

"He wants a confession," I said.

As soon as the words were out of my mouth, his eyes fell like the sun sinking into the ocean. He took the phone away from his ear and held it by his side. This was the part I wasn't sure about. Do I follow up with an explanation, try to make him understand the gravity of this request, or just sit in silence? I wanted to keep going, explain more, but something inside told me to wait.

He stared at me with the hollow eyes of the condemned, and I had seen those same eyes before, years ago on another death row watch, a stare that still haunted my dreams. This is one of the visions I was sure I would have in the future—this place, the sounds, sights, and smells of this room.

He lifted the phone and spoke in guttural tones, like this news had taken everything out of him. "I confess to this and nobody will believe what you're putting in that book."

"I promise I'll tell it straight, just like you want it."

"But signing a confession would be an out-and-out lie. And I can't do that. Plus, there's somebody out there walking around free who deserves to be in here. What happens to that guy?"

I nodded, searching for words that wouldn't come.

"What would my kids think of me? My mama? My wife?"

"They'll know. We'll explain it to the media, in the book, to anybody who will listen. The governor forced your hand. This was the only way to save my son."

"Is that true? You think this is the only way?"

"He was forceful. My guess is there are other people behind the scenes telling him to stay away from this. It's too messy for them."

Terrelle shook his head. "It's not enough that they take my life. They take my dignity, too."

"From what I've seen, nobody can take that, Terrelle."

He looked off into the distance, or maybe into the past, as if he couldn't have imagined this choice. "There isn't anybody going to listen to a guy who changes his story at the last minute. If I lie now, everything I believe in goes down the toilet. The only thing I have left is my self-respect. The only thing that keeps me going is knowing that someday people will know the truth. This cuts the legs out from under me."

"Yeah. And while you keep your dignity, I go to a funeral." I said it with my teeth jammed together. But I said it.

"To you it's just signing a piece of paper. You get your son back."

I shook my head and looked away. "There's no guarantee the operation will work anyway. He may not last until your execution. Something could go wrong with the procedure."

He smirked. "Procedure. Makes it sound like I'm having my tonsils out. It's funny how people use words to make things you can't imagine doing seem normal."

I nodded. "The only thing I really know is that Aiden's not getting another chance. This is it."

Terrelle sat back again and ran a hand through his closely cropped hair. He muttered something under his breath I didn't catch. Finally he said, "You go back to the governor and tell him I'll sign a paper that waives every right I've got to any other appeal. He can move up the execution. He can cut my chest open personally if he wants to. But I can't admit to doing something I didn't do."

I stared at him for as long as I dared. "He's gonna say no, Terrelle."

"I'm sorry. Tell him he can string me up to a tree. Use the electric chair." His face was contorted with pain, sweat beads popping out on his forehead. He leaned into the glass. "You gotta know this, Mr. Truman. I want to help your boy. I'd let them rip my heart out of my chest right now if it would save him. But I can't confess. I can't see how telling a lie would honor God."

The guard behind Terrelle stepped forward and I knew I was running out of time. "Terrelle, listen to me. Nobody knows the kind of pressure you're under. And I don't blame you for sticking to your story, but—"

"It's not my story. It's the truth."

I couldn't answer. I couldn't speak.

"You tell him I'll swear on a stack of Bibles that I won't fight this," Terrelle said. "Oleta won't sue the state after I'm gone, my children won't say anything—I'll even cancel this book idea. Tell him I'll do anything but confess. I just can't do it."

The call came from Reginald as I was driving back on I-10, the roadway stretching between trees bursting with green. I had borrowed Ellen's car for the trip. Traffic was light, so I had time to think of how I might respond to the governor.

"The governor is very interested in your conversation with Conley," Reginald said. He had that superior tone like a stenographer at a court proceeding. Just the facts. "How did it go?"

There are no guardrails on that stretch of I-10. Sometimes roads are like life.

"I need to talk with Townsend."

"That's not possible right now, Mr. Wiley. The governor is a busy man." There was a slight laugh as if old Reg was rolling his eyes at my naiveté.

"Well, tell him to call me when he gets a spare minute or two. You've got my number."

"Mr. Wiley, I assume by your tone that Conley refused the governor's request. He's not going to confess."

I knew if I told Reginald the gist of the meeting, I would have less than a good chance with Townsend. I also knew this guy had a job to do and that was get information so the governor didn't have to. "He's probably sitting right there in the room with you. Just pass the phone to him."

Smarm seeped through the phone line. "I can assure you he's not here, Mr. Wiley. The governor is on his way to a press conference and you already know about the meeting he has with members of the legislature."

"Yeah, sounds like a few shrimp will lose their lives today."

"Mr. Wiley, the meeting this afternoon is vitally important in moving your son's case forward. I suggest you cooperate."

"I am cooperating. I've done everything the governor asked. He can call me himself so I don't have to filter."

"I assure you that you can trust me."

"Just tell him to call me. I have news."

I clicked the End button and wondered if I had just created more problems. Ticking off the governor's right-hand guy probably wasn't the best way to get what we wanted.

I flipped on the radio and watched 18-wheelers pass and tourists from the north make their way back home in minivans stuffed to the gills with suitcases and trinkets. Mothers with their feet on the dash, passed out in the passenger seat while dads struggled to stay awake. Kids firmly plugged in, staring out at me with headphones or earbuds or playing mindless video games to pass the time. Kids have it way too easy these days.

The radio station was preparing for the arrival of Rush Limbaugh's program like it was the Second Coming, pummeling each break with teasers and well-crafted promos. The news sounder ushered in the latest traffic and weather—mostly sunny (what a surprise) and watch out for an accident on US 90 near Capital Circle. Another Florida service member had paid the ultimate price in some distant country. There was bleak economic news coming from another report just out, as well as surprise at the latest unemployment numbers. And the governor was still deciding on the fate of a death row inmate who wanted to donate his heart.

The reporter set up the story, giving as many details of the case as he could in twenty-five seconds—one of the drawbacks of TV or radio reporting—then played a sound bite from a Miles somebody who represented an evangelical think tank and spoke with a British accent that gave me the feeling he would do well on NPR.

"The problem, of course, is the complexity of issues surrounding the transplant. We don't want to diminish any life, so the idea of harvesting organs from a condemned man is problematic, even if the man is willing to be a donor."

My blood pressure rose. It sounded so academic coming through the speakers. So reasonable and carefully thought out. Maybe that was my problem with Christians to begin with: it wasn't about doing good to other people; it was about figuring out what was *right*. That sounds fine on the face of it, but when people try to judge what the Almighty wants, things get more complicated. That's why there are Catholics and Protestants and Jews and Muslims and every other religion. We all want to believe we have the truth about God and know exactly what he wants us to do.

Just thinking about it made my speed increase, a reflex of my foot. If Miles had a son dying in a hospital, I wondered if he would feel the same way. If his view of God would change. It's a lot easier to talk about ethical issues from the ivory tower or the pulpit than it is in the waiting room or on death row.

My phone vibrated and I gladly hit the Power button on Miles and his willing journalistic accomplice. I didn't bother looking at the screen. "This is Truman."

There was a slight pause, then a click and a deep whirring that sounded like it came from a limousine lined with leather and a well-stocked minibar.

"Truman, I don't have much time but I wanted to hear how things went with our man."

He said it like Terrelle was a second-string running back just returning from a hamstring pull. "Thanks for calling me, Governor. Yeah, we had a good talk this morning."

"And . . . ?"

"He was totally on board with the idea of waiving any delays or last-minute appeals. He'll swear on a stack of Bibles or whatever you want him to swear on. No lawsuit from his family. He said you can even move up the execution date because of Aiden's condition. This is a guy who is resigned to this eventuality. He knows it's going to happen."

"But? No confession?"

"I explained your position; I told him this was the best way to make sure Aiden gets a new heart. But he has this thing about not lying in a sworn statement."

Townsend cursed. "And I have the legislature boys all ready to sign off."

"Terrelle got religion. God's a big part of his life. I don't pretend to understand it, but he feels like this would be an affront to the Almighty."

"Truman, you have to go back and put pressure on him. Get him to understand."

"He understands. He offered to let you rip his heart out with your bare hands, pull out old Sparky from the back room, do whatever. He's not afraid to die, to give somebody he's never met his own heart. But what he does seem to be afraid of is letting Jesus down. That's important to him."

"I don't understand these people," Townsend said, almost spitting out the words. "You need to go back there and push him. I can't get this done without a confession."

"With all due respect, sir, this is his last request. To die with dignity. You may get some flak on the campaign trail, but you can charm your way out of that." *Just hold up a few orphan porpoises with rickets.* "This is all he's got."

"Do you believe him?"

"Excuse me?"

"About his innocence. Do you think he's telling the truth?"

"He sure believes he's innocent if that means anything. Bottom line, I don't know."

"It's a sticky wicket, Wiley. If he maintains his innocence, I have to wash my hands. Deny the transplant."

"You don't think that will be difficult to explain on the campaign trail? A grieving family. The governor who had the chance to do something good. Liberals will make hay out of the conservative who has little compassion and even less of a spine."

"Either way, if I get down in the mud on this one, I'm getting dirty."

"You're already in the mud, Governor. And the blood. Take the high road. This guy is begging. Ellen and I are too."

The governor sighed heavily and I could see the little refrigerator opening and someone pouring Dewar's over ice. "Truman, I didn't call you to the house last night to make some hollow pronouncement. If I don't have a confession, Aiden doesn't get a heart."

"And if you make Conley do this, you don't have one." I let that sink in, taking my exit and hitting traffic headed into the city. "Everyone will know about this, Governor. Before election day. They'll either see you as a man they can trust, who makes tough decisions on principle rather than what it does to him politically, or as just another politician on a power grab."

"You don't want to do this, Truman."

"You're right. But you know I will. I'll do it for my son and for Conley and to make you pay." My words hung there and I could hardly believe I said them in such measured tones. "But I don't have to. Nobody has to pay, except for Conley."

"Good-bye, Truman," the governor said.

CHAPTER 29

ABIGAIL SAT IN A PLASTIC CHAIR in the waiting area of Mane Street Hair and Nails. In front of her was a coffee table from Walmart with four screw-in legs. She knew it was from Walmart because she had purchased the same table a few months earlier for Philip's apartment.

An older stylist with bright-red lipstick and Doublemint gum returned to the front, her arm skin jiggling as she walked. "He'll be with you in a minute, hon."

Abigail thanked her and pulled out her purse, her cell phone ringing with Philip's tune, "On Fire." The other stylist, the one that talked with a thick, Eastern European accent and wore black eye shadow and a tongue ring, glanced at her. The waiting room was empty except for Abigail.

"Hey," she said into the phone. "What's up?"

"That's what I was going to ask you." That voice. There was something warm and comforting about it, but it had an edge today. "Why haven't you called?"

"Things are a little crazy. My brother's not doing well. Just kind of hanging on, you know?"

"Are you at the hospital?"

"No, a hair salon. I'm applying for a job."

"What? Abigail, I thought—"

She cut him off. "It's a long story. I promise I'll tell you all about it. Now's not a good time."

He paused and the silence frightened her. When she had left school, they had spoken every day. Almost every hour. But as the days increased, it felt like they were growing apart.

"I'm worried," he said. "About you. About us. That you're going to find somebody to take my place."

He sounded like a hurt puppy. Like a lost little boy who needed his mother or a blanket. Abigail hated that sound. She loved him because he was strong and confident. She was attracted to him because he was different from other guys who needed a girl to complete them. Philip wasn't vulnerable. He was the most whole person she had ever met, so hearing this side of him sent a shiver down to some hidden place in her soul.

"There's nobody here. There's nobody in my heart but you. I'm just on the edge, trying to figure out how to take another breath. I don't think I can take care of you right now."

The strength returned. "I understand. I guess I just needed to hear your voice."

A stocky man approached her, the floor vibrating with his footsteps. The first glance was the scariest. Dark eyes. Dark hair. Hairy arms and chest—the top button undone on his shirt. He walked like an alligator wrestler, arms out from his body, swaggering.

"Sorry, Philip. I have to go," she said and flipped the phone closed.

Curtis Tompkins's hand was pudgy and soft, and he took hers gingerly. "Nice to meet you, Cheryl. Come on back to the office."

She followed him, avoiding piled-up hair, and entered a musty, dimly lit room with exposed ceiling and water pipes overhead. He held the door for her and closed it as she sat in a slightly nicer plastic chair in front of his desk.

"I'll probably ask you to lose the cell phone if you work here," he said as he wedged his way around the desk. "Last thing I want customers seeing is a Chatty Cathy. Eye contact, a smile—that's what I'm looking for. Invite them in. Make them feel welcome. A cell phone makes them feel they're intruding."

"Oh, I understand completely. I was just talking with . . . my ex-boyfriend. You know how that goes."

"Problems with your love life, huh? Pretty girl like you? That doesn't make sense." He smiled and leaned back. "How long were you dating?"

"It's been more than a year now."

"Serious. You'd probably already moved in with him."

"Fortunately I didn't have much furniture."

"Only important piece of furniture is a bed." He laughed and his eyes twinkled. "What school do you go to?"

"State. But I had to leave because of money problems. My dad wasn't able to pay for the last year, so I thought I'd work and save up."

"What's your major?"

"Communications. Journalism."

"That's good. So you have typing skills." He put his hands together and stared at her like she was meat hanging in a butcher shop. She sat up straight.

"You could be a model, you know that?" he said. "Just gorgeous. I should take some pictures of you and hang them in the front. People will be knocking us over to get in the door."

She laughed nervously, pulling her hair behind an ear.

"I might know other ways you can pick up some quick cash, too. Help you out with your school bills."

"Really? Like what?"

He grabbed a clipboard from a filing cabinet that looked like it had been used in WWII. "We can talk about it later. Let's get your information first. Just fill out the front and back of this."

"You mean I got the job?"

He smiled. "Absolutely. You're exactly what I'm looking for. A bright spot at the front of the store. Great smile. Great figure. What's not to hire?"

She looked at the page, complete with Social Security number and address. "Um, do we have to do it this way?"

"What way is that?" he said.

"You know, with taxes taken out and everything. I'd rather get less money and not have to deal with all of that government stuff."

He raised his eyebrows. "Now you're talking my language." He took the clipboard back.

"How much would I get an hour?" she said.

"Minimum wage. But as I said, if you're in a tight spot and need extra cash, we might be able to work something out."

"When do I start?"

"How about now? Come out to the front and I'll show you the register."

He showed her how to run the credit card payments, pointed out the security cameras that recorded every moment of every transaction so he knew she wouldn't steal from him. "You wouldn't want to do that," he said. "Believe me."

He got a little close, brushing against her from behind. He put his hand on her shoulder and she tried not to recoil. The phone rang and Curtis answered, gesturing for her to listen as he correctly spoke to a customer. He showed her how to transfer a call to his office and gave her a short list of numbers and names he wanted to avoid.

"For any of these people, I'm not here."

He left and she settled in, her mind exploding with questions. An hour later he returned and asked how she was doing and if she wanted to grab some lunch.

"Sure."

He opened the door and Abigail noticed the blank stares of the stylists as if they'd seen this happen before. Many times.

They walked to a sandwich shop that advertised a five-dollar special for a sandwich, chips, and drink. Curtis said it was on him, and Abigail wondered how much obligation a five-dollar sandwich was. There wasn't one thing about Curtis that attracted her and she wondered if somehow Diana had been lured by the prospect of easy money.

Booths were taken, so they sat at a tall table and Curtis tried to get comfortable on the stool, but he kept tipping to one side every time he picked up his pastrami. He asked how she liked the shop, if she had any questions, small talk designed to allow him to nod and chew and listen. She wanted to run. Her stomach turned as she watched him chew and the oil run down his chin. Every time the door opened and an ambulatory female walked in, he ogled her. Then she thought of Aiden in the hospital and Mr. Conley in prison. And her father. She didn't understand it, but she felt drawn to this scene. The fact that she'd gained employment and the man's confidence so quickly made her think there was a deeper purpose. Not that God was directing her, like her mother believed, but more like fate was drawing her to its dinner table.

"What are the chances I could make more money, like you were saying? How long would I need to wait to find out about that?"

He laughed and winked at her, wiping his hands with a napkin but still missing the chin. "All in due time. Patience is a virtue. You've heard that before, right?"

"Yeah, but there's no virtue in being broke. I can get patience later. Right now I need to pay my rent and the electric bill."

"Hey, at least you have a place to stay. Where do you live?"

She hesitated. "At some apartments near the university. If I get kicked out of there, it's on the street or back with my parents, and that's not going to happen."

He seemed to like that answer and took a long draw on his soda. "Let's get to know each other a little better. But I promise, with your brains and looks, you could make plenty of money."

"How could I use my looks to make money?"

"You ever dance? You move like a dancer. I got a friend who has a couple of clubs. I bet you could pick it up fast, smart girl like you."

She felt her stomach clench and wasn't sure if it was the black olives on her vegetarian sub or the look in the man's eyes. "You mean, like, stripping?"

"That's such a crass term. Your mother and father probably called it that. It's an art form. Entertainment. It's not as bad as you think."

"I don't dance," she said. "Is there anything else?"

"Don't knock it till you've tried it," he said, crunching a chip. "Some of his girls make a grand a night."

"A thousand dollars?"

"Think about it. Say you work three nights a week. You clear twenty-five hundred easy. You could do that. Ten weeks you'd make twenty-five grand. Forty weeks you'd be at a hundred thousand."

Her jaw dropped, feigning wonder and awe.

"And it's safe," he continued. "He runs a clean place. Lots of security, especially for the girls. But that's just one option."

She was playing it well, trying to act interested and not repulsed. Not that the $100K didn't sound good. It did. But she instinctively knew this was not a guy to trust. *Make eye contact. Smile. Make him think you're interested, hungry, need money.*

"So you have a car, right?" he said.

She nodded, her turn to take a bite and listen.

"Is it dependable?"

"It's old but the engine runs. Why?"

"Just wondering."

She wrapped up the rest of her sandwich and stashed it in her purse. "Why are you being so cryptic? Don't you trust me?"

"Trust you?" He laughed. "In my business, you have to build trust. That takes time."

"You mean in the hair business?"

"Hair is only part of what I do. It's the day job. The less glamorous way of making a living." He rose and tossed his trash, then held the door for her. "But it still pays the bills, especially for the stylists. I try to have multiple income streams."

"So you have the hair place and the dance club?"

"I don't own the club. I just help my friend find new talent."

"And is that all you do?"

He navigated the undulating sidewalk, great slabs that had moved upward over the years. "I do a little *consulting*. A little video work. But we have to get to know each other better before we get into that."

"And how am I going to be able to do that?" she said, stopping on the crest of one slab and crossing her arms, striking the attitude pose.

"Have dinner with me tonight and we'll hash it out." He pulled out a card and wrote something on the back. "Meet me here at nine. You can see the club and I'll answer all of your questions."

CHAPTER 30

I DROVE BACK TO THE HOSPITAL and without gathering much fortitude managed to ride the elevator to the eighth floor. Somehow the hospital had lost its imposing edge. Of course, I could still feel the money draining from the hole in my pocket as I passed the business office.

Aiden lingered in a drug-induced coma. No change in his condition. His heart was beating. That was the good news. The bad news was he was still in the hospital and probably wouldn't come out with that same heart.

Ellen wouldn't leave his side. Her pastor was there again, which made me want to leave. They were in the corner, heads down, eyes closed, asking God to invade, I suppose. I stepped back into the elevator and got some lunch in the cafeteria. By the time I returned, the pastor was gone.

Ellen asked how it had gone with Conley and I told her he was thinking about the confession, which I'm sure was true to some extent, but that if she had any pull with Oleta, now was the time to use it. I worked my way to Aiden's room so she wouldn't press me. She followed, telling me to touch him and talk to him, explaining that studies have proven those in a persistent vegetative state can sense things. She talked about some other study on the effects of the human voice but I couldn't hear any of it. I was struck by the sight of my son.

I touched his lifeless hand. Not the temperature of icicles— more like a lizard on a desert night. I leaned down and whispered in his ear, "Hey, bud, there's a young nurse who's been trying to get your phone number. If you don't get out of this bed fast, you might miss your chance."

Nothing. Not even a blip on the EKG. No eyelids fluttering or squeezing my hand or wiggling a toe. Just chilly skin and a day's worth of stubble on his face.

"Hang in there, Aiden," I said, patting his arm.

In the hallway, Ellen asked again about Conley and I gave her a more accurate picture. As usual, she was a step ahead of me.

"Did you speak with Reginald?"

I smelled a dead fish, my journalistic antennae fully extended. "Did he call you?"

She nodded. "Then Carlton called."

"Wow, you're more popular than I am. I had to hang up in order to get a call from the governor."

"Tru, he said there's nothing more he can do."

"Yeah, that seemed to be the talking point coming from the mansion. Or limo. I don't buy it."

She stood in front of me, her brown eyes piercing. "What are you going to do?"

"After the Townsend call, I got a flash of inspiration. How this thing might play out in our favor. I called Gina and left a message."

"I thought she dropped you. She's not your agent anymore."

"Yeah, but things can change. I explained the way this is playing out, the political ramifications, the life-and-death struggle. I think she'll bite. And we might get some money for the Conleys."

"Truman, this isn't about the money—"

"It's always about the money. And if Gina sends out a blast, maybe she can get a bidding war going between a few publishers who see the merit of the story. By then the press release alone will ramp the pressure up on Townsend."

"The last thing we want to do is cross him. We want him on our side."

"Exactly. And he's not on our side. He's not on Aiden's side. He's on his own side."

"It's too big of a risk."

"Ellen, sometimes the only way to get people on your side is to play hardball."

She shook her head. "I don't think that's the way to go."

"Trust me, I've done this a long time."

"Yes, you have," she muttered. "And look where it's gotten us."

The nurses at the station were nervously eyeing their computer screens. I walked Ellen into a corner closer to the elevators and lowered my voice.

"Here's the deal. Townsend is not going to take this risk because of his generosity. I'd love for him to use his power for good, but he only understands political viability. If it serves his interests, he does it. If it doesn't, he makes a speech or sends an apology. I guarantee you, he'll send a big wreath of flowers for the funeral. Maybe he'd even show up if he could get some press coverage."

"You're sick."

"I'm right and you know it. We have to figure out how to convince him that it's in his best interests to make this happen. He has to see it as counterproductive to block the transplant."

She turned her head away and I sat beside her, trying to pull her back. "What? What do you know that I don't?"

"Tru, I have a feeling about this—and I know you don't share these types of things—but it tells me to wait. Humble ourselves. Let this come to us."

"Is that what the pastor said? Or did Townsend try to convince you to talk sense into me?"

"This has nothing to do with anyone but you and me. I have an impression. I feel like God wants me to stop fighting. To give him control."

I cocked my head sideways and tried not to let the feeling inside show on my face. But incredulity leaks. I turned her to face me—not hard, not manhandling, just guiding her face back to my eyes.

"Are you sure you're my wife? Because my wife has been fighting for the last eighteen years for my son. She's been there when I wasn't. She's carried the ball I dropped."

Ellen had tears in her eyes. "There's a difference between fighting and striving. Between reach and overreach. I've been thinking that maybe . . ."

"Maybe what?"

"Maybe this is as far as it goes. Maybe Aiden is tired. Maybe he's hanging in there for me. All the pain and the procedures—he hates it. Maybe it's time to think of him instead of myself."

"How can you say that?"

"There's more to life than *this* life, Tru."

It sounded like something she'd heard on the radio. "So you're giving up? Isn't that a sin?"

"I've never given up hope."

"Then stand with me and fight."

"I've been fighting. It's time to let him go. I don't want to put him through any more."

I ran a hand through my hair and it stuck up in the back. "And what if your *impression* changes the day after the execution?"

She put a hand on my chest and held it there. "I'm asking you to trust me. You don't have to agree. Keep writing. Keep going with the story. If Gina can sell it, great. But I've stopped striving about this."

She leaned close. "Tru, it's like I'm floating down a river. Untethered from the world. Swirling in a river I didn't know was here. I've had to let go of everything I've ever known or understood. I don't know what's ahead. I don't care what's behind. I just know I'm where I'm supposed to be."

It sounded like she really needed sleep. Or maybe coffee. Maybe these long stays in the hospital had done something to her head. Maybe she needed a break, a vacation from nurses and medication and eighteen years of stress. I suggested she go home and crawl into bed, but she smiled condescendingly, like Christians do when they're staring into eternity and you're looking at a picture on a wall.

"I know this seems weird," she said. "But I'm not scared anymore. I'm not afraid of what's going to happen, what might happen. I'm settled, and that's what I want to give Aiden. No worry and concern, but peace."

Resignation, I thought. "What Aiden needs is somebody with strength who can pull him through, not somebody pushing him toward the light."

She nodded. "I understand. And if you want to be that person, his bedside is empty. I won't fight you."

I wanted to probe more, but I knew I would get Scripture verses and glimpses of heaven and tears wiped away and all that unconditional love of God stuff that can't be true because he *is* conditional. If he's up there—which is a big if—he's enjoying the view: humans scurrying about trying to make sense of life and death and pain while he enjoys the divine entertainment.

That's what I was thinking. But instead of lashing out, I gathered her in and held her. Not in a lover's embrace—I had lost that a long time ago—but the embrace of two travelers, coming from differing paths and headed for different destinations, who meet for a strange season.

My cell phone buzzed and I saw it was from Abby. I answered and held the phone close to Ellen.

"Dad, great news." Her voice was animated like I hadn't heard in a long time. Like she'd just found a puppy and wanted to bring it home. She squealed, "I got the job!"

"What job is that?"

"At the salon. Remember, I told you. And I just had lunch with Tompkins. You wouldn't believe some of the stuff he said."

"Abigail, this is not a good idea."

Ellen punched me in the arm.

"I mean, this guy could be dangerous," I corrected.

"Exactly what I was there to find out. And he's a player, no doubt. Personal questions. Inappropriate. The guy's a creep if there ever was one."

"Where are you now?"

"I'm in a restroom down the street from the salon."

"You need to get away from there. If he finds out your connection with me, things will get ugly."

"Dad, that's the best part. This evening I'm having dinner with him at this club."

"A club?" Ellen said. She was leaning closer. She reached for the phone when Abigail said, "Dad, I think I know what happened to Diana."

CHAPTER 31

ABIGAIL WOULDN'T ELABORATE, saying she'd see me at home. Ellen was concerned and showed as much by staring off and rubbing my arm as we sat in the waiting room, nowhere to go and nothing to do.

My stomach was in knots and I knew I had to get back on the book treadmill—there's no substitute for having my rear in the chair and staying in front of the screen. This is the only way I know how to work. It's the only way I know how to live. And maybe something bigger was drawing me, pulling me like some kind of relational tide to make sense of the inconceivable.

With Ellen's blessing I headed home, grabbing an extra-large, bladder-buster coffee from the local caffeine vendor. I hunkered down in my literary bunker to save the world or at least make sense of it. As a North American male, I have the ability to compartmentalize, to put my head down and throw myself into the task and continue. Take my cottage, my car, my cat, my marriage—take it all and leave me with just one task and I will get the job done, no matter how consequential or meaningless.

But whether it was an adverse reaction to the caffeine or all the thoughts, I couldn't work. So much for the laser focus. I took two or three open runs at the story, but the compartment that had always been so tight sprang a leak and I couldn't think of anything but the dripping.

I clicked open a news website and checked out the latest. In a red banner above the local news I saw a headline that read, "Governor Townsend Meeting with Lawmakers."

It was a rehash, nothing earth-shattering—just that at this hour, in a closed-door meeting with the governor, they were deciding whether to move ahead with plans to allow the heart donation of condemned inmate Terrelle Conley. It was said to be an uphill battle with some of the conservative delegation. Protests were planned outside. For all his efforts to keep things quiet, this had the ring of subversion. Would Townsend intentionally leak information about the meeting in order to sabotage it?

On-screen a link popped up for an online gaming site. *"Visit us again and your first $100 is on us!"*

It's hard to describe the lure that has for someone with my proclivities, especially when it pops up in front of you at a time of great stress, when you need to be doing something else. You tell yourself you'll just spend ten minutes there and two hours later you're looking at your virtual losses and wondering how you wasted so much time. The bigger question, of course, was how you would ever leave the site. Like a fish on a hook—wriggle and squirm all you want, you're not getting that thing out of your mouth.

Maybe it was my willpower, maybe it was divine intervention, but somehow I had the ability to click the X in the right-hand corner and take a walk.

I've always said writer's block is for those people with too much money or time until their next deadline. But here I was, walking down the street assessing the finely manicured lawns of my neighbors, watching sprinklers squirt with the sun still out, drying up the precious droplets before they could get to the roots. I counted three different pool maintenance companies outside homes on the trek.

What I wouldn't give for the sound of children splashing in a backyard pool. I longed for another chance, for the ability to turn the clock back to the days when our biggest concern was whether to go private or public with their schooling. Of course, with Aiden, the concerns were always just short of cataclysmic. Whether to go ahead with a surgery that could give him a chance at being normal or could take his life. All of them turned out to simply be short-term solutions to the longer-term problem.

I suppose I chose to create my own little compartment for that piece of my life and now I was paying the price. My son was dying, my daughter estranged, my wife unfulfilled and unloved. I've heard that the opposite of love is not hate but indifference. Was the distance I felt with my family because of that indifference? Was there any hope for connection?

A black car passed, tinted windows, thin, shiny wheels. I kept walking, then felt something stir inside. I turned and ran back quickly enough to see the car turn onto our street. It slowed and the brake lights flashed as it passed our house. I hadn't thought to get the license number and it was too far away now.

The *chug, chug* of a little Honda with muffler problems came up behind me and I waved at Abigail. She pulled to the curb and I jumped in the passenger seat on top of a McDonald's bag and her purse. "Go around the back way."

"What for?"

"Suspicious car in front of our house. We'll come at them from the other side."

She processed it pretty quickly, then sped around the block to the connecting street. "Who do you think it is?"

Good question.

"Maybe your pals from New Orleans?" she said.

Good answer.

"I don't think so. They promised more time. I was thinking it might be your friend Tompkins."

"He doesn't even know my real name. I told him I have an apartment near Florida State."

"You sign a W-4?"

"I didn't sign anything; he's paying me in cash. Under the table."

"Stop here," I said. From this street I could barely see through shrubbery to our house. The black car wasn't there. "Okay, keep going. And you better watch what Tompkins puts under the table."

"What, you think I'm some little girl who doesn't understand the ways of the world?"

"No, you're plenty smart, but if this guy—watch out!"

She met the black car nearly head-on. The driver laid on the horn and she corrected and kept going. I lowered my head as we passed, then turned to get a look at the plates. I got the first three numbers and wrote them down on the coffee receipt in my pocket.

We drove through the neighborhood and parked across from a playground. Silence hung between us as I watched two kids climb the monkey bars and run giggling toward a slide, chasing each other and squealing just like Abby and Aiden. Finally I got up the nerve to speak.

"Sometimes I wish I could go back and do it all over again. Get it right."

"What are you talking about?"

"Our family. My life. The choices I made to chase the career and the stories I thought were so important."

"If you're looking for me to make you feel better, I won't. You were a terrible dad."

"I'm not asking for that. I just need you to know that when I was on the job, I was always thinking about you."

She rolled her eyes. "You think that helps a little kid who wanted you to show up at her class? When all the other parents were at school, I used to look at the doorway, hoping you'd walk in."

I fought the urge to tick off the list of times I did show up. They were pitifully few. "I wish I had another chance. And that's what I think this could be for us. A chance to fully connect, fully invest ourselves in this story and in Aiden's recovery."

"Dad, you're not fully invested in anything but yourself. You never have been."

Please don't hold back on your criticism. Tell me what you really think. "You have a right to feel let down, but—"

"Let down? Try crushed. Try crying yourself to sleep every night until your heart turned to stone."

"Then why did you come back? Why did you look for me?"

Her chin puckered and I could see the water forming in her eyes. She shook her head and a tear wandered down her cheek. "Maybe I thought there was a chance you still cared."

"You were right. I *do*. That's why I'm here."

"Crabbing at me because I'm actually getting information."

"I'm not trying to squash you. We have to be a team on this and I feel like you're freelancing with this guy—"

"Freelancing? I'm getting information we'll never get any other way."

"Like what?"

"Like the fact that he's connected with this dance club. That could have been how Diana made extra money. And he wants me to be a courier."

"Drugs?"

"He didn't say."

"It wouldn't surprise me. I don't want to see you get hurt."

"And you think that's what I want? You think I want to hang out with this slimeball?"

I let things settle for a minute, then asked, "You said you knew what happened to Diana. What did you mean?"

"No. I'm not talking about this. You give no support. You don't thank me for busting my hump to get information. You just play the concerned father that you've never played before."

"I do appreciate—"

"You said we were on the same team. Why don't you trust your teammate to follow her instincts? I think they're pretty good."

"I agree. I think your instincts are great, but you don't know what guys like this are capable of. They take their time and make sure they have leverage before they reel you in. Not you, of course. I'm just saying it doesn't work this fast."

"So you're saying I'm naive. I'm your innocent little girl who's still on the playground. Well, I'm not, Dad. I've been around the block a few times. I've made some bad decisions just like you. And I can take care of myself."

There are some things you can't say to your children, things they have to discover for themselves. There are other things you want to protect them from, mistakes you've made that you don't want them to repeat. And then there are things you want to do that you know you can't because your problems have stolen the right. That's where I was, sitting in the stifling heat of her Honda, the gas gauge nearing empty and the muffler sounding like it had more holes than my credit rating.

"So you think Diana was mixed up in his drug deals? And that Tompkins murdered her?"

She stared at the kids on the playground. "That's one theory. I'm hoping to get him to talk about it tonight."

"What's happening tonight?"

"You don't want to know. You'd just shoot me down."

"No, I'm on your team. A hundred percent. Tell me."

She told me the club where he wanted to meet. "He wants to buy me dinner and talk."

"Sounds like a good idea," I lied. "Get him to talk. Sometimes alcohol and an agenda can get people to loosen their tongues."

She looked at me. "You mean it?"

"Yeah, it's a public place. His turf. He'll feel comfortable. Just be careful . . ."

The look on her face stopped me. "Of what?"

"Watch what you drink. They can slip you something to knock you out."

"You think I don't know that?"

"Just a reminder."

Darkness had descended by the time we drove back to the house. We couldn't find the mysterious car on any street near us but

Abigail parked a few houses away and I made a sweep of the house. There were no signs of entry and no one inside.

While she ate a sandwich from the dwindling food supply, I checked the latest news. There was no update on the governor and I had a sick feeling about my son's future.

My cell phone rang. It was Gina with the wonderful news that she and her team were going to pass on Terrelle's story. She assured me it wasn't a lack of faith in my abilities to deliver a manuscript, just that the climate of the publishing industry was cold to this type of book at the moment. I told her Townsend was perhaps the best contender for the White House. Her answer contained smoke thicker than most steel mills produce. I thanked her for the chance and told her to call me if she changed her mind.

Abigail came out of her bedroom dressed the part of the young, hungry intern, ready to impress the boss. Her hair styled, lots of makeup, tight black jeans. Everything a father hates to see.

"You look great," I said.

"Thanks."

"I'm going with you."

She laughed, but not in a good way. It was a hard-edged, get-out-of-my-way-or-I'll-run-you-over kind of laugh. "No, you're not."

"Abby, I just—"

"Abigail," she snapped.

"Sorry. Old habits die hard. I just want to be there in case something happens. It will free you up."

"Tell me how I'll feel free with you looking over my shoulder."

"I won't even be close. I'll stay outside."

"The guy will know something is up if you're seen with me. I have to build his trust."

You have to dig your grave.

I held up both hands. "All right. Just keep your cell phone handy. Dial me if anything goes wrong."

She grabbed her purse and keys and headed out the door.

"Okay?" I said, a little pleading and whining.

She slammed the door behind her.

CHAPTER 32

LOCAL ZONING ORDINANCES prohibit the type of establishment Curtis Tompkins visited. That's probably why it was called Outskirts. It was a squarish, cinder-block building placed in the middle of a few other squarish buildings that housed tattoo artists, a used bookstore, a couple of bars, and a leather shop. Sort of a little bohemian village with lots of bicycles and men with dreadlocks and couples pretending not to have much money walking back to a Lexus or BMW around the corner in a lit parking lot.

I drove past the club's lot and saw Abby's car. She was still in it. I had waited a total of six minutes after she left before I followed. It had taken me that long to find and map the address.

I parked near some houses and watched the lot, calling Ellen to ask about Aiden. Her voice sounded as if she had surrendered to the enemy and was being led off as a prisoner of war. I wasn't about to follow. She asked how I felt about Abigail's "meeting." I was sure Abby had explained excitedly what she was going to do, and of course Ellen had encouraged her to follow her heart. That always infuriated me, when I was actually around long enough to find out how she lived her life. Abby would decide to climb a sheer rock face in Keds and Ellen would encourage her to chase the stars. I wanted to scream into the phone, "Isn't one death in the family enough?" Of course, I didn't do that. I kept my mouth shut until she asked, "Are you working?"

"I'm taking a drive."

"Tru . . ."

"No, I'm not headed to a casino."

"Where are you going?"

"Just a drive."

When she didn't speak, I gave her a heavy sigh. "I want to make sure she's okay. This guy isn't right."

"Don't mess this up for her."

"I'm protecting her."

"Think of *her*, Tru. She knows you don't believe in her."

"It'll show her I care."

"That's not the way. You're saying she's not up to the task. She's a big girl. Trust her. Let her fly."

"Okay. But this has nothing to do with trusting her. I know too much about guys like Tompkins. And there's something she doesn't know."

"What's that?"

"I think this guy might be in with a friend of mine. Guy from New Orleans I owe."

"Why do you think that?"

"The car we saw drive past the house this afternoon. Same shady types. And if he finds out she's connected to me, they may use her to get their money. Or revenge."

She paused. "So this is related to the gambling."

"It could be. She swears he doesn't know her full name or where she lives, but these guys are resourceful. I don't want him to use her to get to me."

"Truman, why didn't you tell her that?"

Her words hung there as I watched Abigail step from her car, cell phone to her ear. The phone illuminated her face as she briskly walked toward a side door, a big wooden thing that looked like it had been fashioned from a gangplank of a pirate ship.

"I didn't want to scare her, I guess. I want to support her. I want her to fly. But something has kicked in. Maybe it's my father instinct."

Ellen didn't say anything. She didn't have to. I knew what was going through her head.

"I don't know where that instinct has been, if that's what you're wondering. But it's here now. I don't think I should push it down."

"Truman—"

"Trust me," I said. "You're asking me to trust her. I'm asking you to trust me. She wants to follow her dreams, to follow this story. I need to follow my instincts. Okay?"

Meekly, timidly, humbly, the answer came. "Okay."

The door opened and the darkness and strobes sucked my daughter in like a spaceship envelops grazing cattle in one of those B horror movies. The door closed and the sound was the only thing that remained, pulsing and reverberating through the stucco.

A car pulled to the curb across the street from the pirate ship door. Every car at this time of night seems dark, but this one seemed particularly dark and, unfortunately, particularly familiar. Out of the passenger side came a hulk of a man with long, blond hair and arms that dripped with anabolics. He crossed the street and opened the door like he was pulling Styrofoam.

"Gotta go," I said to Ellen.

I grabbed the Yankees cap I had taken from Aiden's room and pulled it tightly to my eyebrows on the walk toward the club. I hid my face from the black car's driver as I attempted to pull open the ship's anchor that was the side door. A barrel-chested man with a tattoo that ran up his neck and wound around his ear stood between me and the pulsing, deafening noise. A toothpick stuck out of his mouth.

"Is there a cover charge?" I yelled.

Toothpick held up ten fingers and I knew I didn't have it but reached for my wallet anyway. "You take—?"

"Cash only."

"Is there an ATM near here?"

He shrugged and two gentlemen walked in behind me, handing the fellow a twenty. I quickly looked past Toothpick but couldn't see much through the smoky haze besides the young woman in the spotlight. No sign of Abby or the long-haired blond guy.

"I'm looking for someone. She just came in a few minutes ago. Won't take but five minutes and I'll be out of here."

He actually smiled, then took me by the arm and led me outside. His voice was soft, with a slight lisp. "Get thum cash, friend."

Back in the car, heart beating quickly, wondering if there was an ATM at the grocery store a few blocks back, wondering if there was some other blond guy sitting behind the steering wheel of the black car watching me, I mulled my choices. Stay? Look for another way inside?

I hurried to the grocery and found an ATM. My first card was rejected. The second went in and I thought I heard the machine laugh. Somehow I got a twenty and drove back, parking a block away on the other side of the club. The dark car idled across the street and I saw the first three numbers of the license, confirming it was the car we'd seen earlier.

I handed Toothpick the bill and he begrudgingly returned a ten. "Have a nithe night," he thaid.

Inside, I stumbled down a couple of stairs and stayed in the shadows to let my eyes adjust. I shouldn't have worried because nobody was watching who was coming in. They were focused on the stage.

The bar was to the left, and a gaggle of servers in skimpy outfits moved in beelike fashion from the watering hole to the tables. One looked like a Dallas Cowboys cheerleader. Another was in a cat costume and the biggest part of the costume was the whiskers. Seriously. I looked past the stilettos and fishnet stockings to the other side of the room, bathed in the muted glow of the stage. Booths lined the wall but there was no blond guy and no daughter. My mind raced. If Ellen could see this, would she still encourage Abby to follow her dreams?

I texted Abby. R U OK? R U @ club?

I walked closer to the bar to get a better look at the booths. A waitress in a gladiator outfit intercepted me. She wore what looked like a real sword in a belt around her waist that loosely held all the other pieces. "Can I get you something to drink?" she said.

"I'm looking for a friend. Do you know Curtis Tompkins?"

She smiled and I tried to keep my eyes on her dark wig.

"Everybody knows Curt." She pointed to the other side of the stage and said, "Private room B. Is he expecting you?"

"No, I'll wait until he comes out."

"Could be a while," she said. "There's a group back there. What about that drink?"

"Not yet."

She gave me a wet-lipstick pout, then walked away, back toward the Colosseum.

My cell vibrated. I'm OK. @ club. Leave me alone.

I hit the Reply button and quickly typed, I'm here 2. Black car outside. Get out.

I sent the message, then had second thoughts. What if Tompkins saw it? How would she cover herself? I replied again. Go 2 bathroom. Meet u there.

I wandered in the dark until I found the narrow hallway with restrooms and stood in the space between men's and ladies' like some pervert. After a few minutes I went into the men's room. It was small, just one stall that was occupied. I washed my hands and walked back outside. Abby stood there with a not-happy look.

"What are you doing here? And why are you wearing Aiden's hat?"

I grabbed her elbow. "We need to get out of here."

"No," she said in a not-so-subtle voice, jerking away. "I'm getting good information. Why are you doing this?"

"The guys in the car are here. One has long blond hair and arms the size of telephone poles. Is he in there?"

She put up a hand like I was threatening her in some way and moved backward, toward the ladies' room door. "I haven't seen anybody like that. And I'm not going anywhere. I'm seeing this through. Just go home, Dad."

A new song began onstage and men hooted and hollered. More pulsing and pounding and clapping.

"You can't be serious," I said. "Get out now, while you can."

"If you don't like it in here, leave."

"Ith there a problem, mith?" a high-pitched voice said behind me.

I closed my eyes as Abby said, "This man is bothering me."

"Come with me, thir."

He put a vise grip on my elbow and pulled me around the stage toward the door. I looked back, trying to see Abby, but he pushed me forward into the darkness, as if he had night-vision goggles.

"You don't understand," I said, but he wasn't listening. When I was outside, he let go of my arm. I thought about telling him Abby was my daughter, but I decided just to ask for my ten dollars back. He smiled and closed the door.

I walked the perimeter of the club looking for another way in but the place was a bunker. There was a locked front entrance, which probably broke several fire codes, and another back entrance that looked like it exited from the private rooms. It, too, was locked. I walked back to the car and drove to another street and parked.

Waiting is not my strength. I'm a man of action, running into a story when I don't even know the questions, so sitting there imagining what might be happening inside private room B was more than my mind could take. You learn as a journalist to anticipate the story, figure out all the possible angles to cover.

I closed my eyes and pictured Abby, smiling, laughing, Tompkins at her side with powder in a ring he dumped into her drink. Then her eyes rolling back in her head as she passed out. Someone hustling her limp body out the back entrance into another dark car. Or maybe Abby was fully conscious and screaming for help right then as Tompkins and his friends overpowered her.

Or maybe they were just talking.

About thirty minutes after he went in, the blond guy exited the club. His face was punctuated with a long, crooked nose. He walked with military precision and entered the car; then it pulled into the shadows, waiting. Just like me.

An overwhelming fear washed over me. I had challenged Ellen to fight for Aiden, and I was ready to do that. But as a realist and a reporter, I knew even if the Conley situation came through, it was a long shot that Aiden would respond well to the organ. Though we all hoped for the best, it was clear from what the doctors said that his body had endured too much. That fear had turned into resignation, especially after Ellen's discourse. She was the biggest fighter on Aiden's side, and if she was willing to release him, I had to find a way to do the same.

But the mushroom cloud in my stomach now turned to Abby. Sitting there, wondering what was going on inside, made things worse.

I have heard stories of fathers using superhuman strength when an adrenaline-laced situation presented itself, like lifting a car off a pinned loved one, and that's what I felt as I opened the car door. Like a kid coming back from a superhero movie who walks into the parking lot and figures he can put his arms out and fly, I got out and walked down the moonlit street with all the bravado of Captain America.

I noticed a group of about five guys headed toward the club, rowdy and raucous, a roving bachelor party, bobbing and weaving like they had already been to a couple of bars. I hurried across the street and shoved the Yankees cap into my back pocket, catching up with them. There was clearly one leader, a guy about six-five with close-cropped hair who walked slightly ahead of them. I've been around enough military guys to know how others simply follow. As he neared the club, he reached for his wallet.

"Mind if I join you guys?" I said.

The guy turned and I handed him my last ten.

"It's a divorce party," he said. He nodded toward a friend who seemed a bit more inebriated than the rest. "Tim here is losing pretty much everything in the settlement. Thought we'd cheer him up."

"I might need friends like you in another month or two," I said.

Tim slapped me on the back and said something unintelligible, a mixture of laughter and tears and Michelob Light. We hit the door and the leader told the guy there were six of us and we all pushed through, my head down. While they made their way to a table near the stage, hooting and commenting on the current dancer, I let the music carry me back to the restroom. No text this time.

On the wall of the men's room I found what I was looking for. I wrapped my hand in the Yankees cap and gave the fire alarm a punch. Nothing happened, so I punched it again and felt something give inside. I pulled down the lever and immediately the alarm sounded. As I exited the room, the lights came on full force and people headed for the door, crowding and pushing. The girl on the stage skittered about in high heels, picking up pieces of her schoolgirl outfit. I piled in with the rest and kept my head down, looking behind for Abby.

The strobe lights had given the room that "happening" feel, but in full light it looked like a dive with mismatched chairs and pockmarked tables. I guess light will do that to a room. But the light not only gave away the room's condition, it gave me away, so I tried to rejoin the group I had entered with. The divorced man, Tim, guided now by the military guy, spun a string of profanities and saliva at the wall and no one in particular. Cursing his luck, his former wife, people who were messing up his life, and several political figures, he spread the invective over the alarm until he reached the front door.

"Thorry for the inconvenienth, thir," Toothpick said. "Thomebody mutht have pulled the alarm. We'll have you back inthide in a minute or two."

I could smell the fresh air outside, but I also felt pressure at my elbow and shoulder as a crocodile bit me. At least that's what it felt like.

"Thir, you were told to leave," Toothpick said. His breath smelled like rotten fruit at a roadside market, and to be honest, I didn't want to be close enough to smell his breath.

The military guy turned and put a hand on Toothpick's shoulder. "He's with us."

That was enough for me to break free from his grip and skitter into the night, running toward an oncoming fire engine. I hadn't thought through this part of my plan, but when I was across the street, I turned to see a police car arrive and Toothpick talking in an animated, steroid rage. For a fleeting moment I also spotted Abby at the side door, laughing, one hand on the chest of a bearded guy and the other to her forehead. Every instinct in me told me to get her, but with Toothpick pointing in my direction, the better idea would be to remain a free man.

I hurried to the corner, past a convenience store, and found an alley behind it that looked like it might run back to the street where I'd parked the Sequoia. I pulled out my phone as I hurried along and texted Abby, U OK? I had to stop while I texted because I'm not a teenager.

There was a *blip-blip* behind me and I turned to see a police cruiser at the end of the alley with his side light out. Looking back, I shouldn't have done it; I should have stayed right where I was. I have superior communications skills, I wasn't inebriated, I had good cause to be concerned about my daughter, and how many years can they give you for pulling a fire alarm? But some inner sense of injustice kicked in, some feeling that this might be my best chance to save my daughter. I ran to the end of the alley and turned the corner as the cruiser accelerated. I was parked about five cars to my right and across the street, so I hit the door lock on Ellen's key fob and the Sequoia lit like a Christmas tree. I hopped in, closed the door, and leaned over the passenger seat as far as I could, hitting the overhead light and praying the cop hadn't seen me. Yes, I do pray in foxholes.

Blue and red lights strobed past me and I managed to insert the key in the ignition, hands shaking. My phone buzzed and I sat up, looking in the rearview. The police car had slowed, its brake lights mixing with blue and red.

Fire alarm. Headed to Tompkins's place, the text read.

"No!" I yelled to the phone. I threw the car into drive and sped toward the club with my lights off. The street was blocked by the fire engine and I took a quick look at the parking lot illumined by the blinking lights, but in the blur I couldn't pick out my daughter. I also spotted another cruiser pulling up to the scene.

I took a right without stopping and threw on my lights, ran through a yellow at full gallop and checked behind me. Ten minutes later, I pulled into a mostly empty Dunkin' Donuts parking lot and dialed the same number I'd dialed fifty times only to get a recording of "Hey, it's Abigail; leave a message."

I called Ellen and asked if she had her laptop handy.

"What's wrong?" she said.

"Abby went off with the guy and I don't know where they're going." I didn't tell her about the fire alarm.

She typed his name into a website I gave her. "It just gives the salon address," she said. "Have you tried calling her?"

"I think she turned her phone off."

"Let me try. I'll call you back."

I checked my watch, checked the street, then stared at the donut rack and the counter, which had a total of three people hunched over coffee, all in various stages of dishevelment. From the shadows of the street came a man carrying a Bible. Wild-eyed, hair touching his shoulders, he walked in and held the book above his head. All three patrons looked up, then returned to their coffee. The man behind the counter, a Middle Eastern kid with a beard, scratched his neck, then leaned back and folded his arms as if ready for a show he had seen before.

I had no idea what the man was saying, but he seemed convinced. The veins in his neck stood out as he yelled. Finally the guy behind the counter said something to him and pointed toward the door. The confrontation seemed to energize the guy as he paced behind the stools, railing. Dunkin' Donuts was part of his Battle of Armageddon.

My cell phone buzzed as a car pulled in beside me. I glanced right and saw the familiar blue-and-white cruiser of Tallahassee's finest. I flipped my phone open and casually brought it to my ear as my heart puckered. The officer looked at me and climbed out of the cruiser without a blink or nod.

"Hi," I said as calmly as possible, waiting for the man to pull his revolver and tell me to exit the car with my hands up.

"I just talked with her," Ellen said. "They moved from the restaurant because some jerk set off the fire alarm."

"Some people," I said derisively.

The cop adjusted his belt, put on his hat, and walked to the front of my car.

"She said she's fine," Ellen said. "No need to worry."

"Did you get the address?"

Instead of heading inside, the officer moved to my window and pecked at it. I didn't hear what Ellen said next. I was busy getting my heart rate under control.

"You been watching this?" the officer said.

It took me a moment. "Oh, the Bible-thumper? Yeah, he walked in a few minutes ago."

"You might want to give me some room—maybe park toward the end?"

"Sure thing, Officer."

I gave a sigh and pulled the car to the end of the lot. Ellen asked what was going on and I told her. "Did you say you have the address?"

"Tru, Abigail is fine. She doesn't understand why you're doing this."

"I'll admit I've been an absentee, but now I'm here. Just tell me where she is."

"She's following him. Somewhere in Old Town."

"And this doesn't bother you? Do you have any idea what type of people she's dealing with? Drugs, exotic dancing, maybe murder?"

She paused. "I'm only going on what she told me and that I trust her judgment."

Silence. The officer talked with the man outside, the man holding up his Bible and making his case. I put the car in reverse and headed toward Old Town.

"Let me have her call you when she gets there," Ellen said.

"Good."

"There's something else, Tru," she said. "I got a call from Reginald, Townsend's aide."

"Let me guess. They don't feel that under the current political climate they can follow through on their promise."

"That probably would have been the call a few hours ago. But all that has changed."

"How so?"

"Terrelle signed a confession."

CHAPTER 33

I LET ELLEN'S WORDS sink in as I drove. What seemed like an impossibility that morning had become the game changer we were looking for.

"Did he read the confession to you?" I said.

"No, he just said the governor had received word. They're ready to proceed. It sounded like it came during the meeting and that things wouldn't have gone well without it. Aiden's getting a new heart after all."

Something inside didn't feel right. Maybe it was Ellen's voice and how flat it sounded. She should have been jumping up and down and screaming for joy. Instead she was reserved.

"This is what we've been waiting for," I said. "Why do I feel so hollow?"

285

"Probably because you feel like you've forced someone to do something that goes against everything he stands for."

"Maybe that's it. Or have you considered he could be finally telling the truth?"

Another long sigh from the other end. "I'll call Abigail again and have her phone you when she gets to the house."

I drove into the night, streetlights illuminating my life, with that vacant feeling reverberating in my chest, wondering what Terrelle had said, if it had been a qualified confession, leaving room for doubt, or if he had categorically said he pulled the trigger and dug the grave. It was obviously convincing enough for the governor and his friends from both sides of the aisle. Had Terrelle felt pressured into the confession or did he simply see this for what it was: the last, best chance to have something good come from something terrible?

My cell vibrated and I clicked it open, expecting to hear Abby's voice. "All right, tell me where you are."

A slight pause. "How could you do that, Mr. Wiley?" It wasn't Abby. I couldn't place the voice or the number on my screen.

"How could I do what? Who is this?"

"How could you convince Terrelle to sign a confession?"

Oleta. The last voice I expected to hear. "Look, I know this must be hard for you—"

"*Hard* for me?" she interrupted. "You think taking the last shred of dignity from my husband is *hard*? The truth is the only thing he's been able to hang on to. His story has been consistent every second of every hour since he was accused. You took that away from him in one day."

"Oleta, I'm as surprised as you are. Ellen just told me—"

"You saying you had nothing to do with it?"

"I met with him this morning and discussed what the governor told Ellen and me."

"Which was what?"

"He said the only way the transplant procedure could go forward was if he had a confession. I tried not to press Terrelle. But I thought he deserved to know the truth."

"Right. And you probably didn't suggest he sign it today, either."

"When I left him, he was adamant that this was something he couldn't do and I respected that. But obviously he—"

"And you'll respect the fact that you can forget about writing his story," Oleta said. She muttered something under her breath, then took another run at me. "How does a person like you live with himself? How do you go to sleep every night knowing the pain and hurt you've caused your own family? And now this?"

When a person wants to talk, it's best to let them. As a reporter I've known this truth and have seen it in action more times than I can count. I stayed quiet and listened, hoping Oleta wouldn't threaten Murrow's life at the end of her tirade.

"I trusted you. We all did. Why didn't you just go in there and cut his throat? That's basically what you did to him."

Her voice trailed. I put on my most sincere tone. "If it makes any difference, I want you to know I'm having real problems with his guilt. From the start, things haven't matched up, even though the evidence was so against him."

"Then why would you pressure him to give a confession?"

"Talk with Terrelle about our meeting this morning and what I said. My guess is he knows this is the only way. He cares more about Aiden and helping him than about himself. For that you should be proud."

Silence on the other end, then the familiar sound of a woman crying, always the first tune on the sound track of my life. Weeping women have dogged me.

"You took something from me today, Mr. Wiley," she choked.

"What's that, Oleta?" I could see her face, shriveled and contorted with pain and speckled with tears.

"Hope," she said. "You took hope from me today." More sobs that led to an openmouthed wail. "I know I told you I didn't have any to begin with. That I was resigned to the fact that he was gonna be carried out of that prison in a hearse. But in the back of my mind there was always this hope that somebody like you could uncover something that would show he's telling the truth."

"Believe me, I never wanted to cause him this extra pain. And what it's doing to you . . ." My phone buzzed and I saw Abby's number come up.

"You never got to see him in any other context than in a prison jumpsuit. I know you wondered why anyone would hitch their ladder to a guy like that, but you didn't know him."

"Oleta—"

She kept going with some fond memory of how tender Terrelle was with the kids, and though I didn't want to cut her off, I couldn't miss that call. I hit the button and said, "Abby?"

"Dad, did you pull the fire alarm?"

I ignored the question. "Where are you?"

She reluctantly gave me an address on a street I didn't recognize. She mentioned the cross streets, which I did. About ten minutes away.

"Listen to me. Get out of there. This guy is no good."

"I can't, Dad. I have to see this through. I found out something about Diana. I have to follow up."

CHRIS FABRY

"Follow up on it at work. Tell him you don't feel well and need to get home. Anything. If he finds out you have different motives than he thinks—"

"I know how to take care of myself. I'll be home later. We'll talk then."

"Abby—"

Her call went dead and I mashed the accelerator, returning to Oleta midsentence.

"—and all this time I've been able to share those memories with him in letters and visits. His mother called me, Mr. Wiley. His mother called me and asked what it meant. What am I supposed to say to her?"

"You tell her that her son is doing something selfless. He's putting the needs of my son ahead of his own. To me, that's heroic."

"It doesn't feel very heroic to me. It just feels bad."

What could I say to that? "Oleta, I wish I could tell you exactly how this is going to end. I'm going to do everything I can to tell people what really happened with Terrelle. And when I get done, you're going to be proud of him."

"I don't need your help to be proud of him."

"You're right about that. But I need your help to keep telling his story. And to get to the truth. Don't back out on me now."

More tears, sniffs, some gasps. "You have no idea the pain of this."

"You're right. But I know your faith in God has brought you this far. Hang on to that."

"That sounds funny coming from you, Mr. Wiley."

"Believe me, it felt funny coming out of my mouth. But I mean it."

"So are you saying you believe?"

"No. I have to be honest. But I'm seeing something real in you and Terrelle. Something I can't explain. Hang on to that and we'll get through this together."

"If you're right and this is Terrelle's way of being the hero, you need to promise me something," she said.

"Anything. Name it."

"You have to be there with me for the execution."

Anything but that. I promised myself I would never attend another execution after what happened with the last one.

"Absolutely," I said. "I wouldn't have it any other way."

Chapter 34

It was almost midnight when I pulled past Tompkins's building. It was a three-level brownstone and there were no lights on in the two bottom floors. The house was in a run-down area on a darkened street with not one spot to park. I drove down an alley and found Abby's car and another in a tight space behind the building. There was a metal fire escape hanging on to the side of the building for dear life, and a metal fence enclosed a ratty-looking lawn with a few patches of grass and an outbuilding that could have been used by the Unabomber. I know what it looked like. I was at Kaczynski's place soon after it was raided by the ATF. This looked like the perfect spot to dig a hole and toss a body and I wondered if Diana had ever seen the inside of this place. Maybe on the last day of her life?

I parked next to a fire hydrant in the alley. I had a view of the kitchen through an anemic palm tree. There weren't any window coverings and the lights were blazing inside. I rolled down my front windows to get some air movement and killed the engine. In the moonlight I noticed a rickety patio built only on the third floor, supported by several wooden beams that looked like long toothpicks—the kind of place where newspapers report deaths because of the structure. A wooden set of stairs wound down from there into the backyard.

I dialed Abby and got her voice mail again. I am not a fence climber, but in a pinch I knew I could. There was movement in the kitchen and I saw Tompkins's face, presumably over the sink, laughing and saying something. He moved away from the window, opened the door for a moment, then shut it.

There's a feeling you get when something is not quite right. I was covering a story once on a drug cartel in Mexico and you'd be surprised at how easy it is to sense an attack on civilians when a couple of big trucks roll in with armed men in the back. That's what I had right then, but it was more than a feeling. Something had changed in the backyard, a noise, a creaking of the stairs, the intake of air by some machine. I moved into the passenger seat and had my head near the open window when a black pit bull barreled against the fence, jaws dripping saliva, viciously barking like Old Yeller after the hydrophobia kicked in. I thought it would rip through the chain-link and jump straight into the car after my jugular vein, but the fence held the dog.

I moved back to the driver's side while he tried to scale the fence for a late-night snack. The patio door opened again and obediently, midsnarl, the dog turned, panting, slobbering, and moved back to the house. Silhouetted in the doorway was Tompkins. He yelled something. A flame appeared, and then he stood at the edge of the railing, a cigarette glowing orange. I stayed still. If I could see him, he could see me. The dog made several visits to his favorite spots in the yard.

My phone buzzed and lit brightly in my shirt pocket. I bent below the dash and pulled it out.

"Dad, you need to stop calling me," Abby whispered.

"I'm in the alley outside. Come out now and I'll follow you home."

"That's crazy. I'm finally alone with him. We were just talking about Conley. This is my chance, but you have to trust me."

"Looks like his dog is headed inside—get out of there."

"Dad, do you know what's downstairs? I found out they make movies."

My heart sank. I could see how it all played out with Diana and how it might play out with my daughter. "Probably not *Citizen Kane 2*."

"I don't want to know what they shoot down there," she said.

"Abigail, leave the phone on and put it in your purse or something. Let me hear what he says."

"It'll make noise," she said. "He'll hear you."

"I'll mute my side. Let me listen."

I looked up as the door opened and a cigarette spiraled into the yard. The dog disappeared inside. I hit the Mute button.

"What was that all about?" Abby said.

The man said something I couldn't hear and Abby laughed. He moved into the room and said, "He'll bark at anything that moves. And somebody's parked in the alley. Probably a couple of high school kids."

"You should bring them up to the second floor," she said.

He snickered. "Hey, not a bad idea. You think pretty fast. But how do you know about the second floor?"

"One of the guys at the club. Thin mustache."

"Larry. Yeah, Larry needs to keep his mouth shut. You sure I can't get you anything to drink?"

"I'm good," she said. There was a grating sound like a chair being pulled across a wooden floor.

"Was Diana into that? You know, the second-floor stuff? Movies?"

"That's the second time you've brought her up. Why are you so interested in a dead girl?"

His choice of words sent a chill down my spine.

"I've been reading about Conley. Wondering what her life was like. Who she was. Her dreams."

His voice was even closer. "I can think of a lot better things to talk about."

Abby giggled and her voice became distant. Perhaps she stood when he got close. *Good girl. Stand up and run.*

"Did she ever come over here? Make a video?"

Tompkins paused. Maybe he was drinking. Maybe he was trying to remember where his nearest gun was or the duct tape and rope he had hidden.

"Diana was a prude. A mama's girl. Stayed close to home. You've seen her picture. Not the face of a beauty queen. I told her we could make a movie called *Plain Jane* and she could show off her body. She wasn't that bad looking."

"Did she make deliveries for you?" Abby said.

"No. I asked a few times, even tried to hold her freelance over her—you know, 'you want off Tuesday afternoon, deliver a package,' that kind of thing. She would have been perfect, too. Clean-cut. No priors."

His words were beginning to slur. It sounded like he was rubbing his face as he spoke.

"So she did have some kind of freelance work," Abby said. "Making money on the side."

"Yeah, every couple of weeks she'd ask for time off, a stretch of three or four hours during a shift. She'd usually give me enough notice, but there at the end she'd get a phone call and rush out. I accused her of turning tricks at a local hotel and she just laughed. Even thought of following her a couple of times. I'm not excusing what the guy did, but if you're in the wrong place at the wrong time and you meet some unsavories, I say that's on you. Know what I mean?"

Abby didn't respond.

"I still don't get why you're so interested in her," he said.

"She was close to my age. Just a life snuffed out. That kind of thing haunts me, you know? I mean, what did she do to deserve getting killed?"

"Life and death, little girl. It's part of the plan. You can't escape it. You just have to live. Ours is not to reason why; ours is but to do or die."

Oh, give me a break. If you're going to quote Tennyson, at least get it right. "Do and die," you numskull. I hate men who use poetry to woo young women to their deaths.

"It was a real shocker for all of us," Tompkins continued. "Picture in the paper. News trucks out front."

"What was she like?"

He sighed. "Shy, sort of. Kept to herself. And quirky. Always carried around a notebook. When it was slow at the salon, she'd sit in the chair and write. Probably her way of coping. We all have our ways, you know."

There was an uncomfortable silence; then Abby laughed nervously. "No thanks," she said, moving farther from the phone. "Do you think this Conley guy really did it?"

Tompkins cursed. "You kidding me? The body was buried outside his shack. They found the murder weapon inside. You're not one of those anti–death penalty people, are you? Wait, don't answer that. You're a college student." He laughed; then came a snorting sound.

"I just want to know more about it."

"That Conley guy was constantly out on the street, bumming money for a drink, getting into it with people. He was like clockwork. About the same time every day he'd be out there, getting angry if he didn't have his daily bottle, like a spoiled kid. I called the cops a few times and they'd run him off to some shelter but then he'd show up the next day."

"Didn't you testify at the trial?"

Careful, Abby.

"How'd you know that?"

"I saw it in an old article online."

"You probably have read more than I remember. I'm done talking about it. The guy should fry. The needle is too easy. He deserves the death penalty, if not for that girl, then probably for something else they didn't catch him doing."

Something creaked. Maybe his chair. His voice was farther away now, matching Abby's distance.

"Look, it's getting late," he said softly, seductively. "No sense you driving all the way back to your place. Just stay here tonight. I've got an extra room."

"I don't think so."

"I make a mean Denver omelet. We'll get up early and watch the sun come up. Or we don't even have to sleep."

He said something else I couldn't make out and Abby's voice rose. "Stop it!"

My blood, already boiling, surged with adrenaline and I grabbed the phone and opened my door, turning off the speaker and holding it to my ear. If I unmuted the phone, I could stop the guy fast—letting him know he was being watched. But that would give Abby away.

I ran to the fire escape, panting and straining to hear what Tompkins said. A sprinkler kicked on behind me and began its swishing back and forth, spreading water into the alley. The dog barked inside and Tompkins yelled at it.

"No, I'm sorry," Abby said. "It's just that I had this bad experience when I was in school. A guy took me to his apartment and said the same thing. 'Just stay here tonight.'"

"What happened?" he said.

The creep actually sounded like he cared.

"He gave me something to drink. Next morning I woke up not remembering anything, still in the guy's apartment."

"I hate weasels like that. I say if you can't get a girl with your charm, you should never resort to chemicals."

What chivalry.

"I'm sorry that happened to you. But don't judge all guys because of one bad one."

"I don't. It's just that sometimes the feeling comes back and I don't handle it well."

"Completely understandable." Tompkins had moved back toward the phone.

"I'd better go. See you at the shop?"

He sighed like he had just lost a million-dollar bet. "I won't be there until late tomorrow. But I might stop by to see you. You want to go out for a drink afterward?"

"I'll think about it. And sorry for the overreaction."

Don't apologize, Abby.

I hurried back to my car and watched as she walked to hers and pulled away. She picked up the phone and said, "Did you hear that, Dad?"

"Yeah. How much of that college story was true and how much did you make up?"

"Not telling. But did you hear him say that Conley deserved to die even if he didn't kill Diana?"

"Yeah. He almost seemed to blame Diana for getting killed. And what about that notebook stuff?"

"Has to be a diary. Did you see anything like that in her room?"

"Not that I recall. Maybe she had it hidden."

"Or maybe the police have it. I'll head over to her mother's house before work tomorrow."

"You're going back to work for him?"

"Dad, there's more here we haven't uncovered. And I think we're close."

I looked in the rearview to see if anyone was following us. Something in my gut said she was right, we were close. Something in my gut said we were too close.

Abby's voice rose over the road noise. "Dad, thanks for being there. Even if you didn't trust me."

The words washed over me like a baptism. Like she was giving me another chance. Like the mistakes of the past were just that—in the past.

"I've got your back, little girl."

CHAPTER 35

I awoke with sunlight stirring dust and the sound of percolating coffee in the kitchen. At this point in the book process, I usually beat the sun by an hour and have the coffee going myself, but the late night kept me on the air mattress too long. I found Abby in her bathrobe with her wet hair up in a towel, hovering over the toaster like a lion choosing which wildebeest to pick from the herd.

"You're up early," I said, testing the relational waters. She had gone straight to her room and we had not spoken after the drive home.

"Going to Mrs. Wright's house."

"You want me to tag along? I have a relationship with that little dog of hers."

"From the sounds of your first meeting it's probably better if I try this alone."

I nodded, though she was focused with laser-like attention on just the right amount of butter for her bagel. Then she turned and pointed the knife at me as some dripped on the floor.

"I was thinking you might get in touch with the lead detective you talked with and see if they have any record of a diary."

"I left a message at his office when we got home last night. Plus the other detective, Sawyer."

"Great minds think alike," she said, then went back to buttering.

"I've checked the trial transcript, all the evidence presented, and I couldn't find any reference to a diary."

Abby pressed the knife to the crusty surface of the bagel and pulled it across until the butter was a memory. "If she left the salon for good that evening, she probably had it with her, don't you think? She would have had it in her purse and whoever killed her would have tossed it. That is, if she carried it with her all the time."

"We could ask Conley."

"Not funny, Dad."

I poured a cup of her coffee and she scolded me for taking it too soon. The Starbucks bag was nearly empty and the aroma was too heavenly to wait. "We don't know she was headed home that night. I think we have to find out about this freelance gig she had and where it might have taken her."

"I think Tompkins knows a lot more than he's telling. I think he knows exactly what freelance gig she had and it was for him. If we look at his stash of tapes, we might see Diana's face—"

"Abby, there's no way you're going back to his place again."

She pointed to the calendar. "Time's running out to find the truth."

Like the tides along the shoreline, constantly lapping, pulling at the sand and shells, I felt like we were being drawn into something bigger. Or maybe we were being drawn together. Maybe that was the whole point of telling this story. The continent of Abby and the continent of me drifting toward each other, jagged cliffs and fault lines finally within sight, but still far away.

She took an angry bite of her bagel and spoke around it. "You think I want to spend more time with this creep?"

"No, it's admirable what you've already done. Sometimes when you want to get the whole story, you have to go to bad places. You did that and it paid off, but you have to stop."

She looked up at me. "Is that what happened to you? At the execution of that guy?"

I looked at my reflection in the ripple of coffee. "That's not a good topic."

"What happened? Why did it hit you so hard?"

Frozen in time, the memories began to thaw and rise. Memories I did not want to keep but that had stayed seared into my mind by the emotion and chaos. Sounds. Smells. Faces. Darkened rooms finally illumined like some circus sideshow.

"If you could have been there, if you had met this guy, maybe I could get you to understand."

"I saw his picture," Abby said. "I wrote a paper about it for an English class."

"Hope you got a good grade."

"My prof said it was the best she'd read in years. She said it was moving."

"If you moved her with the paper, you probably know enough."

"No, I want to hear it from you. I heard it from Mom, what

she remembers, how you struggled. What you were like afterward. But I want to hear it from you."

I took in a shallow breath as if crawling through a narrow passage of time. "That was the lowest point of my career. My life. His name was Ronnie James Lawson. He was seventeen when he committed the crime. There was an older guy involved who influenced him—told him to pull the trigger. He got the plea deal. Ronnie got the death penalty. It was a terrible crime. The fellow who found the girl's body a few days after the murder quit the job not long afterward. He just couldn't take it."

"The defense said Ronnie had mental problems."

"Low IQ. Borderline mentally retarded. I did an interview with him a few days before the execution and he wasn't very articulate. The family said he had a degenerative brain disease but the state didn't buy the medical evidence. If there was ever anyone who deserved clemency, it was this guy, but the governor felt he should side with the jury."

"And they didn't use drugs back then to do the execution."

"No, it was the chair. Electrocution. He said his last words, they put the hood over him . . ."

The hood and Ronnie's tapping finger came back to me. There are things you don't tell your daughter about death. There are things you don't want to remember. There are things you can't forget. Just when you think you're over them, they knock at your door or stand by the foot of your bed waiting for you to awaken.

"And you were the media reporter?" she said.

"Unfortunately, yes. I was chosen from the pool. I remember sitting there before they pulled the curtain back, wondering if this was really going to happen. Would they lead this twenty-five-year-old guy in and just kill him? And they did. They brought him in, sat him down, strapped him in as tight as they could, and asked if he had any last words."

"Do you remember what he said?"

I'll be able to recite it word for word until the day I die.

"Just something about asking forgiveness and being forgiven by God and going to a better place. He mentioned his family and thanked us for being there with him. He was tapping his finger on the arm of the chair. It was about the only part of his body he could move. And then the warden nodded to another man and he put the hood over his head, hit the button, and the lights dimmed. They stopped the electricity for a minute, then hit the button again."

"And that was it?"

"The doctor checked for a pulse, pronounced him dead, and they wheeled him out on a gurney. It was like clockwork. Moving a sack of potatoes."

There was only one bite taken out of the bagel. Abby looked at me with sad eyes as if I were the one who had been executed. "I would worry if that didn't affect you."

"That's what a lot of people told me."

There was a silence between us. I would have dropped the whole thing, but something inside felt better talking about it instead of bottling.

"Ronnie's face haunted me for a long time. That hood. The way his body moved when the electricity hit him. I didn't really have an opinion on the death penalty before that. I figured you had to be guilty of something to get to that point. And there was no question Ronnie was guilty. He deserved to be kept from society. But he didn't deserve what he got. And the same thing is going to happen with Conley. And with others."

"Does that bring it back, when you see an execution scheduled?"

I nodded. "I've seen death on the battlefield. I've crossed the yellow tape at crime scenes. I've seen bodies in trees after floods and tsunamis. Dying is part of life. I get that. But there was something different about that day. About taking a man's life."

"You went to a counselor afterward?"

"Not right away. I just lived with it. Gave it the old college try. And that story paved the way to the network. Even that bothered me. I was using Ronnie's death for my own purposes. I had a hard time sleeping. And not just for a few weeks or months but years."

"Depression?"

"That and panic attacks. The whole routine. It felt like the world was closing in. I'd get short of breath; my heart would race. Your mom knew I was hurting but I didn't have the courage to get help until it got so bad I couldn't function. I was about to go on the air one day, subbing for one of the anchors, and when the camera light flashed, I saw Ronnie's face, the hood. That was the longest half hour of my life."

"When did you get over it?"

"I'm not sure I have. I cope with it better now and don't have the flashbacks, but walking into that prison to see Conley the first time set off a lot of bells. And now Oleta wants me to be there. I promised I would. I just don't know if I can."

Abby put her plate on the table and sat, hooking one foot around the chair leg. Her toenails were red. I remembered painting them when she was little, cotton balls between her toes, playing spa in one of my more lucid, engaged moments as a dad.

"If we can prove who really did this, you won't have to go there."

"He confessed."

"He did that for Aiden."

"Yeah, what about Aiden? What happens to him if we prove Conley innocent?"

She looked at me with moist eyes. "I don't know. Maybe instead of seeing the hood or Conley on an operating table, Aiden's face is the one you see the rest of your life."

"I don't like either possibility," I said.

Abby left alone, and instead of surfing the Internet, I got my news the old-fashioned way: I retrieved the newspaper from a neighbor's driveway. I would return it later.

The front-page story carried Terrelle's confession, complete with a picture of his jailhouse scrawl on lined notebook paper. Reading between the lines, I could feel his desperation to save both my son and his dignity.

> I hereby confess to the murder of Diana Wright and I
> also will not ask for any more extensions or appeals. I am
> hoping this will convince the authorities that the transplant
> I wish to provide will go through.

I wondered what Diana's mother would think of his confession. It was clear from the story that the governor and his friends in the legislature saw this as a win-win situation and wholeheartedly embraced the confession. From a couple of statements made by anonymous sources, it seemed that the wheels of justice had been duly oiled.

"I see no reason why we won't move forward swiftly now," the source said. "With this confession, there is no need for any further appeals. The medical community has given us the green light, so we'll need to interface with them to make this procedure humane and orderly."

It sounded like Reginald to me. Or some other behind-the-scenes bureaucrat. It also made the execution and heart transplant, as Terrelle had said, sound like a tonsillectomy.

CHAPTER 36

ELLEN TRUDGED UP HER DRIVEWAY after getting a ride from a nurse who had worked a twelve-hour shift in the neonatal intensive care unit—a church member who had just happened by to say hello and wound up offering the ride. That's how it worked in God's economy. Things like this just worked out without her having to orchestrate it. Why couldn't God do the same with the rest of her life?

Aiden was stable and resting comfortably, not much change in his condition, so she felt she could leave. A quick shower and change of clothes would go a long way in helping her frame of mind. But she knew it would take more than water to clear her head. Her energy, all of her silent praying that had normally been focused only on Aiden, was now being split between her son and the rest of her fractured family. Was this diluting the power or adding strength? She wasn't sure.

Something was stirring, brewing and percolating in the family pot, and Ellen equally feared and was excited by the possibilities. Normally she knew everything about her daughter, even things she didn't want to know. They communicated every day by phone and Facebook and texts, a constant stream of information going back and forth. Most of the time Ellen could handle the things Abigail shared, could quell the fear that her daughter was making the same mistakes with her boyfriend that she had made with Truman. She had a deep and abiding knowledge that God had used even her mistakes long ago to help bring her to himself, but she hated to watch Abigail struggle and squirm under a similar weight. Ellen wished she could cut the nets free and let her swim to the surface for air, but she knew from her own life that sometimes the things that dragged her under revealed her need. So as hard as it was to just listen, that's what she tried to do. Just be there as a sounding board—a praying board, really.

However, now that Truman had become involved, Ellen was in the unenviable position of not knowing, and this bothered her. It was one thing to know what to pray about, how to intercede about specific issues. It was totally different to not know what had happened between Truman, Abigail, and the man at the salon. To not know the dangers they were facing. Being on the outside and her husband suddenly moving toward the inner circle of her daughter's life somehow felt like a betrayal.

When Truman was away on some story or, in the past few months, when he was staying at the beach house, she could give up on him, abandon him to the rising tide of his life. Out of sight, out of mind. But now he was home, rekindling a relationship with both children. No matter how imperfect that rekindling was, he was in the house and the closeness brought with it angst and uncertainty. It was easier when her husband had failed her, when he was oblivious that his choices had hurt her so deeply. This was life, routine, what she expected. The sun came up in the east every day and Truman was indifferent to her pain.

But in the last few days she had sensed a change, perhaps an openness that hadn't been there. A look, a way of communicating, a sense that instead of being on opposite sidelines, they were moving closer to each other, closing ranks and fighting a common opponent. She hadn't felt this since the early days when they were scraping by, trying to set sail on life together, pulling for each other rather than competing.

She paused at the front door, watching the nurse pull away from the curb. Maybe she was making all of this up, trying to manufacture hope from hopelessness. Perhaps that feeling she had when she sat next to Truman on the bed, the stirring that moved within her, was hormonal. It had been so long since they had been together *that* way. It had been so long since she had felt any warmth at all. But that moment, sitting next to him, had been like the slow thaw of a Thanksgiving turkey. The hardness and coldness of the bird in the fridge was still there, just under the surface, and the neck and giblets were still firmly trapped, but with a little time and perhaps some running water, there was potential.

Maybe all this mental exercise was her desire for desire, a longing within her to *feel* something other than pain. Anything but that. It was work just getting up the energy to feel disdain. She couldn't imagine what kind of work it would take to feel desire, but there it was, stuck in her mind like gum to the bottom of her shoe. Sitting next to him with nothing between them but her towel and the past had ignited something primal and urgent. Something dangerous. And she didn't need any more danger or drama. She needed stability. Strength. Faith.

She needed love.

She made a little more noise than usual coming in, closing the door with gusto rather than tiptoeing inside and holding the latch so it wouldn't bang. There were two coffee mugs and an unfolded newspaper on the kitchen table. Abigail's car was gone, so she assumed she and Truman were alone.

Instead of looking for him, calling for him like a mother calling her son from the playground, or waiting until he appeared from his writing cave, she headed to the shower and stood under the uninterrupted flow, steam rising, half-hoping he would join her, half-dreading the awkwardness of what might happen if he did. She could go to him, of course. Just get out and walk dripping down the hallway and surprise him at his computer. No one would have to know.

Funny. A clandestine meeting with a stranger she was married to. Just the thought made her laugh. Then she wondered how he might react. What if he recoiled?

She waited, water cascading, then the shampoo that felt like a warm release. She turned off the water and grabbed a towel taller than herself and stepped out, almost expecting to find him standing there waiting. But he wasn't. Just an empty room. An empty bed. Pictures and mementos staring at her from the dresser. And her reflection in the mirror across the darkened room.

Ellen dressed quickly and returned to the kitchen, a towel draped over her shoulders to catch the errant water, and found the newspaper gone. She looked for anything mildly healthy to eat but she hadn't been to Whole Foods in days and there was nothing green to juice. In a fit of hunger and with a lot of guilt, she popped a frozen waffle into the toaster. Something she had bought for Aiden in a moment of weakness, when he pleaded for a waffle and agave nectar. From early on after his diagnosis she had felt the one thing she could give her son was healthy food, fuel for his heart, and that had sent her on a quest for the healthiest of foods. Not just the stuff on the shelves that said *organic*, but truly natural foods that came from the ground. The closer to the dirt, the better.

All of that felt like striving now and she wondered how much the goat milk kefir and homemade yogurt had really helped Aiden and how much it had simply made her feel better, given her something to focus on instead of waiting for him to collapse. How much of it was accomplishing something good in his body and how much of it was about her doing something—anything—that might help prolong his life and make him healthy? She couldn't know the answer to that, probably wouldn't know, ever.

Truman came in the front door and smiled, saying he had to return a neighbor's newspaper. There was a flash from the past, a gleam of the old Truman, connected and inviting. He asked about Aiden and she updated him on the latest from the team, a designation Truman had hated because he said he felt like he was paying the pitching staff of the Yankees. But he listened intently and seemed genuinely interested, not preoccupied as he normally was when he was working on a project. When he was in the zone of his writing or reporting, it was even more difficult to get him to focus on a crisis.

Ellen countered with a question about Abigail and got a few details she didn't know. Truman was sketchy about the night at the club, and his version of what had happened at the salon owner's apartment was even sketchier, but she decided not to pry.

"You two seem to be working well with each other," she said.

"I don't know if I'd go that far," he said. "But it's good having two pairs of eyes on this instead of one. Have you read Terrelle's confession?"

She nodded. She'd read it at the hospital earlier when the newspapers were first dropped off in the waiting room. "It seemed stiff to me. Obligatory. What do you think?"

He told her, but instead of listening to his opinion, she lost herself in his voice, the soft, smooth flow of consonants and vowels over his tongue and lips. It was a natural gift he had, not just with the language but with the mastery of the big picture. He could tap into an issue, some world event or complicated legal battle, and reduce it to its least common denominator. It was an innate skill, along with asking the questions that cut to the heart of any story. He'd had it in the newsroom in college. He had it in the classroom, when professors would ask them to decipher which stories should lead a newscast, what priorities to place on the competing time demands of viewers or readers or editorial directors.

But if he was so good at this on the journalistic level, why couldn't he use that same discipline in their relationship? Why couldn't he see the truth of "If it bleeds, it leads" when it came to her heart? There had been plenty of bleeding in the past few years that he had pushed to the end of his lifecast, after the final weather report.

He washed his hands and poured another cup of coffee. She moved closer and touched his face, just lightly with her thumb. He didn't recoil from her touch but seemed to lean into it, like a pastured horse leans into a farmer's hand. Could this actually work? Could the dead limbs of their marriage be broken away to give room for new growth?

"How's the bruise?" she said.

"Doesn't hurt as much when I chew," he said. "Not ready for a family picture, though."

Ellen traced her index finger across the wound, the dried blood and discolored skin, and looked into his eyes. She wanted to say she was sorry. For what? She didn't know. She had nothing to be sorry for. Still, there was something down deep that compelled her to speak the words. Called them from her.

His cell phone buzzed before she could open her mouth. It was Abigail, talking excitedly about something. Ellen took the half-charred waffle from the toaster and broke off the black pieces until it was one bite-size chunk.

Truman laughed at the end of the conversation, shook his head, and closed the phone.

"What was that about?" she said.

"She went to Diana's house before work. Mrs. Wright is not the easiest person in the world to talk to, especially when you wake her up. But Abby did it." His eyes sparkled. She hated it, but they were actually glinting with something just this side of glee.

"What was she looking for?"

"Diana evidently had this legendary obsession with journals. She was always carrying one and writing in it. Abby schmoozed her way in and asked if she could see any of Diana's diaries, and Mrs. Wright said there weren't any."

"And Abigail found them."

"A whole stack of spirals hidden way back in her closet. I don't think Mrs. Wright has been able to go through Diana's stuff. It's like a museum in there."

"Abigail has them, then?"

"She brought half of them with her to work, the most recent, and Mrs. Wright gave her twenty-four hours. Abby said she's gonna devour them and let me know what she finds out. She said that fortunately her writing is legible, unlike mine."

"You think it'll lead to anything?"

"It's a long shot, but that's the process. Every little rock you turn over can lead you to something else or to a dead end. But you can't stop turning over rocks."

He was in reporter mode, only looking at the story and not thinking of the ramifications. He always lived somewhere between the edits and she had to exist in the real world. But she had given this over to God, right? It was all in his hands.

"I just hope you don't run out of time," Ellen said.

Truman looked her square in the eyes. "Even if we do find something that backs up Terrelle's story, we don't have much recourse now that he's confessed. This train just kicked into high gear and there are no brakes left."

CHAPTER 37

When Ellen touched my face in the kitchen, something happened that scared me. Something electrical. So when I went back to the computer, all I could think about was that touch and the ache it awakened. Not an ache to be bound by promises made and broken so long ago, but to be tethered to something other than my own aimlessness. To find some kind of relational footing that worked. To be "even" again, on level ground, and moving together with her instead of against her.

The noise of the mail carrier's muffler took me from the screen and I wondered what legions from hell this representative of the government might deliver. Stacked inside the box were a car insurance bill, a reminder that my life insurance payment was overdue and if I didn't comply within a specific time frame I would forfeit my opportunity to provide for my family in a potential time of need. There was a nice notice from the hospital billing department that gave me warm and fuzzy feelings about them. And on the heels of that, a collection agency notice that they had now taken over my hospital bill and would I please contact them at my earliest convenience. I decided to do that, but I also decided it wasn't convenient today. A letter from the admissions department of Abby's school offered further financial assistance and a toll-free number. Such nice people. Generous. And the generosity extended to an embossed envelope with a message inside from a credit card company congratulating Aiden on his new card and the hefty credit line that was available.

There was, of course, a common denominator in these pieces of correspondence: money. And since I had none left, it made no sense to spend time fretting about them, but since when has my life made sense? I stacked the envelopes in the kitchen on top of all the unopened mail we had received in the past few days and went back to my cave.

Abby called late in the day to say she hadn't found anything in the journals about Tompkins, but there was enough loneliness and angst in Diana's writing to depress Jane Austen. She read me a section that one of the stylists could have used to curl hair it was so fraught with longing and questions about life and love and why it had passed her by. Diana also talked about the usual workday struggles with other stylists, her boss, and customers who were tightfisted with tips.

"Nothing in there about running drugs for Curtis?"

"The closest she comes is talking about the shady characters he brings into the shop and the passes he made, though she says he seems more interested in a couple other girls at the salon. They don't work here anymore."

"Maybe you can contact them," I said. "Do these entries have dates?"

"Yeah. The newest journal I have ends about six months before her death."

"How much time does each journal cover?"

"A few months. Some entries are pages and pages, front and back, and others are short with intervals in between. She talks about some past guys and heartaches. A lot of stuff I can relate to—are you in the car?"

"Yeah, had to run an errand. So you have to get these back to Diana's mom tomorrow morning. You going to make it all the way through?"

"I'll make it, but I don't have a lot of hope I'm going to find anything. I keep wondering if there's another journal in that closet or hidden somewhere."

"I'll phone Sawyer and check," I said as I pulled into the casino parking lot. "Gotta run. Let me know if you find anything else."

Part III

And I will give you a new heart, and I will put a new
spirit in you. I will take out your stony, stubborn
heart and give you a tender, responsive heart.

Ezekiel 36:26

CHAPTER 38

Suffice it to say the next few days did not go well with Abigail and Ellen because they somehow noticed that I didn't come home until early in the morning that next day and that I had left Aiden's opened credit card envelope on top of the trash in the kitchen. It's tough having bloodhounds as your relatives but I suppose it's in the gene pool. My daughter cried and Ellen didn't run her thumb across the scar on my face or sit on her bed in a towel. I said I was sorry, that I needed help, and that I would be out of their lives soon. They didn't protest.

The missing journal or journals didn't turn up, and neither did my dignity. Abby called in sick when Tompkins put the pressure on for a return engagement at his club. Diana's mother turned sour to our search for the final journal and neither Chandler nor Sawyer had any independent or dependent recollection of a journal Diana had left behind in her purse or in Terrelle Conley's car.

I banished myself to the bedroom, threw myself back into Terrelle's story, and came up with a few last questions, holes in the narrative I needed to wrap up. Oleta arranged my final meeting with him, but the day before, I met with the doctor who would coordinate the execution medical staff.

Dr. Lyle Granger was a short man with perfect posture, mainly because of a childhood bout with scoliosis, who was very good at cutting directly to the main artery of my questions.

He explained how the procedure would work, the difficulty in fulfilling the demands of the state to have Terrelle pronounced dead at the prison and still have a viable heart to transport and transplant.

"We'll use the governor's helicopter for transport of the heart. We have a window of four hours, and our estimates are that from the severing of the aorta to the time of transplant will be between fifty-two and fifty-six minutes. We've already timed the flight."

Something in his voice sent a tingle down my spine. When your son's life is on the line, you want someone who knows within four minutes how long it will take to transport a human heart from point A to point B.

"So you'll be doing the actual procedure . . ."

"The harvesting," he said. "Yes."

"How will that work?"

"Like any execution, we have to go on the state's timetable. We'll prep him for the surgery. He'll have the opportunity to speak his last words to his family and the witnesses in attendance. We'll take him to the surgical room and keep him alive until after the harvest. Then he'll be taken off artificial support."

"Not a usual amount of time for the witnesses to wait."

"No, but these are not usual circumstances. If we didn't have Terrelle's full cooperation in this, there would be no way we could do it."

With military precision he told me how long the procedure would take. He must have sensed some hesitation on my part, which was my growing concern that Terrelle might be innocent.

"Mr. Wiley, I've practiced on nearly seven thousand patients in the last thirty years. I'll bring all that experience into that sterile room at the prison. Terrelle's life will be treated with the dignity he deserves. And I promise you, when his heart gets to the doctors who are treating your son, they'll have everything they need to give him a new shot at life."

"I don't doubt your abilities. Will this environment pose a challenge?"

"I was a trauma surgeon in one of Chicago's biggest hospitals, where kids were coming in with gunshot wounds, bleeding like stuck pigs. I operated on soldiers coming off the battlefield. I will guarantee you Terrelle Conley's heart will make it to your son."

Terrelle seemed tired and listless during our final interview. His eyes were more vacant than I had ever seen them. I had sent him the first few pages of the book and he thanked me for what I had done.

"It almost sounds like me talking on those pages. You did a real good job."

"That's my goal—to capture your voice and let it come through. I have to get out the way."

"Well, for what it's worth, I'm glad we chose you."

I stared at him, trying to figure out how to say what I wanted. "The confession you gave . . . I know that was difficult. Thank you."

He dipped his head to one side and gave a wry smile. "I warmed up to it after a while. I realized it's not really about me. The point is to give your boy a shot at life. I'm going to die one way or another. But people will know the truth because of what you're writing. That's what keeps me going."

I began asking the questions to fill in the holes of his story, some about his earlier life, a few about the descent into alcohol and days on the street.

"I have one source who says something a little different from your view. He claims that you were like clockwork on that street outside the salon. You were there just about every day, same time, same place."

Terrelle squinted and the lines on his forehead were deep furrows. "It's hard to say for sure because by the end I was pretty far down into the bottle. Or maybe it was far down into me. I wouldn't deny showing up at the same places because that's where I got the money to head back to my trailer. You know?"

Just like finding a new credit card in the mail.

"Do you remember . . . ?" I changed my mind midquestion because it was too far-fetched.

"What were you going to ask?"

"The woman who was killed kept a journal. You don't remember anything about it, do you?"

"If I had killed her, maybe I would. You're talking about a diary?"

I nodded.

"I don't recall anything. They found her purse in my car, so if it was in there, the police got it. And they never brought it up at the trial. Did she carry it around?"

"I've heard she wrote in it all the time."

"Look at the surveillance video. They played it at the trial and magnified it. Made it real clear so they could show me yelling at her."

"It's not important," I said, regretting I had gone down that rabbit trail. The question seemed to upset him and that's not what I wanted with time ticking down and the big question ahead of me. "Have you thought about your last meal?"

"I was thinking about one of those big charbroiled burgers they serve at expensive restaurants. And maybe a whole pound of boiled shrimp. I don't want to do anything to hurt my ticker, of course. How's your son doing, by the way?"

"Not too well, to be honest. This last hospitalization has really done a number on him."

"Do they need to move the transplant up?"

Interesting that he would call it a transplant and not an execution. Even in Terrelle's mind, this was about life for Aiden.

"I doubt that'll happen, no matter what condition he's in. But I appreciate you asking."

"I'll do whatever it takes."

"Thanks, Terrelle," I said, and the emotion in my voice caught me off guard. He smiled sadly at me.

"Any thoughts about your last words?" I said quickly, looking away. This was the big question. I wanted his thought process about what he was going to say. Ronnie Lawson had memorized his speech meticulously. I wanted to know if Terrelle was doing the same thing, spending all his waking moments thinking about what he would leave the earth saying.

He thought a minute. "I got a speech I been working on. I was hoping you'd be there to hear it."

"I will be. But how about a preview?"

He nodded. "I figure I'll thank the people who are there, the doctors and whatnot, friends of the family. Press guy. I'll pay tribute to Oleta. She was the best thing in my life. Period. And then my kids. I missed my chance with them and I'll go to my grave regretting that. But I want to tell them not to let what happened to me get them down. I'll thank the warden and the governor for letting me have something good come out of the bad. And of course I'll thank God for constantly being there with me through all these years."

"Nothing about being innocent?"

He chuckled and coughed. "I'll probably tell them to look for a new book coming out about that."

"I don't think they allow you to plug books with your last words."

"Don't see how they can stop me. You got a title yet?"

I still had several floating around. Sometimes titles appear in a flash of creativity before the writing starts. Most of the time they come after the writing ends. "I was hoping you would think of the perfect one."

He smiled and sat for a moment. The guard behind him looked at his watch. Almost time to go.

"There's a verse in one of the Gospels," Terrelle said. "Jesus says it, so it's in red. It's about a man laying down his life for his friends. That's what I want to start with, you know, before chapter 1 or wherever. If you could look that up and put it in there, I'd appreciate it."

"Be glad to."

I started to get up, but Terrelle wasn't finished. "There's one thing before you go," he said. "One thing I have to ask you."

"Shoot."

Bad choice of words.

"When the blood stops flowing to my brain, when they've cut

the main artery that keeps me alive, I know what's going to happen. I will be in the presence of my Savior. I don't have any doubt of that. But I wonder about you. What hope do you have in eternity?"

"I'm good, Terrelle. I've grown closer to my family in these last few weeks. And whatever happens down the road, I think I'll be okay."

He shook his head. "That's not good enough. When you stand before God to give account, you have to have more than a good feeling. You have to know where you're headed."

"When I'm there, I don't know that I'll be able to say anything."

"That's true."

"But if I can talk, I'll say I did my best. I messed up my life big-time, but I tried hard. Tried to kick a few habits. Tried to overcome some stuff from my past."

Terrelle launched into the short version of the Conley catechism. With all the verses and the blood and sin and atonement. It wasn't easy not paying attention to a dying man's last words, but I somehow managed. Just shut him right out with glazed-over eyes. I just wanted to get out of there.

"Ask him to forgive you," Terrelle said. "He'll show you what to do."

I told Terrelle I would seriously consider what he had said.

"Please, Truman. Jesus is the only way."

The guard moved in and touched him on the shoulder. I told him I'd try to get back and see him one more time before the big day but we both knew this was it.

"Whatever happens from here on out, I appreciate what you've done, Mr. Truman."

I nodded and tried to say something but the words wouldn't come.

When I returned home, I searched for the DVD in the Piggly Wiggly bag. While I waited for it to load, I typed *Jesus laying down his life* in my search engine and up popped John 15:12-13.

> "This is my commandment: Love each other in the same way I have loved you. There is no greater love than to lay down one's life for one's friends."

I'm not a student of Jesus. From what I understand, he was a good teacher and promoted peace and love. My problem is his followers. Most think they know how everybody else ought to live. They whip the truth around like a scalpel and wave it at homosexuals and adulterers, until a pastor is caught with a prostitute. Then they talk about forgiveness and restoration. Either that or they hang their own guy and hire another.

I know that's being hard on Jesus, because there are some of his people who aren't jerks, like Ellen. She tries to love people as they are and not who she wants them to be. Take me, for instance. I'm hard to love. I admire her Herculean efforts.

To be honest, I can't buy into the whole church/Jesus thing. Maybe it would change my life if I tried it, which is why I haven't tried it. I think God, if he is really up there, accepts us the way we are and doesn't have a problem with people who are just trying to get by. Of course, I could be wrong about that and if I am, I'll be disappointed when I hit the shores of eternity. I prefer to think of it that way rather than me coming back as an ant or a caterpillar. Stepping onto a shoreline somewhere with the water lapping against golden sand. It's either that or just nothing—you live, you die, and that's it. Unless . . .

Unless Terrelle and my wife are right and there's a God who

really does care enough to make a way back to him. I guess out of all the possibilities in the world, that's an alternative. And if that's true, Abby and I are on the outside looking in, and I won't get to walk the shoreline.

I had watched the surveillance footage early on, but it was more of a cursory viewing to get me into the story. I had skipped the longer version that showed the before and after of the verbal attack. The DVD showed a time stamp in the lower right-hand corner of the screen. Since there was no audio, a lip-reading expert had been called in to interpret what had been said. The defense objected, but the woman who testified corroborated what was said by eyewitnesses who were on the street. Terrelle's profanity-laced statement at the end and his two fiery-looking eyes were grim reminders of his previous life.

He approached Diana as soon as she came out of the salon and followed her. Terrelle looked like a different person, wild-eyed, with darker and longer hair that had a mind of its own. In a word, he looked scary, and when he called to Diana from the street, it sent my stomach to the floor. As he approached her, I wanted to stop the video. Even I could read his lips when he threatened her. She kept shaking her head and trying to get away but he wouldn't stop.

"I'm going to kill you!" he shouted, the veins on his neck sticking out.

The first angle caught Diana from the front as she exited the salon and Terrelle confronted her. The second view was from the top, so the viewer mostly saw everything from above as Diana hurried away down the sidewalk. There were others on the street that day. A woman carrying a grocery bag. A young mom with a child in a stroller. Why had Terrelle picked out Diana? Why not anyone else?

I stopped the DVD and focused on what she carried. Even though it had been enhanced, the picture looked grainy and in some places I couldn't make out her face. It was weird seeing Diana move. She was a still photograph in my mind, an image captured and frozen in time. Something for the bookshelf or the pages of a photo album. But the video showed how she walked, how frightened she was of this man, the way she pushed her glasses onto the bridge of her nose with the back of her hand, her awkward gait. Instead of confidently striding forward, she had more of a self-conscious shuffle that leaned toward the wall of the stores. Timid. Like a cat wanting to get something floating on the water but unwilling to stick a paw in for fear of getting wet.

Her purse was slung over her shoulder but there was nothing in her hands. Perhaps it was in her purse. Or perhaps the person who killed her also took the journal. It was tossed into the trash. Maybe the police discovered it and disregarded it. Or destroyed it by mistake. No matter what happened, it was a dead end.

I took one more look at Terrelle as he came back into the picture. He was headed to the other side of the street, yelling, flailing his arms, as if in defeat. I was about to pop the DVD out of the player when a thought occurred. As Diana walked, she kept looking back. I thought it was toward Terrelle.

I hit the forward button on the DVD but didn't find the full video I was looking for. I wanted the longer version of the events of the day the trial transcript talked about. I dug back into the bag and found the second DVD. There was only one long file on this recording, shot from the angle that showed the top of Diana's head. But that angle also gave the best view of the street. The video began a full forty-five minutes before Diana came out of the shop and I fast-forwarded until I saw Terrelle shuffling back and forth across the street. He leaned against a chain-link fence with one foot up behind him, then sat on the curb and put his back against the fence. His head dipped in a stupor or perhaps in slumber; then he leaned to one side on the hot concrete slab until he lay stretched out. People who walked by went out of their way, even crossing the street, to avoid him.

Just as I was about to fast-forward again, a shadow passed in front of Terrelle. Someone just out of view of the camera. Terrelle stirred, propping himself up on one elbow, speaking to the shadow. His head lolled back and then he sat fully up, shaking his head and pointing a finger. The shadow lingered, straight as a telephone pole, and if I hadn't seen it move there, I would have thought it was a sign or a tree.

Terrelle stood and moved out of the picture, then back in, bobbing, weaving, walking back and forth like a prizefighter waiting for his title match. I strained to see him, wishing I could reposition the camera after all those years. He would return for a few seconds, then shuffle out again. When he returned to the right side of the screen, I paused the DVD. Instead of talking in his stream-of-consciousness rant, he seemed to be listening now. I hit Play again and he shifted out of view. It was agonizing. The sun went behind a cloud. Cars parked and people hurried along the sidewalk.

I hit fast-forward and kept my eye on the right side of the screen and the two shadows that now lingered. A car pulled close to the curb and parked. Terrelle moved into the picture, gesturing, smiling, then pushing back on a man who slowly walked toward the car. I stopped the DVD and tried to see the man's face. He was dressed in a polo shirt and jeans, a baseball cap pulled low. Terrelle followed him to the car, nodding and smiling, rubbing his hands together, almost gleeful. The man opened the rear door of the car, pointed toward the next street, and Terrelle pointed as well, nodding and saying something.

Something about the man in the hat seemed familiar. Perhaps it was the way he carried himself or a gesture that sparked something in the back of my mind. From this angle it was impossible to see the license plate and the windows were tinted, so I couldn't see the driver. It wasn't until the man took off his baseball cap as he entered the vehicle that I saw the blond hair that reached his shoulders.

I backed the DVD up and got the best, clearest view of his face. My heart racing, I knew I had stumbled onto something others had missed. Some connection between Terrelle and this mystery man.

The car pulled away and Terrelle seemed energized, pacing across the street from the salon and watching the front door. The car disappeared from view. A few minutes later, Terrelle walked into the parking lot, behind the chain-link fence, and gestured toward the street as if acknowledging someone.

Twenty minutes later Diana walked out of the salon and the ugly scene played out again. This time I watched all the way through. When Terrelle went out of view of the camera, there were people on the street walking to the other side, avoiding his verbal tirade, shocked and appalled at what they heard. In that pool of people no one had noticed the solitary figure who stood like a sentinel, baseball cap pulled low, observing the scene from the chain-link fence across the street. As soon as Terrelle followed Diana, yelling obscenities and threats, the man exited, hastily heading out of the picture in the other direction.

Terrelle came back into the picture once again after the altercation, walking purposefully, as if in search of someone, but his gait betrayed him and he wound up pacing again on the hot sidewalk. The DVD ended with many more questions than answers. Had the police disregarded this? Had they even noticed it? Could this video jog Terrelle's memory? And was this blond guy linked with both Diana and Curtis Tompkins?

I wanted to call someone, anyone—Abby or Ellen, the police; I had to tell someone what I'd found. But who? And if this meant what I thought it did . . . could I reveal this new information knowing that it might mean the end to any chance of life for my son? Wouldn't it be better for everyone if this evidence just slipped through the cracks?

I sat back and hit the Off button on the DVD player. Time was running out for Terrelle. Time was running out for Aiden's ailing heart. And I suddenly felt a shudder of fear. Time was running out for me to decide what to do about both.

CHAPTER 39

I WAS ATTEMPTING to get back in the zone, pecking away at the computer and filling in much of what Terrelle had told me, trying to get the image of the blond-haired man out of my mind, waiting for a return call from Detective Sawyer, and having this pain in my gut that wouldn't go away. They call it hunger. But it was more than that. A growing realization that I had to make more important choices than cuisine.

Every few minutes I would get up and go to the refrigerator and see the same thing I had seen fifteen minutes earlier, which was six eggs, a head of cabbage, and some frozen chicken. What can you make with those ingredients? I calculated how long it would take to drive to the nearest fast-food place but that seemed like a huge time waster, so I trudged back to the room.

I was considering the ramifications of breaking in to a neighbor's house and stealing lunch meat and bread when the door to my room flew open and Abby burst in with a wild look in her eyes, a black book in one hand and a Pizza Hut box in the other.

"I found something," she said, thrusting the book in front of me.

"Sausage or pepperoni?"

"No, Dad, this."

"Her diary?"

"No, it's one of those time management books—a calendar on steroids they had before cell phones took over the world."

My daughter. A chip off the old block.

"Look at this," she said.

She opened a page and pointed at a dark circle around January 22 while I opened the pizza box and saw almost an entire thin-crust cheese pizza inside. Who in their right mind orders only cheese? And thin crust? Made me wonder if this chip off the block could possibly be related to me.

"Throughout January and February there are dates circled every two or three weeks."

"Back up," I said. Actually it sounded more like "Bmmm ummmm" because I had a mouthful of pizza that was putting a serious dent in my hunger pangs. "How did you get this?"

"Diana's mom had a plastic bag in her closet. All of the evidence that was returned after the trial. She never touched it. Just put it in the closet and kept it there. Diana's purse and all of its contents."

"No diary."

"No, but this is interesting." She opened the calendar and held it in front of me, presumably so I wouldn't get pizza sauce on the pages. That just enabled me to use both hands, but I'm not that uncouth.

"Early on, back in January, she has notes down at the bottom of the page. Grocery lists, supplies for the salon, that kind of thing."

"'Freelance,'" I said, staring at the dead girl's note. Her handwriting wasn't that much better than mine. Squiggly *F* and no real form if you ask me. The word had a question mark beside it.

"Now look at February," Abby said. "The twelfth has a big circle around it and *Freelance* is written at the bottom."

"At four thirty," I said. "Probably one of the days she asked to leave early. But it doesn't give any clues about what she was doing."

Abby flipped the page. "Then at the end of February you see the initials *CT*. And again here, on March 4."

"Curtis Tompkins. This proves his whole story to you was made up. He knew exactly what her freelance was. But what was she doing for him?"

"Who knows? Making a delivery. Running drugs. Whatever it is, I think it got her killed, because look at the frequency before she died. As you get into March and then April, there are more circles, more meetings. Only a few days separate the jobs."

My mind raced with the information and I jammed the rest of the piece of pizza in my mouth, wiped my fingers on my shorts, and took the calendar, flipping ahead to April 28, the day Terrelle accosted her outside the salon. There was a circle around the date and again the initials *CT* were scribbled underneath.

I sat with that for a moment, waiting for the realization to kick in. Waiting for the images of Diana walking down the sidewalk to clear my head. Wondering what her last moments were like and who had pulled the trigger.

My phone buzzed—Detective Sawyer. As I explained what

Abby had discovered, I pulled up the video on my computer. Abby hovered over my shoulder, which I knew she would do because she was as interested in the shadows and faces of the past as I was. I skipped forward a little, telling the man what I saw and mapping out linear observations of Diana's last day on earth. Terrelle's final day as a free man.

"Did you review this video after Terrelle's arrest?" I asked.

"Yeah, we saw it. It just confirmed what Chandler believed. Made the case that much stronger."

"But did you see what happened with the guy who approaches Terrelle? The blond-haired guy?"

The man sounded annoyed. "What are you talking about?"

I explained what I'd found on the surveillance video and told him I believed I had seen the man caught on tape in the past few days.

"What's his name?"

"I don't know who he is, but it looks like he's telling Terrelle to do something, and then he keeps watching him."

"Wait, didn't Conley already confess to this?"

"He did, but it was the only way the transplant for my son could go through."

"And you're trying to get the governor to change his mind?"

"Detective, I don't know what I'm doing. I'm just telling the truth as I get the information and this guy on the street doesn't look right to me."

"So what do you think he says to Conley? You think he says, 'Go up to the girl when she comes out of the salon and tell her you're going to kill her'?"

"I don't know what he says, but he's talking with Terrelle for a long time. It's really suspicious."

"Suspicious doesn't get you much at this point, Mr. Wiley. It may have at the trial or a few years ago as new evidence, but at this point it will just look like grasping."

"I don't know if he did it, Detective."

The man sighed heavily as if he had just eaten an entire pizza. Wait, that was me.

"Have you talked to Terrelle?" he said. "Does he remember the guy?"

"He said he only remembered what happened that day because he saw the video."

"Show it to him. See if it jogs something. You'll probably have to work through his lawyer to get him to see evidence. My guess is, this changes nothing, and you'll only endanger your chances of the transplant if you go further."

"One more thing. You know anybody who can run a license plate for me?"

"Wiley, I think it's time to give this up. I'm sorry to say that."

I hung up. Abby stared at the screen watching the time code. "You have to take this to the police. His lawyer. The judge. Somebody."

"We just talked to the investigator who agrees with us. The police and prosecutor used this to convict Terrelle."

"Yeah, but there's no way they saw that. They didn't look closely enough. And if the police aren't going to help, go to the governor."

"Abby, Terrelle confessed. He waived all of his appeal rights."

"Then why are you showing me? You can't spike this."

"You think I plan to?" I got up and walked to the window and looked out on our backyard. The old swing set was back there. The one I had sunk in the ground with concrete. It had settled at a weird angle. Abby's handprints were out there along with Aiden's.

Swinging was one thing he could do and I remembered pushing his little back as gently as I could and the squeak and squawk of the metal on metal.

For some reason I thought of my father. Maybe because I remember sitting on the swing set behind our house in the dark. He would come home drunk or would get that way downstairs watching football on Sundays and come upstairs. I learned to hate Sundays. But then Sundays turned into Mondays and just about any day of the week was a good one to drink and things spiraled down, out of control.

Though I had tried to live my life differently, never taking Aiden to an NFL game or watching much more than the play-offs and Super Bowl because of my father's rabid and drunken obeisance, I saw the swing set as a monument to my own mistakes. I hadn't inflicted pain on my family with drugs or booze, but I had damaged my wife and children by crawling into something equally as damaging. My work. My ambition. Myself. And the swing set was the sullen reminder of all I had missed, all I had sacrificed so I could chase fame and wind up alone in a room typing a story. As my father before me, I had escaped pain, or at least numbed it for a while with gambling and my work, but I had ultimately lost what I was really looking for.

"What are you going to do?" Abby said.

I tried to think of something snappy, something humorous to say. I wanted to give her a steely look, like in one of those men's magazines, and assure her everything was going to be okay. But the only thing that came out when I opened my mouth was "I don't know."

Chapter 40

6 DAYS BEFORE EXECUTION

Abigail watched the clock tick toward nine, glancing back at the empty stalls and the one man still getting a haircut. She had wanted to quit the job after the scene at Tompkins's apartment, but something told her to hang in there. It wasn't bad having some extra money, of course, but working there gave her a creepy feeling. It was partly the section of town they were in but mostly the personnel.

Tompkins had returned in the afternoon and she gave him a stack of call slips, including one of her own at the bottom of the pile that said, "I need to talk to you after work." He had called her phone and made her go through the whole spiel: "It's a great day for a style at Mane Street Hair and Nails. This is Cheryl; how may I help you?"

341

"I saw your note. What's up?"

"I need to talk. After work, if that's okay."

"Sure thing. Lock up after everyone leaves and come on back."

Even the way he said it made her stomach turn, but she shoved that feeling down and helped Dexter sweep the hair and wipe down the stations.

"You don't have to do that," Dexter said.

"I know. I can finish up in here if you'd like."

The man looked at her like she had a third eye in her forehead. "You don't mind?"

"I'm fine. Go ahead."

Seizing an opportunity he acted like he'd never had, the man gathered his backpack and flew out the door. Abigail locked it behind him and turned off the flashing Open sign. Then she hit the Off button to cut the classic rock station that played more Lynyrd Skynyrd than any other station on the planet. She shut off the lights, took a deep breath, and knocked on the office door.

"Come," Tompkins said. He covered the phone when she entered and nodded toward the chair. The room was dimly lit by a banker's lamp with a green shade that cast the requisite glow.

"All right, I got somebody here. Maybe we can talk about it later."

He had the phone up loud, probably because most of his hearing was gone from the excessive noise levels at the club.

"What can I do you for?" he said when he was finished.

"I was just wondering about your offer. You said there might be more I could do for you than be a receptionist."

"Money getting a little tight, or are you just looking for some adventure?" He smiled and leaned back in the chair. "After what happened at the apartment, I figured you weren't interested."

"I am," she said.

"All right. The way it works is this. I give you something to do. You do it. You don't ask questions. I pay you. Everybody's happy."

"How often?"

"I don't know; how often do you want? Maybe once every couple of weeks?"

"And how much would it pay?"

"I'd start you out at a C-note. A hundred bucks. I'd just add it to your pay. At any point you don't like it, you let me know and you'll be done." A pause. "What's the matter?"

"I just . . . I mean, I need the money, but I'm worried about what happened to that girl who worked here before."

He rolled his eyes. "Diana? You got nothing to worry about. That was a fluke. And the guy who did it is buying the farm. That had nothing to do with this job."

She eased forward in the seat, pasting a look on her face that showed concern. "I saw a guy in the club the night we were there. I've seen him before but I don't know where."

"A guy? Honey, there are a lot of guys at the club who scare me, but I don't let that stand in the way of business, you know what I mean? What did he look like?"

She used her dad's description to paint a picture and watched Tompkins's face for any sign of recognition. She made a big deal about his blond hair and how long it was.

"Doesn't ring a bell. I'm not usually afraid of anybody with long blond hair, but maybe that's just me."

"He creeped me out. I thought you might know him."

"You see him again, point him out. In fact, why don't you come with me tonight? We'll get to the bottom of this mystery blond guy."

"I'd rather get started with the delivery, to be honest."

"Well, that happens when the need arises, on my schedule, not yours."

"I understand," she said.

He sat there looking at her as if she were some exquisitely wrapped present. "What else is going through your mind? Why would you stay late instead of heading home? There must be something."

The look was knowing, inviting, seductive, stomach-turning. "Come on, tell me."

Abigail winced. "I don't know. I just can't stop thinking about that girl. Can't get her out of my mind. Working here one day and the next she's gone, buried in some junkyard."

His phone buzzed and he looked at it. "You seriously need to stop living in the past. Are you her sister or something? Related to her? Trying to put some pieces together?" He hit a button on the phone. "Yeah? . . . All right, I'm almost on my way."

Abigail beat him to the door and walked out. She could feel his stare. "I'm not related. It's just one of those stories I can't get out of my head."

He moved past her toward the front door and she reached inside the top drawer of the reception desk and pulled out a weathered notebook. "I've been reading her last diary."

He stopped and turned. "Her what?"

She held it up so he could see it and he moved toward her.

"I'm thinking maybe the police would want to see it. Or maybe the lawyers for Conley's defense."

"Where'd you find it?"

She pulled it away from his grasp and glanced outside. "Have *you* been looking for it?"

"No, not me. Right after she died, there was somebody from her family who got in touch. Said they wanted it. We looked at her station but there was nothing in the drawers. Let me see." He held out his hand. "Listen, they offered a reward. You could probably still make a few bucks."

"Her family offered a reward? Her mother was this close to eating cat food." She took a step back. "What family member called?"

"I don't know. It was a man. A little while after her body turned up. And then a few days ago."

"A few days ago?"

"Yeah. I got a call from a guy who said they were still looking for that diary and could I help. I told him I didn't know about it. And now you come up with it."

"What if I told you it tells everything? About what you did. About how you wanted to frame Conley. How you used her to make your little deliveries."

"I'd say you're crazy because she never worked for me outside of . . . Look, who are you?" He moved toward her with a hand out. "Give me that diary. If you found it here, it's not your property."

Abigail moved around the reception desk toward the front door and Tompkins followed. She shoved it into her purse, knowing this wasn't Diana's diary but her own from middle school. Her dad had suggested they try to age a notebook they bought at Office Max, but Abigail had a better idea.

"Where did you find it?"

"You tell me," Abigail said. "Maybe your safe?"

His face scrunched in incredulity. "Now you're talking stupid. Why would I keep her diary in my safe when I could have gotten a reward?"

"You're right. You wouldn't have kept it; you'd have destroyed it. What are you hiding, Tompkins? Why did you kill Diana Wright?"

Tompkins lunged for her arm and grabbed it. He pulled her closer and grasped her purse. At that moment, glass shattered in front of them and a brick landed in a chair near the magazines. Tompkins covered his face and let go of her arm. Abigail moved behind the desk as a masked figure ran down the sidewalk.

"Hey!" Tompkins shouted. He unlocked the door and rushed outside, giving chase.

Abigail followed him out but quickly turned right and hurried away. Her car was parked on the next street and she was to rendezvous with her dad at a predetermined location. She glanced back a couple of times to make sure her boss wasn't following her, then broke into a dead run, her heart racing, a smile forming on her lips. Their plan had worked, at least somewhat. She would have to play back the audio she had captured with the microrecorder, but she felt sure this new information would be useful.

At the corner, she found her car parked right where her dad said it would be, but when she reached it, she heard footsteps behind her and a voice. She turned in time to see a figure before he pushed her to the ground. Metal glinted in the streetlight. She threw her hands up and screamed, and then the assailant was gone, along with her purse and everything in it. Her keys. The decoy diary. And her wallet and every bit of identification.

She struggled to her feet as the figure ran toward a streetlamp. He paused by a trash can, pulled something from the purse, then tossed the purse inside. The last thing Abigail saw of the man was the blond hair flowing down his back.

CHAPTER 41

I STOOD ACROSS THE STREET from a Subway restaurant, sweating like a pig, panting like a dog, and smelling a little like both, waiting for the police to pounce, worried about Abby, and wondering where she was. From my vantage point, the plan had worked. I had no idea how the conversation had gone, but when she brought that diary out, Tompkins tipped his hand. As I had assumed, he wanted to chase me down. I figured in his overweight condition he would lose steam and Abby would get away. I didn't know that he would have such fortitude, and he actually closed the gap between us. The closer he got, the heavier my heart beat, the shorter my own breath. He lumbered closer and his breath sounded like a freight train. The nine fifteen murder express was catching up.

Fortunately for me he pulled up lame, holding the back of one leg. I slowed to a trot. He pulled out his cell phone and I took off again, darting around a corner, ditching the ski mask I had picked up at Goodwill, and headed for the rendezvous point. When Abby didn't show in what I thought was plenty of time, I wanted to double back to her car, but the screaming siren and pulsing blue and red lights sent me into the shadows, then across the street to the Subway for something to drink.

Abby pulled up a few minutes later and showed me the cut strap and described the guy who had pushed her down and given her a nasty scrape where she hit the pavement. With her face and my eye, we made quite a pair. That razor could have been used on her instead of her purse strap, and that fact was chilling.

She drove from the area and I let the information sink in. The blond guy and Tompkins had to be working together. Unless they weren't. Unless the blond guy was watching the salon just as closely as I was. And the club as well.

Abby pulled into a deserted Mervyns parking lot. Looked like the place had been shuttered for a while. Perfect spot for a father-daughter chat.

She told me about the conversation she'd had with Tompkins, how she tried to lead him into giving more information about Diana, but that he wouldn't bite.

"He's a liar and a drug dealer and a cheat; there's no doubt about it," she said. "But some of his responses . . . I don't know. Either he's a really good actor, or he doesn't know anything about Diana."

"He's mixed up in it somehow," I said.

She played me the audio of the entire conversation, right up to the point of the brick crashing through the window. She reached to stop it, but I told her to let it go. She had kept recording as she ran, breathing heavily as she rushed to her car. I was glad I didn't have a recording of myself after the brick-throwing incident.

The audio was muffled and rattled inside Abby's shirt pocket, but at the point when she turned, a man's voice rang out. I grabbed the recorder to replay that section and hit the wrong button, taking us back to the beginning. Abby rolled her eyes and fast-forwarded to the spot and played the voice again.

"One more time," I said.

She played it again.

"He said, 'Abigail.' He knows your name."

"That's creepy," Abby said. "Tompkins doesn't know my real name, so how would the blond guy?"

"Maybe they know a lot more than we think. When you showed him the diary, he was all over it."

"Maybe there's something in there that incriminates him— stuff that was going on at the salon. But everybody who has worked there knows stuff is going on behind the scenes."

"Makes you wonder why he hasn't been caught at something." I ran a hand through my hair, thinking through the possible scenarios. "Maybe she threatened him. He got her to make some deliveries and then she got scared. Said she would go to the police."

"Which would make sense that he said she was a prude. She wouldn't keep working for him. But what about the blond guy?"

"Maybe Tompkins hired him to track her, to make sure she wasn't going to the police. He confronted her, and things went south."

"But why go to the trouble of framing Conley?" Abby said. "Before she was even murdered, he was out there."

"And why would he be hanging around after all these years? At the club and watching you tonight?"

Abby touched my shoulder, a look of horror on her face. "Dad, that car at our house. Maybe somebody planted a bug. Maybe they're listening."

I gave her a deadpan stare. "Maybe they'll check my mail and pay some of our hospital bills. This is not some grand conspiracy. This is a little criminal trying to cover his tracks." *I hope.*

"Murder is not a little crime and neither is framing an innocent man. That'll be two deaths to his account if Conley is executed."

She had a point there.

"What should we do?" she said.

"If we find this blond guy who knows your name, we have to deal with the sharp razor."

"If he would risk coming out in the open like that for what he thought was the diary, it has to have something in it. Dad, what if the police were involved? What if one of them found it and kept it?"

I rolled my eyes. "Their motivation?"

"Money. Maybe they're collecting it from Tompkins."

"You've been watching too many bad cop movies. These cops aren't pure by any stretch but—"

Abby snapped her fingers. "Wait, you said Diana was looking back at the street in the video. What if she'd seen the blond guy through the window? Maybe that spooked her and she ditched the diary before she left."

"Wanda said she was agitated that day and thought it could have been because of Conley. But if she saw the blond guy . . ."

"The surveillance camera clearly shows him there. And if she was scared, she might have left it."

"Why?"

"To speak from the grave. To show everybody who killed her."

"That's a pretty huge leap."

"It's what I would have done."

"Well, there's no diary there now."

"How do we know?"

"Abby, it's been—sorry, Abigail—it's been a lot of years. Anything she may have hidden in the drawers or some secret compartment is long gone."

"But think about it. If you were going to hide something incriminating, where would you put it? Right under the nose of the guy who could be hurt the most. Right?"

"No, I would have mailed it to my mother in a sealed envelope and marked it 'Open at the event of my untimely death.' But that's just me."

"Dad, the diary is in Tompkins's office. Stuffed in a filing cabinet, duct-taped under his desk, concealed in a bookshelf—I don't know, but it's there."

"Well, we shouldn't have too much trouble getting it now that we've broken the front window and there are police crawling all over."

"We need to go back."

Good idea. Let me find my ski mask. "That's crazy. We're not going near that place."

"Dad, we'll find something."

"Maybe so, but not tonight. Take me home."

"No, I'm going."

"Abby, you don't have to prove anything more. Let's go."

She smiled. For the first time I saw some kind of satisfaction in her eyes, like she had reached the top of a mountain she'd been climbing all her life.

CHAPTER 42

ABBY PARKED ON THE CORNER near where I had left her car earlier that night. Such an obedient girl. A mind of her own and instincts she was willing to follow. Just like her old man, unfortunately.

A couple of streetlights buzzed and flickered above us and the other side of the street was almost totally darkened, so we crossed over and walked toward the salon, navigating the broken sidewalk. A police car was parked in front and there was yellow tape across the broken window.

"Can they get fingerprints from a brick?" I said.

"You should have bought the matching gloves at Goodwill," Abby said.

"Let's get out of here."

"No, wait. I can report the purse theft and give them a description of the guy."

"If Tompkins is there, he'll have you arrested."

"Let him try. I'll say he was trying to rape me. The police will believe me."

There was no talking this girl out of something when she set her mind to it, but I tried again.

"Dad, this might be my last chance to get in there. He'll change the locks, tell me I can't work there anymore."

"Good. I don't want you going back."

She looked at me with that stare that most females in my life have given at some critical juncture. All my women, from my mother down to Abby, have been right about the big decisions they've made. It has taken me this long to realize that fact.

"Do you want me to hold your purse?" I said, the closest I could come to tacit approval of her plan.

"Doesn't go with your ski mask. Plus, I need it." She headed toward the salon, then turned and whispered, "Stay out of sight."

I slid to one knee behind an aging Pontiac whose bumper was held together with a wire hanger and prayer. The right brake light was a piece of red tape. I watched Abby navigate the street, her hair bouncing as she crossed onto the illumined sidewalk. She knocked at the front and waited, waving. The police officer exited, ushering her inside. The front light was on, so I could see them kibbutzing, Abby gesturing, leaning forward and pointing to her forehead, holding out her purse. I couldn't see Tompkins, but I could see his shadow moving and the officer with folded arms.

I was so intent on watching the scene that I didn't hear the footsteps behind me. I should have been alerted by the smell.

"Excuse me, sir," a man said in a high-pitched rattle and rasp. My eyes had adjusted to the moonlight and general haze of the city, and I turned and saw his salt-and-pepper beard stained with something black or red. He wore layers of clothes, too much for the evening chill. His shoes, if you could even call them that, looked only a little better than the Pontiac's rear end. I was just glad it wasn't the blond guy with the razor.

"Excuse me, sir," he said again.

I have never, ever had anything good happen to me after someone said those three words. Usually I either wind up walking away and feeling guilty or giving the person some money and feeling equally as guilty for supplying the habit.

"Just back up and get out of here," I said firmly and quietly.

He put up his hands in a defensive posture. "Don't mean no harm. Don't mean no harm. Just admirin' that nice little lady you have with you. Must be nice havin' a hot young thing like that." He gave a phlegmy laugh without covering his mouth.

"You need to move on, friend," I said in my most authoritative voice.

He nodded, then glanced at the salon. I wanted to look back but my fear kept my eyes on him, thinking he might make a move.

"Wonder what's going on," he said as if he were wearing headphones with Coldplay turned up as loud as it could go. "Don't look good, what's going on over there. *Poe*-leese and all that. Don't look good at all."

"Would you keep it down?" I said.

"Sure thing, sure thing. Gotta be movin' on anyway. You wouldn't happen to have some spare change, would you, sir? Just some spare change is all I'm looking for."

I shoved a hand into my pocket and looked back quickly. Abby was still inside. If I had a twenty-dollar bill right then, I would have considered it an investment just to get the guy to shut up and leave. But about all I had was loose change from the soda at Subway.

"This is all I have; now please, be quiet and leave me alone, okay?"

He cradled the change in his grimy hands and sneered. Seriously the guy sneered at my offering like I had asked him to fish for pennies in elephant dung. On a parade route.

"Man, if this is all you got, you better keep it," he muttered. Then, raising his voice, he said, "And last I checked this was a free country and a man could stand anywhere he wanted."

"Look, that's my daughter over there. She has some cash in her purse. If you move on down the street, I promise you . . ." The words struck a chord somewhere.

"You promise me what?" he shouted, angry now. Teeth bared. Eyes bulging.

"You just made me think of something." I looked up at him, then stood. He stepped back, fearful, like a child who has pulled the tail of a rabid dog. His watery eyes betrayed him for who he was, just another scared, addicted man on the street trying to get money from another addicted man.

"Thank you," I said, patting him on the shoulder. The touch sparked something inside him. How many times had he been touched as an adult? How many people had walked to the other side of the street just to get away from the sight and smell or to avoid his verbal ramblings?

"Thank you," I repeated, and I meant it.

"Well, if I helped you so much, why don't you just give me a fiver and call it even?"

"Wait down at the corner," I said. I couldn't believe I was saying it but there it was. "When my daughter comes out, I'll bring you a fiver. Go now and I'll make it a ten."

"A ten would be good. That would do the trick."

"Then go."

"You promise? You promise?"

"Cross my heart," I said. Yeah, it was cheesy, and I even crossed it like some little kid about to double- or triple-dog dare him to stick his tongue to a cold flagpole. That was the scene. That was my desperation.

He squinted and pointed a grimy finger toward me. "You'd better give it to me. You promised."

"I'm not giving you anything unless you move now, you hear me?"

He shuffled away, muttering and gesturing. I crouched again, then moved to my right to see inside. Abby was nowhere in sight, but the officer and Tompkins were standing by the front desk in an animated conversation.

"You better bring it to me!" the drunk shouted from halfway down the block.

The officer turned and stared out the window at the man, then went back to his conversation. The drunk staggered toward the corner obediently, shaking and muttering. Cars passed on the street and he waved at them, then back at me, saying something that ended with "You promised!"

I told you nothing good ever comes of "Excuse me, sir." But I had just proved my postulate wrong. Something good had come of it.

Abby appeared from the back of the salon and Tompkins turned his attention to her. The officer moved closer as if to protect her. She pointed toward the street, the window, then held up her hands. She showed the officer her purse and forehead. I was sure he would ask her to fill out a report of some kind but in a few minutes she came out of the salon and headed toward the car, not even looking at me.

I ran to the car and hopped in as Abby started it. "Do you have a ten-dollar bill?"

She looked at me like I had just said I had decided to become a Benedictine monk.

"I need it for that guy down there. He helped me understand something."

"I've got something better than that," she said. She pulled a moldy, wet notebook from her purse and held it up. "I found it."

My jaw dropped. She pulled away. The drunk guy a block away ran after us, whooping and yelling, waving his arms, leaving one shoe behind. "You promised!"

A half block away I told her to stop. "You have any cash?"

She handed me a twenty and I told her to back up. I held it up, showing it to the man, then put it under the windshield wiper of a parked car.

"That's the trick!" the man yelled, running toward me now. "I knew you'd come through for me."

I jumped back into the car and Abby drove away.

CHAPTER 43

I CRADLED THE NOTEBOOK like some holy artifact lost for centuries. A piece of Diana's cross, as it were. I didn't want to open it but couldn't help leafing through it in the dark as we drove home, the curled pages rattling with age, giving off a musty smell.

"How did you . . . ? Where . . . ?"

Abby kept her eyes on the road but reached over and took the notebook from me and pulled it back into her lap. "I explained about the purse snatching and gave a description of the guy who slashed it. I told him I thought Tompkins and the guy knew each other, but he denied it. Said I had made the whole thing up."

"What did the officer say?"

"He said I should file a report. I told him I would. I looked straight at Tompkins and said the guy left my wallet and cell phone but took a notebook."

"How did Tompkins react?"

She shrugged. "Didn't seem to faze him. I couldn't read any fear, but who knows. Anyway, I needed to get alone and think, so I told them I needed to use the restroom. I went back and locked the door and just sat and closed my eyes."

I do that a lot, too, but I didn't want to say that right then.

"I tried to put myself in Diana's shoes. Scared. Thinking someone might be trying to hurt her. Keeping some kind of secret. Being paranoid about being paranoid. Knowing I'd recorded stuff in a notebook that I wasn't supposed to. And then I thought about my own diary. She didn't want to leave it for someone else to find; she wanted to hide it to come back for later. Someplace nobody would look."

"She taped it inside the back of the toilet?"

She rolled her eyes. "No. It wasn't something she planned. It must have just happened. She saw the blond guy across the street. She got scared. She hid it."

"Where?"

"The bathroom floor is built up a bit. The ceiling in that building is low anyway and with the floor raised, you get that closed-in feeling. I looked at the ceiling tiles—they're all water stained and some are broken and falling apart. But the tile just above the toilet was popped up. And I thought, if I was scared, I might come in there and hide what I treasure most. So I stood on the toilet and pushed the tile up and reached in."

"You should never reach into dark places."

"Believe me, I didn't want to. At first I just felt cobwebs and water. But when I moved to the other side, I brushed against it."

"Have you read anything?"

"Enough to know it's hers. A lot of it is ruined by the water damage. I knew I had to get out of there. When I came out, the cop and Tompkins were talking about some drunk across the street."

"He was hitting me up for money. He helped me."

She gave me a quick glance, the cousin to the quizzical stare that shows up when you're driving.

"You know how drunks will seek you out and ask you for stuff? Follow you until they get what they want? It struck me, that was exactly the opposite of what happened in the video. The blond guy followed Terrelle. He was the initiator."

"You think he put Terrelle up to chasing Diana?"

"I'm sure of it. Now maybe that journal will tell us why."

My cell buzzed. It was Ellen. But when I answered, it wasn't her voice.

"Mr. Wiley, it's nice to finally meet you."

A thick German accent. Noise in the background—perhaps the ding of an elevator? Someone speaking through an intercom?

"Who is this?"

"I am the man who knows too much about your daughter's teenage crush on . . . what is the name? Tommy?"

"Who is it, Dad?" Abigail said.

I covered the phone, wondering if I should tell Abby he had Ellen's phone. "Our friend who took the bait. You had a crush on Tommy Spence?"

"The blond guy?" she whispered, slowing down and pulling to the side of the road.

I nodded and mouthed, "Go toward the hospital."

"This is all very interesting," the man said. "Your daughter gets an A for penmanship. But this is not what you purported to have."

Some people clam up when they're scared. Others cry. For me, humor and sarcasm take over. "Listen, Dieter—it's okay if I call you Dieter, isn't it? You probably don't want to give me your real name. I can make it Klaus or Wilhelm, if you'd like."

"I prefer Adolf."

Menace and a sense of humor. Perfect.

"Good, Adolf. First of all, I don't know how you can say we've purported to have anything unless you have a bug inside the salon. Or maybe you're working with Tompkins. Did he talk to you?"

"Is that what you think?" There was derision in his voice.

I hate derision in the voice of a bad guy. Especially one who has my wife's cell phone and pushed my daughter to the ground.

"I'm new to this, Helmut. I'm just trying to tell a story of a guy who got framed for something he didn't do."

"You have no idea what you're doing." He said it with a bit of pity. "You have no idea the danger you're putting yourself and your family in."

"Sounds like a threat, Jurgen. How did you get my wife's cell phone?"

"I sliced your daughter's purse quite easily. I could have sliced her face. You're a smart man. You know when you're in too deep."

"Illumine me, Fritz. What am I into?"

"Your son's condition is very fragile. If you don't drop this, he won't make it to the transplant. And your wife will pay the consequences as well."

I thought about telling him we had the real diary. I thought about threatening him with a buzz cut at the salon. I thought about rolling down my window and throwing up because that's what my stomach told me to do. But I shut up instead.

"This is your final warning," he continued. "You follow this trail any farther and your life will get even more bleak than it already is. Your debts have just increased."

This guy knew a lot more than I wanted him to. I steeled myself to that fact as Abby neared the hospital.

"Thanks for caring about us, Sigmund. Really appreciate that. I do have to say you really looked photogenic on the surveillance video with Terrelle. Don't think the police or Terrelle's defense noticed you all those years ago. Your hair was a little shorter, but I couldn't mistake the cocky walk. Do you use help on your color now? Or maybe extensions?"

I could feel his anger seething through the phone, which was a good thing. I wanted him to show emotion.

"You are a fool, Wiley."

I wanted to be all hard-nosed and say something like "You and Tompkins will pay for what you did to Diana, I guarantee you," but I had run out of courage, valor, and German first names.

The call dropped and Abby let me out at the emergency room entrance. I looked around the lobby, down hallways and corridors, then rushed to the elevator and up to the eighth floor. Ellen wasn't in the waiting room. I hurried to Aiden's room, my heart beating wildly. My breath was even more labored now than running away from my window-smashing episode.

She wasn't by Aiden's side. His room was darkened, monitors and machines assembled, working overtime to keep him alive. His face was gray ash, lifeless and sallow. I put my hand on his chest, lightly, just enough to feel it moving. Maybe I breathed a prayer. Maybe the touch was my prayer. He didn't stir and I had turned to head out when something caught my eye. On the bed next to Aiden's hand was Ellen's cell phone.

CHAPTER 44

THOUGH I DIDN'T WANT TO TELL ELLEN, I felt compelled to give her the information about her cell phone and the man who had taken it. She turned white when she heard where I had found it. She tried to retrace her steps to figure out if she had seen him, how he had taken it. The thoughts tripped her up and I assured her the man wanted to keep us quiet and wouldn't make contact again. "He's like the big, bad wolf, huffing and puffing and threatening to blow our house down."

"Remember how that story ended," Ellen said. "He ate two of the pigs."

Bad analogy.

She showed me a glazed look, her words coming from some deep pool. "That means you're onto something. Someone's scared about what you're doing."

"I don't know what it means, but I can't stop turning over rocks now."

She nodded and gave me a trembling hug.

From a purely literary standpoint, this was no diary of Anne Frank. From a spelling standpoint, Diana got a C at best. She didn't reveal much about her inner life and struggles; I didn't discover what made her the person she was, her hopes and fears and losses. Her entries were simply observations and laundry lists of things she'd done, things she needed to do, and how much certain customers ticked her off. But there were flashes of revelation, lightning strikes of creativity where she was able to expose more than just the surface.

Of course, she had not meant for anyone else to see these words, and since much of it was incomprehensible because of the moldy pages and water stains that had caused the ink to run and pages to stick together, she had nothing to fear. But there were snippets from her life that provided insight into her elation and fear.

March 4

Saw CT today. Had the day off from the salon and we spent some uninterupted time together. Things are pergressing, but he says we still need to keep everything a secret. I can't wait for the day when we don't have to hide our love. Some day that will happen and I look forward to the freedom of it.

He says [unintelligible for several lines]. I am just trying to hang onto my heart until this can all work out. Part of me feels really bad about all of this and when it comes into the light it will be talked about a lot. I know it's wrong, but I can't help it.

Just reading it made me feel sick, which was happening a lot lately. The stress mixed with the uncertainty and all of the relational/emotional/physical/financial clouds over my own life made me want to run to Walgreens every other hour for something that would calm my stomach, help me sleep, or both. Maybe I could invent MaaQuil, the new upset stomach/sleep aid.

The first thing Abby did was take the diary to the nearest Kinko's to copy every page we could even remotely read. Unfortunately, there was a prohibitive cost for that, so a quick call to Oleta gave us use of the aged copier at her office. Abby took it there, not telling Oleta what we had found, fearing that might give her false hope.

Over the next few days I worked Diana's words into a separate section of the book, putting the pieces I understood together, knowing there was much more I didn't understand.

Abby and I were particularly interested in the dates circled in her planner. Unfortunately, some of those diary entries had been destroyed by the water and aging process. However, we did find the earliest date that was circled.

January 22

Freelance opurtunity this afternoon. Very exciting. I was aproached after work Monday. No idea what or who but it could mean a couple hundred extra each month. Supposed to be a secret, I guess. I just have to be avaleable and they pay. I can handle that. Maybe Mom and I can get a new TV.

Abby and I went back and forth on what to do with our find. I wanted to show the diary to Mrs. Wright and get her reactions, but Abby thought Diana's mother would be brokenhearted by seeing her daughter's scrawl. If she hadn't touched Diana's room after all this time, why would she want to read her last words, even if it did help find the real killer?

The police were another matter. It was clear they didn't want to be bothered with the facts; they already had their man and were going to put this all behind them with Terrelle's death. I figured Detective Chandler would dismiss the information outright. Abby thought it was worth one more shot.

All of our mental gymnastics were futile until we answered the question of the mysterious blond man.

The next afternoon at a local Starbucks, away from any possible bugs in our house (though I had checked the phones), Abby and I talked freely about what we knew.

"The freelance has to involve Tompkins, right?" she said.

I pulled up the section I had typed into my manuscript, an entry from early February that said, *I don't have any contract, it's all on a handshake, but I was handed $500 for January.*

"Nice handshake," Abby said. "What would she have done for five hundred dollars?"

"Maybe she painted somebody's house." That was from an old joke that went right over Abby's head.

"Seriously, Dad, this has to be her delivering drugs or doing something worse for Tompkins. She writes his initials all over the place. I just can't understand how she could fall for a guy like that."

"A little green will make a plump old guy look a lot more

appealing. And who knows, maybe she got strung out on something and he held it over her."

There was one section of the diary we didn't talk much about, one I wanted to hide from Abby. I'm not a prude when it comes to sex, but there are some things you don't want your daughter to see, even though I assume if she has a boyfriend . . . Well, never mind.

I don't read romance novels, but it appeared Diana had. Turgid, misspelled prose of things she and Tompkins had done and where they had done them and details of the quick seduction. How she had never planned to do anything like this, especially with someone like him. How surprised her mother would be if she found out. How surprised everyone was going to be. Details included specifics about the existence of a tattoo in a curious spot on her lover. This revelation made me want to join the same gym as Tompkins and catch him in the locker room, but even if I did find the tattoo, it wouldn't mean that Tompkins had killed her, just add to the mounting evidence.

Of course all of these thoughts took away from the writing of Terrelle's story, but as I saw it, this *was* his story. I felt I had stumbled onto the B side of a hit record from the past, and both songs tied the sickening melodies together and could lead to a resolution that none of us had expected.

Most troubling were the last few entries. Diana questioned her involvement with CT and there was remorse mixed with confusion, doubt, and outright fear. *I think I was followed last night after work. I can't understand why this is happening.*

In another entry she wrote, *That funny feeling is back this morning. I'm seeing CT tomorrow and am struggling with whether to talk to him about my fears.*

Against Abby's judgment, which I weighed heavily, I decided to stop at Mrs. Wright's house for another heart-to-heart. Her mangy mutt held me at the front door until she unlocked it and spoke through the small crack.

"Where's the Piggly Wiggly bag?" she said.

"I'm shopping at Kroger these days. Can I come in and ask a couple more questions?"

She opened the door just enough and put one of her misshapen legs in front of the dog. I entered and she turned the volume down on the dusty TV.

"Did Diana buy that for you?" I said, sitting on the worn couch.

She nodded and settled into her faux leather chair with a few creaks, mostly from the chair. "One of the last things she did. Every time I turn it on, I think of her."

What a sad legacy.

"Where did she get the money?"

She shrugged. "I didn't ask. She just seemed so happy to be able to give it to me. To buy it for *us*."

I sat forward on the couch, noticing the hair remnants of the dog and its pungent smell. I realized as he curled up beside me that I was an intruder, though he seemed to tolerate me a bit more than the first time. "In the last few months of her life, did you notice any change in Diana?"

"What kind of change?"

"Anything. Was she more happy? Sad? Scared? Upset?"

She ran her tongue over her lower dentures and stared at the wall. "In those last months, she seemed like she was happier. Preoccupied with something, but she'd never talk about it."

"Did you suspect she was seeing someone?"

"It crossed my mind. I even asked her if there was someone

and she laughed at me. But it was the kind of laugh that made me think I'd hit something. We'll never know, will we? And it doesn't matter anyway because Conley confessed."

"Why didn't you tell me this before?"

"You never asked. And I was intimidated by you, after seeing you on TV."

Funny, she did not act the least bit intimidated. I let it slide. "Who do you think it might have been?"

"I assumed, because she never said anything, that it was Curtis from the salon. She knew I didn't trust him and would have wanted to hide that from me."

"Did you ever think he might have been involved in her death?"

"It crossed my mind when she disappeared, but when they found her and all the evidence against Conley, I knew Curtis didn't do it. Plus, I told you he was kind to me."

I paused long enough for her to look at me. "We found Diana's diary. The journal she kept."

"I know. Your daughter took them from the closet."

"No, not those. The last one she was working on. She'd hidden it."

She closed her eyes. "Don't you do this. Don't bring up all that old stuff. It's almost over, and here you come bringing up everything I've tried to forget."

"Mrs. Wright, your daughter was murdered. She didn't deserve that. Her words speak from her grave. I think there's a lot we don't know."

"What does she say?"

"Lots of things. But we're pretty sure it shows the killer wasn't Terrelle."

"Then why did he confess?"

"Because he wants to help my son. He sees his execution as something that's going to happen no matter what, so if good can come from it, so be it. But if he didn't do it, I want to help him."

"What kind of father are you if this cuts off your chances for your son to get a new heart?"

I stared at her. "You think I haven't wrestled with that? I go back and forth every three minutes—leave it alone, let my son live, shut up. But what kind of human being would I be if I let an innocent man die?"

She chewed on that for a moment. I chewed on it as well. I remember a book Ellen left by her bed, written by a reporter who had been an atheist and turned to Christianity. He asserted that Jesus was the only person in history who didn't deserve to die but did it willingly. I read the whole thing. It wasn't enough to make me jump off the deep end of the faith pool, but right then it kind of hit me hard, with Mrs. Wright's words hanging in the air.

"Are you saying I let my daughter down all those years ago?" she said.

"You didn't let her down. You didn't know."

"I should have known. If what you're saying is true, I should have been able to pick up the signals. What does she say in the journal?"

Where do I start? Certainly not the romance material. "She talked about the love she had found and how excited she was about the future. She talked about her freelance work and making money on the side. That must have been where she got the money for the TV. And then things turned pretty dark."

"What do you mean?"

"We can't say for sure what happened—"

"We?"

"My daughter, Abby, and me."

"You're the only ones who have seen it?"

"So far, yes."

"Your daughter is a nice girl. I'm surprised she came from you."

"Her mother's side of the gene pool is better than mine."

She smiled, at least as much as Helen Wright could smile under the circumstances.

"From what we can piece together," I continued, "she had a relationship with Tompkins that somehow went south. One entry talks about a 'funny feeling' she had in the morning and telling him about it. Abby is not with me on this, but I wonder if there's a chance she thought she was pregnant."

Helen put her head back on the cracked cushion and let out a painful yelp, then covered her face with her hands. "Oh, for heaven's sake, why do you tell me this? Why do you want to rip my heart out?"

The dog jumped into her lap, which helped calm her. She put her hand on the dog's head and held him to her chest.

"I checked the autopsy results. There was no pregnancy. The blood test showed that. But the important thing is she thought she was."

"Why is that important?"

"If the killer knew this, that Diana thought she was pregnant, perhaps he encouraged her to get an abortion, and—"

"She would never have done that. It's hard enough for me to imagine her pregnant, but there's no way she would have done that. She knew that would have killed me."

"I understand. But let's say she resisted and there was pressure put on her, perhaps that explains part of her fear. If she had become involved in some of Tompkins's questionable side business endeavors, she may have gotten in too deep. Things came to a head and someone was hired to take her life."

"Hired?"

"Tompkins had an alibi for every moment of the day she was killed. That seems suspicious for a guy who spends a lot of time alone. Plus, there's evidence of a man who may have followed Diana."

She thought about that for a minute. "The night before she went missing, she looked out the window a lot. Several times."

"How do you remember that?"

"Because we were watching *Jeopardy!* and she kept getting up at the worst moments. I told her to sit down and relax and she would; then she'd get back up and check again, even right when they were about to give the final question."

"She knew something was going on. She knew she was in trouble."

The dog's mangy ears went up and his body went rigid. He climbed up Helen's front and looked over her shoulder and growled.

Helen struggled to stand and handed the dog to me.

"Where you headed?" I said.

"We need to call the police."

I looked at the front door and thought I saw a shadow moving. "Wait, I've got my cell phone."

I heard something click and looked up at a .38, cocked and loaded.

"You go ahead and call the police. I'm ready for Tompkins."

I put the dog on the ground and he ran to the front door, barking and sniffing. Just as quickly he darted to the back of the house, yipping, the fur on the back of his neck standing on end. Murrow had never done that. Maybe there's something to this dog idea.

Helen turned, holding the gun out like she was ready for a fight with a rival gang of grandmothers. You've heard of the Bloods and Crips. She was with the Aarps. I had to admire the woman, and part of me wanted to stay with her because she made me feel safe, but I pulled the curtain and looked out a side window. Nothing. No Wiener schnitzel salesman with blond hair.

"If you're right, Mr. Wiley, there are going to be some people who are really unhappy you're telling this story. I'm not saying I agree with you. I still think Conley is guilty. But if you turn up dead at the side of the road or that pretty daughter of yours winds up missing, I want to be prepared."

What a comforting thought.

"As a matter of fact, you'd better take this. You're going to need it. I got another one in my nightstand."

You've heard of a pistol-packin' mama. Helen was the poster child. I thought for a moment about the implications, but only for a moment before I pocketed it.

Helen looked out the window and whispered, "What are you going to do now? The execution is Tuesday."

"I'll think of something," I said, unsure how to answer.

I drove home, looking in my rearview and side mirrors constantly, waiting for someone to cut me off or pull alongside with an Uzi. Though nothing happened, the feeling was there, and I have learned to trust that feeling and not push it down, no matter how far-fetched it may seem.

Abby's car wasn't in the driveway, but the front door had been left ajar. As soon as I walked in, I knew something was wrong. Call it my reporter's instinct if you'd like, but I immediately deduced that the stuff strewn all over the house was a clue. I went straight to my writing cave and just as I suspected, my laptop and jump drive were gone. So was the pile of pages by my printer. I hurried to Abby's room. Nancy Drew books and the rest of her bookshelves were trashed. The diary was missing. Ellen kept a small safe in her room and that's where we had stashed the copy. The bedroom was darkened and unlived in, almost a ghost town of forgotten memories. The safe hadn't been opened and rifled through; it was just gone.

I dialed Ellen quickly and she picked up. There was fear in her voice, a strain I could hear, and I asked her what was wrong.

"Oh, you know, just the usual. More tests. More prep. Trying to decide if his heart will hold out. What's new with you?"

"I need you to do something for me on your laptop."

"Seriously? Tru, right now I don't think I can even find my laptop."

"It's okay; I understand." I said it compassionately, my heart racing, wanting to know the information, but also knowing she was not the one to give it.

"What do you need?"

"I'll call Abby."

"Tru, Abigail is here. Tell me what you need. I have my laptop open."

I gave her the website and my password and asked her to open my mail. She logged in successfully and asked what to look for.

"Click the in-box and tell me what you see."

"There's nothing here, Tru. The in-box is empty. In fact, There's no mail at all."

Other than the few pages I had given to Terrelle, I'd lost everything. My computer, all the files, my hard copy, the surveillance video, everything but the Piggly Wiggly bag. This guy had taken the last of the Who-hash and roast beast.

You might think this was the point at which a guy like me gives up. You would be wrong. This is the point at which a guy like me gets angry. And an angry reporter is not a good thing.

CHAPTER 45

I PROBABLY SHOULD have called the police. I probably should have had them come over and catalog everything that had been stolen. I probably should have gone to a Gamblers Anonymous meeting a long time ago or gotten counseling about my bad childhood and alcoholic father. But I didn't do any of that.

Instead, with my trusty sidearm provided by the geriatric Helen Wright, I headed to the ground zero of evil: Tompkins's apartment. I had prepared my speech and was fully ready to pull my gun, or at least hold it out so he could admire it, and make threatening pronouncements about what would happen if he didn't hand over my files. I also expected him to wither into a mass of emotion and spill the facts about Diana and how sorry he was to have taken her life and swear that he would do anything to undo that wrong.

It was just after dusk and the orange glow of the sunset was in full bloom over the horizon. Of course I couldn't see the horizon for all the buildings and trees, but I could feel the glow in my bones.

I looked for a doorbell but the front door was unlocked. I took the stairwell to the third floor and stepped into a long, dimly lit hallway.

I chose my steps carefully to cut down on the creaking floorboards, but there's only so much a man can do. I stopped after a particularly loud creak and listened, hoping some madman with a chain saw wouldn't jump me from behind. All I heard was the sound of weird music.

As I got closer, I realized it wasn't just music, but also sound effects from what had to be one of Tompkins's videos made on the second floor. The door was open a few inches and I knocked, though I knew no one would hear me over the pulsing bass and the staccato shouts that were as fake as the hardwood floors in the front room.

I pushed the door closed behind me and said, "Hello?"

The sound overwhelmed my voice and I inched toward the living room. I fully expected to find Tompkins watching with a friend or two or maybe to see him walk from the kitchen in his robe.

The shades were drawn, no lights on except for the fifty-two-inch Sony. But I wasn't looking at the screen. I was looking at the floor in front of it, where the body of Tompkins lay in an expanding pool of blood. Fresh blood.

I backed to the door, wanting to run, knowing I couldn't, and knowing that life was about to get even more complicated.

CHAPTER 46

Terrelle Conley was calm and collected, as much as any man can be who is about to lose his life. The prison staff had done their job well of prepping him. He walked with an IV bag behind him and looked more like an out-of-place patient than an inmate. It was not an actual breaking of the rules to let me speak with him, but the warden didn't want me upsetting his model prisoner in his last hours.

"They say you had your last meal early," I said, trying to break the ice of my own heart. Trying to keep the emotion and fear in check. The kind of fear that comes with sand nearly gone from the hourglass and every one of my choices a dead end for someone.

He smiled. "Yeah, can't have anything right before the surgery,

379

so they brought it yesterday. Fried shrimp and catfish. Hush puppies. Not as good as my mother's, but it was all right. Your boy might have high cholesterol for a couple of days, but he'll get over it." He laughed like a condemned man, short and incomplete. "I heard you spent some time with the police over that salon owner."

"Yeah, it's been a long couple days."

"They know who did it?"

"I do, but they don't. They say it could have been any of a hundred people with what they found in the building. The police think it was a drug deal gone bad. Or it could have been about his video empire. Somebody who decided they didn't want to be a movie star after all."

"That's not your theory."

"No. But now the evidence I had is gone. Which I think is the point. Get everything out of the way."

"Whoever it was did a good job."

"Yeah, unfortunately for you."

"I appreciate all you did," Terrelle said. "I know you tried hard and that's all a man can ask. Don't beat yourself up for how this whole thing came out. You did more than anybody."

His words brought relief. But they also brought torment that I was out of options. I asked him again about that day with Diana, trying to jog any memory of the blond man, but Terrelle came up empty. His first few pages of the book would be turned over to Oleta after the "procedure." At least I had that.

"You're still going to be here this evening, right?" Terrelle said, a bit of pleading in his voice.

"I promised I would be," I said.

"I knew I could count on you. Oleta will appreciate having you there—and the reverend. I can feel the prayers, you know?"

"What do you mean?"

"The prayers from all the people who care. Prayers to help me be strong and get through this. Prayers for your son."

I couldn't believe a guy facing death would have the ability to get outside of himself to that degree, but that was Terrelle. He wasn't bitter. He wasn't angry. He was at peace.

The guard looked at the time and moved forward a step.

I thanked Terrelle and promised I would be back with Oleta that night.

"I know you will. And God's people will watch over her and my kids. Thanks again for what you've done with the book, even though it's gone. I've been praying you'll get it back."

"I still have it up here," I said. "They can't steal that. I feel bad you have to pay for this crime."

"Tomorrow they're going to write that I'm dead. That my life was taken. Don't believe it. I'll be more alive than I've ever been. I'll just go to sleep here and wake up on the shores of glory."

"How can you be so sure, Terrelle?"

"Because it's like I said—I'm not going to heaven because I've been good. It's because God has been good to me. Kind and merciful and full of grace. He's true to his word every time. If God says he'll do something, he does it. I put my faith fully in what he said about how to get to him. That's how I can go through this with my head up."

The guard told him it was past time to go and Terrelle said one more good-bye. "See you tonight."

I met briefly with Dr. Granger, who was ready for the transplant that evening. Aiden had been on artificial life support for fourteen days. It was touch and go; his condition slipped and slid down that ventricular chasm, and Ellen was right there. I was not, of course, but since he was in a coma, I felt okay about it.

I had managed one more visit to the hospital the night before to sit beside Aiden's bed and hold his hand. It was just him and me and the sounds of time ticking. I felt regret and shame for not being there for him. I felt hope for the future, but I wasn't sure why.

"One way or another we're going to get you out of here," I whispered. "The doctor's going to fix that bum ticker. You'll be chasing nurses down the hallway."

I almost saw a smile on his lips. Almost.

After the prison meeting, I joined Abby for a late lunch, though food was the last thing I wanted. I sat in the parking lot and waited for her car to pull in. One of those north-Florida storms was brewing and I was glad I had brought a jacket so I could be chivalrous to my only daughter and protect her from the malicious raindrops.

My phone buzzed and the number was restricted. I expected to hear a German accent but my reporter's intuition was way off. Instead of bratwurst, I smelled gumbo coming through the line.

"Truman, good to hear your voice again. I understand today is a big day for you and your family."

"Yeah, thanks for caring. Did you send flowers?"

"I was thinking about that. Seriously. Give me the address. Well, I actually already know the address, so don't bother."

Such a humorous fellow.

"I believe we had an agreement, Truman. And the time period for that agreement is about at its end."

"You have impeccable timing, Mickey."

"Yes, I've been told that. Have you made progress in the fund department?"

"Oh yeah, I've been racking up some deep debt with the hospital, with specialists, with my mortgage company . . . you'll need to get in line."

"And what about this book? That should net you some kind of advance, correct?"

"If I had a book left, it would, but it was stolen. You wouldn't know anything about that, would you?"

"That makes a lot of sense. Take away the very thing that will allow a client to pay his debt. You're becoming conspiratorial in your old age."

"I get that way when people drop dead of gunshot wounds."

"Well, how you come up with the money is none of my concern. I don't care if you rob a bank or get an inheritance."

"You can forget the inheritance."

"As I said, not my concern. But you do understand that we will collect."

Abby rattled up beside me and parked.

"And how will that work out?" I said. "Your goons come back with a crowbar?"

"I wish it didn't have to end this way, Truman. Such a tragic legacy for your family."

"Well, as they say, you make your bed, you lie in it. Do what you have to do, Mickey, and I'll do what I have to do. I'll be at the prison tonight. You're welcome to join me."

He laughed and there was pity in it. "I'm sorry it has to be this way, my friend. You've hit your deadline."

I hung up and got out to give Abby a hug. I tried to hide my feelings but she had been around me enough in the past few weeks to recognize the inner turmoil. In spite of everything going on, I was grateful to have reconnected with her. She'd grown a lot in that time. Or maybe she was the same. Maybe I'd grown to love her for who she was.

I gave her my coat and held it over her head as we ran to the door.

"We don't have to eat," she said. "I don't much feel like it anyway."

"Let's at least sit down and have water," I said.

We were seated in a restaurant we couldn't afford, around people who had no idea what was happening, people living life with no gravely ill children or condemned friends. Nice people with no gambling problems. Marriages intact. Mortgages current. They'd never visited death row.

Abby asked about my meeting with Terrelle and I told her. The server, a young man with a prickly beard and blue eyes, focused on Abby and paid no attention to me. I hate prickly beards and blue eyes. But our order of two waters with lemons didn't seem to faze him, so I can't complain.

Abby withdrew the latest *People* magazine from her purse and leafed through it as we talked. An article had just been published about the execution and the role the governor had played. It was a new day in medical ethics and a majority in the public-opinion-poll-saturated society approved this procedure for the condemned.

She slid the article around so I could see. There were few words and pictures galore, as if the American public couldn't live without a colored collage that illustrated every jot and tittle. Just like television news, in a way. Leaning on the horrific video, the debris of a plane crash, a bull goring people on its way down the streets of Spain.

Abby said something about going back to the hospital with Ellen when Aiden went into surgery.

"You'll drive Oleta up afterward, right?" she said.

"Yeah, that's the plan. . . ."

I was stuck on something in the photographs. A blur of images sifting through the cerebral cortex, slipping through one by one, face by face. Something didn't fit. A stray image that wasn't supposed to be there. I'd found Waldo but didn't know what to do with him. Initials. Payment. Puzzle pieces that looked like they went in the left upper corner suddenly came together in the opposite corner—not fitting all the way, but I had found all of the edge pieces and the rest were right there in front of me.

"Dad, you're going to be okay tonight?" She said it with concern, compassion, and a generous measure of love. It was like water to my thirsty soul. But I couldn't enjoy the feeling because the world was suddenly spinning and dominoes were falling in my brain. Consequences of actions long ago.

I glanced at my watch. "Yeah. I'm going to be all right. We're all going to be all right." I looked into her eyes. "Honey, I'm sorry about this but I have to go."

"What? I came all the way—"

"Trust me, Abigail."

I took the *People* magazine with me.

I left a message on Ellen's cell phone, then called the nurses' station and they looked for her. My phone buzzed.

"I was on the phone with Abigail," Ellen said. "She's worried about you, Tru."

Ellen was outside Aiden's room, of course. I told her to give him a hug for me and then asked her to listen carefully.

"I want to ask you a question that's not going to make much sense. A personal question."

"Truman, now you're scaring me. What's going on?"

"This is about Terrelle. I think it could help him. It's going to come out of the blue and you're going to think I'm crazy, but I need you to trust me."

"Okay."

"How well did you know the governor? In college, before I came along. Were you and Carlton ever intimate?"

She paused and lowered her voice as if others nearby could hear. "We've been over this. You know I had a history."

"This is not about your history. This doesn't affect my love for you. And I do love you. I know I don't say it and I sure haven't shown it. But answer me. Were you ever together . . . that way?"

"We went as far as you can go without, you know . . ."

"All right. Thank you. Now think hard. Did he have any . . . distinguishing marks on his body? Anything you recall?"

The phone made a crinkling noise as if she was cradling it closer, as if I had stepped over some invisible line.

"Please," I said. "Does anything come to mind?"

"What do you mean by marks?"

"I don't know. . . . I don't want to suggest anything and plant a thought that—"

"There was a tattoo."

My heart fluttered. "Where?"

She told me. I couldn't speak. Couldn't breathe. I pushed the accelerator to the floor.

"Truman, what's this about?"

"It's about Diana's murder. Everything has come together. It makes sense now."

"What makes sense? What are you going to do?"

"Something I'm going to regret. Something that may mean we lose Aiden."

"Tru . . ."

"Something I have to do."

She was silent on the other end and I heard the *beep, beep* of the machines around Aiden's bed. "I need one more thing."

"What?"

"Call Oleta. Tell her I have good news and bad news. The bad news is I'm not going to make the execution."

"You promised her you would," she said.

"But you haven't heard the good news. There still might be something I can do to save Terrelle's life."

Chapter 47

48 minutes before execution

One step at a time, one foot in front of the other, letting the truth take me where it would, I headed for the governor's mansion. I was slowed by the rain pooling on the streets, in gutters, on my windshield, and generally raising the water table several inches. When it rains in Florida, it's not a slow, steady drizzle; it's usually a go-for-broke, all-out onslaught of pelting droplets big enough to bludgeon small animals.

Phone service was in and out but I managed to get in touch with the aide of the governor's aide to tell him I needed to speak with the governor. That was met with a swift and curt push of the Hold button, followed by a "That would be impossible, I'm afraid."

I asked to speak with Reginald, who promptly reiterated the "much too busy" schedule and added another "impossible" to the mix. A dinner party with some foreign dignitary, probably from some far-flung, exotic place like Pennsylvania. The aide actually laughed out loud when I said I was on my way for a private, face-to-face meeting. I explained the matter was urgent, dealt with my son and the execution. He explained some more. I made a couple of threats and then pulled out the one card I had left, which was the PR nightmare this would be for the governor if my son didn't make it through the surgery. He was supposed to be holding our hands in the hospital waiting room, not dining with the queen of Sheba.

I simply said I was on my way and left it at that, hoping someone would be there to greet me when I arrived, or at least that there wouldn't be anybody with a shotgun at the security checkpoint.

About a mile before the exit, a car pulled beside me, which wouldn't be a big deal or out of the ordinary on most days. However, for conditions like these and how fast I was already going, it seemed a little obtuse for someone to try to race me for the middle lane. Instead of passing me, the car stayed there splattering my windshield and side windows.

I could barely see with the torrent cascading. The sun had descended and the cloud cover made things pitch dark. Amid the water streams along the side of the car I noticed the passenger window coming down in the car next to me. Upon closer examination I saw a man smiling—another dead giveaway that something was wrong because sane people don't smile in rainstorms. The guy had a handlebar mustache. I suddenly recalled the glint of a tire iron and searing pain in my face.

I hit the brakes and the car zoomed ahead, then hit its own brakes. We were now off the interstate, heading for town, and I couldn't turn around and go the other way because of the median. But never let a little thing like that stop a determined reporter. I swung the car around and went the wrong way, unable to see anything in my path. In my rearview, I noticed my friends doing the same thing, following me with haste and bravado.

Don't these guys know I have something important to do?

The first semitrailer I met sounded his air horn and I nearly flooded the driver's seat, if you know what I mean. He swerved to miss me, and my friends from the interstate zoomed up to my rear with brights and flashers on, which was not a bad idea. I thought it was going to be one of those chase scenes from the movies where the main character drives amazingly well against traffic, bobbing and weaving through oncoming cars, but as soon as I hit the next intersection, a line of cars met me, blocking my way, honking their horns and being generally unhelpful in my getaway.

When the passenger door of the car behind me opened, I mashed the accelerator and went up on the median, a concrete barrier that was tall enough to prevent drivers, but the old Sequoia did admirably well. That is until my back window blew out. I ducked way too late, but it was reflex. When I sat up, I was headed north, this time flowing with traffic instead of against it. There's one advantage to having your back window blown out by a shotgun and that is you can actually see. And what I saw was the car chasing me smash into the front end of a Camry or a Civic—I can't tell the difference anymore—spinning that car around before it continued.

It was at this moment that I remembered the gift I had received from Helen. All unwrapped and ready to go. Instead of speeding up, I slowed a bit. My heart surged with adrenaline, my body alive and alert. I rolled the window down and let the car catch up.

I wanted to shout some epithet toward the guys about Mickey and what a loser he was, but I knew they wouldn't hear me over the roar of the road and rain.

They seemed genuinely excited to pull up close, but that look of excitement changed when they saw Helen's .38. One of the things my dad had done well was teach me how to shoot. I hadn't held a gun in my hand in twenty years, but I took dead aim and fired three times before I saw their right front tire deflate. That sent them swerving toward me and I accelerated. Through the rearview I watched the driver try to regain control before the tire disintegrated. The passenger put his gun out the window and fired again but I was gone. Long gone with a date at the governor's mansion.

CHAPTER 48

A security guard in a trench coat met me at the gate and pointed to the parking area. He looked askance at the holes in the side of my car and the missing back windshield, but I kept moving. In the parking area I was met by an aide's brother's pet sitter (it must have been someone like that) who came to the car with an umbrella the size of Iowa and ushered me to an entrance, the rain thundering on the roof and rushing from the eaves. Heart beating wildly, looking behind me for Mickey's goons, I was at the door before I remembered Helen's gun in my jacket pocket. Fortunately it was a rear entrance and there was no metal detector.

The music of Mozart wafted from surround-sound speakers in the small meeting room at the back of the mansion. I hung my jacket on a coat tree near the door and watched it drip into a pool on the immaculately vacuumed carpet. The jacket sagged grotesquely to one side, the weight of the .38 pulling it down, and I positioned it as well as I could, taking the *People* magazine from under my arm and placing it on an end table.

The pet sitter left and it was just Amadeus, me, and my thoughts about the conversation ahead. I was so focused on getting here and taking the next step that I hadn't let the full force of my actions sink in. Could I really do what I was about to do? Pulling the plug on the execution automatically meant pulling the plug on Aiden. Which choice could I live with more? Which choice would haunt me the most when I was old and gray?

I've heard of atheists having deathbed conversions. Was it this type of situation that caused them to turn toward God, or were those reports just the imaginations of hopeful believers interpreting last-gasp words as honest confessions?

Instead of dealing with eternity or shooting up a halfhearted prayer, I turned to Mozart. Classical music has a tendency to make people feel calm and collected. It makes me want to find an overstuffed chair at Barnes & Noble and read *Jane Eyre* or sip a double latte frappe-whatever so I can experience the yang to the yin of all that calmness, the caffeine stirring up the inside while the cells try to float along unhindered and happy. But tonight the violins caused more stress and I was unable to focus. All that *ba da ba bum bum bum bum bum* stuck in my craw. That's the funny thing about Mozart: you can't turn him down like you can Billy Joel or U2. Mozart will seep into your soul and force you to deal with him.

Mozart is like God in that way, I guess, because through all of the day's events I couldn't shake the feeling that I was being followed, hounded, pursued, not just by Mickey's goons but by the hand of some unseen being. Maybe Ellen was right. Maybe there was something to this Jesus thing. It had certainly given her a measure of peace in the midst of the storm. It had also changed Terrelle's life and given him freedom inside that prison that I had never known outside it. Was God better than the slots? Could I trust him?

What was I doing? I couldn't think about the God quotient right then, but that's what flooded my mind. And if I gave him a chance, if I simply said, "God, if you're up there, I'm open," what would happen?

I stayed away from the window for obvious reasons and glanced at my watch. According to the timetable set in motion by the state, Terrelle Conley would at that very moment be on a gurney in his cell, strapped and prepped for the surgery that would take his life. In less than thirty minutes two groups assembled outside the execution chamber would hear his last words. Terrelle would be given the chance to make that statement with his head turned sideways, facing his family and friends. Then the curtain would be drawn, and he would be taken to a sterile operating room prepared by the warden at the request of the governor, a cost the taxpayers would shoulder. When the procedure was complete, the warden would reappear with a doctor who would pronounce the prisoner deceased, and everyone would either celebrate or grieve.

I found the radio clicker in the top drawer of the ancient end table Ponce de León had probably used on his last vacation trip. That's when the governor waltzed into the room in a tuxedo and black shoes so shiny I could have applied mascara—if I used mascara, that is. Reginald tagged along, as well as a buff bodyguard type who looked like he could tag-team wrestle after his stint with the government.

"Truman, I'm surprised to see you. Why aren't you at the prison?"

"That was the plan. But the plan has changed."

"You should be with Ellen, then. This is a big night for your son."

"It's a big night for you, too, isn't it?" My tone was not conciliatory.

It was getting a little tight in the room, all four of us, and the governor decided to thin the herd with a glance and a nod. The two others reluctantly left. The governor held out a hand to the nearest leather chair that smelled like a cow had very recently given its last full measure. I stood, preferring to look down on him.

"What do you mean, it's a big night for me? The dinner?"

"In a few minutes your problems are all going to fade. You'll be hailed as the magnanimous hero who turned sewage into wine."

"I'm not sure I understand. You're getting everything you wanted. Your son is getting a new lease on life. What's the problem?"

"The problem is Terrelle Conley didn't kill Diana Wright and you know it."

"That's preposterous. I have a signed confession."

"From a guy who knew he was going to die anyway. A confession you forced."

He ran a hand through his perfectly combed hair. "After all I've done. After all the chances I took. I'm under considerable political scrutiny here, and I took those risks to help you and your family."

"You took the risk to cover your mistake."

"What mistake?" he said, his eyebrows arched, his brow furrowed.

"Your relationship with Diana."

Ba da ba bum bum bum bum bum.

He stared at me.

"You put her on a monthly retainer to trim your hair. This was when you were in the legislature—even before you stepped into the mansion. You sent the limo to pick her up in some undisclosed place, swore her to secrecy. Paid her well."

His face was tight now. "I don't know what you're talking about and I resent the insinuation that I am part of this conspiracy you've concocted."

"Well, why don't we just forget the formalities here, Carlton. Stand up and drop your pants."

"I beg your pardon."

"Diana described your tattoo. Gave the exact location. So let's see if I'm concocting or if—"

"That would prove nothing."

"Diana said you two were going to run off and be soul mates. That your hearts beat as one. That she'd never felt as loved and as whole as when she was with you. How does it feel, Townsend, to have that girl on your conscience when you go to sleep? You covered it well. You framed a drunk and figured nobody would care."

"I did no such thing."

"Conley's defense thought he was guilty. The prosecution followed blindly along the crumb-strewn trail. You and your German friend—Dieter, or whatever his name is—did a good job."

I plopped the magazine in his lap and pointed to the picture where the blond man was shown behind Townsend in a rally a few years earlier. He was inside the perimeter, obviously part of the governor's detail.

"This is the guy who's been following us, accosting my daughter. He's probably the one who broke in to my house. Maybe even planted bugs. Ever seen him before?"

Something like fear coursed through Townsend's eyes. His mouth opened but nothing came out. For once in his political life.

"Diana did more than your hair, didn't she? She believed the tripe you shoveled her way, just like your voters."

He sat forward, a blank stare, his hands on his face. Then he looked up. "I didn't kill her or have her killed. Our relationship was innocent. At first. She was not a beauty queen. We agreed she would be good—personal appearance is important in this line of work, as you know. And she didn't pose quite the threat that others may have."

"Threat?"

"To my marriage, Truman. You've heard the stories of my indiscretions. There are others who have knowledge of my tattoo."

Yeah, I know.

"But I know nothing about her death. I was as shocked as anyone when her body was found. You can't know the pain."

Amadeus had turned to a more happy tune, lots of frolicking and high string action. Tugging at the heart. Kind of like a sound track to the sob story Townsend was spilling.

"I wouldn't talk about your pain on the witness stand."

Townsend continued, "I've gone under the same assumption as the authorities. Conley was the killer and deserved full punishment."

"Well, Carlton, I'm not buying it. There are too many trails leading back to you."

There was a quick knock at the door.

"Not now," the governor snapped.

The door opened anyway and in walked Mrs. Townsend in a stunning black dress, low-cut neckline, and shiny shoes just like her hubby's.

"What is it, darling?" she said. "We're waiting for you."

He looked up at her with something akin to childhood pleading. A diabetic kid with his hand in the Snickers jar. "Truman believes I'm responsible for that hairdresser's death. I told him she cut my hair, but . . ."

Jennifer strode toward me, head straight, posture perfect. "Truman, this is counterproductive to your son's situation. It's idle talk. Tabloid conjecture."

"Mrs. Townsend, did you know about Diana Wright and your husband?"

She looked at him, then back at me.

"I hate to break this to you, but he was getting more than a haircut," I said.

She put a hand to her mouth in mock horror. "My husband? An affair? There's a shocker. You think I haven't heard this before?"

"I don't know what you've heard, but it's true. And when the media gets hold of it, you can put a nail in the coffin of moving this little political road show to DC." I turned to the governor. "Now I suggest you get on the bat phone to the warden and tell him to stop the execution."

"Not yet," Jennifer said. "He has no proof. An out-of-work reporter trying to put together something to land him another job. Obviously he's emotionally distraught."

"Let's say I'm wrong," I said. "Let's say CT here didn't actually have her killed. He had a dalliance with a young hairdresser who knew how to keep a secret. That alone is enough to plunge the public opinion polls. And then the cover-up. That's not exactly what the American people are looking for in a leader. They've been there, done that. And the fact that this young lady had her life snuffed out only adds fuel to the story."

"How would you know what the American people want in a president?" she sneered. "I couldn't care less what you think or know or think you know."

"Well, you're going to care; I can guarantee you that." It was as close to a John Wayne line as I could get.

Jennifer put out her hand and walked closer, touching my chest. "Truman, listen to reason. Of course this raises troubling questions. But think of your son. This means life or death to him."

I looked her straight in the eyes. Behind all the shadow and eyeliner were dead, blue pools. Eyes that desperately wanted an all-expense-paid trip to Washington for eight years.

"For once I *am* thinking of him. He wouldn't want an innocent man's heart. Even if it cost his own life. And if he pulls through this somehow, I want him to know his old man finally did something right. Something good."

I looked at my watch. Precious seconds ticked away. I hoped my words were true. I hoped Aiden would forgive me. I hoped Ellen and Abby would forgive me. And to tell the truth, I hoped God could.

There, I said it.

And right then I opened up just a little bit to the thought that perhaps he had been part of all that had gone on. Perhaps he had been not only hounding, but calling out to me all this time.

Forgive me, I prayed. *Show me what to do.*

It wasn't that hard. And something washed over me as soon as I said it in my head.

I glanced at the governor. "Call the warden."

Jennifer turned and opened the door. "Ron? Would you mind stepping in here a moment?"

Townsend put his head down. A man stepped into the room. Jennifer smiled at the look on my face as the blond guy passed her. He wasn't in a tux and shiny shoes, but he also wasn't in camouflage. He smiled, and after he let it sink in, he reached into my jacket pocket for Helen's gun. I had the feeling early on that it was a little too easy getting past security into the mansion. Now I knew why. I was a fish lured into a barrel. And Mozart, good old Amadeus himself, would play the benediction at my demise. Ignoramus. Incompetatus. Benedictus Dominoes falling all around me.

"Jennifer, what are you doing?" the governor said. It was the most believable thing I had heard from him all evening.

"I'm taking care of this," she snapped. "Something you should have done long ago."

The governor looked at his wife and her aide. "You?"

She rolled her eyes. "Please, Carlton. You were as subtle as a dog in heat. I had to put a stop to it."

Townsend stood. "You had her killed?"

"After it came to light, we tried paying her. She wouldn't let go of the fantasy."

"Wait," I said, not in any position to ask questions, but still, I'm a reporter. It's kind of in the bloodstream. "You and *Ron* had contact with Diana before the murder?"

"It wasn't murder. It was a good plan that . . . got out of hand."

My mind reeled. "So it was you, Jennifer. You found a frumpy stylist for him. One you felt your husband couldn't possibly fall for. But he and Diana began this relationship—he scheduled extra sessions—"

"That's enough," Ron said.

"No, let me get this straight." I did my best Columbo, hand to the head, pacing. "You controlled the appointments, but Carlton set up other clandestine meetings. You discovered the relationship and tried to end it, but she wouldn't comply. You threatened. She believed there was a future for her in his life."

"I never meant to mislead her," the governor said. "And I didn't want to hurt you." He looked at his wife with doe eyes. "But I never dreamed you would—"

"You've always known, Carlton. Don't pretend."

"No, I never suspected." He looked at the two of them, crestfallen.

"Do you think I would let a simpleton, a stylist *I* had suggested, keep us from our goal? Yes, it was regrettable. Ron never meant to harm her. We wanted her to leave and offered to help make that happen."

"Especially since she was carrying the offspring of the future president," I said.

"That's not true," she snapped. "The autopsy stated she wasn't pregnant."

"But she thought she was." I looked at Townsend. "And she told you that."

"I told her I would provide for her and her child. Not to worry. Things would work out."

Ron pointed Helen's gun at me. What kind of name is *Ron* for such a menacing figure?

"That girl was not going to keep us from the White House and neither are you," Jennifer said to me.

"And Ron here offered Conley a bottle if he'd approach Diana after work that day," I said. "Or maybe just some money."

Ron smiled but it did not warm my heart.

"So how does this end?" I said. "There's no drunk on the side of the road you can frame."

"We tried to warn you, Mr. Wiley," he said with perfect diction. His words came out as if he were reading a script.

I looked at the ceiling, deep in thought. "So the story will be that a disgruntled father showed up with a gun at the mansion? Why would I be disgruntled when you're doing so much for my son?"

Jennifer smiled. "Now you can phone the prison, Carlton."

"What?" the governor said.

"He's right. That's how it happened. Truman heard you were considering a stay."

I took a step forward. Sometimes you wait; sometimes you have to push things ahead. "And Ron here, trusted aide to the First Lady, heroically intervened, saving the governor's life."

"Former trusted aide," Ron said. "Who happened to be invited at the last moment."

"Right. You had to go freelance after the murder. Distance yourself. How did you know I had a gun?"

"Perhaps it was a lucky guess," Ron said. "Perhaps I have been monitoring you a little more closely than you knew."

"And Tompkins? Part of your handiwork?"

He smiled but didn't reply. It was really all I needed.

Jennifer looked at her husband. "Call the warden."

Ron raised the gun and pointed it at my chest. I could see it then, with Mozart sprinting off on another familiar melodic line, the haphazard, winding hand of God moving the chess pieces of our lives in such a way as to have me at this place at this time on this night. My son in a hospital bed. My wife at his side. My daughter and I reconciled. And a man on a gurney at Starke with a doctor and some sharp knives, the full weight of the law hovering over all of them. Over all of us. Did God really work this quickly? Was this his answer? I had to believe it was.

I had to believe.

I looked at Ron, then at Mrs. Townsend, then at the gun.

"Please. Not in the heart."

Before the man could pull the trigger, the governor shouted, "No!" He sprang from his seat and lunged for Ron's arm, but the gun went off and I felt a weird sensation. It wasn't searing pain like I expected. I staggered back against the wall and must have hit the radio because Mozart went silent. But I could still hear him in my head.

Ba da ba bum bum bum bum bum.

At least, it sounded like Mozart.

It was the strangest thing, like some brother I'd never had putting pressure on an artery. And a deep feeling of peace washing through me, past all of the questions and doubt and hard-heartedness.

The door opened and people rushed in. A radio squawked. Someone called for an ambulance. Now more people in the room. Someone pressing on my neck.

"There's a lot of blood," someone said.

"Sir, can you hear me?"

Flashing lights. Movement.

"Just hold on," I heard someone whisper. *"Hold on."*

CHAPTER 49

ELLEN SQUEEZED HER SON'S HAND but received no response before they wheeled the gurney away. Her pastor was there, along with his wife and several members of the church keeping a silent vigil in the waiting room.

Abby stepped off the elevator and fell into her mother's arms. "Something's off with Dad," she said.

Ellen couldn't shake the same feeling, one of dread or a growing sense that something was taking over his life. She filled Abby in on his last phone call but since then he hadn't made contact or answered any texts. Another family came into the room and Ellen and Abby stood by the far window, the one overlooking the emergency room.

A nurse found them and the room got quiet. The woman let them know Aiden was being prepped for the procedure. It was a matter of waiting now. Everyone in the room looked at the clock. Ellen thought of Oleta and what she was going through at the prison. The television was muted but showed the scene outside Starke and protesters lined up with placards. Ellen had to turn away and saw an ambulance racing toward the hospital. Then an urgent report cut in from a reporter outside the governor's mansion who seemed frantic to read information from a notepad.

"Mom," Abby said. It was a plea of helplessness, and Ellen recognized it. She pulled her daughter to her shoulder and the two wept together.

Moments later, Dr. Fanelli hurried into the waiting room and found Ellen and pulled her into an empty hall. It seemed to her that bits of information were flowing through his brain she would never understand. Until he spoke.

"Ellen, listen carefully. There has been a stay of execution."

"What?"

"The governor just gave a stay order. Terrelle's heart is not available."

As if those words weren't enough to take her breath, he spoke again, measured, gentle.

"Ellen, your husband has been shot. Truman was injured. He's being brought to surgery. But there has been a massive loss of blood, as I understand."

The room spun, moved like an amusement park ride. There was no air. No sound. No light. Just death.

"What happened? Was it . . . self-inflicted?"

"No. Something happened at the governor's mansion. We don't know the details. But I need your decision. Truman is an organ donor. . . . Are you able to make this decision? Do you want your pastor with you?"

"What decision?"

"If we can't save him. If we can't resuscitate . . ."

Ellen listened, processed the information, and through tears nodded. The doctor hurried away, barking orders. Ellen was met by Abby and the others and fell to the floor, sobbing.

After the surgery, Dr. Fanelli allowed Ellen into the room where her husband lay. The body had been hastily prepared and the room sanitized. There were no blood-spattered garments, no gaping holes. He was covered from the neck down. All she saw was his face and the tousled hair and the lines drawn by time and stress.

"I've never seen anything like it, Ellen," Dr. Fanelli said. The man wasn't weeping, but close to it. "It was as though he knew he had to hold on, just the right amount of time."

Ellen couldn't speak. Couldn't breathe.

"The bullet missed the heart but struck a major artery," the man continued. "He never really had a chance. The blood filled . . . He just would not let go. Through willpower or some power greater than his own, he held on."

The doctor left her alone with Truman, and Ellen touched his cheek again as a tear fell. She had dreamed they would be together, prayed that God would allow them to live until they were old and had grandchildren. But here was Truman, ashen, his life taken in an instant.

She couldn't think, couldn't breathe, couldn't process the loss of a husband and the gain of a son—if that's what would eventually happen. How could she process that? It would take a lifetime.

Through the blur of tears and the memories, she noticed something she hadn't seen on his face in a long time. Maybe she had never seen it. It was a look of peace.

Epilogue

"Put that down!" Abigail Wiley told her brother as he lugged a box into the entry.

"It's not that heavy," Aiden said. He wiped some sweat from his brow. "Dr. Granger said I can do just about anything I want now. And there's two more out by the frog."

She shook her head at him and focused on the box. The familiar logo of the publishing house stood out and something electric shot through her. Like Christmas and her birthday and wedding day rolled into one.

"Mom! They're here!"

Ellen came running and stopped short when she spied the box. She quickly retrieved a pair of scissors and cut away the clear tape. It was all too slow for Aiden, who grabbed the cardboard and ripped the top apart.

Inside were the brightly colored book covers with the catchy title. Terrelle Conley's face appeared in a photo that had circulated the globe. Hands raised, arms outstretched, being embraced by his wife—it was a bittersweet photo that captured the elation but not the loss Abigail and her family felt.

Abigail picked up a copy gingerly and held it like it was a piece of her father. In fact, it was. It was a piece of all of them and what they had been through the past year.

Aiden opened to the pictures in the middle of one copy. "They got the funeral in here." He pointed out the network news personalities and political and sports celebrities who had paid their respects. He looked at his mother. "Did you ever figure out whose arrangement that was from New Orleans?"

"No," their mother said, then opened a copy to the dedication page. Abigail watched as her mother put a hand to her mouth and turned away.

Abigail stared at the cover and the words at the bottom: *Written by Truman and Abby Wiley*. It felt like cheating to have her name there, but having it as "Abby" made sense. It would honor her dad in a small way.

She had gone back and forth about the attribution with the publisher and Gina Lessinger, her father's former agent, who had a change of heart after his death. With all the work she put into the manuscript and the interviews that were sure to come, it was only fair to name her. But she felt unworthy.

"We should call Oleta," her mother said, but before she reached the phone, there was a knock at the door. Oleta held a copy and tears of joy brimmed. Behind her was Terrelle, shy but beaming.

"We won't come in because we've got the cat dander on us,

probably," she said. "But we had to come right over when the UPS guy delivered these."

The three of them joined Oleta and Terrelle outside. There was a nervous pause as they all focused on the book cover, then read the back.

"I never thought I'd see my husband on the outside again," Oleta said to Abigail. "We have your father to thank for that."

"Your father would be proud," Terrelle said, his voice deep and plaintive.

"He would have loved to be there when this picture was taken," Abigail said.

"He'd have loved seeing Ron Detmüller with his blond hair shaved off and on his way to prison," Aiden said. "And what it did to Townsend and his wife."

"I don't think he would have rejoiced in their demise," Oleta said. "I think he would have felt a little sorry for them."

"I'll never forget his visits to me at the end," Terrelle said.

"I'll never forget the detective who found Dad's flash drive," Abigail said. "He had tears in his eyes. You don't see that every day."

Her mother held the book to her chest and looked toward the trees. Birds were getting antsy to leave the coast and fly north.

"What are you thinking, Mom?" Aiden said.

"That we should go to the beach. Take a walk down there to celebrate. I think Truman would like that."

And so they did. When Terrelle and Oleta left, the three of them hopped in the Sequoia and drove straight to the beach, recounting stories of Truman Wiley on the way. They spoke of his failures, the love they felt, their regrets, and what he taught them in his imperfect way.

As the sun was setting, Aiden and his mother waded into the

surf arm in arm, pant legs rolled up, laughing and enjoying the moment. But Abigail walked behind, her feet just outside the reach of the incoming tide. She thought of her father's heart and how it now beat in the chest of her brother. His last gift to them.

She wished she could tell her father what she had learned. About life. About him. Even about God and possibilities. It felt like all God needed was an open door. An open heart.

And then she waded in after them, splashing and running toward her family, into the ocean.

Acknowledgments

Thanks to my Tyndale family for letting me tell another story from the heart. Sarah Mason helped rescue my ramblings and get Truman's voice. Karen Watson continues to encourage—thanks for giving me a chance. Thanks also to Sherry Parmelee, who read an early version and provided Tallahassee pictures and technical help, especially with Murrow.

Thanks to Sean Callebs for his friendship and allowing me to use a tiny slice of his career as the catalyst for this tale.

Thanks to all who read my stories. I'm humbled at your feedback and that you continue to read. May your tribe increase.

Thanks to my nine children for being constant inspirations, and to my own Ellen, Andrea, who puts up with much too much of my Trumanness.

And thanks to God for his indescribable gift, which changes anyone who will open their heart to him.

ABOUT THE AUTHOR

CHRIS FABRY is a 1982 graduate of the W. Page Pitt School of Journalism at Marshall University and a native of West Virginia. He is heard on Moody Radio's *Chris Fabry Live!*, *Love Worth Finding*, and *Building Relationships with Dr. Gary Chapman*. He and his wife, Andrea, are the parents of nine children. Chris has published more than seventy books for adults and children. His novel *Dogwood* won a Christy Award in 2009. In 2011 *Almost Heaven* won a Christy Award and the ECPA Christian Book Award for fiction. You can visit his website at www.chrisfabry.com.

READING GROUP QUESTIONS AND TOPICS FOR DISCUSSION

1. How did you react to Truman's character? Did you like him?
   Would you call him a good guy? Did your opinion of him
   change over the course of the story?

2. Have you ever known someone with an addiction? What
   similarities did you see between that person and Truman?
   Why do you think Truman gambles?

3. What did you think of the way Ellen dealt with Truman?
   Should she have divorced him like her parents wanted? How
   did she show genuine love to him?

4. The money for writing Terrelle's book came from someone
   other than Oleta. Do you think that was a good decision,
   even though it was clear what Truman would do with it?
   Why do you think that person provided the money?

5. Why is Truman closed to religion? Have you ever felt the
   same way or known someone who has? Oleta, Terrelle, and
   Ellen all share their faith with Truman in different ways.
   Which do you think had the most impact and why?

6. In chapter 17, Truman remarks, "Religion has always seemed an opiate to me, something to numb a person to reality." Discuss the irony of that statement in light of Truman's addiction. How do you see him changing throughout the story in regard to faith?

7. Why can't Truman bring himself to go see Aiden in the hospital? Read Romans 7:14-15. What parallels do you see between Truman and Paul?

8. If Abigail were your daughter, would you have let her investigate Curtis Tompkins? As a parent, how would you balance protecting your adult children with allowing them to learn from the consequences of their decisions?

9. Do you think it should be legal for death row inmates to donate their organs, as Terrelle wanted to? Would you want one of your family members to receive an organ that was donated this way?

10. In chapter 24, Ellen tells Truman that "there are things you learn about life and yourself in the valley that you can't learn anywhere else." What does she mean? Have you ever experienced this in your own life?

11. Truman says in chapter 31, "I've heard that the opposite of love is not hate but indifference." Do you agree?

12. Do you think Terrelle should have signed the confession? Why or why not?